D1393598

☆

F/225/792

The Queen's Man

The Queen's Man

RORY CLEMENTS

**HODDER &
STOUGHTON**

First published in Great Britain in 2014 by Hodder & Stoughton
An Hachette UK Company

1

© Rory Clements 2014

The right of Rory Clements to be identified as the Author of the Work has been asserted by him
in accordance with the Copyright, Designs and Patents Act 1988.

Maps drawn by Rodney Paull

A CIP catalogue record for this title is available from the British Library

Hardback ISBN 978-1-84854-844-2
Trade paperback ISBN 978-1-84854-845-9
Ebook ISBN 978-1-84854-846-6

Typeset in 12.5/16 pt Adobe Garamond by Servis Filmsetting Ltd, Stockport, Cheshire

Printed and bound by Clays Ltd, St Ives plc

Hodder & Stoughton policy is to use papers that are natural, renewable and recyclable products
and made from wood grown in sustainable forests. The logging and manufacturing processes are
expected to conform to the environmental regulations of the country of origin.

Hodder & Stoughton Ltd
338 Euston Road
London NW1 3BH

www.hodder.co.uk

For Jean and Roland,
with love

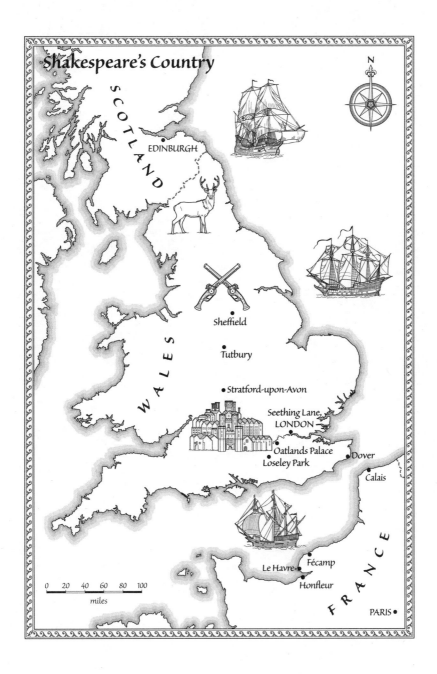

Shakespeare's Country

SCOTLAND

EDINBURGH

WALES

Sheffield

Tutbury

Stratford-upon-Avon

Seething Lane
LONDON

Oatlands Palace
Loseley Park

Dover

Calais

FRANCE

Le Havre

Fécamp

Honfleur

PARIS

0 20 40 60 80 100
miles

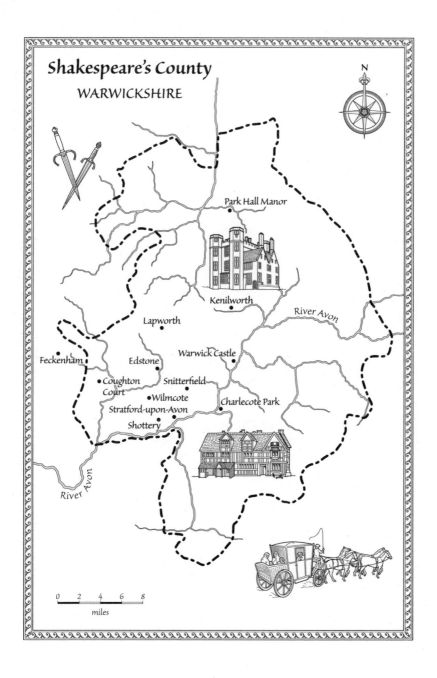

Shakespeare's County
WARWICKSHIRE

Park Hall Manor

Kenilworth

River Avon

Lapworth

Warwick Castle

Feckenham
Edstone

• Coughton
Court

Snitterfield

• Wilmcote

Stratford-upon-Avon

Charlecote Park

Shottery

River Avon

0   2   4   6   8
miles

N

Prologue

1578

S IR FRANCIS WALSINGHAM peered across the great hall of Gray's Inn. 'Which one is he, Paul?'

'At the end of the far table, the one just standing up from the bench.'

Walsingham picked out the young man. He was tall, perhaps six feet, with long hair and hooded eyes. 'Is he a good student?'

'He has wit enough, though he is not a university man; he came to me after his Barnard's year.'

'He looks a little thin.'

'Well, he is not yet twenty. Give him time to grow. I certainly think him strong.'

'I like thin men. They slip through doors unnoticed.'

Paul Ballater threw a sideways glance at his old friend and laughed. Walsingham could have been talking about himself, for he was gaunt and angular, with a dark, sunken face that spoke of too many hours hunched over documents and too little time for nourishment.

'And what makes you think your Mr Shakespeare might be suited to my purpose?'

'As I told you, he has an inquiring mind and a keen sense of justice, but little love for the intricacies of the law. I think he is not made for dusty tomes.'

'He will not escape dusty tomes that easily. A hundred papers pass my desk each day. And he will need to learn languages and politics.'

Walsingham watched as John Shakespeare clapped his fellow diner on the back and seemed to share a jest, for they both smiled, then he strode away across the echoing hall. Was this the man he was looking for? He needed an apprentice to learn every nuance of the war of secrets that must be waged if Elizabeth was to hold on to her throne. He needed a man of courage and honesty; rare qualities in the world of the intelligencer.

'Try him, Frank. If you don't like him, send him back here. I'll make a barrister of him in time.'

'Do we know his family?'

'His father is a burgess of some standing in the town of Stratford-upon-Avon in Warwickshire.'

'Are they sound of faith?'

'I have no reason to believe otherwise.'

Walsingham was silent for a few moments, then nodded. 'Very well, Paul. Talk to him. If he is amenable, send him to me at Seething Lane on the morrow. Let us see what stuff your Mr Shakespeare is made of.'

Chapter 1

1582

S HE WAS TWENTY-SIX; he was eighteen. They lay naked on a mattress made from hay with a covering of canvas that they had found on an old cart. Had *stolen* from a cart.

By their illicit bed stood a half-empty jug of cloudy cider. A light warm rain dripped through the rafters. Otherwise the only sound in this ancient ruin of a manor house was their breathing, growing softer with each moment.

The lovers had been coming to this place all summer long, believing that they were unlikely to be disturbed. It was known in the district as the Black House and fear kept people away, as it had done for more than two hundred years since the Black Death raged through its halls like the scythe of God. It was said that a family of ten had lived here with a dozen servants and retainers, and not a soul had survived. The building had been locked up and shunned ever since. Now it was overgrown and skeletal. A tall oak had grown in the middle of the great hall and much of the roof had crumbled, but the stone walls still survived, covered in a tangle of ivy and briar.

The house was largely forgotten. It stood three miles to the north of Stratford-upon-Avon; the park that once surrounded it was now dense woodland and the old walls were unseen, save by the occasional poacher or curious child.

The woman looked at her lover apprehensively. Initially, it had been his idea to come here, for he was not afraid of the place. He had told her that he first visited it seven years ago with another boy. His friend offered him a farthing to enter the ruin, so he had no option; he had to go in. He had won the coin from his friend and a badly gashed leg when a rotten board gave way beneath him. To his friend, the injury proved that the place was indeed accursed and haunted. But Will knew otherwise. He liked the house and had begun to come here alone, to read or think or merely to watch the sky.

And then, this spring past, he had brought her here. Together they had cleared a corner that offered enough shelter and a flat stone floor that would serve as a base for the straw mattress and that would not give way under their energetic couplings.

A drop of rain fell on his chest.

'Summer is done,' he said, looking up at the damp, grey September sky.

She kissed his face. She had a secret that she must tell and another that she would keep to herself. Tentatively, she took his hand down to her belly. Her flesh was warm, but she was nervous. She had been wondering how to tell him of her pregnancy. He had been besotted when this all started, exultant at having won the prize, the fairest young woman in the county, the one who had evaded the confines of marriage all these years. But how did he feel now, this boy, with summer gone and so much passion spent?

He allowed her to clasp his hand there beneath her own curling fingers, enjoying the quiet intimacy. At first he did not seem to comprehend the silent message she was trying to convey, but she held his hand to her soft mound all the harder and suddenly she sensed a tension. He turned to her and she met his gaze.

'Are you . . .?'

She nodded. There, it was out now. No going back.

'Is it certain?' he said, raising himself on his elbows.

The sharpness of his movement alarmed her. Was he angry? 'I believe so,' she said as evenly as she could. 'My flowers are three weeks late. Normally, they are as regular as the moon.'

He said nothing, his face a puzzle. She wished he would say something, not merely look at her. *Will. Oh, please say something.* Then he took her in his arms. Perhaps he had seen the desperation in her eyes. God in heaven, what would he say? Would he run from her? He had spoken often enough of leaving Stratford and Warwickshire. Now, he might think he had even more reason to leave. To *flee* . . .

They had both known the risk. She had been his teacher in love, and he the eager pupil. She had thought him grateful for such schooling. What man of eighteen would not? But now she noted the change in his demeanour. As though he were the master, and she the novice.

He pulled away from her and smiled, then kissed the tears from her cheeks. At last he picked up the fired-clay jar of cider, drank from it, then held it to her lips. He whispered in her ear words of love, the sorts of words that had wooed and won her; words that fell sweetly from his lips like honey from the comb.

The words and the cider warmed her heart, but they did not calm it. For there was still the other matter, the one she dared not confide in him. The secret that could kill her.

Chapter 2

FRANÇOIS LELOUP, DOCTOR of medicine, and known this day as Seguin, walked beside the young Scot across the inner bailey or courtyard of Sheffield Castle. His journey from Normandy had been long and tiresome, riding a flea-bitten horse down pitted byways and peasant paths, all the time trying to avoid scrutiny. He felt dirty and unrested, despite a night's sleep at the local inn and a handsome dinner here within these ancient walls.

This castle was an abomination. The stench of an overflowing midden hung heavy and cloying in the air. With his one hand, he held a small silver pomander of musk and ambergris to his nose, but it did little to keep the smell from his wide nostrils. These English! How could they live like this?

Ahead of him, at the bottom of the steep flight of stone steps that must lead to the entrance of the castle keep where Mary was held, he saw half a dozen guards closing ranks. The guards were armed with ceremonial halberds, but the real weapons were at their belts: fighting short swords and loaded pistols. This was not merely for show. The Frenchman stopped and threw an inquiring glance at his young companion.

'They have to do this, monsieur.'

'Of course, Mr Ord.'

The Scotsman turned to the guard. 'This is the physician, Dr

Seguin.' He held out a paper. 'There, you will see the earl's mark. Monsieur Seguin is to be granted admittance to Her Majesty's presence.'

The guard thrust his pistol into his broad, hide belt then examined the paper carefully and slowly, occasionally looking at the Frenchman with an impassive face. He clearly knew the elegant Mr Buchan Ord, resplendent in his expensive black doublet studded with beads of jet and coral, but not his companion.

What the guard saw was a one-armed man in his late forties, perhaps even fifty, with dark, greying hair, a large nose and a sharp beard. He had a tanned skin and his slanting eyes seemed amused and clever. His attire was dark and sober.

'So this is the Frenchie is it, Mr Ord? Her Scottish Majesty not satisfied with her own physicians?'

'Be pleased to show some respect, Sergeant. Our visitor is a renowned doctor of medicine, held in high esteem throughout France. I believe the earl's steward has told you all you need to know. And you must recognise his lordship's mark and seal.'

'Yes, it's Shrewsbury's mark all right. I've seen it often enough.' The guard grinned and handed back the pass. 'That seems to be in order.'

'Then be so good as to let us enter, Sergeant.'

'Forgive me, Mr Ord, but first, as you must know, we are required to search you both. Don't want no dags or knives going near the Queen of Scots, do we? Don't want no nasty accidents.'

The Scotsman sighed and held out his arms, Christlike, to be patted down.

Still holding the silver ball of exotic perfumes in his hand, the Frenchman lifted his one arm with as little enthusiasm as he could muster. '*C'est vraiment nécessaire?*'

Ord looked at the newcomer apologetically. A body search

was, indeed, a tiresome condition of their entry. 'And we shall have to endure it all over again from her own men before entering the privy chamber. I am sorry.'

'It is nothing.' Leloup sighed and allowed a pair of guards to grope him intimately, all down his ribs and between his legs, their well-practised, insolent hands lingering at his balls. He found their attention quite pleasurable and wondered whether they understood the effect they were having. From their blank faces he guessed probably not; but this was a thing the English never did understand. At last the guards nodded to their sergeant, who stood back to allow Leloup to step forward and ascend the steps into the great hall of the keep.

The Frenchman laughed and leant towards Ord's ear. 'I am surprised they try so hard to keep her alive.'

'It is not such a mystery. They do not acknowledge her yet, but she *is* Queen of England. One day she will take the crown from the usurper, God willing, and these men will be her subjects. There will be many days of reckoning for those who scorned and mocked her and deprived her of liberty.'

'Vengeance . . .'

'. . . is golden. Like the sun after rain.' Ord looked sombre. There was a moment of silence, then he touched the French visitor on the shoulder. 'Before we go to her, Monsieur Seguin, I must warn you that she is in exceeding poor health. The black choler assails her.'

'Which is why she has summoned me, is it not?'

'Indeed, but I fear she will not wish to be seen, even by you.'

He had heard as much.

'Her hair is thin and patchy, her body is . . . a little stout. Her gut ails her with much farting and defluxions, and she goes days without sleep. I think that no woman, certainly no queen, would wish to be seen in her present humour. If you have a wife of your own, you must understand this. And, please, I beg you, speak softly in her presence.'

'I am a *médecin* of long standing, Mr Ord.' The Frenchman laughed again. 'I have faced many delicate situations over the years. You may place your faith in me.'

'Good. Once again, I crave your forgiveness if I seem a little too protective. But those of us who love Mary spend our whole lives safeguarding her from the slights and barbs of this infernal regimen – this imprisonment – to which she has been subjected these fourteen years.'

Leloup studied Ord. From his accent, he seemed Scottish, like his royal mistress, yet he was a very young man. Why would such a person devote his life to caring for this woman in her incarceration? He could have been no more than a child in 1568 when she came to England seeking refuge, and found only imprisonment. Had Ord been inspired by tales of her great beauty and saintliness from his Catholic parents? Inwardly, he shrugged; it was hardly worth speculating.

The presence chamber was lit by dozens of beeswax candles, and yet it somehow contrived to be funereal. A dozen people, both men and women, stood or sat in groups of two or three, stiff like mannequins that might crumble to dust if touched. They played cards or talked in low voices, their movements exaggeratedly slow. The scene was horribly cold, thought Leloup, like a badly wrought tableau. The retainers looked up at the two men as they entered, saluting Buchan Ord in slow acknowledgement.

At one end of the hall, against a high wall, a tall-backed chair rested on a dais. It was burnished with gold leaf so that it looked like a throne of solid gold. Above it hung Mary's cloth of state, in dazzling threads of scarlet and silver, with the words '*En ma fin est mon commencement*'. In my end is my beginning.

Leloup glanced at it and smiled. So she had taken the motto of her mother, Mary of Guise. Perhaps it was an omen.

Set into the opposite wall was a small doorway. Two liveried sentries stood to attention on either side of it.

'Those are Mary's own guards, monsieur,' Ord said. 'They are unarmed but as strong as wild cats and would fight like tigers to preserve Her Royal Majesty from harm.'

'Well, then I will not resist.'

The privy chamber where Mary, Queen of Scots, lived and slept was lit by the glowing embers of a fire in the hearth. Leloup followed Ord's lead in going down on both knees by the large curtained bed, waiting for a word from the world enclosed within. He heard a snuffling noise, then the touch of something wet on his hand. A dog. No, three or four little dogs. They seemed to be everywhere, panting and sniffing and licking.

Gradually, as they waited in silence, Leloup's eyes grew accustomed to the desperate gloom and his hearing picked up the soft sounds of her breathing. Was she asleep?

'Mr Ord?'

The voice, when it came, was suprisingly firm and clear.

'Your Majesty.'

'Have you brought le docteur Leloup?'

'I have, ma'am. He is here with me. He is going by the name Seguin.'

An arm snaked from the curtain and a hand was held out, palm down and loose at the wrist. Buchan Ord took the hand in his and kissed it. He did not take it as a signal to rise from his genuflection.

'We bid you welcome to our humble prison, monsieur,' she said in French, instinctively moving her hand towards her visitor. 'Which name should I call you?'

'My real name while we are alone, Your Majesty,' he said.

'And may I say that it is to my eternal honour to be admitted to your presence.' He kissed the plump hand, which hovered a few moments before retreating behind the curtain.

'What news of our cousin Henri of Guise?'

'Monseigneur le Duc sends you his felicitations, ma'am.'

'I pray he has sent me more than that. Have you brought mithridate for my ailments? And horn of unicorn? Surely he has received my letter begging him for these precious elixirs.' An edge of frustration in the voice; so many of her letters to the great men and women of Europe had gone unanswered. Even her former mother-in-law, Catherine de Medici, ignored her missives and her pleas for succour.

'The duke has sent you something yet more valuable to him, his ring.'

'His ring?'

'As a token of his great love and as a pledge that he will do all in his power –' Leloup's voice lowered to a whisper – 'to free you from your present predicament and raise you up to your rightful place. He believes this will do more for your health than any potion, powder or tincture.'

The hand emerged yet again from the curtains. He already had the ring out. One of the little dogs leapt up to lick its mistress's hand. With the ring clenched in his fist, Leloup pushed the animal aside, a little too forcefully, so that it yelped. Now he uncurled his fingers and placed the ring in the Queen of Scotland's upturned palm. For a brief moment he looked at it in the glow of the fire. He had carried it for three weeks, secreted in a small pouch within his clothing, wrapped against his body, and all the time he was ready to kill any highway robber who might try to steal it. It was a broad gold band decorated with the cross of Anjou or Lorraine, part of the Guise crest. Mary's fingers closed around the ring and took it back into her tent of silk.

'Is it really his, Monsieur Leloup?'

'The duke placed it in my own hand. He wishes you to accept it as a token of his great goodwill – and as assurance that we will secure your freedom.'

'There is a candle by the bed, Mr Ord. Light it and give it to me.'

The Scotsman took the candle, housed in an ornate silver candlestick, to the hearth and lit it with a taper. Its long flame relieved the gloom and cast light along the delicate cream canopy and curtains that surrounded the enormous bed. 'Your Majesty.' He handed it into her and there was a gasp of pleasure from her as the bright gold shone.

'Oh, it *is* his. I know it well. Then I am not forgotten.'

'Indeed, you are most certainly not forgotten.'

'Monsieur Leloup, when I was a girl at the French court, the seer Michel de Nostredame came to me with foretellings. Queen Catherine had demanded he draw up my chart. He said I was to be Queen of France and also Queen of the isles. He said that I would live to a very great age and be known as a beloved sovereign to all the peoples of these islands. Is this still to come true as Monsieur de Nostredame foretold?'

'With God on our side, yes.'

'I have scarce dared hope it these long years.'

Leloup turned towards Ord. 'How freely may we talk here?'

'It is safe, but while Walsingham draws breath it is best to be circumspect. His spies are everywhere. Let us speak without specifics. No names. No details.'

'Could we be overheard?'

'No. We have searched every inch of this chamber, tapped at all the walls. One of our own stands outside the window alongside Shrewsbury's guards. Nothing can be heard, but still I do not trust them. If there is any way in heaven or on earth to do so, then Walsingham will listen.'

'Very well.' Leloup kept his voice low, then moved yet closer to the curtain of the bed and began speaking in French again. 'Your cousin has charged me with the holy office of bringing you away from this place. I concur with him that there can be no better medicine than this.'

'Then you are indeed a harbinger of good news, monsieur.'

'Mr Ord has discovered men and women of the true faith who will escort you from here to a place of safety and thence across the narrow sea to await the downfall of this heretical regime, which will not be long in coming.' He lowered his voice yet further. 'The invasion fleet is already under construction – at Le Havre, Fécamp and Honfleur.' And so, he thought, is the band of would-be assassins. *Englishmen trusted by the court of Elizabeth who will not hesitate to strike home the blade.* But he would not burden Mary with such knowledge. Not while there was any chance of a spy within earshot.

'Should you be saying all this, Dr Leloup?'

He laughed gently. 'I think it fair to say that they have always assumed you will try to escape. Hearing it will make no difference – so long as they do not know the method.'

'Mr Ord, can this be true that I am to have my freedom?'

'I believe it will happen, ma'am.'

'But why have you not told me this before?'

'I did not wish to raise your hopes, only to have them cruelly dashed as they have been so often in the past. Monsieur Leloup's arrival here changes everything. He brings gold for weapons and the great expense involved in concealing you as we carry you across England, thence over the narrow sea to France. The plan is almost in place.'

'But how? How will this be effected?'

The light inside the tent seemed to blaze closer to the cream curtain and for a moment Leloup feared it would all go up in a burst of flames.

'Your Majesty, I beg you to ask no more. Not yet.'

'This is not good enough, monsieur! I must be sure. The she-cat knows I would escape if I could, so do her sharp-toothed minions, Burghley and Walsingham. They have the eyes and claws of rats, and there is an army of their guards around this castle. If your plan is attempted and fails, they will consign me to some dungeon like a common criminal. I cannot bear to have this fail, for I would become a worm, trapped deep within the earth.'

'Nothing will go wrong,' Leloup said. 'On the Bible and in the name of our Holy Mother of Christ I swear this.'

'The Holy Mother . . .'

From within the curtained bed, there was a gasp, then silence.

'Your Majesty . . .'

They heard a sob, which became a wail, deep and horrible.

Leloup felt Ord's breath in his ear. A whisper so quiet that Mary could not hear. '*Mother.* It is a word we must not use in her presence. She is a mother, too. Her son is fifteen years of age and never once has she heard his voice nor even had a letter from him. What torture is this for a mother?'

The Frenchman was silent a moment, then moved closer to the bed. 'Your Majesty, your ordeal will soon be at an end. I entreat you to trust us in this. I will send word to you with every detail when all is secured.'

The sobbing subsided.

'Madame?'

'You must come yourself.'

'That may not be possible. I doubt I will be trusted by the Earl of Shrewsbury again. But there is yet one favour that I must ask of you. Those who would help you in this noble enterprise require some sign from you – some article that will convince them that their work is indeed done in your name. I beg you to do this, for they will be risking their own lives.'

Mary's hand came once more from between the curtains. She held another ring in her hand. 'Take this. It was my mother's and bears the sign of the phoenix rising from the ashes. Her sign and now mine. Show it to our loyal people. And then, when I see it again, I will believe that all is prepared. As you have come from my beloved cousin Henri, so must I put my trust in you, Monsieur Leloup. Do not let me down.'

François Leloup took the ring. 'I pledge I will not fail you, ma'am.'

Chapter 3

As John Shakespeare came over a small stone bridge, he reined in sharply. Ahead of him, in the trees, he saw movement.

A large animal burst from the woods. Shakespeare recoiled in shock as a hart with a majestic crown of antlers and eyes distended like bowls came charging straight at him. Only at the last second, within a foot or two of Shakespeare's startled horse, did the enormous deer sheer left with breath-stopping violence, stumbling in the mud at the river's edge, and then plunging into the water.

The Thames here was only a hundred feet across, nothing like the great tidal flow downriver in London and beyond, but it was deep enough and the frightened beast had no choice but to swim, scrambling for the northern bank.

Shakespeare watched it in astonishment. Never had he seen a more magnificent beast. Its antlers were huge with a multitude of branches and points, swept back now across the water. Its nostrils skimmed the surface drawing in breath in short gasps. So proudly did it hold itself, it might have been swimming for joy. The truth lay concealed beneath the water where, Shakespeare knew, its legs would be frantic and its heart would be racing.

He heard barking and the piercing blare of horns. And then

the first dogs appeared from the woods, snarling, slavering and baying, all their senses alive at the hot, acrid scent. Without hesitation, the leading hounds plunged into the river after their quarry.

Shakespeare narrowed his eyes, peering deep into the woods. There, he saw more movement, the unstoppable advance of the hunt. The trees were suddenly alive with horses, mastiffs and men. He looked back to the water. The hart was almost across the river, but the northern bank was nothing but black, oozing mud and the animal struggled to get ashore, the mud sucking its hoofs down, holding it like a fly in syrup.

And then, somehow, it was up and out, but still not safe. Standing on the lush meadow, it appeared to be dazed, not knowing which way to turn or what to do. Immobile and weak, all its energy had been sapped by the panic-stricken swim and the battle with the deep, unyielding mud. It stumbled and seemed about to fall, its forelegs buckling, surely too spindly to support its great bulk. And was its head not too fine to hold such a forest of antlers? Its wide eyes seemed glazed, fixed on some distant point.

Then the first of the hounds was across the water, snapping at the deer's hind heels. The attack brought the hart to its senses. It kicked out, sent one of the dogs flying, found purchase in the grass and wildflowers and drew on deep reserves of strength. It began to run and soon it was in the cover of woods again. Shakespeare smiled. There was hope for it yet; it was too beautiful to die this day.

Shakespeare's musing was interrupted. His horse was buffeted from side to side. He swivelled in his saddle and found himself looking into the muzzle of a wheel-lock pistol. The horseman holding the weapon wore a quilted doublet of many colours, almost like a harlequin. But there was nothing amusing or merry about this man. He nudged his mount forward aggressively.

'Who are you?' the man asked. 'Speak now or I'll grow you a second arsehole where your belly-button now resides.'

'I am John Shakespeare.' Shakespeare noted the well-known escutcheon on the man's bright-coloured breast, the heraldic device of the bear and ragged staff of the Dudleys. 'In the service of Sir Francis Walsingham.'

'Walsingham? Then you should be in your kennel, whipped and starved like all his scurvy whelps. You have no right here. You are intruding on the royal hunt. What is worse –' he glanced at Shakespeare's sword and dagger – 'you go armed on Queen's land. I could blow you away and make a royal jest of it at supper.'

Despite the man's smooth, unbearded face, there was something darkly threatening about him, a simmering shadow of violence that could explode with the slightest tic of his slender finger on the trigger. Shakespeare kept his calm. 'Then you would have to answer to Mr Secretary, for I am here on urgent business.' As he spoke, he glanced over the man's shoulder. The main party of the hunt was emerging from the woods.

Among them was the Queen.

Their attention was focused on the far bank, watching the dogs as they raced across the meadow on the scent of the hart. As the rest of the hunt surged forward into the river, Elizabeth, riding sidesaddle, spotted the guard holding the interloper at gunpoint. She stopped momentarily, caught Shakespeare's eye, then touched the sleeve of the horseman at her side. He spurred his horse away from the company and trotted in the direction of the little side drama.

Shakespeare recognised the Earl of Leicester instantly, bristling with the haughty masculinity for which he was known throughout the world and which had won him the Queen's jealous love these many years. He was a proud, rugged man with broad shoulders, and fine attire. It seemed to Shakespeare that he was the human incarnation of the hart.

'What is this, Mr Hungate?' he demanded in a voice that required obeisance.

The guard bowed low in the saddle and as he did so Shakespeare saw that one of his ears was studded with red stones. 'He says he's John Shakespeare, Mr Secretary's man. I think him a mangy cur and worthy of putting away.'

'Is this so?' Leicester addressed the question to Shakespeare.

Shakespeare judged it wise to bow as low as Hungate had done. 'My lord, I am here with intelligence for Sir Francis. Intelligence that I believe has import for the security of the realm and the safety of Her Majesty.'

'Tell me more.' The earl's eyes drilled into Shakespeare like a mastiff watching its dinner.

Shakespeare was having none of it. 'My lord, forgive me, I must convey my information to the Principal Secretary alone.'

'I think you know who I am, Mr Shakespeare. Do you think it wise and prudent to deny me?'

'On pain of death, I have no option. Sir Francis is my master. I am certain you would not wish one of your own servants to pass secret information to another, even to one you considered a friend.'

Leicester laughed. He looked at Shakespeare yet more closely, as though measuring him up for a coffin. 'Then tell me a little about yourself, Mr Shakespeare. Are you a fighting man like Mr Hungate here? Good with blade and pistol and fists? You have no scars . . .'

'I can shoot and I can wield a sword, but I have never been in battle, if that is what you mean, my lord.'

'No, that does not surprise me. What then does Mr Secretary see in you?'

'You must ask him that.'

'Fear not, I shall. And whence do you come?'

'I was born and bred in your own county, Warwickshire, in the town of Stratford-upon-Avon. From there I went to Gray's Inn to study at law. That was where Mr Secretary found me.'

'Warwickshire?'

'That is so, sir.'

'So you will know it is become a hive of treachery.'

'If you say so, my lord.'

'It is not what I say, it is what is truth.' A flash of anger rose in Leicester's eyes. 'If you work for Mr Secretary, you should know this.' His anger subsided as quickly. 'Escort this man to the house, Mr Hungate.' He turned once again to Shakespeare. 'You speak boldly, sir. Be careful it does not cost you your head.'

Shakespeare bowed.

'And Mr Shakespeare . . .'

'My lord?'

'You might just be the man I seek.' Leicester wheeled his horse's head and kicked on to rejoin the hunt.

In a forest beneath a Scottish mountain, two men looked down at the remains of a rider. He was fifty yards from his bay stallion, which was also dead. The animal was still in harness, but its saddle and bags had gone. The rider was sprawled naked on open ground, not a trace of clothing – not even a shred of stocking or shirt – left on his corpse. Much of the body had been gnawed away by animals, and all the skin was gone. There was nothing left for them to identify him.

The cause of death seemed clear: the thin rope knotted around the neck, tightened with a six-inch wooden peg. Garrotted, as the Spaniards do.

The ghillie and his apprentice looked on with fascinated horror.

'How long has he been here, Mr Laidlaw?' the younger man asked.

'From the look of him, I'd say it must have been a while, Jamie. A good while.'

'Do you think it's him?'

'He's the right height and form, but otherwise hard to say. I recognise the horse, though. A fine steed he was. I'd swear the horse was his, so we must assume the worst.'

They wandered back to the horse and peered down at it. Bones protruded, white and innocent, from the decayed flesh at its exposed flank. Laidlaw put his hand into the wound and delved in among the stinking, dried-up mess of its vital organs. He grimaced as he went about the work, but quickly found what he was looking for. He pulled it out, rubbed it on his jerkin, then held it up to the light: a ball of lead. 'This brought the horse down. I think he tried to run, but they caught him.'

'They?'

'He could handle himself well enough. I don't think he would have fled from one man, even one with a petronel.'

'What do we do now?'

'Tell his father. It will break the old man's heart.' The ghillie looked again at the body and felt more unnerved than ever he had before. The stripping of the skin did not look like the work of animals, but of man – and a skilled man at that. He could not have done it better himself.

Chapter 4

As they rode up to the palace of Oatlands, Shakespeare tried to brush the dust from his doublet and hose; appearances were important in such places, so that men might think you worthy of note. He was not sure that he desired any more of Mr Hungate's attention, however, for he was uncomfortably aware that the guard's eyes were on him constantly, and that the muzzle of his pistol was pointing directly at his heart. The man discomfited him with the juxtaposition of harlequin colours and his cold, blue eyes, and the strange line of red stones running down the edge of one ear. This was no commonplace bodyguard or serving man.

Oatlands was not the most beautiful of the royal houses but it was one of the largest, covering nine acres in all. Once through the main gate in the long wall that enclosed the front of the stately residence, the visitor was immediately confronted by a row of what appeared to be twenty or so cottages, all interlinked and with sloping tiled roofs; these were the lodging chambers for the administrators who made everything run smoothly for the Queen and her senior courtiers. To Shakespeare, the buildings looked like nothing more glorious than the centre of a small market town. And certainly the main gatehouse in the middle of this terrace seemed more like one of the gates into London – such as Newgate or

Bishopsgate – than the entrance to one of Elizabeth's finest homes.

But the palace had a pleasant aspect. Set on a rise with views across a vast sweep of Surrey, twenty miles south-west of London, Oatlands was built of brick and surrounded by gardens and delightful deer parks which dipped down to the winding thoroughfare of the Thames.

After presenting his papers at the first gate, Shakespeare rode with his escort through into the outer courtyard where he was confronted by a much grander gatehouse that led through to the inner courtyard and the main palace hall and royal apartments. They rode without conversing and all the while Hungate kept his hand on the hilt of his pistol and the gun pointed in the direction of his charge.

Above them, rooks circled in the late summer sky. The air was still sweet for the royal court had been in residence only two days. In a week or two, the place would stink like a jakes in July and the court would move on. The fact that there were instances of plague in the nearby town of Windsor might also spur them to depart sooner rather than later.

At the inner gatehouse, a sentry listened to Shakespeare's story, then sent off an underling to tell Walsingham that a visitor had arrived.

'I believe you can lower your pistol now, Mr Hungate,' Shakespeare said, looking at his escort.

Hungate stifled a yawn. 'I believe you would make a fine pair of shoes, were I to flay you and cure your scrawny hide, but we must live with what we have.'

Shakespeare ignored him, turning away with deliberate indifference. A few minutes later a familiar face arrived: Walter Whey, a diplomatic servant and close associate of Walsingham over many years.

'Good day to you, Mr Shakespeare.'

Shakespeare slid from his horse and handed the reins to a groom. 'And to you, Mr Whey. I must see Sir Francis with all haste.'

Hungate caught Whey's attention with a jerk of his hairless chin. 'You know this useless, festering piece of waste, do you, Mr Whey? He says he's a Warwickshire man. There are many traitors in that county.'

'This is Mr Shakespeare.'

'Yes, I've heard of traitors called Shakespeare. And their cousins the Ardens. Lower than vermin, all of them, as my master will testify.' He jutted his chin at Whey. 'He's yours.' Hungate pulled on the reins, turned his horse's head and rode away, without another word.

Whey raised his eyes to the sky.

'You know Mr Hungate?'

'Don't ask. I will inform Sir Francis that you are here as soon as he is free. For the present, he is occupied so I must ask you to bide your time in an ante-room.'

Shakespeare indicated the retreating horseman. 'I ask you again, Mr Whey, what man is that?'

'That is Ruby Hungate. He is my lord of Leicester's thing. Do not be fooled by his rough manner. It is said he is the finest swordsman in all of England, and that there are no better shots with dag or hagbut. It is said he can shoot dead a bird on the wing from the saddle of a galloping horse.'

'What is his place in his lordship's retinue?'

Whey grimaced. 'Do you really want to know?'

'His doublet tells me he is a jester, but he does not make me laugh.'

'Ah, yes, his coat of many colours? Well, you are right, he is no Tarleton. I fear there is little to amuse about Mr Hungate. No, I am afraid I can tell you no more – for everything is court tittle-tattle and not to be trusted. All I would say is this: be wary. Mr Hungate is a man who bears a grudge.'

It was two hours before Shakespeare was summoned to the presence of his master, Walsingham. As Principal Secretary, he was England's second most senior minister, in thrall to no one but Her Majesty and his friend Lord Burghley, the Lord Treasurer.

They met in his private quarters in a large, cold room with a plain oak table and a stool on each side.

Walsingham gestured Shakespeare to step forward. 'John. I have a mission for you. One of great significance. But first I believe you have some intelligence for me.'

Shakespeare knew better than to expect a word of welcome from Walsingham, the man known to one and all simply as Mr Secretary. His war of secrets against England's enemies in the Catholic world allowed no time for pleasantries or idle conversation and anyway it was not in his nature.

'I do, Sir Francis. Intelligence has reached me from the searchers at Dover that an agent or emissary of the Duke of Guise is in England. They believe he has been here ten days.'

'And if they know this, why did the searchers not stop him?'

'He had already passed through the port before they found out. They believed him to be a merchant, but learnt his true identity two days ago, from a contact in Calais.'

'And what is this man's name?'

Shakespeare turned around sharply. The question came from behind him.

The Earl of Leicester was sitting on a cushioned seat set into a window alcove, one booted foot on the seat, the other on the floor. He was still in his hunting clothes, spattered with dust and mud.

Shakespeare bowed. 'My lord of Leicester. Forgive me, I did not see you there.'

'So had I been an assassin, you would now be dead.' He tilted his head languidly towards Walsingham. 'Do you not teach your young intelligencers to look about them, Mr Secretary?'

Walsingham smiled briefly. 'Do not be taken in by Mr Shakespeare's scholarly appearance. I believe he will be hard enough when the time comes.'

'God's faith, he looks scarce out of swaddling bands. How old are you, Mr Shakespeare?'

'Twenty-three, my lord.'

'You tell me you have not seen battle, yet you must have killed men in the service of your sovereign. How many?'

'I have killed no man.'

Walsingham tapped the hilt of his dagger on the table. 'There is more than one way to fight, Robin. And so back to business. Who is this Frenchman stalking our land, John?'

'The man had but one arm, his left severed at the shoulder.'

'Leloup . . .'

'Yes, that is the name I was given. François Leloup.'

Walsingham leant forward. His brow darkened. 'Well, well.'

'Does the name mean something to you, Sir Francis?'

'Yes, indeed it does. So the Wolf's Snout is here, is he?'

'The Wolf's Snout?' Leicester laughed.

'*Le Museau du Loup*. François Leloup has a rather magnificent nose. Long and sharp, like a wolf. Like his name. He is a doctor of medicine, but much more than that, he is as close to the Duke of Guise as I am to my prick. They are indivisible. When not healing the sick, he plots deaths on his master's behalf. I have always believed he was the go-between connecting Guise to the assassin Maurevert. It was Leloup who paid the blood money and gave the order for Maurevert to shoot Admiral Coligny. And yet Dr Leloup is so discreet that he keeps his own hand clean. I know Leloup of old. Like his master, he is a man of infinite charm.'

'If you delight in the company of wolves . . .'

'He was there ten years ago on the day of infamy,' Walsingham continued. 'August the twenty-third in the year of our Lord fifteen seventy-two. The day the streets of Paris ran red and the cries of dying Protestants outsang the pealing bells. Leloup was at the side of Henri de Guise as they finished off the work begun by Maurevert and killed Admiral Coligny as he lay wounded. And yet I have reason to believe that he also saved Protestant lives when the royal mob ran riot and slaughtered women and children. The Catholics were killing, killing, killing, but Leloup saved my friend Jean d'Arpajon and his family from the sword. He took them to the Hôtel de Guise, where they were safe. I heard this from d'Arpajon's own lips when he came to England seeking refuge, like so many Huguenots. And so when I have heard tell of the wickedness of Guise and Leloup, I have had pause for thought. Did they save d'Arpajon merely for money – for certainly he paid three thousand livres for his life – or out of pity?'

'Guise show mercy!' Leicester almost snorted with derision as he spoke. 'He was at the very heart of the massacre. It is said his men were painted crimson, their hair tangled with gore, their hands sticky with blood.'

Walsingham spread his hands as though to show they, at least, were free of blood. 'Guise had cause to kill Coligny. He believed the admiral had assassinated his father. Perhaps, too, he took the opportunity to kill others among his enemies. But I do not believe he murdered the wholly innocent. Did Leloup marshal the wolves? Was he one of them? He is a puzzle to me, as is his master.'

'But it sounds as if you *liked* them, Mr Secretary? You liked Leloup . . .' Leicester was aghast.

'He was amusing. It was hard not to like him. I felt much the same about Guise himself. At that time, before the massacre and years before his leadership of the Catholic League, I did not even believe the duke was a man of particular faith. He was not insane like King Charles, nor wicked like the Medici devil, and yet somehow she shifted the blame for all that happened on to Guise. Catherine de Medici could learn nothing from Machiavelli . . .'

'So who plotted the massacre?'

'The whole royal council of France. They were all in it, up to their very eyes in gore. But that is all by the by. Blood in the gutters. What we must now divine is where Leloup is and *why* he is here. Your thoughts, John?'

'It must involve the Queen of Scots.'

Walsingham looked towards Leicester. 'You see, my lord, the young apprentice is already thinking like his master.' He clapped his hands together lightly. 'Yes, John, this most certainly involves the Scots witch. Guise wishes to secure her liberty and set her on the throne of England. He makes no secret of this. Why else is he building ships at the Normandy harbours if not as an invasion fleet?'

'So Leloup is here to set her free?'

At his side, Walsingham had a small silver cup. He picked it up and sipped delicately. 'This is part of a greater plan – to seize the crown of France, too. King Henri is vulnerable. Like a fool, he goes away on retreat just as Guise reaches the height of his power. The people of France love Guise. The Catholics would crown him in an instant. He believes that if he can seize the thrones of England and Scotland, Henri would be powerless to withstand him. This is what the Guise family have desired and conspired towards for many years.'

'Then we must stop him,' Leicester said, hammering his right fist into his left palm. 'But surely Mary is safely guarded.'

Walsingham stroked his dark beard as though trying to lengthen his sombre face. 'I pray it is so.'

'Do you have reason to think otherwise?'

'We have been receiving reports for eighteen months now of Guise's intentions to secure her freedom. Every week, we hear more reports of greased priests in the region around Sheffield Castle where she is held. And nor can we trust the northern lords who inhabit – *infest* – those parts. Beware former enemies. Never trust a man whom once you have harmed.'

Never trust a man whom you have harmed. It was a familiar refrain from Walsingham, one of the first things John Shakespeare had learnt from his master when he left his law studies at Gray's Inn and entered the great man's service four years since. What Walsingham meant was that though the noble families of the north had been punished and humiliated when their rebellion was quelled in the bloody year of sixty-nine, it would be dangerous to believe them chastened. And while that vicious event now seemed long gone, the northern lords still felt aggrieved and would do anything in their power, seize any opportunity, to take revenge on those who had brought them low.

'Has the time come to move Mary Stuart south?' Shakespeare suggested tentatively. 'Away from such people.'

'The Queen will not hear of it. She does not wish her cousin any closer to her than is absolutely necessary. But there are *other* possibilities. We need to prove to Her Majesty that Sheffield has become ill-equipped for the task. I want you to go there, John. Use your judgement carefully. Is Sheffield Castle a fit place to hold this Queen of Scots? Is it well-guarded? If there are holes, find them. Then bring me a full and detailed report.'

Shakespeare bowed. 'Yes, Sir Francis.'

'Look for Leloup while you are there. For I believe you are right in suggesting that is his motive for coming to England. And in Sheffield, you will have assistance. You will find one of my seasoned men there. His name is Richard Topcliffe. He is there on another matter, but I would like you to work together.' Walsingham paused and pressed his fingers together. 'Dick Topcliffe is a very different man to you, John, so you may not agree with him on every point. However, your opinions will both be of great interest to me. To that end, you will take letters from me ordering him to help you. I merely warn you of this: you will doubtless find Mr Topcliffe to be strong meat, but he has the Queen's trust, and mine. You do not need to like him, but you *will* work with him.'

Shakespeare bowed.

'Return with Mr Topcliffe by way of Tutbury where Mary was held before. It is far enough from the north and a good distance from the court. Sometimes, I wish we had never moved her from there. See what state of repair the castle is in. How soon could it be brought into service again? Mr Topcliffe's help will be of great value, for he knows Tutbury of old. Do you understand this? And most importantly, set the search for Leloup. Return to Seething Lane this day and have Mr Phelippes send out word to all our intelligencers and agents to find him. He may have headed north, but we must not take that for granted. If he is in London, Tom Phelippes will find him soon enough.'

'Very well, Sir Francis.' Shakespeare bowed and moved towards the door.

'Wait.' Walsingham stayed him with a flick of his deeply veined hand. 'I have not yet told you the true reason I wished to see you. The mission I mentioned.'

Shakespeare paused expectantly.

'It involves your own county, John. My lord of Leicester tells me he touched on the subject when you became tangled up in the hunt. Robin, you know Warwickshire better than any man; explain your fears to Mr Shakespeare.'

Leicester was up now and pacing. 'The peril is not merely in the north, you see. It is in my own lands in middle England. Sir Thomas Lucy, my chief man in the county, has a war on his hands trying to put down the papist vermin that run free like rats in a sewer. I do not exaggerate when I tell you that my county – *our* county, Mr Shakespeare – has become a Judas nest of conspirators.'

Walsingham turned his penetrating gaze on Shakespeare. 'You begin to understand, John? We believe you may be the perfect man to help Sir Thomas Lucy counter this terror. Indeed, I am *certain* you are ready for this important task and that you will not let me down.'

'Conspiracy abounds in Warwickshire like a high summer stink,' Leicester said. 'You could draw a ten-mile circle around the town of Stratford and within that roundel you would find half the papist traitors in England. First there was this Simon Hunt, a teacher at the grammar, who now licks the Antichrist's arse in the Vatican. Then the traitor Cottam. Now the fugitives Dibdale and Angel.' He locked eyes with Shakespeare. 'Do you know these people?'

'Yes.' Shakespeare knew them all well. Hunt had taught him at school. Benedict Angel, the same age as Shakespeare, had been his classmate for a while. His sister, Florence Angel, a year or two older, had been his friend in their youth. Now Angel had been ordained a Catholic priest and was on the run. He knew the Cottams too. Thomas Cottam was brother of John Cottam, Hunt's successor as schoolmaster. Thomas Cottam had been executed earlier in the year for treason, having entered the country secretly as a priest. Robert Dibdale was also a priest and, like Benedict Angel, was on the loose, his whereabouts unknown. They all had close links with Stratford-upon-Avon and they were all deemed enemies of the state.

'There are others,' Leicester continued, warming to his vehement harangue. 'What of Catesby of Lapworth? Some say he harboured the deluded Campion. Nor do I trust the Throckmortons who live close by at Coughton Court. These people conspire against God and the Queen.'

'This priest Angel,' Walsingham said, taking up the earl's thread. 'I took pity on the man and ordered him released from the Gatehouse gaol and sent into exile. Well, he *has* been freed – but there is no record of him leaving the country. Find out where he is. Often such men make contact with their families. I am sure you will discover the truth soon enough. This so-called Angel should not be at large. Go home to Stratford after Tutbury. It cannot be far. Find Angel and the others. Root out treason, John. Root it out and destroy it. This is what I want from you. This is what I have been training you for. It is what I saw in you when I snatched you from the tedium of your law studies.'

Shakespeare bowed again, but said nothing. Beneath his linen shirt and plain doublet, his body was soaked with sweat. Angel and the others were the people he grew up with. Was Walsingham testing his loyalty – seeing whether he had the stomach to turn in his neighbours? Was that what this was all about? Was that why Leicester was here?

'And there is Arden, too. Do not forget Arden,' Leicester went on. 'I raised Edward Arden up as county sheriff, but then I saw his true colours. The devil take him. Do you know this Catholic viper, Mr Shakespeare? Are the Ardens not kin to the Catesbys?'

'I have met Edward Arden, my lord,' Shakespeare said in what he hoped was an even voice. Oh yes, he knew Arden. How could he not know him when his own mother, Mary, was born an Arden? Their blood was his blood. He knew, too, that Edward Arden had insulted Leicester publicly and with utter contempt, calling him 'whoremaster' at a time when the earl was dealing lewdly with another man's wife. The Earl of Leicester, a man ruled by pride, did not forgive such slurs.

It felt to Shakespeare as if he were manacled to a wall in the coldest Tower dungeon and that these two men, Walsingham and Leicester, had red-glowing irons in their gauntleted fists. *Bring your old friends and your family to the gallows or we will know that you are not one of us. Turn in the traitors – or we will consider* you *the traitor.* He had not foreseen this when he agreed to enter the service of Sir Francis Walsingham. This was torture of the soul.

Suddenly Leicester clapped him about the shoulder and growled a laugh. 'I am told you are an honest man, Mr Shakespeare, an honest witness. Did you hear of the great hart in this day's hunt? He escaped us! Now and for all time he is a royal hart. Tell me: do you have the heart of that hart? Can *you* earn such royal favour? Will you hazard your very life for England?'

Chapter 5

SHAKESPEARE REINED IN to a slow walk, easing his mount after the long ride from Oatlands to London. He turned left and rode north along Seething Lane in the east of the city, stopping at last before the woodframe house, ancient and weathered, that he counted as home. It stood four storeys high and melded into the night sky. His hired man, Boltfoot Cooper, opened the door to him and bowed. 'Boltfoot, we ride north tomorrow. We will go armed.'

'Yes, master.'

'Is there food in the house?'

'Perhaps some old bread. A little ale . . .'

'Did I not ask you to buy some food from the market?'

'No, master.'

'Well, in future you will think to do so, unasked.'

Boltfoot grumbled something inaudible.

Shakespeare shook his head and wondered, not for the first time, whether he had made a terrible error in hiring this lame seafarer. His tone hardened. 'You must earn your keep.'

'Yes, master.'

'Take the horse to the stable and see it fed. And then go to the Blue Boy and get their kitchens to provide some pie or meats. Anything halfway edible.' Could he not have at least brought some eggs and meat into the house? Shakespeare handed over the reins of his mount and watched Boltfoot limping along the road, dragging his club-foot through the dust. Neither servant nor intelligencer, he was a gnarled ship-wreck of a man who looked as ill at ease on land as a fish and the truth was he had hired him because he liked him and trusted him – and because he had fighting skills. Shakespeare was all too aware of his own lack of experience in that regard. Though he was a great deal stronger than he looked to the Earl of Leicester, yet he was untested; he had never been in a fight, not even a taproom brawl.

This was where Boltfoot came in. He knew how to defend himself and would not flinch in the face of enemy fire and shot. He was skilled with cutlass and caliver, his weapons of choice. And what if he had no conversation, and had little in the way of background save his time as a mariner? On the rare occa-sions when he did open his mouth to speak it was usually to pour scorn upon his former captain, Drake. 'Drake a hero? He would sell his own mother to the Spaniard for a groat.' Shakespeare smiled at the thought. He hoped Boltfoot would speak in more flattering terms about him. He took a candle into the pantry, and found a crust of bread and examined it in the guttering light. It had an unpleasant coating of blue mould. He shook the keg of ale. Some liquid and lees sploshed around, so he drew it out into a tankard. Sniffing at it, he put the mug to his lips, then spat. It was undrinkable. He cursed. This would not do. He needed a maidservant. When Boltfoot returned with the unwelcome news that the Blue Boy had closed its doors, he took himself to bed for want of anything better to do.

In the morning, hungry and ill-rested, he took breakfast at the tavern, and then strode along Seething Lane, avoiding the piles of horse-dung and human waste that clogged the way. The stench did not help his mood. Why in God's name had the gong farmers not cleared this path overnight? A kite wheeled overhead, searching for its dinner. Another perched on the roof of St Olave's, pecking the juicy muscle meat from some rodent. London, once a lion among cities, was becoming more and more like a sick tomcat.

Arriving at Walsingham's mansion, he sought out the senior intelligencers. This house, close by the Thames and the Tower, was one of Sir Francis's two residences. On Walsingham's advice, Shakespeare had deliberately found a house close by for his own dwelling. 'If you wish to work for me, I expect nothing more than your body and soul, John. That means you either live with me, or near me. I cannot be doing with sending messengers to fetch you.'

Near to him seemed the better option.

He found Thomas Phelippes in a back office. The room was stacked high with books and documents and smelt of sweat. Phelippes was peering down hard through his small round spectacle-glasses, examining a scrap of paper, his lank yellow hair falling about his pox-ridden face.

'Mr Phelippes.'

'Wait.'

Shakespeare pulled the paper from the table. 'No, Mr Phelippes, this will not wait.'

Phelippes tried in vain to snatch back the paper. 'So the fledgling crow thinks it has talons?'

He ignored the barb. 'I have come from Mr Secretary at Oatlands. A Frenchman named François Leloup has landed covertly and is at large in England. It may be that he has gone to Sheffield. I am to ride there this day. You, meanwhile, along with Mr Gregory, are to raise a search for him in London and the south.'

'Do you think to command me?'

Shakespeare had had to put up with Phelippes's goading ever since he joined Walsingham's service and it was becoming tiresome. Phelippes knew very well that the order had come from Walsingham. 'I will tell you about Leloup.'

The codebreaker laughed. 'I know all about the good Dr Leloup. I know more about him than does his own mother.'

'Then you will know under which stone to look.' Shakespeare replaced the paper on the table. 'Good day to you, Mr Phelippes. You know what is required of you.'

Shakespeare turned to walk from the room, but he felt the clasp of Thomas Phelippes's hand on his sleeve.

'Wait, Shakespeare. Let us talk more of this Frenchman.'

Shakespeare paused, shaking off Phelippes's hand. 'Very well. What I know is what Mr Secretary has told me, that he is about fifty, elegant, assured, dark-haired when last he saw him, with a prominent nose and only one arm. He will not find it easy to hide.'

Phelippes nodded. 'His arm was carried away by a cannon-ball at Jarnac, where he was helping the wounded. In France they know him as *Le Museau du Loup*.'

'The Wolf's Snout. Mr Secretary mentioned that.'

'Guise will have ordered him to prepare the way for his invasion fleet. He wants the bosom serpent free and our own sovereign lady murdered. These are all parts of the whole.' Phelippes leant forward excitedly, all signs of hostility gone. 'I have come from Bruges this week. I learnt there that Guise and the English exiles have sent priests to England who have been told that their mortal souls are safe however many they kill, so long as their victims are Protestants. It accords with everything that Mr Secretary's man Lawrence Tomson discovered from the papal agent in Bologna.'

'Did your Bruges contact name the priests?'

'He named one. Benedict Angel, originally of Warwickshire. Find him and we may find Leloup too.'

Father Benedict Angel made the sign of the cross and bowed low. Then he turned, away from the crucifix, the missal, the chalice and paten on the little table that served as an altar. His heart was a flood of raging fire, fanned by the glory of the mass. At times, he could not breathe, so overwhelming was the passion and joy of Christ within him. Every sinew told him to shout it loud amid the heavenly choir of trumpets and voices, the fury of bliss in the storm. Yet his voice was as quiet as his manner; no one would ever see the torrent and turmoil within.

Once the mass was said, the sacred objects must be hidden without delay. He quickly removed his robes – the exquisitely embroidered chasuble, the cincture and the white alb. Who knew when the door would be hammered down with a ram? The aroma of incense could not be hidden so easily. 'Florence, if you would pack away the mass things.' His sister bowed to him and set about her chore, wrapping the precious artefacts in a woollen cloth. With her golden hair tied back and concealed beneath a coif, it seemed to him that she looked very much like the nuns at Louvain. But the life of quiet contemplation would never be her lot; she must fight like him, a soldier of God.

'I have here a letter,' he said, holding aloft a folded paper, the seal broken.

He stood small and neat by the fire. He kept his hair and beard short. Now that his robes were removed, he wore a dun-coloured doublet and hose. He thought they made him look like a gentleman of Calvinist persuasion, which was the guise he adopted while travelling through England. Here in Warwickshire, however, he could not walk abroad, for he was too well known. He had come to this house by night and had stayed hidden away by day. He had been here all summer long and had reconciled many souls to the true faith. There was but one more task to be undertaken, and then his mission would be complete.

He looked around him at the faces of his companions and it seemed to him that they glowed with ardour in the glimmer of a dozen candles. Here in this well-appointed room, light and shadow flickered on the walls. The windows were shuttered against the moonlight and against prying eyes.

Apart from Benedict Angel and his sister, Florence, there were five others present: three men and two women. They would do Christ's holy work. The forces of repression, of Walsingham, Burghley and the pseudo-Church, would call them conspirators; he called them God's agents.

They watched him expectantly, their eyes on the letter he held, awaiting word of what they should do next.

'This letter is a precious treasure,' he said in a low voice. 'It is written in the hand of our most gracious sovereign lady, Mary. The true Queen of England, Ireland and Scotland. Look –' he unfurled the paper and pointed his finger at the bottom of the page – 'this is her name, in her own hand. *Marie R.*'

His eyes were caught by a movement. The young man named Somerville had pulled out his pistol. He was dangerously excited. 'Put away the pistol, Mr Somerville.'

But Somerville was not listening. He waved the weapon around, pointing at imaginary targets. One moment, his eyes were on Father Benedict Angel, the next on some object such as a book or cup. He pretended to pull the trigger and made a little popping noise with his pursed lips. 'There she is. Look, I shoot the usurper dead.' He stared at Angel, looking for approbation.

'I know you have come here this evening in the hope of final orders,' Angel said, 'but in the name of Jesus Christ and His

Holy Mother, I beg you to have patience.' He looked at the other faces. 'All of you. Trust in this letter.'

'What does it say?' Somerville demanded urgently. He had lowered his pistol. 'What does it say?'

'It is encoded in a cipher no man can break, not even Walsingham and his demons. But –' Angel waved aloft a second piece of paper – 'I have here a concise version of her words, written for me by one of those closest to her who helped her write it and who knows the code.'

One of those closest to her. Buchan Ord, the man who had devised this at the English seminary in Douai. When would he come here? Soon, God willing. Soon.

'What does it say? What does it say?'

'Be calm, Mr Somerville. I entreat you.' As an ordained priest of the Roman Catholic Church, Benedict Angel was used to making himself heard without shouting. Leave the shouting to the pseudo-priests who now infected so much of this benighted land. And yet he worried that he had been a little sharp, had betrayed his irritation. 'What I can tell you is that she calls on us to be strong and to do what we are bidden to do by those who come to us in her name. It says the plan is advanced and that we will be required to hazard our lives very soon. She knows we will do all that is asked of us. By the grace of God the father, God the son and God the holy ghost, Marie Stuart. Our true monarch.' He scrunched up the second paper in his fist and threw it into the hearth where it blazed up, then died down, reduced to blackened ash. The other letter, the encrypted one, he re-folded with care and handed to his sister. She took it with reverential awe, kissed it and bowed to her brother.

Somerville was still agitated and had begun waving his pistol around again. 'We must act now, before it is too late,' he said. He grasped the stock of his gun in both hands and pointed it at Angel. 'If we do not do this now . . . no, I say again, we *must* act now.'

'I beg you, put up your pistol, Mr Somerville,' Angel said calmly. 'It is better that we *pray* for guidance than brandish guns. They have a tendency to go off when least expected or desired. I can be of no service to God or our sovereign if you kill me.'

'You are too cautious, Father. The slow fox wins no hens. My pistol burns with holy intent. Has the Holy Father not ruled it lawful—'

Angel raised his right hand, palm open, to stop Somerville's flow. 'In good time. We will wait until all is confirmed. We *must* wait. There is another who will come and bring word of what is expected of us. He will come soon. I pledge this to you. If we are over-hasty, if we move from here, we will likely die and nothing will have been achieved. I have no fear of death, but God would not thank us for shedding our blood without first fulfilling His holy mission.'

For a few moments they were all silent. Angel bent his head and began to intone a prayer in Latin.

There was a sudden gasp. His sister jerked back her head as if seized by ecstasy. Her back arched, her generous red mouth opened and exhaled a guttural rush of air, and her body began to jerk violently. She fell on her knees on the wooden floor and shook like an ash leaf in a stiff breeze.

The mass things tipped from the unfurling cloth and clattered to the floor. She fell backwards, convulsed once more, then became rigid and remained still.

'It is the letter,' Somerville said. 'It is holy. It has burnt her.'

Benedict Angel clutched his hands to his thin chest. The seraphim sang in his burning heart. The maid had come to Florence again. He was *sure* it was the maid. He knelt at her side and put an arm around her quivering shoulders. 'What is it, Florence? What do you hear?'

Florence Angel's breathing was fast and shallow. Her eyes were wide open and fixed at some point directly above her. Her lips seemed to be quivering, as though she were trying to say something.

Her brother put his ear close to her mouth. 'Is it her, Florence? What does she tell you?'

Her voice – if it *was* her voice – was the quietest of whispers. Was it the whispering of the wind outside the window or was she speaking? It was so hushed that none in the room save Benedict Angel could hear it. He clutched her quivering hand and nodded soothingly, as though he understood, as though Florence were a vessel pouring forth words like holy water into the cup of his ear alone.

The conspirators watched in dread fascination. They believed they heard sounds, but still could make out no words. Finally she shook again, her body arched once more as though her spine would break, and then went utterly limp, like a rag. Father Benedict signalled to one of the other women in the room and together they helped Florence up and on to a settle and made her comfortable among some cushions.

Angel stroked her brow. 'Fetch her some water, Margaret. This will pass in a short while. The holy spirit has come to her.'

'What did she say, what did you hear?' Somerville demanded.

'It was the maid . . .'

'The Maid of Orleans? Joan of Arc?'

'I heard her so clearly . . . she was burning, burning. She spoke through Florence, as she has spoken before. Her young body was bound to the stake and the flames devoured her. I could hear the crackle of blazing wood, the sough of the rushing wind and the cries of her passion. She was in the throes of death and yet she spoke to Florence. I heard her voice. I heard it all, as clear as I can hear you.'

'What? What did she say?'

'She said that God would give us a sign when it was time. She said there would be an omen and no one would be in any doubt. She begged us to stand strong, as she stood strong, to trust in Mary, and then she breathed her last and gave up her saintly spirit to the Lord.'

Chapter 6

ON THE WAY north, Shakespeare and Boltfoot rested just one night at an inn, ate, slept and then rode on by day and night, coming at last out of Sherwood Forest into the hills surrounding the prosperous market town of Sheffield. They trotted into the main square, close to the castle, half an hour before dawn on the second day, tired and hungry. In front of them, dark and asleep, stood a coaching inn. In the pre-dawn gloom, they made out a sign that revealed the inn's name as the Cutler's Rest.

'Wake someone, Boltfoot.'

Boltfoot dismounted and limped to the locked door and hammered at it with his fist. Shakespeare heard soft footfalls from inside, then the drawing back of an iron bolt. The door opened and a young woman appeared on the threshold, lit by the candle she held in her left hand.

'Good morrow, gentlemen.'

For a moment neither Shakespeare nor Boltfoot said a word. This was the last place or time of day that they had expected to find such beauty. She wore a plain linen smock and apron. Her hair was long and fair and tousled as though she had just risen from her pillow, her eyes blue and a little bleary. But it was the exquisite imperfection, the gap between the otherwise perfect teeth, that caught the eye and set her apart.

'Are you wishing to break your fast or do you seek a chamber?'

'We need food,' Boltfoot said. 'So do our horses.'

'And a chamber. Somewhere to wash and dust off our apparel.'

'Then you have come to the right house,' the woman said.

She smiled and Shakespeare thought that he had never seen such a lovely face, not even among the ladies of the royal court. He could not take his eyes off her and was irritated to note that Boltfoot, too, was staring at her longingly.

As she bustled about, preparing food and lighting a fire, she told them that her name was Kat Whetstone and that she was the daughter of the innkeeper. 'And what brings you two fine gentlemen to Sheffield town?' she said as she brought them jugs of ale and large trenchers of butter, eggs, bacon and roasted blood pudding.

'We have business at the castle.'

'Well, then you will find more comforts at the Cutler's Rest than you will within those cold fortress walls. We offer all the pleasures, master . . .'

'All the pleasures?' Shakespeare raised his eyebrows.

She smiled. 'Why, honest English food, soft feather beds and great good cheer. We have them all – and the price is fair.'

'Where is the castle gate from here?'

'To the right, down by the river. Not more than a furlong.'

'We shall see.' In truth, Shakespeare thought, it was not a bad idea. He would like to hear about the castle from outside as well as in. He took a deep draught of ale and began to eat. He needed to be at the castle quickly, to present himself to the Earl of Shrewsbury, the long-suffering keeper of Mary, Queen of Scotland, the woman Walsingham referred to as *the Scots devil* and others called *bosom serpent*.

*

Sheffield Castle nestled at the confluence of the rivers Don and Sheaf, which defended its northern and eastern walls. The water was channelled around to form a moat on the other two sides.

Shakespeare's first impression was of an old-fashioned motte-and-bailey fortress with impressive earthworks and a stone palisade. From what Walsingham had told him, it had been built in the days of the third Henry, three hundred years since. Its high stone walls then would have held the local people in thrall and would have been a deterrent to any opposing host armed with simple swords and pikes. Even a siege engine of those days, such as the trebuchet or catapult, would have had little impact. Yet those same walls would crumble before today's mighty cannon. A battery of culverins would reduce the stones to rubble.

At the gatehouse, to the west, Shakespeare handed over the papers bearing Walsingham's seal. Within a few minutes, he and Boltfoot were relieved of their weapons and ushered through to the earl's great chamber, in the outer bailey. The hall was hung with tapestries and to Shakespeare's surprise some carpets were laid out on the floor for walking on, something he had never seen before, even at court. Boltfoot stayed outside the door.

George Talbot, Earl of Shrewsbury, was sitting at the end of a long, oak table, carved with mythic beasts and polished to a shine. He was writing, a secretary standing at his side with inkhorn in his outstretched hand. The earl occasionally dipped his quill in the ink, but he did not look up. At last, he decided he had finished and read the paper through. Finally, he added his mark with a flourish and handed the paper to his man. 'Seal it and send it,' he ordered. Only then did Shrewsbury look up at Shakespeare, who was standing at a distance from him. The earl gestured briskly with his hand. 'Draw near, sir, draw near.'

Shakespeare approached and bowed, all the while studying the old nobleman's face. As he neared the great age of sixty, Shrewsbury looked tired. His skin was thin and lined like parchment, his beard long and wispy and grey, his eyes heavy-lidded and distant.

'I am John Shakespeare, my lord, in the employ of Sir Francis Walsingham.'

'So I see from your papers. Why are you here? Are you sent to spy on me?'

'No, sir.'

'Then what is it? Do you seek dirty little morsels for the shrew my wife? Are you in *her* pay? Has the shrew sent you?'

Shakespeare was disconcerted by the earl's tone. Shrewsbury seemed like a lighted match, hovering over the touchpowder of an arquebus, and even without digging further he knew he would have to recommend change: the earl had borne the onerous task of keeping Mary Stuart prisoner for almost fourteen years – far too long for one man to endure. It was said at court that his health was diminished and his marriage to Bess of Hardwick long gone to perdition. Now, looking at the man in the flesh, it was clear that the gossips spoke true.

'I have never met your wife, my lord. I am here on the orders of Mr Secretary, as you can see from my papers.'

'Then why are you here? Get it out, man. Speak plain.'

Shrewsbury was the wealthiest noble in the land and he was angry. Most young men of modest birth would be intimidated by him, but Shakespeare looked the earl straight in his watery blue eyes. 'I am here to seek a Frenchman named Leloup, whom we know to be in the country. It is thought possible – no, *likely* – that he intended coming here to Sheffield.'

'A Frenchman?'

It seemed to Shakespeare that the ragged lines in Shrewsbury's face were suddenly deeper, his pallid skin paler. 'A one-armed

Frenchman with a nose that has been compared to that of a wolf's. He would be difficult to miss.'

'Seguin.' The earl sighed heavily. 'One arm . . .'

'Have you seen him?'

'I fear I have. Yes, yes, he was here. He called himself François Seguin, doctor of medicine. And like a fool I allowed him to see her.'

Shakespeare was appalled. 'He was permitted to meet the Queen of Scots?'

'Four days ago. The papist had been begging me for months to allow her a visit from a new physician, one she had heard of in France when she was married to the French king, one who she said would be able to save her where other men could not. She told me that her own physician, Dr Burgoyne, and her surgeon, Jarvis, lacked knowledge and potions and that she would die without Seguin's care and ministration.'

'Did you meet this man?'

'I entertained him to dinner. He was good company. I do not have much in the way of company, Mr Shakespeare. As you must know, I am forbidden to leave my post as custodian and come to court. And so I take my cheer where I may. Visitors are welcome at my table. Even young factotums of Walsingham if they have wit. Anyway, continue, if you will. Who is this Seguin?'

'His real name is Leloup. He is the Duke of Guise's man.'

'Guise?' The little colour left in the earl's face drained away.

'When not ministering to the sick, he organises assassinations on the duke's behalf.'

'God's blood, what have I done?'

'That is what we must discover. Is Leloup still here?'

Shrewsbury shook his head. 'He left soon after their meeting. He came to me and thanked me for allowing him access, but said that he could not stay, for he had to bring mithridate to her, or she would most certainly die. He said he would be back as soon as he could. I shook him by the hand and hurried him on his way, for I feared the worst. Mary has ailed for many months now. My duty is to keep her alive, Mr Shakespeare, whatever other men might wish.'

'How long was Leloup with her? Was he accompanied?'

'He arrived here alone. He did not even have a servant. The only one with him when he met Mary Stuart was her own man, who resides here in her apartments, a young Scot named Buchan Ord. My chief of guards, Mr Wren, told me they were with her an hour.'

'I will need to speak with Mr Ord and Mr Wren.'

'That will be easily arranged.'

Shakespeare was appalled. The earl had clearly been guilty of a shocking dereliction of duty. At the very least, he should have requested permission from the Privy Council before allowing Mary such a visitor. As a Privy Councillor himself – even one who was never able to attend meetings – he should have known as much. And Shakespeare was aware that this was not the first time the earl had taken such matters into his own hands. Perhaps the scandalous talk at court that he was becoming altogether too close to the Scots Queen had some foundation in fact. Shakespeare kept his expression carefully neutral.

'Tell me more about your surveillance of Mary, if you would, my lord.'

'Surveillance?'

'Did anyone manage to overhear Leloup's conversation with her?'

'What are you implying, Shakespeare?'

'Is she spied on at all times?'

'Do you think I am a man without honour? This may be a garrison but it is also my home. Mary is my royal guest, Queen of Scotland. I will not countenance Walsingham's damnable practices in this place. It is enough that I must hold the wretched woman captive these interminable years . . .'

Shakespeare needed no more evidence; however suitable the earl might once have been as a gaoler, those days were past. He needed to be replaced. The next question was over the security of the castle. If Leloup was plotting to break Mary free from her cage, then someone must have spotted a hole in the security arrangements. John Shakespeare had to seek out that hole and close it. First, however, he had to send a message post-haste to Walsingham.

'I will need access to every part of the castle and everyone within it.'

'As you will, Mr Shakespeare, though I cannot believe you will find anything that Mr Beale missed when he was here last year. He was painfully thorough.'

'What of guards? Is the garrison at full strength? Do you require more?'

'And what if I do? Will you give me some?'

'My lord, you continually answer my questions with questions.'

'And you are damnably impertinent questioning me in this manner. If you wish to know about the sentries, speak to the chief of guards.'

'No, sir, I desire *your* opinion. If you need greater strength, I am certain the Privy Council will provide it.'

'Mr Shakespeare, who do you think pays for all this?' Shrewsbury swept his long arm in a circle to indicate the entirety of his property. 'Who do you think pays for the two hundred sentries that patrol this castle and grounds? I do, sir. All of it. I pay, too, for Mary and her entourage. Her gentle-men demand eight dishes at every meal, while her ladies consume five apiece. All their wine and food and depredations are costed to my purse. Her courtiers are barbarians. They ruin or purloin my plate and they despoil my hangings. An inventory has been done this year and I am appalled at the loss that my stewards have uncovered.'

'Surely this will be paid for, my lord? Does the Scots Queen contribute nothing for her own keep?'

'Nothing, nor will she while she is not allowed her freedom. Worst of all are the habits of her people. They care not for privies or garderobes, taking their easement where they will, in the corners of their chambers. Her apartments stink like a midden! And for this, I am paid thirty pounds a week – *reduced*, I say, from fifty-two! Do Her Majesty and her Council think this is enough to pay for a royal court, for that is what Mary has here? I tell you it scarce covers the wine and food they consume each day! I have worn out so many quills requesting Burghley for more money that I fear Yorkshire will soon be void of geese. I do believe my letters are the source of much merriment for the Lord Treasurer and Her Majesty. Ha-ha, the old fool George Talbot is asking for money again!' He paused for breath and shook his head wearily. 'It seems you have no notion of the way things work.'

'Then I must learn, my lord.' And quickly, he thought.

'Well, you are here now and I know you will report everything you see and hear to Mr Secretary, so it is better that you hear my side too. Come to me at noon.' The earl's tone seemed a little less sharp. 'We will eat together and I will answer your questions. My friend Mr Topcliffe will most likely join us after his morning hunting.' Shrewsbury smiled and waved his hand in dismissal.

Shakespeare and Boltfoot walked to the guardhouse. The sentries eyed them with suspicion.

Their leader, the sergeant of guards, took the paper Shakespeare proffered. It contained instructions from

Shrewsbury that they were to be given all the assistance they required. 'I have seen it all before, Mr Shakespeare,' the sergeant said, giving the paper the most cursory of glances. 'Every year there is a supposed plot to break her from her gaol. And every year someone like you comes along and tells the Privy Council she should be moved somewhere more secure. It all comes to nothing, of course. No plot, no move except for the occasional sojourn at the manor or summer trips to take the waters at Buxton. But we'll go through it all with you as always. Now, where do you want to start?'

Shakespeare was silent for a few moments as he looked the man in the eye. The sergeant, a strong-armed man with a shaven face and no neck, looked straight back at him, unblinking, his open face a portrait of benign innocence. But Shakespeare knew better. This was insolence. 'Mr Wren, I wish to see and hear everything about this place. If there is a stone loose in the wall, you will tell me about it. If a bluecoat has lifted a scullion's skirts, then you will pass me the knowledge of it.'

'Thy will be done, almighty sir. And there will be unicorn pie for supper . . .'

Shakespeare looked at Boltfoot, who shook his head slowly. Shakespeare turned back to the sergeant, held his gaze and frowned. 'Speak to me in that manner again, Mr Wren, and I will have you removed from your post, and worse.'

'You have the power to do that, do you, sir?'

'I have the power to do it and I *will* do it. I am here on Queen's business and I will tolerate neither slackness nor impudence.'

At the mention of the Queen, the sergeant's demeanour changed as swiftly as the weather. 'Forgive me, sir. I intended no disrespect.'

'How long have you been at the castle?'

'Since the Scots Queen first arrived here in November fifteen seventy. I was promoted sergeant of guards in seventy-four.'

Like his master, Shrewsbury, he had probably been in the job a great deal too long, Shakespeare thought. The danger in a man holding such an office over many years was the carelessness that came with familiarity and too much confidence. But one thing was certain: Wren would know the castle and grounds better than any other.

'Good, then you will be my escort, Sergeant. Within and without the castle walls. I wish to hear everything you know about the Scots Queen and those who attend upon her. I wish, too, to know everything you have heard from the goodwives and gossips and in the taverns hereabouts. Do you understand?'

'Yes, sir.'

'A room has been set aside for me by the hall. Have the steward send me a courier within the half-hour. Not just anyone – your fastest, most trustworthy rider.'

'Yes, sir.'

'You will come to me at one o'clock.'

The sergeant snapped his heels together and bowed obediently.

'What is the watchword this day?'

Wren's mouth opened, then closed. A look of desperate bewilderment crossed his brow. 'I – I am not permitted to say, master.'

'Would you cross me?'

'No, sir. I would happily tell you, but I cannot.'

'You speak well, for had you revealed the word I would have had you dismissed on the spot. Now go about your business.'

The guard clicked his heels again and saluted. Shakespeare touched Boltfoot's arm and they walked back towards the hall.

'I have work for you, Boltfoot.'

'Yes, master.'

'You will go from here and examine the castle walls from the outside. And when darkness falls, you will break in . . .'

Chapter 7

SHAKESPEARE DESPATCHED THE courier with his letter to Walsingham at Oatlands. It told of Leloup's visit and subsequent disappearance, that was all. He would reveal his doubts about the Earl of Shrewsbury to Walsingham in person; such opinions were not to be consigned to paper.

He wondered for a moment whether Shrewsbury might intercept the letter, for he would guess it was not flattering to him. But Shrewsbury would know, too, that the information the letter contained could not be held back for long. Walsingham would learn of Leloup's visit to Mary eventually. One way or another.

After the courier had gone, Shakespeare walked out into the bailey and ascended a flight of stone steps to the battlements. He was stopped at every turn by guards. Was this a special display for his benefit, or were they always so thorough?

From the ramparts, he looked out over Sheffield. It was a fair-sized market town, renowned for making steel cutlery. He gazed all around for ten minutes, trying to work out the lie of the land. Below him was one of the rivers that formed a moat most of the way around the castle. Not far off, he saw the Cutler's Rest, and thought briefly of Miss Whetstone. He would take a chamber there rather than here in this grim castle.

He turned away and looked to the north. Across the ditch,

the castle keep where Mary lodged was raised high on its motte. Shakespeare studied the ancient earthwork and fortress for a few minutes, then made his way slowly back to the great hall. He had clearly missed the start of the midday repast, for the place was already as raucous as a lawyers' dinner at Gray's Inn. The table was packed with senior officers and administrators, eating, talking and laughing with abandon. At the table's head, the earl was chewing at the wing bone of a fowl. At his left side sat a comely woman. Shrewsbury hammered the haft of his knife on the table. 'Mr Shakeshaft, you will sit here beside me,' he boomed across the hall. All eyes turned to Shakespeare. 'Have you met Mistress Britten?'

Shakespeare bowed, not bothering to correct his name. So this was the earl's pastry cook, Elinor Britten. Walsingham had told him of her. She smiled at him and pushed forward her large bosom in welcome and the image of an appetising apple pie came to mind. No wonder the countess, Bess, had absented herself from the marriage bed. She was at Hardwick Hall with her young grand-daughter Arbella Stuart, and was said to be in a towering rage that her husband had taken this wench as his mistress.

'Good day to you, Mr Shake*speare*,' Elinor Britten said, laughing. 'You see, *I* know your name even if my lord does not. He is most forgetful these days. With that and the gout and the prattling, one could imagine him a feeble old man soon. We shall have to feed him potage with a babe's spoon.'

'Enough of that, Mistress Britten! How can a man be old when he has a warm woman in his bed to keep him up? Do I not rise and crow when duty calls?'

Elinor graced his lordship with a tolerant smile, then turned back to their guest. 'Please be seated, Mr Shakespeare.' She swept her plump pink hand in the direction of the bird in the centre of the table. 'Have you tried ptarmigan? It is really quite delicious. One of Mary's men had a dozen sent down in cages from his estates in Scotland for us. I think it has the flavour of swan. It is a fine royal roasting bird.'

Shakespeare was astonished at the manner in which the earl's bed companion flaunted their relationship. He was just about to reply when the room fell silent. All eyes swivelled to the doorway and Shakespeare turned to see what they were looking at.

A dark shadow of a man stood there, the light of the sun behind him. All Shakespeare could make out was the whiteness of his hair, like a demonic halo, and the heavy stick that he held in his right hand.

'Ah, Mr Topcliffe,' the earl bellowed. 'How went the chase?'

'Too simple, my lord, too simple. No sport at all.'

'And poor eating.'

'Indeed.'

'Step forward, sir, and say well met to our guest. His name is Mr Shake*speare*. There, I have it, Mistress Britten.'

Richard Topcliffe strode forward, tapping his blackthorn stick at every third step, and Shakespeare now saw him clearly. From his skin and strength, he looked fifty or so, yet his hoary white hair was that of a man many years older. He was not tall, but he emanated a brutish power. He was grinning through yellow-brown teeth which, rather oddly, matched the colour of his marigold silk doublet. Shakespeare wondered exactly what manner of work he did for Walsingham.

'Mr Topcliffe,' the earl continued when the white-haired man came to a halt. 'I am pleased to introduce you to Mr Shakespeare who has letters of introduction from Mr Secretary.'

Topcliffe stood square like a mastiff at bay. 'If you are Walsingham's man, then you are indeed well-met, Mr Shakespeare.' His voice was a dark and unpleasant syrup. 'Any friend of Mr Secretary is an enemy of the Antichrist, and so you must be my friend, too.'

Shakespeare was surprised. Was this truly one of Mr Secretary's men? 'It is my honour to meet you, Mr Topcliffe.' He proffered his hand, but it was not taken. Instead Topcliffe slapped his blackthorn into the palm of his own left hand. It had a heavy silver grip and the dark wood tapered to a narrow tip which was also wrought in beaten silver. There was something of the cudgel about it.

'Good, then let us eat, for the hunt has made me as hungry as a hog.'

'What was the game, sir? Stag? Boar?'

'No, no, the finest chase of them all. Topcliffizare! Priest-hunting – and I smoked me out a fine one, a boy-priest, hiding in a coffer among women's undergarments. Christ's fellow cowering in a coffer and shaking as though he had the ague! Did he think I would not look there? Well, soon we shall have him in his traitor's coffin – with worms not petticoats for company.'

Topcliffe roared with laughter at his own jest, and some of those present joined him politely. They had all ceased their own conversations to attend the words of this man, as though he held some power over them. He pushed his way forward on to the bench into the place that Shakespeare was about to take, with Shrewsbury at his left hand. He then elbowed the neighbour at his right sideways to allow a little space for Shakespeare. 'Come sit by me and tell me news of the court.'

Shakespeare hesitated. Opposite him, Elinor Britten smiled and gestured towards the tiny space between Topcliffe and the diner on his right. 'Push and squeeze, Mr Shakespeare. We have no courtly daintiness here. Push and squeeze. Take us as you will, sir.'

*

As he ate a leg of ptarmigan, which was every bit as good as Elinor Britten had promised, Shakespeare began to notice a stink. It came not from the food, but from the man at his side with the white hair. At first he could not identify the smell. It was partially sweat, partially the rancid dirt of a man who wore fine clothes but neither washed nor perfumed himself. Smoky, too, as though he had been too near a bonfire. But there was something else, something unholy. And then he realised what it was. It was the stench he knew from Bladder Street in the city of London, as you approached the shambles; the smell that greets the beast at the slaughterhouse on its final journey and drives it into a cold panic with fear. The smell of spilt blood.

Shakespeare gagged and could not swallow his meat. Surreptitiously, he put a hand to his mouth, but his right-hand neighbour, a young squire, noticed his discomfort and handed him a tankard of ale. Shakespeare drew down a deep draught and caught his breath.

'A bone in your throat, Shakespeare?' Topcliffe demanded.

No, your stink in my nose. He breathed deeply, regaining his composure. 'Something of that ilk,' he said.

'Take care. It is most discourteous to die while men are at their meat.'

'I have never died at the table yet.' He managed a smile. 'You mentioned a priest, Mr Topcliffe. What priest is that?'

The white-haired man looked at him for a moment as though he were not sure he wished to be asked such questions. 'Why are you here?'

'As his lordship said, I have been sent by Mr Secretary.'

'You have papers?'

Shakespeare dug into his doublet and pulled out the sealed paper addressed to Topcliffe.

Topcliffe read it carefully, and then stared into Shakespeare's eyes. 'Well, then, I can tell you that the priest was a sodomising traitor and he will suffer a traitor's death. He says his name is Cuthbert Edenshaw and that is all he will say. But I know him to be a priest ordained at Rheims and sent back here by the devil's turds that inhabit that sink of wickedness. I shall have him racked in the Tower, and then we shall have the truth from him. And names. We shall have the name of every traitor he has met.'

Shakespeare did not try to disguise his distaste. 'A man will say anything when tortured.'

'Indeed he will. And when I go to the places he tells me and find those I have been seeking, I will know whether he has spoken true or not. If not, then he will face worse. Now, Shakespeare, you still have not told me why you are here. The paper merely says I am to work with you.'

'He is after the Frenchie I mentioned to you, Dick,' the earl said. 'It turns out he was not a doctor of medicine.'

'Is this so, Shakespeare?'

'Did you meet him, Mr Topcliffe?'

'He left before I arrived. Who is he?'

'This is not the place to talk about it. Let us eat, then meet in private.' Shakespeare forced another smile, then turned away and made conversation with the young squire to his right.

'Never do that to me again, Shakespeare.'

'What is that, Topcliffe?'

'Turn your back on me.'

'You are making something of nothing. Let us get to business.'

They were in the office that had been set aside for Shakespeare by the earl. Shakespeare sat at a table. Topcliffe paced angrily.

For a man of mature years, Topcliffe seemed charged with a remarkable energy and fervour. But there was something worrying close to the surface, and it was not simply his odious gloating at the taking of a priest and the prospect of having him tortured and executed. For the moment, Shakespeare decided he would simply have to pay no heed to his doubts. If Walsingham said he was to be trusted, then so be it.

'The Frenchman's true name is Leloup, not Seguin. What Shrewsbury told you was wrong; he *is* a doctor of medicine. But more than that he is the Duke of Guise's man. He should never have been allowed within a hundred miles of Mary, and Shrewsbury knows it.'

'Beware your tongue, Shakespeare, lest someone cut it from you. I will not have you speaking ill of the earl to Mr Secretary.' Topcliffe's threat was alarming, coming from one who was supposed to be a colleague, but Shakespeare declined to rise to the bait.

'There is no need to. His poor judgement speaks for itself.'

He went on to explain all he knew of Leloup and raised the possibility of moving Mary Stuart somewhere more enclosed and secure. 'Mr Secretary wishes us to form a common verdict on the matter and go from here to Tutbury. But his foremost wish is that we capture the Frenchman.'

'Then let us hope for fine hunting. I will be the hunter; you will be my houndswain.'

'We will go as equals, Mr Topcliffe,' Shakespeare said firmly. 'The problem is that there is no reason to think Leloup is still in Sheffield, or even in Yorkshire. By now, he could be approaching Dover, his mission completed.'

'I say he is still here, conspiring with the northern lords and other lewd popish insects. This county is a very ant-heap of them. Maybe my petticoat priest will have something to say on the matter.'

'Then let us go our separate ways. You can seek out Leloup as you think fit; I will examine this castle for holes and look for Leloup in my own way. Let us meet again in twenty-four hours and discuss our progress. Then, depending on that, we can consider riding south to Tutbury together.'

Topcliffe pointed his blackthorn stick at Shakespeare. 'Very well, but first I will show you this castle.'

'There is no need. I am going with the sergeant of guards.'

Topcliffe snorted with scorn. 'The sergeant of guards is sly. Wren will only show you what he wants you to see. You will be better dealt with in my company. I know every inch of this castle – I have been here many times.'

Perhaps it was a good idea, Shakespeare thought. He and Topcliffe had got off to a bad start. If he had to work with this strange man, it would probably be a good idea to get to know him. 'Very well,' he said. 'Thank you, Mr Topcliffe.'

'We shall make a fine team. Let us go to it.'

Boltfoot stopped at the bank of the Sheaf river and gazed across it up at the huge stone walls of the castle. If he took one of the small rowing boats he could cross the stream here, but the wall was sheer and too high to scale. Perhaps another man, a soldier trained in climbing fortress walls, might be able to do it, but with his club-foot, he could not.

'What you looking at, friend?'

Boltfoot turned at the voice. A man in a torn smock had come up behind him. He held the bridle of a bullock harnessed to a long, heavy wagon.

'I'm looking at the wall,' said Boltfoot. 'Folks that built those walls knew what they were about.'

'Aye, that they did,' said the carter. 'Strong enough to keep the Scots fartleberry locked away where she do belong. You new to these parts, friend?'

'I travel with my master. He has business in the castle. Told me to bide my time out here.'

'What's his business?'

'His business is his own and I am not at liberty to divulge it.'

The carter laughed. 'You want to be careful folks don't take you for a spy. This town is riddled with spies of every shade. More spies in Sheffield than you'll find weevils in a hundred-weight of grain. Looking too closely at castle walls could cost a man his liberty and his head hereabouts.'

Boltfoot weighed the man up. 'Spies? What they spying on?'

The carter shrugged. 'Each other mostly, I reckon. They can spy on each other all they want for all I care. The innkeepers are happy, too, because they bring London gold to Sheffield town.'

'So how would you get in the castle?'

'That's easy. Just drive in with provender. Carts like mine go in and out all day and sometimes at night, too. They got a hundred or more horses in the stables. Those beasts need a lot of feed day by day. Then there's the guards and the fartleberry's own crew to be provided for . . .' The man tailed off and looked at Boltfoot more closely. 'Now enough of your questions or I'll begin to think you *are* a spy . . .'

Boltfoot grunted. 'Who'd have a cripple like me as a spy?'

'True enough, friend, true enough. Now with your leave, I'll be on my way.' The carter tugged on the bridle and the bullock lumbered on after him, leaving Boltfoot staring thoughtfully in their wake.

Shakespeare reckoned the castle walls enclosed four or five acres of land. Many of the buildings within its confines were lodging chambers of varying degrees, the rest storehouses, kitchens, workshops, arsenal and stables. He would need to ask Shrewsbury for a chart, because the many narrow ginnels and dead-ends did not seem planned. The buildings must have been altered and added to on numerous occasions by different owners in the past three hundred years.

'A man could get lost in here, Mr Topcliffe,' Shakespeare

said as they rounded yet another corner in what had seemed a blind alley.

'Indeed, he could. It's no place to keep the heifer. I'd put her in Newgate, and then take her to Paddington Green for despatching.'

'On what charge?'

'Plotting the overthrow of our own Royal Majesty, whose favour and love I do value above pearls of the orient.'

'Plotting the Queen's overthrow? Do you know of some conspiracy then?'

'There is always a conspiracy when one or more popish beast is gathered together. I tell you this: the matter of the Frenchie will not be without blood.'

'So you do think Mary should be moved from here?'

'Don't *you*, Shakespeare?'

'Yes, I do. But from your fears that I might impugn the earl's reputation, I had thought you might be happy with the present arrangements.'

'My friend George Talbot, Earl of Shrewsbury, has done his duty. His health and wealth are brought low from keeping this foul woman in his home. No man has done the realm greater service. He deserves a rest, for he will not live long elsewise. I tell you, Shakespeare, he has aged twenty years in these past ten. It is only the love and favours of Mistress Britten that save his sanity, for his marriage to Bess, who is also my good friend, is now a bitter wreck. And so, yes, I wish the Scots heifer away from here, but in doing so, I do not want George slandered.'

'Then I think we are almost agreed, Mr Topcliffe.'

By now they were close to Mary Stuart's apartments. As they approached, a youth emerged from the entranceway. He was slender and handsome and finely attired. Topcliffe gripped Shakespeare's arm a shade too tightly and nodded in the man's direction. 'See that one?'

'What of him?'

'That's one of her pages, or that's what she says. None of them are what they seem. She keeps nuns disguised as seamstresses and priests in the guise of footmen. I know not what they all do, but this I tell you: they are all lower than vermin.'

The young man, no more than sixteen years of age, strode past the guards, waved to them with familiar carelessness, and carried on at a brisk walk. His red hair caught the breeze.

'Is that Buchan Ord?'

'I do not know his name. If I did I would spit on it. All I know is that he is the scion of a noble Scotch family of Calvinist persuasion. If they could see him now clutching at the heifer's skirts, they would stab their own throats from shame.'

The youth wore a suit of fine red velvet which matched his long red hair. There was something feminine about his face and the neat, smooth way he walked, like a cat. He was coming towards them and slowed down because the path was narrow. Shakespeare stopped to let him pass. Topcliffe did, too. The young man smiled and bowed his head in an exaggerated gesture of thanks.

He was a yard past them when Topcliffe swung his black-thorn stick, heavy end first, at the young man's head. He landed a crunching blow and the man crumpled and fell sideways on to the unforgiving flagstone pathway. Shakespeare was certain he heard a crack of bone as the velvet-clad shoulder slammed into stone, then his upper temple smacked down like the tip of a whip.

'God's faith, what have you done?'

But Topcliffe wasn't listening. He stood astride the fallen figure, lifted up his stick once more and smashed it into the back of the injured Scotsman's head. The man's back arched but he did not scream. Topcliffe threw down the stick, then knelt over him, got his neck in a stranglehold in the crook of his right arm and began to pummel the side of his head with his left fist.

'Stop, Topcliffe, stop!' Shakespeare was on him now, pulling at his arms, trying to drag him away. With a mighty wrench, he pulled him off, and they both sprawled backwards, away from the injured man, who now lay still, face down, blood seeping from his head in a little rivulet, across the grey stones.

Two guards from outside Mary's apartments were walking towards them. They seemed to be in no hurry.

Topcliffe was panting like a dog, his lips foam-flecked.

'God's tears, Topcliffe, what have you done?'

Topcliffe spat on the ground in front of Shakespeare. 'Done for a rat. Isn't that what you do? Would you have me cosset the Queen's foes like babes at the teat?'

With languid indifference, the two guards examined the fallen man. He moved and groaned as he tried to sit up.

'He's still alive, Mr Topcliffe.'

'I'll leave him to you lads then. Throw him from the castle walls into the river. Let him swim back to Scotland. That's the way to dispose of rodents.'

'No,' Shakespeare said. 'I'll see to him.'

'Do as you will, Shakespeare. I believe I know *you* now.' Topcliffe dusted down his doublet and hose, picked up his blackthorn stick and walked away in the company of the guards, all of them laughing.

The young Scot had an aching, bloody head and his upper arm appeared to be broken, but he seemed likely to survive.

'Come with me, we will get you help,' said Shakespeare. 'The earl must know of a physician who can put a splint on that arm and bandage your head.' He moved to help the young man to his feet.

The Scotsman shied away, the pain in his eyes replaced by a

look of contempt. 'I'll not be tended to by an Englishman. The Queen's physician will see to me.'

'As you wish.'

'Aye, I do wish.' He winced, then tilted his chin in the direction of the departing Topcliffe. 'Your man's the devil made flesh, do you know that? Do you not note the stink of brimstone about him? He's Satan himself. And that makes *you* his familiar. Whoever you are, I want nothing to do with you and would not accept water from you even though I were dying.'

Shakespeare stayed him. 'Wait, did I not pull him off you?'

'I have nothing more to say.' The Scots youth shrugged off the hand, gasped with pain from the movement of his damaged shoulder, and hobbled away, back towards Mary's quarters. The English guards grinned scornfully at him as he passed.

Chapter 8

SHAKESPEARE LOOKED INTO his goblet of brandy, swirled the dark liquid, then inhaled its powerful fumes. This place was making him despondent. There was something horribly unwholesome about these two communities – captors and captives – living so close together but so far apart.

After the brutal incident with Topcliffe and the young Scotsman, he had sought out the sergeant of guards and demanded to know what would be done.

'The young man's name is Mr McKyle. I have heard all about it. Has he complained?'

'Not to me, but I witnessed an appalling, unprovoked assault.'

'Then you are free to lay a complaint, Mr Shakespeare, if you so wish. But the way I heard, it was McKyle that provoked Mr Topcliffe.'

There was no point in complaining to the sergeant of guards, Shakespeare realised; the only hope of redress would be with the earl himself. In the meantime, he resumed his examination of the castle and its inhabitants. He was particularly anxious to find Buchan Ord, the man who was said to have accompanied François Leloup when he met Mary, but no one knew where he was.

Shakespeare tried to gain access to Mary's apartments, but

was barred by the English guards. Now he was in the room that passed as his office, awaiting another meeting with the earl. Through the window, he saw that night was closing in. There was a knock at the door and a bluecoat appeared.

'His lordship will see you now, Mr Shakespeare.'

He downed the brandy and enjoyed its warm descent through his gullet, then followed the servant through to a comfortable withdrawing room where he found Shrewsbury and Topcliffe standing before the hearth, warmed by a log fire.

'Mr Shakespeare, you wished to talk with me.'

Shakespeare bowed to the earl and ignored Topcliffe. 'I need to see the Scotsman named Buchan Ord. No one seems to know where he is.'

'That is because he is no longer here.'

The surprise and irritation were evident on Shakespeare's face. 'Where then has he gone?'

The earl shrugged helplessly. 'I know not. After our midday repast, I was summoned to the presence of the Scots Queen . . .'

'The Scots *heifer* . . .' Topcliffe put in.

'The Scots *Queen* asked to see me.'

'And so you crawled to her like a dog.'

Shrewsbury looked at Topcliffe and shook his head, as though he had heard it all before. 'We may not like it, Dick, but she is a Queen and must be treated as such. She may, indeed, be *our* Queen one day. More than that, she is a lonely woman of thirty-nine years and fears herself abandoned and forgotten.'

'Do you know what the world says about you and the heifer, George?'

'Yes, Dick, for you have told it me before. Many times.'

'It behoves me to say it again, however, lest you be in any doubt or forget it. They say you are a slave to her, that she is a lewd Romish worm, with succubus talons and teeth between her legs, and that you obediently grovel beneath her skirts and scrape at her rough-scabbed vileness with your tongue. That everything you do is at her will. That she has borne you two bastards. That is what the court says. That is what men say.'

Shrewsbury sighed. 'Then tell them the truth, Dick, for you know me as well as any man.'

'I should tell them you have gone soft, that you are a jelly of a man. And I would do so, but for the love I bear you.'

'Tell them I am maligned and wretched, that I am caught in a triangular snare of women. A wife who despises me, a guest who uses weeping to rule me and a sovereign who allows me no respite from my over-long years of service. I believe myself the most woebegone subject in this realm.'

Shakespeare grew impatient. 'What did Mary want of you, my lord?'

The earl shrugged his angular shoulders dismissively. 'The usual. She wished to scold me.'

'About what?'

'She demanded to know what had become of Mr Ord, her new favourite courtier. She accused me of sending him away.'

'Why would she think you had done such a thing?'

'Because I have done so with other members of her retinue in the past, usually on orders from the Privy Council, but sometimes because I have had my own doubts about them. Each time I have done it, there has been yet more sobbing and wailing and tear-stained letters of protest to Lord Burghley and Her Majesty.'

'But in this case, you did not send Mr Ord away.'

'No, I did not. Nor did I grant him licence to leave, which he should have sought under the terms by which Mary is allowed certain retainers. When he returns, I shall be minded to have him dismissed anyway. He will not be missed. One less stomach for me to fill with food.'

'And this was the first you had heard he was gone?'

'Indeed.'

'Have none of her entourage any idea where he has gone? What of her secretary, Claude Nau? What does he say on the matter?'

'Monsieur Nau is in London. As for her other secretary, that old fool Gilbert Curle, and the others of her senior aides, they are not saying. The Master of her Household seemed rather pleased that he was no longer there. I think he saw Ord as a maker of trouble, a young man with too much time on his hands and too much prick in his hose for such close-confined society.'

'Why was such a young man put in charge of a visitor to Mary? Why was he trusted?'

Shrewsbury sighed heavily. 'I cannot organise *her* entourage and my own, Mr Shakespeare. This is a matter for them. And Mr Shakespeare, I feel I might also mention some other disturbing news. Some maps of the castle and surrounding area have also gone missing.'

Shakespeare was aghast. 'God's blood, have they been stolen?'

'Well, they are not small items. They would be difficult to mislay.'

'Where were they kept?'

'In my chief steward's office. I have my suspicions . . .'

'Your steward?'

'No, Ord. But I have no proof, nor even evidence. Just my own fear.'

'Then by the blood of Christ where is this man Ord? Indeed, *who* is he?'

Shrewsbury was looking increasingly pained. 'His family

served her mother, Mary of Guise. The Ords are well known in the Highlands. He came with letters. There can be no doubt that he is of noble birth and we had no reason to distrust him. As to where he is now, I have no notion, Mr Shakespeare.'

Topcliffe snorted with derision. 'Well, I have a notion. He is with the one-armed Frenchie, organising the heifer's escape with the help of your own maps, George. Finding a hole for her to scurry through. Arranging the murder of her cousin so that she may steal a crown. There will be others conspiring: massing priests, popish gentry and northern nobles. Men who claim loyalty to our beloved Elizabeth and finger sharp daggers behind their backs.'

Shakespeare had had enough. 'God's death, Mr Topcliffe, you go too far. This is egregious supposition, nothing more.' And yet, he could not help wondering whether Topcliffe was correct, that Buchan Ord was indeed with Leloup. For the moment, though, his anger with Topcliffe got the better of him. He turned to the earl. 'I must tell you, my lord, that this day I witnessed a grievous assault on a member of the Scots Queen's retinue by this man you call friend. Mr Topcliffe struck a boy – and I call him that for he was scarcely out of childhood – to the ground, without cause.'

Shrewsbury sighed again. 'Is this true, Dick?'

'It was not without cause. As he passed he called me heretic.'

'He said nothing, merely smiled in greeting.'

'He said heretic! Perhaps you did not hear it, Shakespeare, for it was said low.' Topcliffe prodded Shakespeare's chest with his blackthorn. 'The effeminate maggot was – *is* – a traitor. Anyway, there was no assault. It was a mere slap. A little birching. A chastisement for a schoolboy. I did him no harm. Did he not walk away on his own feet?'

Shakespeare did not flinch, merely brushed the stick aside

and moved a step closer to his assailant. His hand drew back, fingers curling into a fist to punch the feral dog's hard and cruel face. And then just as his muscles tensed to deliver the blow, a gunshot resounded from the courtyard outside.

Boltfoot was already within the castle walls before night fell. The busy town market had been a source of various items haggled over at great length but which gave him the disguise he required to make his way past the guards. First there was an old knapsack, which had cost him tuppence, then a dozen larks and quails for sixpence. He filled the knapsack halfway with stones, and then topped it off with six of the birds. He tied string around the necks of the other six and hung them from the straps of the knapsack so that they were clearly visible. Lastly he found a stall with items of old clothing acquired from the families of the dead and bought a shepherd's smock and a poor man's ragged wool cap with sidestrings to tie it beneath his chin and cover his face.

Before setting off for the castle gate, he left his weapons at the Cutler's Rest in the care of Kat Whetstone and her father.

'My master has said I should not go armed in these parts, that I might be taken as a highwayman or footpad when not in his company.'

'We'll look after them well,' the young woman said.

Boltfoot gazed at her with a mixture of suspicion and longing. He had brought the caliver and cutlass from the other side of the world and could not bear the prospect of losing them. But nor could he take them into the castle.

'You'll have a penny from me if they are kept safe.'

She laughed. 'I don't want your money for that, Mr Cooper. Don't be worrying yourself. They'll still be here when you return.'

He grunted a word of thanks and limped off into a side

street, where he quickly put the smock over his clothes and pulled his new cap about his face. He then slung the knapsack on to his back and made his way towards the castle gatehouse. His main worry was his club-foot. Would one of the guards recognise him because of it? The gatehouse was no more than two hundred yards from the Cutler's Rest, but by the time he got there, he was wishing he had put fewer stones in the sack. A guard saw him struggling over the drawbridge and offered him a helping hand.

Boltfoot shook his head. 'I'll cope,' he said. 'Got larks and quails for his lordship's table.' He unslung the heavy knapsack and unstrapped it to reveal the birds.

The guard looked in peremptorily then tilted his long pointed beard at Boltfoot. 'Not seen you about before.'

Boltfoot sighed with relief. The guard had changed since he left the castle. 'Helping a friend from the market. A message came to him from the cookhouse that the earl had a taste for the birds and would have them tonight or there would be hell to pay.'

The guard scratched his greasy, lice-ridden hair. 'Hell to pay? Sounds like my wife. I always know when she's with child for she demands baked apples and cheese of the dales, whatever the time of year. I'd rather have a pail of turds about my ears than her pecking if I don't get her what she wants.'

'Well, I don't suppose the earl's due any time soon.'

The guard thrust out his large stomach and grinned. 'Get you along to the cookhouse then, Mr Birdman. Do you know the way?'

'To the left and straight along, so I was told. If I get lost, I'll ask someone.'

'Right enough. And tell the cooks I said you were to have some ale. For that's a mighty load you have to carry there with your crippled foot.'

Boltfoot thanked the guard and walked on through. The sky was darkening over the crenellated battlements. He limped on in the direction of the kitchens and then, when he was no longer visible from the gatehouse, he stopped and looked about him to assess his position. A narrow alley led off to the right with a series of low doorways. Ensuring he was not observed, he ducked down into the ginnel and slipped into the first entrance. It was a storeroom for meat. The slaughtered carcasses of pigs, bullocks and deer hung from hooks along ceiling rails. With relief, he removed the knapsack from his back and set it against a wall.

The only light in the store came through the doorway, which he had left slightly ajar. He took off the shepherd's smock, and then sat on the floor beside the bag of birds, to wait until nightfall. It was unlikely that anyone would come here now; the cooks would already have selected and butchered their joints of meat for dinner.

When darkness came, he pulled himself up, and eased the door open. No one was about. He slipped out into the passageway and walked further into the maze of buildings, avoiding the parts where the lighter of lanterns and torches had done his work. When he saw anyone, he either shrank back into a doorway or walked forth boldly, saluting as he went, as though he were a castle worker.

As he came to the causeway across the ditch to the inner bailey, he stopped. Something was happening. The whole area was lit by wall lanterns, cressets with blazing coals and men holding brands. Above them, at the top of the steps, the doorway to the keep was open and brilliantly lit from inside by candles. A woman stepped out, slowly, like an invalid. She was supported on both sides by women in fine clothes.

She seemed tall, almost six feet, and large of frame. Her hair and face were covered by a black veil. Boltfoot shrank back against the wall and watched as the woman came slowly down the steep steps into the yard and began to walk anti-clockwise in the shadow of the battlements, supported all the time by her companions.

With a jolt Boltfoot realised this must be Mary, Queen of Scots herself. From what the world said, he had believed her to be a woman of stature. But the Mary that everyone spoke of was acclaimed a goddess. This woman was heavy of girth and had the slow gait of a grandmother. Every few paces she stopped, as though to catch her breath.

A dozen or more English guards, easily identifiable by their quilted leather jerkins, watched her and held their hands on the hilts of their swords and pistols. But there were a dozen others, too – her own people – men and women, all mingling around her, like the protective curtain wall of a fort. Boltfoot watched, intrigued. Was this really Mary Stuart? The name itself had acquired mythic status in the long years of her incarceration. Some called her saint; others called her Satan's spouse and murderess.

In the light of the fires, her perambulation among the two groups was an eerie sight. A curious dance of two disparate parties: the guards and the guarded.

As he watched her, it occurred to Boltfoot that she would be difficult to snatch to safety from this place. It would, however, be easy for someone to put a bullet into her – someone like a carrier of game birds with a pistol secured within his knapsack.

A hand clasped his shoulder. Boltfoot froze, horribly aware that he was unarmed.

'She is the very queen of pies, is she not?'

Boltfoot's head went down and he emitted a non-committal noise. The hand rested on his shoulder. It seemed amicable enough.

'Fat as a sty full of sows, she is,' the voice continued. 'I'll wager her three husbands are pleased to be dead and gone. More pleasure dead than in that lump of suet's bed.'

Boltfoot said nothing. He felt hot despite the cool of the evening. Every sinew was strained.

Suddenly the hand on his shoulder tightened. 'Who are you?'

Boltfoot did not answer. He twisted around, wrenching his shoulder free of the clasping hand.

Realising his error, the guard's eyes registered shock and his fingers flailed to keep a hold on the stranger. But Boltfoot was already gone, loping away from the courtyard, back into the labyrinth of buildings. A whistle blew; then a shout went up.

Boltfoot stumbled onwards. Men were always surprised how fast he could move with his club-foot when he needed to.

All he had on his side was surprise and the darkness of the narrow alleyways, for he knew there was no way out of here. Fearing they would loose a shot or bolt at him, he tried to move from side to side to lessen their target. The only thing that was certain was that he was trapped. The alarm of the whistle meant there was no way through the front gatehouse. In a sudden moment of clarity, he realised there was only one thing for it. The great hall. At the end of the ginnel, he stopped and looked left and then right, desperate to get his bearings.

Behind him there was a shout. 'Stop!'

Left. It was left. He heard the boom of a pistol and saw a fist-sized chip of brick fly in an explosion of dust from the wall, no more than a foot from his arm. He turned left and ran. The doorway was fifty yards from him. Two halberdiers stood guard outside. They saw him and moved forward instinctively, crossing their weapons to form a barrier. To the devil with them; this was his only chance. He had not survived a sea journey around the globe with Sir Francis Drake to be shot in the back by a squadron of guards in a Yorkshire castle. He ducked low and dived for the triangular gap beneath the halberds.

'What in God's name was that?' the earl demanded.

'That was a gunshot,' Topcliffe said.

The door to the chamber burst open, and Boltfoot fell in, sprawling across the floor, two guards close behind him, their axe-pike halberds raised as they moved into position to hack him to pieces.

Shakespeare could scarcely comprehend the evidence of his eyes. But then he pushed forward into the path of the halberds. 'Boltfoot?'

Boltfoot was scrabbling to gain his feet and put distance between himself and the guards. Shakespeare dragged his assistant aside by the neck of his jerkin, and then raised his hand to the two guards. 'I know this man,' he said. 'Leave him be. He is no threat.'

'No threat?' Shrewsbury bellowed. 'Who is this man?' The earl grabbed a heavy iron poker from the fire and brandished it. 'If he is your servant, Shakespeare, what in all the circles of hell is he doing here? Why is he in my hall? And who is firing pistols?'

Shakespeare tried to repress a sudden smile. Whatever else Boltfoot had done, he had clearly succeeded in breaking into the castle. More than that, he had managed to defuse a disagreeable confrontation with Topcliffe. 'This is Mr Boltfoot Cooper, my lord. He is indeed my man and he was under my instructions to see if there was a way to gain access to this castle. It appears he has succeeded. Handsomely.'

'And what of the gunshot? Has he killed someone?'

Boltfoot bowed his head. 'One of the guards tried to shoot me.'

'I am not surprised. This is an outrage! A damnable outrage! I will have you hanged!'

Shakespeare moved forward in front of Boltfoot. 'I believe we should be giving thanks to Mr Cooper if he has discovered a hole in your security arrangements. We need to learn a lesson from this. If this man, a friend, could get in, then so could a foe. Mary Stuart is not secure here.'

'No!' Shrewsbury was appalled and disbelieving. 'That man could not have swum the moat and scaled the walls. There is no way in.'

'How did you do it?' Topcliffe demanded.

Boltfoot looked to Shakespeare for confirmation that he should answer this man. He nodded.

'I came in with a knapsack of larks and quails on my back. I told the guards I had been ordered to deliver them to the kitchens.'

'Then I shall hang the guards, too,' the earl said, his normally pallid face now red with rage.

'My lord, might I suggest we take a little time to reflect on these events,' Shakespeare said. 'I believe it would be unjust to lay the blame on your guards. The problem lies not with them but with a regime that has become unwieldy. You have so many people and horses here in this garrison that suppliers must bring in their wagons and drays by day and by night. These carts cannot all be torn apart and searched; nor can every poultryman be interrogated and racked.'

'I have had enough of this!' The earl clenched his hand into a fist. A vein pulsed at his gaunt temple. 'I am going to pay my respects to Mistress Britten. Come with me, Mr Topcliffe. And you, Mr Shakespeare, I demand that you remove that *thing* from my hall.' He pointed at Boltfoot. 'And then you may do as you please. Carry your reports to Mr Secretary and my wife the shrew. Tell them what you will, for I no longer care about any of it – marriage, Privy Council, my duty as a gaoler. To the dogs with them all. And so I bid you good night. Come, Topcliffe.' He turned on his heel and was gone. At the door-way, the earl's white-haired companion looked back over his shoulder and smirked.

Chapter 9

THE LONE RIDER reined in his horse in a small glade at the bottom of a forested slope, a little way south of Sheffield. He wore a dark, fur-trimmed cloak about his doublet, and a large hat to cover his head and face. A wooden cabin stood nearby, but the rider did not go to it. He stayed on his stallion and waited.

The only light came from the moon and stars. The only sounds were the wind in the trees, the occasional snap of a twig in the woods and the breathing of his own fine horse.

For an hour he waited, not moving. He took no drink and ate no bread. Another hour passed, and then he heard a sound – the quiet walking of another horse.

Beneath his cloak, the waiting rider's right hand tightened on the stock of the wheel-lock pistol he held. That was all; the only movement. He acknowledged the approaching rider with a curt nod of the head.

'It is a good night for a hunt,' the newcomer said.

'A good night for a kill.' The accent was Scottish.

'The moon is high.'

'The wind is still.'

Both men laughed. The waiting man's pistol hand eased its grip a little, but not wholly.

'Mr Ord?' the newcomer said.

'Indeed.' Without dismounting, he swept an extravagant bow in confirmation, his right hand across his slender belly. 'Well met, my lord.'

'And well met to you. What do you bring?'

'A message from our true Queen for those who wish her well.'

'And what is the message?'

'That all is well. Her Majesty has given her assent and will play her part. Now you must do your part. We must *all* do our part.'

The nobleman took a deep breath, as though this were the first clean air he had tasted in many a month. 'So it is agreed.'

'The hunt will ride on the appointed day.'

'And when will that be?'

'You will be the first to know, my lord.'

'Is everything to your satisfaction, masters?'

'Indeed, the food and beer are as fine as you promised, Miss Whetstone.'

'Then I am delighted, sir, for it is always our intention to please at the Cutler's Rest.'

Shakespeare and Boltfoot had a table in a high-ceilinged taproom, not far from the large open fire where a haunch of venison was being turned on a spit. The room smelt of roasting meats, woodsmoke and ale. No man, thought Shakespeare, could hope to be in a more congenial spot to while away a dark evening in a strange town, especially with Kat Whetstone standing before them asking after their welfare and comfort.

The more he gazed at her, the more he noted her imperfections: the brow given to frowning, the mole on her wrist, the dipping of her breasts where perfection might have made them pert. And each imperfection made her yet more beautiful in his eyes.

'You must be sure to buy yourself one of these before you leave Sheffield.' She took a small implement from the pocket of her apron. 'It is a penknife for the sharpening of goose quills. Folks say that Sheffield penknives are the finest in the land, so robust and easily honed are their blades. See . . .' She leant forward and handed the knife to Shakespeare.

Shakespeare took the knife, his hand touching hers as he did so. The knife had a long, elegantly curved handle, crafted from the tip of a staghorn, and a short steel blade that shone. He turned it and weighed it in his hand. It was, indeed, a good piece of work. 'I doubt I will have the opportunity to seek out a craftsman. Perhaps you would sell me this one, Miss Whetstone?'

'It's worth a shilling, but I'll let you have it for sixpence. My cousin makes them.'

'And do you have another for my friend Mr Cooper?'

'I am sure I can find another one, master.'

Shakespeare took his purse from his belt and found a shilling within it. He handed the silver coin to Kat Whetstone, wondering whether he was being gulled. He had no idea what such a knife should cost here in Sheffield, but nor did he care. The beer was coursing through him, washing him to distant shores, as was the glow of this young woman. As she closed the coin in her hand, he saw that its skin had a soft sheen to it, a rare thing for a young woman working in such a place where calluses and broken nails were the usual order. He very much wished to kiss the brown mole on the underside of her wrist.

She gave him that warm, generous smile again. 'I shall go now and find the knife for Mr Cooper.'

When she was out of earshot, Boltfoot touched his master's arm. 'I believe I saw her, master,' he said in an undertone.

'Miss Whetstone? Where?'

'No, the Queen of Scots. Coming out of her apartments into

the inner courtyard. Surrounded by her own retainers – men and women – and the earl's guard. I rather thought she was taking a walk.'

'What did she look like?'

'Large, master. And gouty.'

'Large?'

'Almost as tall as you, I would say, but fat about the hips and neck. She hobbled and required support from her ladies. I did not see her face for she was veiled from her hair down to her chin.'

'What happened?'

'That was when I was discovered and had to run.'

'Why did you not tell me this before?'

'I have told you now.'

Not for the first time Shakespeare wondered whether he had been right to hire this man. Yes, he had managed to find a way into the castle, as instructed, but he had nearly got himself killed and had given the Earl of Shrewsbury a genuine reason to feel aggrieved. And why had he not thought to mention seeing Mary of Scots until two hours after the event? 'In future, Boltfoot, tell me any matter of import as soon as possible. I am not saying it is the case in this instance, but on many occasions time is of the essence. Do you understand?'

Boltfoot grunted and gazed into his beer. 'If I had had my caliver I could have killed her,' he muttered.

As Shakespeare digested Boltfoot's news, their hostess reappeared with a second penknife. 'Here you are. Hone her well and oil her and she will keep rust-free. I do believe she will give you many years of good service.'

'I am sure she will.' He had no idea why he was buying it for Boltfoot or what he would do with such a tool. As far as Shakespeare knew he had never learnt to read, let alone write.

Boltfoot put the knife down on the table without even looking at it. He had a sullen expression on his weather-beaten face.

Kat picked up the beer jug, which was empty. 'Shall I bring you another of these, sir?'

'I will have a goblet of brandy, and then my bed.'

She turned away but he raised his hand to stay her.

'Wait. Sit and talk with us, Miss Whetstone.'

She laughed but did not sit down. 'You see how thronged this taproom is, sir. My father would not allow me the liberty to sit down with customers.'

Shakespeare could not imagine her father refusing her the liberty to do anything, but he let it pass. 'At least stay a minute or two and tell me about the people who come here to this place. If it is the closest coaching inn to the castle, many couriers and men of note must stay here. Is that not so?'

'Indeed, they do. Government men aplenty, which is a fine thing for us. The years since the Scots Queen came here have been the best my father ever knew. And no one calls me Miss Whetstone. I am Kat to one and to all.'

'Foreign men sometimes – from Scotland and from France?'

'From time to time.'

'Please, Kat, be seated. I can wait a while for my brandy. Talk with us. There are potboys aplenty here, are there not? They will serve your other customers.' He moved along the bench and patted the warm wood at his side.

This time she accepted the offer of the seat. He could smell her warmth. Her linen chemise was cut low and her bosom was full and rounded and ripe. Her hair was less tousled than it had been at dawn, but there was still an alluring wildness to it.

'First tell me a little about yourself.' Was it his imagination, or had she moved closer to him than was necessary? He could feel her thigh against his. 'There is nothing more to tell, master. My mother went to God when I was ten. My father is the landlord and I do all the work. Even without government men such as yourself we would make a fair living for, as you say, we are on the highway and by the castle . . .'

And because *you* are here, thought Shakespeare. Men might come a long way for a glimpse of you.

'In truth, I would rather hear about you, Mr Shakespeare, sir. Do you hail from London? Some say there are as many folk in the town as you will find in the whole of Yorkshire, that ships sail from London to the world entire, that there is a menagerie of strange beasts, and that there is a great bridge across the river. Tell me true: is all this so?'

'It is so. There are lions of Africa at the Tower. Great cats the size of a horse, with pointed teeth six inches long. They would eat a man were they not caged. Perhaps I will take you there and show you.' He regretted the words immediately. It was the beer talking, but it was a cruel thing to do; hopes could so easily be raised and dashed by a remark made in jest or in a man's cups.

'I should like that very much. Indeed, I should. It has always been my dearest wish to see London. And I would die to see the lion-cats.'

Shakespeare looked at Boltfoot. Did he note a slight shake of the head? Remember who is the servant, Boltfoot, and who is the master.

'But for the moment,' Shakespeare said hurriedly, 'I have much work to do. And a particular question I must put to you, a strange question, you may think: did a Frenchman with one arm stay here recently?'

'Mr Seguin?'

Shakespeare sat up straight. Suddenly he felt a great deal less inebriated. 'He was here?'

'Why, yes, sir. A fine French gentleman. Most generous and with a pleasing manner. I was sorry to see him go.'

'When was this?'

'He left four days past, I do believe. I can check in the black book, if you so wish.'

'Yes, Kat, I do wish that. And I would very much like to inspect his chamber.'

'Well, that is easily done, sir, for he was in the chamber you and Mr Cooper are to share this night. And I can tell you that Mr Seguin spent two nights here.'

Shakespeare recalled his conversation with the Earl of Shrewsbury. He said he had entertained the Frenchman to dinner and that he had seen Mary the next day before departing. So why had he stayed at the Cutler's Rest *two* nights?

'Did he have any visitors while he was here, Kat?'

'Not to my knowledge.'

'Did he have servants?'

'None, sir, which was most unusual, for his standing in the world was clear to see.'

'How did he pay you?'

'With English coin, I believe. My father could confirm that.'

'Did Seguin send any messages from here?'

'Again, you must ask my father. He deals with the couriers.'

'Summon him, if you would, with the black book. And fetch me the brandy.'

She was up from the bench. He wanted to reach out to her and touch her; the way she moved as she rose, the smell and the tone of her skin. Such softness . . . why did men, so hard and brutish in body and temperament, yearn for such softness? And why did women, so soft and nurturing, long for the hardness of men? It was a topsy-turvy world.

No man would have picked out Geoffrey Whetstone as Kat's father. Large and lumbering with a stomach that would have produced as much lard as a well-fed hog, he was saved from being monstrous by a face that was as benign as a fine summer's day.

He bowed low to his guests. 'Kat said you wished to talk with me on some matter pertaining to Monsieur Seguin.'

Shakespeare sipped his brandy then put the goblet down on the table. He met the landlord's eyes. 'I would like to see the black book.'

'Indeed, Kat told me as much. She told me, too, that she believed you to be on government business.'

'I am the Queen's man; that is true.'

'Then the book is yours to look over.' Mr Whetstone dried the beer-wet table with his sleeve, then laid down a heavy tome. Opening it to the middle, he pointed his large, broken-nailed index finger at a name. 'There you have it. François Seguin's appointed chamber, clean linen and feather bed, two shillings and sixpence for room and board, though the first night he ate at the castle to his own loss, I believe.'

'What did you make of the man, Mr Whetstone?'

'May I inquire your interest, sir?'

'I am on Queen's business. Any stranger in the same town as the Queen of Scots must be of interest. Most especially a Frenchman.'

Whetstone bowed again. 'Indeed, sir. Monsieur Seguin made no trouble and paid in full with good English silver, leaving a shilling extra for the quality of the service he found here.'

'Did you talk with him?'

'Only to welcome him and ask his pleasure, sir. We do not tend to ask men their business. Monsieur Seguin was not the first Frenchie we've seen here and I doubt he'll be the last if the Scots Queen remains at the castle, as we must hope she does. I've seen them all here, Mr Shakespeare. Italish ambassadors, Scotch knights and Netherlandish merchants. Come one, come all, they'll have a welcome of good beef and ale at my inn.'

'Did Seguin despatch any letters from here?'

'No, sir.'

'And did he say where he was going when he left?'

'Not to me, sir. I will ask among the others in my staff if they know aught, should you so desire.'

But Shakespeare wasn't listening. His eyes had moved to the far side of the high-ceilinged taproom, beside the entrance door. The light was dim in that corner, but he could see that Kat was there talking with a man. Shakespeare could only see the back of his head, which was mostly covered by a hat. Their conversation somehow seemed to be more than a casual encounter between a taproom hostess and a customer. He was surprised to discover a twinge of jealousy. He shook his head. This was a woman he had just met; he had not slept in thirty-six hours and needed a good night's sleep to regain his senses.

The man with Kat turned and they both looked back in the direction of Shakespeare and Boltfoot. Shakespeare stared back at them. 'Who is that man with your daughter, Mr Whetstone?'

Whetstone turned around to follow Shakespeare's gaze, but the man was no longer there. 'We have many customers, sir.'

'Did you see him, Boltfoot?'

'No, master.'

'Would you like me to ask Kat?'

Shakespeare shook his head. 'It is of no import.' He finished the brandy. 'Have me woken an hour after dawn if you would, Mr Whetstone. I am not to be disturbed until then.'

Chapter 10

SHAKESPEARE TOOK THE great bedstead for himself and slept better than he had done in many days. Boltfoot curled up on the truckle. If either man snored, the other did not hear it. In the morning, they ordered food to be brought to the chamber and although Shakespeare was disappointed that Kat did not serve them, he ate heartily.

'Boltfoot, you are to spend the morning listening. I want you to go into every tavern, alehouse and ordinary in Sheffield. I want to know what men say about the castle, about Mary and about the earl. Everything. Can you do that?'

'I can sit in a taproom as well as any man, master.'

'But can you take note of all you hear? Can you engage men in conversation without yourself coming under suspicion?'

'I believe I can.'

'Then let us meet here when the clock strikes one.'

Before leaving the inn, Shakespeare searched his room for any evidence that Leloup might have left behind, but there was nothing. The maidservant had cleaned the chamber thoroughly, laying fresh rushes.

Outside, the morning was clear with an autumnal bite to the air. Shakespeare marched out of the valley of Sheffield, along the banks of the River Sheaf, and then upwards across a greensward dotted with oaks and herds of grazing deer. A mile or two distant on higher ground, in the lee of a range of hills, he saw Manor Lodge, the mansion Shrewsbury had built as a prison to house Mary when the air in the castle became too fetid. From the far side of the park, it looked a great deal more pleasing to the eye than the castle, and this impression was maintained as he drew nearer.

The gatehouse was distinguished by two high octagonal towers built of brick. He stopped, expecting to be challenged, but no sentries were on duty. The main gate was locked and bolted but beside it there was a postern door, with no lock visible. He lifted the latch and it opened. He walked through into the courtyard.

Like a walled garden, the yard was warmer than the chilly outside. It had a pleasant feeling of neglect. Grass grew between the flagstones, bees buzzed and a mass of butterflies rose up. Shakespeare walked across to the hall door. He was about to try it when it opened. A man in the Shrewsbury livery stood before him, studying him closely.

'May I be of assistance, sir?'

Shakespeare knew the ways of servants well enough. It was only the good cut of his clothes that prevented the earl's retainer from booting him away with a choice insult in his ears.

'My name is John Shakespeare. I am here on Queen's business, inspecting the earl's properties.'

'You will have papers to that effect, sir?'

Shakespeare took his letters from his doublet.

The servant read them carefully, then handed them back. 'How may I help you, Mr Shakespeare?'

'Why was no one in the porter's lodge at the gatehouse?'

'I was called away briefly, sir. When the Scots Queen is not in residence, security is not seen as being of great importance.'

'Who told you that?'

'It is the custom, that is all.'

'I wish you to show me the lodge. Everything, from the cellars to the brewhouse. But first you will take me to the quarters the Scots Queen uses when she is here.'

'That will be the octagonal turret, which is presently locked.'

'And I am sure that you have the key, so let us proceed.'

The servant suppressed a sigh of irritation and bowed his head an inch, no more. 'Very well, sir. Please follow me.'

'What is your name?'

'Flowerdew, sir. Thomas Flowerdew.'

They went through to the servants' quarters. A pair of young men whom Shakespeare took to be footmen, though they were not in livery, were playing at cards and drinking ale at a table. On spotting Shakespeare, they quickly gathered up the deck of cards.

Flowerdew led the way to the octagonal turret and they ascended the staircase. In the main chamber, on the second floor, there was a large fireplace with a fine mantelpiece supported on both sides by pillars in the shape of hounds.

Shakespeare looked out from the window and gazed across at the smoking chimneys of Sheffield and its castle. Below him he saw the complete layout of Manor Lodge. There was a small chapel, stables and some fine brick houses that would probably hold the kitchens, dairy and bakery. In many ways, it was less secure than the castle, for its wall was not as high and there was no moat. But it was smaller and should be easier to patrol.

For the next hour, the reluctant Flowerdew threw open chambers and cupboards, showed the inside of the chapel and the kennels and all the other rooms and outhouses. Shakespeare asked questions sparsely. There was little to be said.

At last, he signalled that the tour was done. 'That is enough. I will see myself out, Mr Flowerdew. And command your card-players to take their posts at the gatehouse for sentry duty.

There was no man to stop me entering; that must not happen again.'

'But Mr Shakespeare, the Scots Queen is not here at present. It is the castle that must be guarded.'

Shakespeare gritted his teeth. 'Mr Flowerdew, start to use the wit God gave you. If a man could enter the lodge when the Scots Queen is not here, then he could bring in arms and secrete them at will to be used when next she arrives. I should not need to explain this to you.'

As Shakespeare strode away, he could hear the clanging of a church bell somewhere to the north. He was heartily sick of the men supposedly holding the Scots Queen; first the insolence of Sergeant Wren, now the idle folly of Flowerdew. The Earl of Shrewsbury's guards needed a kick up their lazy, overfed arses. He stood a minute or two on the edge of the woods and surveyed the parkland and manor house; if Mary were to be the subject of a large-scale bid for freedom, it would be from this woodland that the force would come. By night, a sizeable party of men could get close to the Manor Lodge unseen, and then it was but a short dash to the gatehouse.

Turning away, he walked into the woods, treading a path that seemed to be used regularly, for the dry earth beneath his feet was beaten down and compacted. As he walked he began to sense a sound so soft it barely registered. He did not stop, nor did he look around. He felt the sound again and then he was certain: footfalls. He was being followed.

Taking a turning deeper into the woods, Shakespeare quickened his pace. The trees were more closely packed here. Brambles and ferns thickened and became more difficult to pass. Yet he knew, too, that his pursuer would be finding it tougher to keep track of him.

And then he stopped, in the shade of a tall, heavy-laden horse-chestnut tree, and waited.

The pursuer did not realise until it was too late that his quarry had stopped and was hidden in ambush. Shakespeare was on him from behind, clubbing him to the ground with a double fist, beating at the man's neck and back like a smithy's hammer.

The man sprawled on the ground. 'Stop! Stop!' He was squirming, grovelling in the dust.

Shakespeare stood back, his sword drawn. He touched the nape of the man's neck with the swordpoint. 'Stay on the ground. When I withdraw the point of my sword from your neck, turn over so I can see your face. If you try to escape or attack, I will run you straight through.' He raised the tip of his blade. 'Now.'

The man began to turn and lift himself. He was on his knees. 'Slowly!'

'I mean you no harm. Please put up your sword.' He had his hands in the air, palms forward defensively.

'Who are you?'

'Slide. My name is Harry Slide. I swear to God I am your friend not your foe. I beg you, Mr Shakespeare . . .'

'How do you know my name?'

'Because we work for the same man. I am Mr Secretary's creature, like you.'

'Stand up, Mr Slide – if that is your name – and keep your hands well away from your sword and dagger.'

Harry Slide struggled to his feet. His face and hands were covered in dust. His clothes were torn and dirty from his fall, but Shakespeare could tell that they were of good quality. No, not merely good quality – but exceedingly costly. An ordinary work-man would have had to give up half a year's money in wages for such a suit, for it was of the finest cut. He ran his hand through his long hair, brushed the dust from his face and satin doublet, the colour of daffodils, then bent down to pick up his hat.

'Hand me your sword, hilt first, then your dagger.'

Slide gave Shakespeare his weapons.

'Now, I think you had better explain who you are.'

'An intelligencer.'

It occurred to Shakespeare that this man was vaguely familiar. 'Have we met, Mr Slide?'

'I think not.'

'Then why do I know your face?'

'Perhaps you have seen me at Seething Lane, for I have seen you.'

It was possible. Men like Slide came day by day with tasty morsels of information to sell to Walsingham and his staff. Shakespeare let the matter pass. 'What intelligence do you have for me?'

'Enough. I know that you are looking for Leloup. I know, too, that the Scotsman Buchan Ord has gone missing.'

'Tell me, Mr Slide, if you know this much, where are those two men? I would very much like to find them.'

'If I knew that, Mr Shakespeare, I would have them arrested and brought to gaol.'

'Where do you *believe* them to be?'

'I think they are gone.'

'If you provide me with answers like that, Mr Slide, I may very well thrust my sword through your belly for the mere pleasure of the act.'

'What I mean is that I believe they are gone away from this region.'

'What makes you say that?'

'My intuition, which has saved my life on many an occasion.'

'Your intuition did not tell you I was concealed in the shade of that conker tree, ready to strike you down. I have a notion you place too much faith in this intuition of yours. And you still have not told me why you were following me.'

'I want to offer my services to you. I know Buchan Ord's face. I have heard his voice. None can identify him better than me and so we should work together. Mr Secretary would expect no less.'

'If you know Buchan Ord, describe him to me.'

'He has a pleasant Scottish accent, a fair enough face. I would know him were I to see him again, as I intend.'

'How do you know his voice – *where* did you see him?'

'I had heard of Ord from a certain friend of mine within the castle and I learnt that he was in the habit of taking his wine at the coaching inn each day – when the stink of the Scots Queen's apartments overpowered him. And so I approached him at the Cutler's Rest and tried to engage him in conversation. I fear my renowned charm did not succeed, for he told me he did not drink with Walsingham spies.' Slide laughed. 'I had not realised I was so conspicuous.'

Shakespeare looked at Harry Slide closely. He did not believe a word he said, and yet there was something about him that warranted further inquiry. Had he not known Shakespeare's own name and the nature of his mission? 'Do you have papers, Slide? Some proof of who you are?'

Slide grimaced. 'Mr Shakespeare, you know the way Sir Francis works. I am no more than a kennelhound to him, used to sniff out traitors in return for scraps. He does not grace men like me with official papers, nor would he acknowledge me if I were brought to a court of law in the service of the crown.'

'For a hound fed scraps, you have a remarkably extravagant taste in clothes.'

Slide dusted his left arm with his right hand. 'It is a magnificent piece of tailoring, is it not? And in truth it is my downfall – the reason I undertake hazardous missions for Mr Secretary and our sovereign lady Elizabeth. If I catch a traitor, Mr Secretary will pay me twenty marks or more, and then I will have a new cloak. If I bring him intelligence concerning a seminary priest, I will have two marks in my palm. If I discover the bedroom secrets of a Privy Councillor, I may have a handful of gold and my tailor will eat rare beef. And so I find myself here in these northern wastes on a fool's errand that will likely yield me not a farthing – and my tailor will have to wait for his money yet again.'

There *was* some little charm to this man. Shakespeare resisted the urge to smile.

'And so when you were rebuffed by Mr Ord, what happened next?'

'Why, I left him to his solitary cup of wine.'

'And that is the sum of it?'

'Do you take me for a coney, Mr Shakespeare? No, that was not the sum of it. I waited outside and then followed him. He led me straight to the house of a most notorious recusant gentleman, Sir Bassingbourne Bole. Do you know of him?'

Shakespeare had seen the name on a list of known Catholic sympathisers in the north, but knew nothing else of the man. He shook his head.

'He is of little import, but it is interesting that Buchan Ord sought him out. He stayed an hour and then left, returning to the castle.'

'Could Ord be at Sir Bassingbourne's house now that he has fled?'

'No.'

'How can you be so sure, Slide?'

'Trust me, it is certain.'

'Come,' Shakespeare said. 'Let us go to the Earl of Shrewsbury and see what he makes of all this.'

Slide shrank backwards two steps. 'I fear that is not a good plan. You must know that the earl reviles the spies sent here to watch him. He will clap me in irons.'

Shakespeare poked his chest with the tip of his sword. 'Walk on, Mr Slide.'

'Please, Mr Shakespeare, have you not deduced why I am come here? My mission is to divine the truth about the scandalous nightwork of the earl and the Scots Queen, to wit and to speak plain, are they conjoined in pleasure? Do they know each other carnally?'

'What had Mr Ord to do with this?'

Slide sighed. 'Ord is one of Mary Stuart's most favoured courtiers. He must know almost as much as her ladies concerning her bedtime cavortings. I sought to offer him garnish for detailed intelligence about any assignments with the earl, but Mr Ord was not to be bought with good English silver. Do you not loathe these incorruptibles, Mr Shakespeare? They are the bane of a good intelligencer's life. And now do you understand why I would rather not be taken before his lordship?'

'It makes no difference,' said Shakespeare, prodding him onwards. 'You are coming with me on pain of death.'

Chapter 11

Harry Slide made his escape among the throng of townspeople in the marketplace. He had seemed resigned to obey Shakespeare's command and they had been walking briskly and talking of Walsingham when he suddenly darted from his side.

Shakespeare lunged after him, sword still in hand. But Slide clearly had local knowledge and slipped quickly into one of the side streets leading away from the square. One moment he was there, the next he was gone. For a quarter-hour, Shakespeare hunted him through the narrow alleys and teeming thoroughfares, but the man had vanished like a wisp on the breeze.

He cursed silently and thrust his sword back into its scabbard. How had he let Slide go? Harry Slide: if that was his real name, then it was appropriate, for he was as slippery as an adder. And probably as venomous. Well, it was a lesson learnt: never escort a man to custody unbound.

Across the market square, he spotted Boltfoot Cooper emerging from a tavern. He hailed him and Boltfoot limped across.

'What have you discovered, Boltfoot?'

'I have discovered that Yorkshire ale is as good as London ale, master. Also, that there are many in these parts who believe the Scots Queen to be wronged by our own dear Majesty.'

'And many, I suppose, who would like to see Mary hanged.'

'No, master. The only words I heard sounded very much like treason. They spoke of Good Queen Bess as a . . . no, I must not say the word of her, for fear of my own neck on the block.'

The word was *bastard*. They were suggesting that Great Henry's marriage to Anne Boleyn – the 'concubine' as the Catholics called her – was not legitimate and therefore neither was their daughter.

It was the argument always used by those who would see her deposed in favour of the Scots Queen. Since the day Elizabeth ascended the throne, she had never been recognised by Catholics across the sea, or by many of those who clung to the old faith in England. In France, where the then fifteen-year-old Mary was newly married to the French Dauphin, Francis, it had immediately been ordered that she should henceforth be known as Queen of England, Scotland and Ireland. When she walked in company, ushers were commanded to cry out: *Make way for the Queen of England*. And nothing had changed. Was it any wonder that Elizabeth would not accept her cousin at court, nor grant her liberty?

'So all men in these parts are for the Scots Queen?'

'I could not say that, for most men did not speak of her at all, but discussed the price of beef, the harvest, and the pig-like ugliness of their wives.'

Shakespeare listened to Boltfoot's grim testimony with resignation but no surprise. But it was still worrying that enough men felt free to voice their treasonable thoughts without fear of retribution. How could Elizabeth be safe when so many of her subjects would rejoice if she were deposed or dead? This was the war of secrets to which he was signed. Sometimes in the quiet of the night in London, it seemed the threat was all in the febrile mind of his master, Walsingham. Here, in Yorkshire, it seemed dangerously real. Yet more reason to move Mary Stuart away from this place.

Sir Bassingbourne Bole's house stood two miles to the north of Sheffield. As Shakespeare and Boltfoot rode along the tree-lined driveway, it began to seem that something was horribly wrong. A thin black spiral of smoke drifted into the sky.

As the two riders reined in at the front of the house, all they saw was a blackened husk of what had clearly been a decent, stone-built manor, fit for a magistrate and respected member of the Yorkshire gentry. Smoke drifted lazily from the remnants of rafters, thatch and purlins. Ash fluttered all around them. The air stank.

Shakespeare nudged his horse forward and rode it around to the stables. Looking about in vain for signs of life, he slid from the animal, indicating to his assistant that he should remain mounted.

'Load your caliver, Boltfoot.'

The yard had stabling for a dozen or more horses, but the boxes were all empty. The only sign of life was the steaming pile of horse-dung that had been shovelled high in a corner of the yard.

To the left, the broad open yard was bordered by sties and coops, all empty, as though the pigs had run and the birds flown. There was, too, a huge old barn, so large that it might have been used for the collecting of tithes in former times. Shakespeare entered through the gaping doorway. All about him there were ploughs and carts, some in good repair, others awaiting the wheelwright's attention. At one end, a long ladder gave access to a hayloft.

'Is anyone here?' The words rang through the vast, high-domed space.

He was convinced he heard a sound from the loft. 'Come down, you will be safe. On the Holy Book, I pledge it.'

He waited a moment, but there was no more noise, so he ascended the ladder. As he reached the top, there was a sudden scuttling in the hay. Shakespeare's hand went for his dagger, but then withdrew. He could hear the whimpering of children. There was no threat here. He stood in the slanting light that came through the gaps in the roofing and looked about at the echoing gallery.

'I am a friend. I will not harm you.' He spoke as softly as he could. 'Have no fear.' He held up his hands to show that they did not hold weapons.

Slowly, a woman rose to her feet from the hay. Her eyes were wide with terror. Three, no, four children rose beside her, clutching at her skirts as though they were one entity. None of them was older than seven or eight years. He had chanced upon a terrified family – a mother and her young – hiding from some nameless dread.

The woman was shaking, eyes agog as she stared at the newcomer. One moment she was looking at his face, the next at the sword and dagger stowed in his belt. Avoiding any sudden movements, Shakespeare took out the weapons and laid them flat on the boards of the loft, hilts pointing away from him. 'See. I mean you no injury. What has happened here, mistress?'

'Who are you?'

'My name is John Shakespeare. I have come to speak with Sir Bassingbourne Bole. This is his home, is it not?'

She said nothing.

'Is he here?'

'They took him.'

'Who did this? Why?'

'The pursuivants. They ransacked our home, then torched it.'

'Are you Lady Bole?'

The woman nodded tentatively. She cut a plump, homely figure, more farmwife than lady to a knight.

'Have you any idea why they did this?'

'They said they were seeking books.'

'Papist books?'

She nodded again.

'Did they discover what they were looking for?'

'No, but they found our guest, Father ... *Mr* Cuthbert Edenshaw.'

'Hiding in a coffer among your apparel.'

'You know of this?'

Shakespeare sighed. 'I fear I heard it from the man who discovered him, one Topcliffe. I did not know he had taken your husband, too. Nor did I know he had destroyed your home.'

The blood seemed to drain from the woman's face on hearing the name. 'The white-haired one? I would walk through fire and water never to see his face again. Did he tell you that he and his men smashed the coffer to pieces with a sledgehammer, along with all the other furnishings and panelling in our home? And then piled it up and put a torch to it?'

'No, he did not tell me that.'

'Who exactly are you, Mr Shakespeare?' She seemed to be regaining a little of her courage. 'Why did you wish to talk with my husband?'

'I am on royal business at the castle. I heard of some connection between this house and a certain member of the Scots Queen's household. Do you know anything of this?'

'I know nothing about anything. I know that I no longer have a home and that my husband lies in his soil in a dungeon. I know that our servants have fled and all our horses and livestock are gone. I have nothing save my children, and what is to

✝ 103 ✝

become of them? I know that I live in an England I do not recognise from the days of my girlhood.'

'Do you have any kin nearby – somewhere you can stay for the present?'

'My only family is my brother, but he lives in Grantham.'

'I could try to find you transport there.'

'Then who would be here for Bassingbourne?'

'What of friends nearby, would any take you in?'

She gave a mirthless laugh. 'If I go to them, they will be tainted like us and the pursuivants will destroy them, too. We will stay here. God will provide.'

'But your children . . . they need more than this barn. I would like to help you.'

'Then bring me back my husband and unburn my house, Mr Shakespeare, for that is all my desire.'

Shakespeare felt sick to the stomach as he walked from the barn back to his horse. He mounted up without a word to Boltfoot and kicked his horse's flanks with a savagery born of his anger. Never had he felt so impotent. He threw a last glance at the smoking house and wondered about the man who had done this. Was Richard Topcliffe somehow beyond the law of the land?

As they neared the town, he slowed to a trot. Boltfoot came alongside him. 'What happened, master?'

'The destruction of a family, Boltfoot. Come, I want to see the inside of the town gaol.'

The prison was in a poor state with stones fallen away into the street. It looked more like a farmworker's hovel than a stronghouse to hold desperate outlaws. The studded door was unlocked, so Shakespeare entered unhindered. A gaoler with more hair on his chin than on his head sat at a small, ill-made table in a room no more than eight feet by ten. Behind him another studded door was set into the wall. The cell would be behind that; there was nothing more.

The gaoler looked up without interest from his tankard of ale. The only other thing on the table was a ring with two large iron keys.

'I am looking for Sir Bassingbourne Bole and a man named Cuthbert Edenshaw.'

'Well, master, you have come to the right place.' Dull-eyed, he motioned his bald head backwards. 'They are behind that door. For a short while, leastwise.'

'What are their crimes?'

'One is a priest come secretly into the realm to seduce the Queen's subjects away from the true faith, which is treasonable. The other has been harbouring and assisting the said priest, which must also be considered treasonable. The penalty, master, is hanging, drawing and quartering until dead. And then their several limbs and heads will be displayed about the town at the sheriff's pleasure as a warning to others.'

'Can I see them?'

The gaoler held out his hand, palm upwards. 'If I unlock the door, then you can see them.'

Shakespeare dug a halfpenny from his purse and tossed it to the man, a bone for a dog. The gaoler bent down and picked the coin from the dirty floor near his shoeless feet, where it had landed, then took the keys from his table and turned to unlock the door.

The cell was a dark, foul-smelling hole. There was no window so with the door closed, there would be no light. The slumped hulks of two men sat against the wall to the left, heads in their chests, apparently asleep. Even in the gloom, Shakespeare could see the heavy iron shackles that held their ankles and the manacles that weighed down their wrists.

'Why is there no light for these men?'

'Because there is no window, master.'

'This is shameful. Give me your candle, turnkey.'

The gaoler held out his tallow candle. Shakespeare took it, then stepped into the cell. He guessed that the larger and older of the two men was Sir Bassingbourne Bole. His chest was heaving and an unhealthy rattling sound emanated from his throat.

'Sir Bassingbourne?'

Slowly, the heads of the two men lifted and their eyes squinted into the unaccustomed light.

'My name is Shakespeare. I am on royal business in these parts. I went to your house to speak with you, but I found it burnt to the ground.'

'Yes, I am Bassingbourne Bole,' the elder of the two men rasped. 'Is the house all gone?'

'I fear so. Beyond repair.'

'The unholy curs . . .'

'Your livestock and servants are gone, too.'

The prisoner shook his over-large head. 'The pursuivants will eat well tonight.'

Shakespeare bowed his head but said nothing.

'Did you see Margaret and the children?' Bole spoke at last, his voice raw.

'They are well, though mighty worried about your fate.'

'Are you my friend or enemy, Mr Shakespeare?'

Which was he? He was on the side of England, but Bole might say the same thing. 'I have no desire to be your enemy, sir. If you mean no injury to my sovereign or my country, then you have no cause to fear me.'

Bole attempted to laugh, but his throat was parched and the sound was unpleasant, like a cough that will not come. Shakespeare stepped from the cell into the outer room and picked up the tankard of ale from the table. The gaoler attempted to snatch it back, but Shakespeare drew his dagger and put it to the man's throat. 'Fear not, turnkey, you will be paid for this.' He took the ale into the cell and put it to Bole's lips.

The chained man drank greedily. 'Enough. Give the rest to my friend.'

Shakespeare put the tankard to the other man's lips and he drank the vessel dry.

'I will ensure more ale is brought to you both, and food.'

'Thank you. Please, tell Margaret she must go to her brother in Lincolnshire. She must not wait for she is not safe. Most of all, she must not come and see me here.'

'She will not go to her brother. Her loyalty is to you.'

'Then command her, I beg you. Tell her that if she is loyal to me, she must *obey* me – and go. For the children's sake, she must do this.'

'I will try.'

'Thank you. Now tell me, why were you looking for me?'

'It concerns a man named Buchan Ord.'

At first the name seemed to elicit no reaction. But then Bole gave him a curious look, almost mocking. And it struck Shakespeare that even chained to the floor Bole oozed defiance rather than fear.

'You do not answer me, Sir Bassingbourne. Do you know Buchan Ord, a steward to the Scots Queen in Sheffield Castle?'

'The name means nothing to me.'

'And yet I know he went to your house, for he was followed there.'

'Then, Mr Shakespeare, you know more than I do. Tell me, was the house still standing when he arrived?'

'You seem mighty unconcerned about your predicament.'

'Why should I fear death? Only heretics fear their maker.'

'Who do you consider to be a heretic?'

'Walsingham, Burghley . . . the usurper who calls herself Queen. Perhaps you, too. I have no knowledge of your religion. I know this, though: you are all damned.'

Shakespeare turned to the other man. 'What of you, Mr Edenshaw?'

The man merely stared at Shakespeare.

'Does he not speak, Sir Bassingbourne?'

'He will say his name when asked. What else is there for him to say? All is decided, is it not? We are condemned by your government of traitors, and so we will endure the pain of death. But hear me well, one day it will be your turn on the scaffold – and the usurper's. Unlike us, you will not have the comfort of trusting that you will fly on angel wings into the arms of Christ. When *you* die, you will go down and down. You will burn in hell for ever.'

Shakespeare turned on his heel. He had had enough of these men and their quest for martyrdom. He had tried to bring them a little succour; now he felt sullied by their acquaintance. They would certainly not acknowledge that they knew Buchan Ord, let alone help to find him. Why should they, when their death was ordained whatever they said?

Shakespeare walked from the cell. The gaoler gave him an insolent grin.

'Tell you all you wished to know, did they, master?'

'Do you value your balls, turnkey?'

The gaoler's hand went instinctively to cover his prick.

Shakespeare took two coins from his purse, a sixpence and a penny. He held them up in front of the gaoler's eyes, then placed them on the table before the empty tankard. 'You will use that sixpence to buy good food and beer for the prisoners. The penny is for your ale, which is more than its worth.'

'Why feed them? They will die soon enough anyway.'

'Just do as I say.' Shakespeare was about to stride on by, but stopped. 'Gaoler, what I do know is that those men are human beings – God's creatures like you and me. I like them no more than you do, but you will feed them and give them drink. And you will clear away their straw each day they are here and allow them a little light. Yes, they will die soon, but before that happens, they will be treated with courtesy or *you* will pay a heavy price.'

Turning away, he wrenched open the gaol door – and came face to face with Richard Topcliffe.

Chapter 12

'A H, Mr Shakespeare, I have been looking for you. We must depart for Tutbury imminently if we are to fulfil our mission for Mr Secretary.'

Topcliffe smiled, as though they were confederates with a common purpose.

'I have just met the priest you caught and the man who harboured him.'

'A fine brace of popish worms, are they not? My lord of Shrewsbury has arranged a party of guards to take them to the Tower, where I shall look forward to stretching them longer by a foot. Then they will tell us all we need to know.'

Shakespeare's lips curled down at the thought of Topcliffe being let loose on the two men. The rack was a rarely used device and surely not one to be placed in the hands of a man like this white-haired devil. 'And was it necessary to burn down Bole's house?'

'Is that what he told you? You can never trust a papist. They dissemble to paint the Queen's men in a bad light. You can be certain that even now they are saying evil things about you, Mr Shakespeare.'

'But I saw the smoking ruins with my own eyes.'

'Oh, there was a fire, true enough. But it was one of his own servants as did start it, by knocking over a rushlight on to some sheets. It made a merry blaze.'

'And his wife and children, where are they to live now?'

'The bitch should thank me for not taking her in, too. For certain she was party to the secreting of the priest. Were they not her undergarments in which I found him? Perhaps the greased priest had already groped in her petticoats while they were about her person, for they are dirty dogs these seminary men.'

Shakespeare looked at Topcliffe in disgust. It was not even worth the effort of gainsaying him and yet for better or worse he was affixed to him, like daub to wattle. But he did not wish to go south; not quite yet. 'I still have business here.'

'No, Shakespeare, your business is long gone. The Frenchman has taken his one arm and his wolf snout many miles from here. There is nothing to be done here but to hunt priests, which is wondrous sport, but Mr Secretary has other designs for us. We must pack our saddles and go.'

There was some truth in what Topcliffe said. Yet it vexed Shakespeare to leave this place having found no sign of François Leloup or Buchan Ord. He spoke briskly. 'Very well. I will meet you in an hour at the castle gate. There is enough moon. We can ride through the night.'

'So be it, Mr Shakespeare.' Topcliffe laughed and pushed on into the gaol.

Arriving back at the Cutler's Rest, Shakespeare was immediately approached by the landlord, Geoffrey Whetstone. 'One of my ostlers has information for you, master.'

They stepped out into the yard. The ostler was a strong, confident man of middle years.

'You were asking about the Frenchie, sir. I remember him well. Four or five days since. Rode a flea-bitten jade that had seen better days, but she looked tough enough.'

'Did he say where he was going?'

'To the southern coast, but he said he wished to go by way of the county of Warwick, where he had friends. He did ask me the best highway to take. He gave me a groat. He was a gentleman for a Frenchie.'

'Warwickshire?' What would a man like François Leloup be doing in Warwickshire? Shakespeare felt the sudden chill of alarm. This was uncomfortably close to home.

'Boltfoot, I want you to stay here.'

'As you wish, master.' Boltfoot did not look convinced.

'I do not know how long I will be gone, so I want you to continue to seek out Mr Buchan Ord, and the man named Harry Slide. If you find either of them, you are to take them to the castle guard. I will leave instructions that they are to be held under lock and key until my return. Do you understand?'

'What if I find one and he resists? Am I to kill him?'

Shakespeare sighed. His assistant's loyalty and courage could not be in doubt, but whether he could engage in the subtleties of espionage was another matter altogether. 'No, you are to use your wit and overpower him. And Boltfoot . . .'

'Yes, master?'

'You are to go back to the burnt-down manor house, find the mistress of the house who was in the barn. Tell her that her husband commands her to take the children to Grantham, without delay. Tell her that he is resigned to his death and thinks only of his family.'

They rode through the night and all the next day. Shakespeare either trotted ahead of Topcliffe or a little behind him. He had no desire to ride alongside him and converse.

He was trying to work out the puzzle of Buchan Ord and his

journey to the home of Sir Bassingbourne Bole, but his thoughts kept returning to the luscious Kat Whetstone. He hoped he would have cause to return to Sheffield.

Shakespeare had told Shrewsbury that he might have to return. He had also told him that Boltfoot would be remaining and that he should summon him if he heard anything of Ord or Leloup or the missing maps. The earl was not impressed by the suggestion.

On the sixty-mile ride south, Shakespeare and Topcliffe stopped twice to eat at inns and to refresh their animals. Over their first meal together, Topcliffe had tried to goad his new companion.

'Men like you know nothing of the Pope, the scarlet whore of Babylon, the Antichrist. How old are you? You cannot have been born when blessed Elizabeth ascended the throne to save this realm. You were not there when the devil's acolytes stalked this land.'

Indeed Shakespeare had only been a month old when Elizabeth became Queen, but that was of no relevance. 'I know enough of Catholicism. It is there in all our pasts, is it not, Mr Topcliffe?'

'They are all steeped in venery and sin, idolatry and bigotry. Sodomising boy-priests . . . satanical rites . . . you were not there when the Spaniard and his wretched whore brought their foul Inquisition to England, casting a black cloud of smoke over us. The smoke of burning flesh.'

'I know of it. I have read much of Mr Foxe's volume on the martyrs.'

'But you weren't *there*. They were filthy men, who did evil deeds and sold the bones of cats and dogs to the superstitious, calling them saints. You were not there! You do not know the terror of a child called upon to make confession for his sins. Devils they were, devils in stinking robes. They did not drag *you* into the sacristy and defile you at three years of age and call it penance for your sins.' Topcliffe spat the words out as if they poisoned him.

Shakespeare pushed his half-eaten trencher of food away and downed his ale. He no longer had an appetite. 'I am going for a piss in the yard, Mr Topcliffe. And then let us ride once more.'

'God damn you, Shakespeare. If we are to destroy the popish beast, the country needs men not milksops!'

As he rode towards the ruin of Bassingbourne Bole's home, Boltfoot Cooper was seized by despondency. The problem was that he knew he was inadequate to the task he had been set. Boltfoot was grateful to John Shakespeare for taking him on as his underling but what exactly was his role? One day, Mr Shakespeare seemed displeased that he had not filled the house in Seething Lane with food and ale; now, just days later, he was being asked to hunt down spies. Servant? Pursuivant? He was not sure he desired either of the two jobs.

His life from boyhood had been as a cooper, a builder of barrels, aboard ships sailing out of the west country. Most recently, he had been with Sir Francis Drake during his great three-year circumnavigation of the globe. It was a voyage that had destroyed his love of the sea for ever. He had seen brutality and suffered hunger that no man would wish to repeat.

Sheffield may have been a less hostile part of the world, but it was as unknown to him as Peru or the Moluccas had been. Where was he supposed to start in looking for these two men, Ord and Leloup? He had no idea what they looked like and he knew no one here who might help him.

On arrival at the ruined house, he went straight to the barn where Shakespeare had found Lady Bole and her children.

They were no longer there. Nor were they in any of the other outhouses. Boltfoot picked over the blackened remnants of the main building, but could find nothing to suggest where they might have gone. After an hour of searching, he mounted up for the two-mile ride back to Sheffield. A hundred yards along the track, he spotted a figure standing by a small cart, watching him. Still on horseback, Boltfoot approached the figure and saw a man in peasant rags. Boltfoot lifted his head in silent greeting.

'Good day, master.'

'I'm not your master,' Boltfoot said.

'You're no ploughman or cowherd, that's for certain.'

It had never occurred to Boltfoot that he could be mistaken for anyone's master. He might not wear the ragged smock and hat of a farmhand, but he knew that his face was the lined, weather-beaten face of mariners and working men the world over. No one could take his leather jerkin and plain hose for the attire of a man of note.

'I am looking for the lady of the manor. Lady Bole. She was here.'

'She's gone. Flown with her children.'

'Where to?'

The man blew his nose into his cupped hands, then wiped them on his rags and grinned, revealing his one remaining tooth. 'Who did you say you were, master?'

'My name is Cooper.'

'Well, Mr Cooper, I think she is looking for a place of safety. Nothing left for her here.'

'And who are you? Do you work here?'

'Aye. Wilfred's the name. Worked this farm all my life, boy and man.'

'Where are all the other farmhands and servants?'

'They're about. Mostly in the woods until they be certain the soldiers have all gone for good. None of us got anywhere else to go, unless we can find work on nearby farms.'

'And the livestock?'

'Not for me to say.'

Boltfoot dug his hand into the pocket of his jerkin. Mr Shakespeare had told him that he would be repaid if he needed to give a coin or two for information. 'There's a halfpenny here. It's yours if you can help me find someone.'

'You mean Lady Bole?'

'No. A man named Buchan Ord. Acquaintance of Sir Bassingbourne, so I'm told. Scotch, he is, so he won't talk like anyone from hereabouts.'

'Never heard of the man but I'll ask about. How much would it be worth?'

'This halfpenny for the information, then sixpence if I find Mr Ord. You can share the sixpence as you please.'

'Scotchman, you say? This wouldn't have aught to do with the Scotch Queen, would it?'

'That's for me to know.'

'I may be naught but an old farmboy, but I know danger when I see or hear it. Look what's happened to Bassy Bole. Going for the chop, folk say. So any word pertaining to the Scotch Queen or priests would be mighty perilous and would cost more than a pretty sixpence.'

'Find someone who knows something, then we'll talk money.'

'Fair enough, Mr Cooper. Fair enough. Where can a man find you?'

'Cutler's Rest in Sheffield.'

Shakespeare and Topcliffe arrived at Tutbury in the late afternoon. High on an earthwork mound in the middle of a plain, the old castle stood stark and forlorn against a darkening sky, its turrets and chimneys as numerous as the prickles on a hedgehog.

To the front it looked towards the peaks of Derbyshire. To the south was the small town of Tutbury, backed by the royal forest of Needwood where a wealth of boar and deer roamed wild. But the woodland was far enough distant to pose no threat of cover to an enemy. Indeed, there had been a fortification here for almost a thousand years, so readily defendable was it.

'Should never have moved the heifer away from here,' Topcliffe said as they reined in at the base of the enormous earthwork and looked across the moat to the tower gatehouse and crenellated walls.

'Why is that, Mr Topcliffe?'

'Because she loathed the place.' Topcliffe laughed. 'Cold. Damp. Filthy. Beset by bitter, foul-smelling winds beneath the doors and through the windows. She complained each day with tears and wailing. And to hear her complain and weep would cheer the heart of any true Englishman. Come on, let's get on with it.'

Shakespeare's immediate impression was that Tutbury Castle enjoyed a powerful defensive position, with magnificent views for many miles around in all directions across the town to the forest and the Staffordshire countryside. But he soon realised, too, that that was the sum of its attractions. As Topcliffe had said, there was, indeed, a festering damp and rotten air to the place. In the state rooms at the southern quarter of the castle, where Mary had stayed – the great chamber and hall – water ran in rivulets down the walls along brown-stained grooves. In many places the plaster had peeled back. Mildew assailed the nose.

The grey-haired porter and his pinch-mouth wife clearly

knew Topcliffe well, for they welcomed him like a long-lost son.

'Come in, Mr Topcliffe, come in. This is a rare privilege, sir. Will you be staying with us? Will roast beef and curlew pie suit for your supper, sir?'

'One night is all, Mr and Mrs Harkness. And a piece of your curlew pie would sit well with me.'

They ushered him in with great extravagant bowings and scrapings, disregarding Shakespeare as though they thought he might be Topcliffe's servant. He was having none of it. He reached out and stayed the porter, gripping his shoulder as he turned away.

'My name is John Shakespeare. I am here from the office of Sir Francis Walsingham and you will extend me every courtesy.'

The porter looked at him for a few moments, and then turned back to Topcliffe. 'We shall have a fire laid in your chamber, master, the room you liked so well when last you were here.'

Topcliffe grinned. 'He means the one where the cold does not seep in through the devil's nooks and holes.'

'And for your companion, Mr Topcliffe?'

'Why, I do believe he might enjoy the heifer's privy chamber. What say you, Shakespeare?'

He knew that they were trying to discomfit him, but they were wrong; the truth was, he *would* like to sleep there. It would be instructive to learn how Mary Stuart had felt in the room. A night there might tell him if there was any hope of bringing it up to a suitable standard to house a Queen.

Chapter 13

Boltfoot was in the taproom of the Cutler's Rest, enjoying a quart of ale and the heat from the fire in the hearth. He had finished his supper and was trying to think straight about his next move. Across the room, walking towards a booth, he spotted the sentry he had met the night before, at the castle gate. His instinct was to shy away from the man, for he might desire revenge for the trouble caused him. Instead, he steeled himself and approached the guard.

'Do you recognise me?'

'Aye, I do. Larks and quails! And I should run you through with my short sword, you worthless scraping of dog turd.'

'I am sorry. I had no thought to cause you trouble.'

'You could have got us both hanged. As it is, I've lost a week's wages. Who'll make that up to me?' He gave Boltfoot a searching look.

'How much?'

'Three shillings and sixpence.'

'Will you talk with me? Allow me to stand you a gage of ale?'

The guard grumbled and then smiled. 'I'll let you stand me a gage of *beer* – and I'll have my wages, too. Make it five shillings for the chastisement I endured.'

'Well, I'm pleased to meet you properly. I hope I'm not

keeping you from your wife. She may be in need of apples and cheese.'

'You know what I'd like? I would like to buy my wife a looking glass, so that she might stand in front of it all day long and bully *herself* to an early grave with her sharp tongue, and leave me be. But I fear your five shillings will not be enough for such furnishing.'

Boltfoot handed over a crown to his new companion from the money Shakespeare had left him. It occurred to him that the coins would not last long if he had to keep handing them out like this. A potboy arrived and Boltfoot ordered a jug of beer.

He settled down opposite the sentry. 'I am looking for one of the Scots Queen's men – name of Buchan Ord.'

'Nor are you alone in that.'

'Is there a hue and cry for him?'

'The castle was searched high and low and word went out to the sheriff and justices. But not a sign of him.' The guardsman gulped down a deep draught of beer and wiped the drips from his beard with his sleeve.

'My master was told that Buchan Ord was followed to the home of Sir Bassingbourne Bole, who now rests at Her Majesty's pleasure in Sheffield gaol, awaiting trial and execution for assisting a priest in the harvesting of converts.'

The sentry grunted. 'I heard of it. Sad day when men die for a mass, I say. But I know nothing of Ord going to him. Has your master told this to old Shrewsbury?'

Boltfoot gritted his teeth. This was going nowhere. He wished desperately that he had some tobacco, but there was none to be had in a place like Yorkshire. Nor was there information to be had. He wondered for one dark moment whether he should just head for the coast and board a ship; a good barrel-maker could always find work, and he knew that he was as good as any man at making a cask watertight. At least he'd likely find a pipeful of sotweed aboard ship. The moment passed. At the door of the inn, he saw another new arrival.

It was Wilfred, the one-toothed farmhand from the burnt-out ruin. He was beckoning to Boltfoot with bony fingers. Then he slid away into the night.

'The Queen does love me very well, Shakespeare. Did you know that?'

'I know nothing of you, Mr Topcliffe. I had never heard your name until Mr Secretary asked me to meet you.'

'I may take my Elizabeth away from any company, for she does love her Dick Topcliffe more sweetly than any other man alive. Once, I even lured her from the company of the French Frog when recently he was here a-wooing.'

'Then you are much favoured, Mr Topcliffe, though I think you do your sovereign no honour by speaking of her in such wise.'

'I have seen and touched her milk-white legs and have placed my hand between her soft womanly paps.'

If Topcliffe's intention was to shock, he succeeded. For a moment Shakespeare was lost for words.

Topcliffe laughed. 'You are a boy, Shakespeare. You know nothing of the world.'

'And you, Topcliffe, what are you? Does the Queen know that you talk of her as though she were a Southwark trug? Shame on you, sir.'

'Do you doubt me?' Topcliffe stared at Shakespeare from the far side of the table, seeming to dare him to contradict his assertions. 'And more than that, I know her mind as well as her woman's body. And so I know that she will be very pleased to see her cousin brought to this place. What do *you* say, Shakespeare? Is Tutbury not fit for the papist slattern?'

Shakespeare fought to calm himself. *Stick to the point, the reason for your being here together. Get it done with, and go your separate ways.* 'This castle is easily defended, I grant you, Mr Topcliffe. But it is unwholesome and would require a great deal of money to refurbish it fit for a queen. Even the Queen of Scots is worthy of better.'

They were at the long table in the hall, being brought dishes by porter Harkness and his wife. The castle echoed around them in its near emptiness. Shakespeare rather thought that he would prefer to dine with the devil.

The food was poor, but Topcliffe wolfed it down as though it were the finest fare in the land. Shakespeare ate because he was hungry, and because there was nothing else in this dungeon of a place. He tasted a cup of wine, but it was off and he spat it out.

In all the other rooms Shakespeare had seen, the furniture was covered in linen dust-sheets, yet even the sheets were rotten with damp and falling to shreds. A large portrait of Elizabeth that should have dominated the great hall was scarcely recognisable, for the paint was flaking and coming away.

Topcliffe snorted with derision. 'Worthy of better, you say? I say the Scotch heifer is a head too tall. I would have lopped her many years since. Did she not conspire with the traitor Norfolk?'

'Perhaps.'

'And worse, she is a papist, and should die for that alone.'

Shakespeare said nothing. He would not be provoked, however much he desired to take the haft of his dagger to the man's skull.

Topcliffe finished the curlew pie, then picked up a beef bone and gnawed at it. His lips dripped fat and saliva. He pointed the bone at Shakespeare. 'Oft-times, it does seem to me that

Her Majesty is the only one in this realm with the balls of a man. You should be hunting down papists, Shakespeare. You should be hanging them – not coddling them.'

'I hunt down traitors, not Catholics.'

'Papist, traitor . . . the words are interchangeable.'

Shakespeare had had enough. He rose from the table, shaking with anger. He almost drew his sword, but instead he swept his arm across the tabletop, scattering tankards, goblets and platters. Then he turned his shoulder and stalked from the hall, Topcliffe's scornful laughter ringing in his ears.

Wilfred led Boltfoot away from the inn, into the darkness behind the stables. The only light was the moon.

'Well?'

'Your Scotchman had a woman, Mr Cooper. A local lass.'

'Who told you this?'

'A friend. Do you wish to know her name and where she abides?'

'Indeed, I would be most grateful for such information.'

The ragged farmhand laughed his toothless laugh. 'It is not gratitude I desire, but coin. Such information comes at a price, for it is stepping into hazardous country to be trading in secrets involving the Scotch Queen and her people.'

'What was it we said? A halfpenny if you bring me word. Then sixpence if I find Mr Ord.'

A scratch of laughter came from Wilfred's dribbling mouth. 'You must think northern folk doddypolls, Mr Cooper. I tell you this: we know the worth of bread and beer as well as any southern man. And more besides.'

Boltfoot began to realise he was mighty exposed out here in the darkness of night. Surreptitiously, his hand gripped the hilt of his cutlass. 'What sort of price did you have in mind, Wilfred?'

'Two sovereigns.'

'Two sovereigns! I don't have money like that.'

'Then I don't know the name of Mr Ord's sweetheart, nor where she abides.'

'A crown. I'll give you a crown.' A *crown*? He had just given that sum to the sentry. It was insane to be offering these men such money with no guarantee of anything in return.

'Let's make it *three* sovereigns, Mr Cooper.'

'No, let us not. I do not have the money, nor do I believe you.' Boltfoot let go the hilt of his cutlass and poured the coins from his purse into the palm of his hand. 'There. Look at it. There's not a pound there, let alone a single sovereign. And before you ask, I have no more hidden away.'

'Then you'll have no information. And so I wish you farewell and sweet dreams.'

Boltfoot grabbed his arm. 'Wait. Let us discuss this like Christians.'

'Proceed, Mr Cooper.'

'My master has gone south, but he will be back. If we strike a deal, he will honour it. I can vouch this, I am certain. Let us say ten shillings now and then a pound if the young woman proves helpful and tells us where to find Mr Ord.'

'How much you got in that purse?'

'You cannot have all this. A man must live from day to day.'

'What of your nag? That must be worth two or more sovereigns, for she looks a serviceable mare.'

'Not the horse. I have made you a fine offer, Wilfred. A true offer. I have never cheated any man.'

Wilfred thrust out his hand. 'Put the ten shillings there, Mr Cooper. And a pound to follow, mind.'

Boltfoot counted the coins into the man's hand. He looked at what remained and realised he had left himself mighty short of money. 'Who is she then? Who is Mr Buchan Ord's sweetheart?'

'Why, she's the prettiest girl in Sheffield town. That's all you need to know.'

As he returned to the taproom, Boltfoot was in a palsy of indecision. Should he go straight to Kat and confront her? Or should he watch her and follow her in the hope that she would lead him to the Scotsman? What would Mr Shakespeare do in the circumstances?

Boltfoot sat nursing his tankard for the remainder of the evening, watching Kat Whetstone's every move.

He looked at her for signs of distress. Was she distraught at having been betrayed and abandoned by a lover, or had Ord in fact not left Sheffield? Certainly, nothing in Kat Whetstone's behaviour seemed to suggest that anything was amiss.

Boltfoot downed a gage of ale, then another. He had never been a big drinker, not even at sea when man's only comfort is the spirit of the grape.

Soon after midnight, Kat closed the door, snuffed most of the candles and doused the fires. Boltfoot looked about and realised he was the only one in the room, save her. At last, she came over to him.

'Would you like something, Mr Cooper? A posset, perhaps, to warm your way to bed?'

He shook his head. He had drunk a great deal too much already without adding a hot sweet beverage of curdled milk and ale.

'Do you know when Mr Shakespeare will be returning to Sheffield, sir? I had thought him a fine young man.'

Boltfoot shrugged and stumbled to his feet, holding the table to steady himself.

'Let me give you a candle to light your way.'

He gazed at her through misty, yearning eyes. Her hair was golden in the last of the light, her eyes soft and hazy. The sort of young woman who would never give a lame and grizzled mariner a second glance. She took his arm and led him away from the table.

At the door, she plucked a candlestick from the top of an old oak barrel, then lifted the door latch and took Boltfoot out to the courtyard. He allowed her to help him up to the chamber as though he were an old man. He could smell her sweat and feel the warmth of her breast as she gripped his arm. She opened the door to his room. For one brief moment he wondered whether she would follow him in. Instead, she handed him the candle.

'I bid you good night, Mr Cooper.'

He grunted a word of thanks, and she was gone.

A low, intermittent gust of air whistled and soughed through the panes and beneath the doors, but John Shakespeare slept like a sheepdog when its work is done. He woke to the slant of sun across his eyelids. He turned his head away from the light, burying his face in the pillow. For a few moments he did not move, wishing only more of this luxuriant sleep. But then he stiffened. If the sun was this high, he had overslept. What time of day was it, in the name of God?

He opened his eyes and pushed himself up on the pillows. He blinked away the sleep, taking deep breaths to wake himself. And then his eyes caught the horror that hung before him.

At first he thought he must still be dreaming. He opened his eyes wider, then recoiled at the obscenity that he beheld. A woman was hanging by her neck, suspended from the rafters, on the far side of the room.

She twisted slowly in the chilly draught. She was dressed in a long red dress of velvet and gold, like a queen.

He leapt up and stared at the figure, frozen. His indecision lasted but a moment. His sword and dagger were on the floor beside the bed. He drew the sword, grabbed the small stool where he had thrown his garments and climbed on it. Grasping the figure around the waist, he reached up, slashing at the hemp rope with his honed blade. Two strokes, three, and it was severed. The hanging woman fell into his arms. He had braced himself to take her weight, but there was none. She was light as straw.

Relieved, he laid her upon the bed. There was no substance here, no flesh or blood; this was nothing but an effigy. And then his feeling of relief gave way to rage.

The face was made of linen. From close up he could see that the dead eyes, the mouth, the nose, were but paint. The hair was a wig, like those worn by ladies of fashion at the royal court. It was only the shock of seeing the image straight from sleep that had allowed him to be fooled.

He tore at the face, ripping the linen asunder. Rags fell out. He threw the foul object to the floor, then pulled on his clothes, picked up his weapons and strode from the room, sword in his right hand, dagger in his left. He was ready to draw blood.

In the hall, the porter's wife, Mrs Harkness, was sweeping the wooden boards with a well-used broom. She stopped and smiled. 'Good morning, master, I trust you have slept well?'

'Where is Topcliffe? Where is your husband?'

'Why, Mr Topcliffe was up with the birds and has ridden from here. That was three hours since. He will be twenty miles distant by now, God willing.'

'Did he put that *thing* in my room?'

'Why, sir, I do not know what thing you mean.'

'The effigy, woman! The filthy puppet hanging from the rafter. Was it supposed to be the Queen of Scots – was that it?

Fetch your husband. You will both pay a damnable price for your temerity.'

After a minute, Harkness waddled in with his wife. He was grinning. 'The good Lord bless us, Mr Shakespeare, I was assured by Mr Topcliffe that you had a most uncommon sense of humour and that you would be greatly amused by our little jest. We did believe that any man would laugh until his breeches ran like a river to see the murdering Scotch witch hanging!'

'Where did that effigy come from? It was too accomplished – you did not make it last night.'

'Indeed, we did not. We had it packed away in the attics from the old days when last Mary was here. Is it not a fine likeness? It caused her many tears – and afforded us much merriment.'

Chapter 14

S HAKESPEARE WAS MOUNTED and riding within a half-hour. He followed the road almost directly south, through woods and farmland. The day was dry and bright, but the sun could do nothing to shake away the anger that maddened him. What sort of man was Topcliffe? And what was Sir Francis Walsingham's purpose in making them work together?

You will doubtless find Mr Topcliffe to be strong meat, but he has the Queen's trust, and mine. You do not need to like him . . .

Those had been Mr Secretary's words. Well, Shakespeare had indeed found him strong meat. *Rancid* meat. But why did he have the trust of the Principal Secretary and the Queen? What service could such a man offer? And what did they know of his lewd, fantastical bragging? Other men might die on the gibbet for speaking thus of their sovereign lady.

He would give his opinion forcibly when next he was alone with Walsingham. In the meantime, he would have to entrust his opinion of Tutbury to a letter sent by courier from Stratford, for he had no faith in Harkness nor anyone else in the nearby town.

In different circumstances, his inclination now might have been to return to Sheffield to resume the hunt for Buchan Ord, or to repair to Oatlands to take further advice from Mr

Secretary. But Walsingham's orders had been quite clear: after Tutbury, he was to go to Warwickshire. And had not the ostler at the Cutler's Rest suggested that this might have been the direction Leloup was headed?

He was chasing smoke.

By late afternoon, he had reached Snitterfield where his grandfather, Richard Shakespeare, had tilled the soil. And then he knew he was almost home, a mere four miles or so along the Stratford way before he would see his mother and father, his brothers and sister again.

He eased the horse down to a slow, restful walk and began to soak in the familiar sights of his youth. The avenue of elms shading the byway to the east, the hedges, the dappled woods, the wide open meadows, filled with bees, late summer butter-flies and every songbird under heaven. This place was Eden. He found himself mouthing a prayer, his anger of the morning ebbing away and being replaced by a longing for these familiar fields and paths.

In the distance, he could just make out the tip of the wooden spire of Holy Trinity, the parish church where his father had had him baptised. Ahead of him, he spotted a young man strid-ing along the road, and with joy he recognised the gait. He was walking in the same direction as Shakespeare, but a hundred yards ahead of him. Shakespeare began to smile. He would know that familiar, confident walk anywhere. He urged his horse on and trotted up behind his brother, then leant over and clapped him on the shoulder. 'And where are you going in such haste, Master Shakespeare?'

Will turned at the touch. If there had been anxiety etched on his brow, it vanished in an instant, replaced by a warm smile of delight.

'John!'

Shakespeare dismounted and embraced his brother. He

stood back from him and studied him. 'Will, you look every inch a man.'

'I *feel* it,' he said ruefully.

Will was eighteen now, his whole life stretching out before him. What would he do with that mighty mind? Perhaps Walsingham could find Will a place within one of the great estates of government? He had the brain for it, and Mr Secretary always had one eye open for men of intellect. One thing was certain: Stratford, for all its strategic and commercial importance in the Midlands, would not hold Will for long, any more than it had held Shakespeare himself.

'I do not mean to imply that you look worn down by cares. You look a man in the *best* sense. Strong, well-formed – and with more in the way of beard than last I saw you.'

'And you look dusty.' Will threw his brother a wry expression. 'I have just been to call on Uncle Henry. I have been earning a few pence tutoring his sons.'

'And has he paid you?'

'He promises he will pay me at the end of the month.'

'And promises not written are, as we know, made of air. Still, at least you have his ill tempers to keep you amused while you await your pennies.'

Will did not argue with his brother's assessment of their father's younger brother. 'But whence have *you* come, John? If you have travelled through Snitterfield, then you have not ridden from London or the south.'

'The north.' Shakespeare did not wish to explain further for the present.

'Did you not write to say you were coming?'

'No. I am on Queen's business and my movements are uncertain. But more of that later. Come, let us walk together. The nag has had enough of my weight this day.'

*

A little way to their left, beyond the osier beds, the mild green waters of the Avon flowed slowly towards Stratford. Ahead of them, the way was filled with a cloud of dust and they saw four horsemen approaching at speed. No traveller would drive his mount so hard. Alarmed, Shakespeare stopped, moved to the side of the road, and watched them.

Suddenly, as they were almost upon the two brothers, one of the riders wheeled his horse sharply to the left. Shakespeare sensed the sword in the man's hand before he even saw the glint of steel. He gripped his brother's arm to pull him aside.

Too late. The sword was already thrust forward. With a flick of the rider's wrist, Will's velvet hat was impaled by the sword-point and lifted from his head. A little lower and the blade would have pierced his eye through to his brain.

The swordsman held his prize aloft and shouted, 'Pig!' With another snap of the hand, the hat flew up, billowing, its feather catching the breeze like the wing of a bird.

A roar of laughter and cheers rang from the throats of his companions. They did not stop, nor even slow down, but rode on without slackening their pace. Will shook his head but said nothing, merely strode back the way he had come and collected his hat where it had landed, thirty yards along the lane.

Shakespeare watched the departing horsemen in bemusement and more than a little disquiet, for he rather imagined he had recognised one of the four men. 'What in God's name was that, Will? Who were they?'

'That was Badger Rench. Did you not recognise him?' Will beat the dust from his hat, and then examined it. He put his finger through a hole where the sword had pierced the velvet.

'Rench? You mean Rafe Rench's boy, from the farm out Shottery way?' With his brute strength and lack of wit, Shakespeare had always thought him ideally suited for hefting sacks of barleycorn and nothing more. 'All I recall of him was that he was skilled at tormenting frogs and wrestling.'

'Well, now he rides with Sir Thomas Lucy's men and believes himself a very prince of the county. He does not like me.'

'Why not?'

'He has his reasons. I try to steer clear of all Sir Thomas's men since my unfortunate brush with his gamekeeper last year.'

Shakespeare laughed. 'Ah yes, the deer that you did not poach from his parkland. I could imagine that still rankles with Sir Thomas. He is not one to forget a grudge, I fear.'

'I do not share your amusement, brother. He would have had me hanged if he could. It is my good fortune that the jury liked him even less than they liked me. Thomas Lucy is become worse. He takes an exceeding hard line with anyone he suspects of being Catholic or even vaguely doubtful about the new Church. He believes the county of Warwick to be infested with conspirators, saving the greater part of his bile for the Ardens. In his mind, anyone with Arden blood is tainted and so he has sworn vengeance on our family.'

A hatred shared by the Earl of Leicester. Shakespeare thought back to the conversation he had had at Oatlands. 'Well, at the very least his man Rench owes you a hat.'

The truth was, Shakespeare was not really thinking about his brother's fine velvet cap. Nor was he thinking of the brutish Badger Rench, a brock by nature as well as by name. He was thinking about another of the four horsemen. They had passed at such speed and amid such dust that he was not at all certain of what he had seen. And yet he had indeed recognised one of the men. It was the slightness of the figure, the smoothness of the narrow chin, the brightness of the attire. It was a man he had met at the palace of Oatlands. A man who was some sort of assistant or servant to the Earl of Leicester, a man with foul words for the Ardens and the Shakespeares. A man who wore a multicoloured doublet and a row of red stones in his ear. A man named Ruby Hungate.

Boltfoot loitered around the stableyard of the Cutler's Rest like a hog awaiting its swill. He could think of no way to make himself inconspicuous. Surely, Kat would be going somewhere, anywhere. And then he would do his best to follow her, unseen.

'You looking for something, Mr Cooper?' one of the grooms asked after Boltfoot had been standing around, helplessly, for the best part of an hour.

'No, nothing. Passing the time of day.'

'Well, it's a fine enough day.'

'Miss Whetstone, does she have a swain?' The words came out without thought, blurted like a blabbering child.

'Now why would you be asking something like that? Fancy she'd look at a cripple like you, do you? Like your chances there, eh? Fair pair of paps on her, would you be thinking? Soft rounded belly – don't suppose a mongrel like you gets much of that.'

Boltfoot ignored the insult. The ostler was ugly enough himself. 'Curiosity, that's all. Fine-looking woman like that – how be it she don't have no husband yet?'

'Why don't you ask her yourself? Make her an offer. Shilling should do it. That's what she usually charges.'

Boltfoot frowned at the ostler. 'That's no way to talk about your master's daughter.'

The groom laughed. 'What would Kat Whetstone want with a swain? The whole world loves her – why would she need one man? Don't need a husband to feed her when she's got the Cutler's Rest, do she?'

'What of a foreign man, a Scotch fellow?'

The groom stiffened visibly at the suggestion. 'You're awful inquisitive for a man who's a stranger himself. I think Goodman Whetstone might like to hear about your questions.'

'Wait. I'm just looking for the Scotchman, that's all. Heard he had been sniffing around Kat Whetstone. My master wishes to talk with him.'

The groom, who was only a shade bigger than Boltfoot, grabbed him by the collar of his jerkin.

Boltfoot wrenched himself free and drew his cutlass in one easy move. 'Touch me again and I'll cut you.' He held the edge of the blade close to the man's throat, then withdrew it and replaced it in his scabbard. From the corner of his eye, he saw a figure standing at the back door to the inn. He turned and met the gaze of Geoffrey Whetstone, resting his enormous bulk against the jamb, his arms folded casually on the platform of his great stomach.

He tilted his head towards Boltfoot. 'I do not like to see naked blades on my property, Mr Cooper.' His voice was quiet but audible. 'Unless they be for the slicing of roasted beef. Come with me.' He beckoned to Boltfoot to follow him inside. 'Now tell me, Mr Cooper, what is this about?' They were in the landlord's private apartments, a room with two leaded windows that allowed sunlight to stream across the lime-washed wood. Goodman Whetstone sat on a stool by the hearth, lounging back against the wall.

Boltfoot was in too deep now to dissemble. Better to have the truth out and see what he could learn.

'My master works for the office of the Principal Secretary. He is concerned about the disappearance of a man named Buchan Ord, a courtier from the retinue of the Queen of Scots. And then I was told that your daughter had been his sweetheart. I did not know whether to believe it.'

'Who told you this?'

'I cannot give you his name. But tell me this, did he speak true? Was Ord your daughter's swain or intended?'

'Best ask her yourself. Better than skulking around, prying like a man with something dirty to hide. I'll fetch her to you, Mr Cooper. Then you may ask away at will. Though I cannot promise that she will vouchsafe you any answers.'

Chapter 15

As they entered Stratford, Shakespeare began to spot old friends from his childhood. The draper George Whateley was first, riding his roan mare at the corner of Guild Street and Bridgefoot. He was about to ride on past when he spotted Shakespeare and reined in, then leant down and shook hands with a firm grip. 'Well met, John. Folks around here said we'd seen the last of you.'

Shakespeare returned the greeting and smiled warmly at his old Henley Street neighbour. His damask doublet, puffed up like the chest of a pheasant cock, told the tale of his increasing wealth. Shakespeare knew from his mother's letters how well he was doing. 'He'll have bought up the whole town by next year's Lammastide,' she had said in her last missive.

Others followed. Tom Godwin, cheerful Obadiah Baker, poor Kate, recently widowed of locksmith Richard Bellamy, the handsome young Hamnet Sadler. Faces welled up from his past in a welcome stream: ploughwright, yeoman, mercer, miller, goodwife, bailiff, vintner, gravedigger. He knew most of them by name, and they knew him. This was the place he had been born and raised, a town of two thousand souls, some rich, many poor and others doing well enough, like the Shakespeares.

The market was closing down for the day. Livestock was being herded away for grazing or slaughter. Shakespeare breathed in the familiar air and felt a surge of remembering. Every town had its own smell, though its constituent parts were the same: dung, ale, piss, sweat and woodsmoke. At the corner of the High Street, he spotted John Somerville, son-in-law to his cousin Edward Arden. Shakespeare hailed him, but Somerville affected not to recognise him or note the greeting, and scurried away, rat-like.

'Always was a peculiar one, that Somerville.'

'Grows odder by the day, John. Speaks out against the Queen and Leicester where any man might hear him. I have even heard him say he would kill the witch – as he calls her – if he could. What is worse he has found himself a pistol. A man must have pity on poor Margaret Arden for marrying him.'

'He says those things openly?' Shakespeare shook his head in dismay. If Mr Somerville said such things in his vicinity, he would be arraigned for treason before he knew it. Perhaps there had been some truth in Leicester's description of this region as a *Judas nest*. Somerville might warrant further investigation.

Along Henley Street, the smell of home grew ever more powerful; even in the street at the front of the broad house, the stench of his father's tanning in the back yard was noxious. But it was a necessary evil. Without the tanning of skins into fine leather, how was the old man to pursue his craft of glover and whittawer? A man had to earn his living; and the greater the stink, the greater the profit. This was the background odour of his youth, a smell he had known from birth.

Will shifted the saddlebags off the back of the horse for his brother.

'Why did you say you had come here, John? What is this Queen's business of which you speak? Am I allowed to know?'

Shakespeare spoke quietly. 'Unlikely as it may seem, I am seeking a one-armed Frenchman.'

'Then I shall see if I can find you one. There must be dozens to choose from in Stratford.'

Shakespeare smiled and spent a few moments gazing up at the house where he had been born and raised. It was a broad-fronted, comfortable home of wattle and daub with exposed oak timbers, windows of glass, two chimney stacks and the thatch roof replaced by tiles; a house that most men would envy.

'You go in, John, I'll stable the nag.'

Shakespeare frowned at his brother. 'Is there aught wrong, Will? Something you haven't told me?'

'Nothing. No. I have been thinking much of the future. Your arrival has made me reflect all the more on the path I should take. That is all.'

'Well, let us talk of that over some good Stratford beer.'

He pushed open the door and stepped inside the welcoming hall that stood at the centre of the building and was its heart. A maid was tending to the fire in the hearth. She turned around, scrambled to her feet and bowed her head hurriedly and nervously.

'Good day, Margery.'

'Oh, Mr Shakespeare, sir!'

The maid was young. She had been with the Shakespeares less than three years, since she was twelve years of age.

'Is my mother at home?'

'She is at the back, in the kitchen, sir. Shall I go to her for you?'

'No. I will go myself.'

Mary Shakespeare, born Mary Arden, was supervising the baking of rabbit pies, little Edmund clutching at the hem of her skirt with one hand while the thumb of his other hand was wedged in his mouth. Mary's surprise at seeing her eldest son did not last more than a few moments, before she flung her arms around him. He could feel her sobbing with joy, and stroked her hair.

'Mother, have I been gone that long?' Edmund started to wail, so Shakespeare picked him up and he wailed all the more. 'And you, little man, I see you have learnt to walk.'

'Oh, John, the house is not the same without you. So much has happened in the past few months.'

'Then you will tell me all about it, Mother. I shall be here a few days, I believe.' He inclined his head in greeting to the new kitchen maid.

'This is Margery's younger sister, Amy.'

'Good day to you, Amy.'

The kitchen maid put down the skillet she was holding, then clasped her hands together in front of her linen apron, bowed her head like a hen pecking. She looked even more ill at ease than Margery.

Suddenly, Mary Shakespeare bustled. 'What am I thinking of, John? You must be hungry. I am becoming a foolish old woman. All these children . . .'

'Mother, the day you become foolish will be the day the sun turns blue and the stars fall to earth. Now, do not be anxious on my part. I am as hungry as a horse, but I will save it – and take supper with the family. However, I will not trouble you for a bed, for I must stay at the inn. I am charged with certain tasks on this visit that would be best administered away from here.'

'As you wish, John. We can always find space for you – though they all grow apace.'

There were five surviving siblings. William, of course, Gilbert, almost sixteen years of age and apprenticed to their father, thirteen-year-old Joan, eight-year-old Richard and, most recent of all, Edmund, two years of age and the baby of the family.

'Where is Father?'

'In the workshop.'

'And all is well with you both?'

'Between us? As loving as the day we wed. But—'

'Has trade still not improved?'

She shook her head. 'Nor is it likely to. But avoid the subject if you will, for it casts him into a pit of melancholy.' She lowered her voice in case the cook should hear. 'We have but Margery and Amy here to serve us now, along with two apprentices, one of whom is Gilbert.'

'But men and women will always need good gloves and fine white leather. What has brought the old man to this pass?'

'He has over-reached himself, buying property without the wherewithal to pay for it. Look around you: we now own all this house. But then he bought other properties in town with mortgages, which he could not pay.' She sighed heavily, then mouthed four words. No sound, but Shakespeare understood them well enough. '*My inheritance is gone.*'

His mother's inheritance had been bequeathed by her father, Robert Arden of Wilmcote. It had always been the foundation stone that underpinned this household, this family. It was the bond that showed all was well and that the Shakespeares could be trusted by all shops and tradesmen within ten miles of town. How had the old man managed to lose that?

'The money?'

She nodded.

'And the land at Wilmcote?'

'Everything.'

Shakespeare put down Edmund, who was by now mollified, then hugged his mother again. 'All will be well, Mother.'

She managed to smile, and then laughed. 'If only that was all, John . . .'

'There is something else?'

'Your brother, of course. Will. Oh! You don't know, do you? Well, he will have to tell you himself. He is presently at Uncle Henry's.'

'I met him on the road as he walked back. He told me of the trouble with Sir Thomas Lucy, if that is what you mean.'

'Oh, that. No, it is the other thing.' She turned back to her pies. 'He will tell you soon enough, I am sure.'

Shakespeare found his father coming into the hall from the little workshop, wiping his hands on a rag. They embraced as warmly as he had embraced his mother. It was only since he had been away, first at Gray's Inn and then in the service of Walsingham, that Shakespeare had truly begun to understand what a remarkable partnership his parents made. Their bond was as firm as the roots of an oak in good earth. If he had lost her money, then it had been done with the best of intentions, attempting to improve their fortunes. She might mention her fears to *son* John, but she would never make complaint to *husband* John. Their love and common purpose would endure, come what may.

'What brings you home, John? Yearning for Mother's pies?'

'That and the stink of your tanyard, Father.'

His father laughed and clapped him on the back. 'Come, let us take a draught of beer. My work is finished for the day and I have a thirst.'

'That is a fine notion.'

'You will discover that there has been a rich harvest and all the town is merry.' He raised a weary eyebrow. 'Though some of us will reap *more* than we desired. Have you heard the young fool's news yet?'

'You mean Will? What is it? Mother alluded to something, but would say no more. Don't tell me he has brought a girl with child—'

'What do you think? Here he comes. Ask him yourself.'

The door opened and Will stepped inside.

'John was just asking me if you had brought a girl with child, Will. What think you to that?'

Will looked at his father as though he might kill him, then turned around and strode from the house.

'Well, is it true?'

The two brothers stood on the corner of Henley Street, close to the White Lion, beneath the jettied overhangs of the houses.

'Yes, it's true.'

'Who is she? Do I know her?'

'You know her well enough, brother. It's Anne – Anne Hathaway of Shottery.'

For a moment, Shakespeare thought his brother must be jesting. 'No, Will, tell me true.'

'I am telling you true. Why should you not believe me?'

'But Will, she's—'

'Eight years my senior? More your age than mine? Indeed she is. But what of it? She is healthy; she has lost none of her beauty. And whatever you think of it, she *is* with child. We are to be wed.'

'Well, this is unexpected news.'

'But it is so, and I will not listen to any word but celebration. It is a new life, not a death, though to hear Father's strictures and Mother's sobs, you might think it so.'

'How did it happen?'

Will sighed as though he had been answering these questions every day of his life and was mighty tired of them. 'In the usual manner, John. How else?'

'Be careful your wit does not cut you. I meant you and Anne – how did you fall for each other? When?'

'The May Day revels. Too much cider. A dance around the pole, a kiss, a tryst . . . a tale as old as love itself.'

Shakespeare shrugged in resignation. 'Well, it has happened.'

'John, is that all you have to say? "*It has happened.*" Do you shrug it away like spilt milk? Can you find nothing *good* in this? Do you not wish me well?'

Shakespeare forced a smile, then took Will in a hug. 'Forgive me, brother. I am surprised, that is all. I had no idea that you and she . . . but that is by the by. Please accept my heartfelt congratulations. Both of you. You are a lucky man – and she is fortunate, too. That is my honest opinion.'

'Thank you,' Will said, a little too stiffly. 'And you will be pleased to know that there is no regret here. In truth, I had to *win* her. Badger Rench fancied himself in with a hope.'

'I cannot imagine Anne would have looked on Badger with anything but scorn. However, he will not take well to being bested.'

'Were it legal, he would very much like to kill me. It is to my great good fortune that no law has yet been enacted against winning in love.'

Shakespeare called up a picture of Anne: of middle height, womanly and well-formed, the prettiest of faces and the sweetest of natures. 'As I recall there is none more beautiful in or near Stratford, brother.' But even as he spoke he was surprised that such a woman should even look at a callow young man like Will. She had certainly never looked at his older brother as anything but a playmate, and a junior one at that. An unkind thought entered his mind: perhaps her age and being left in charge of her young siblings since the death of her father last year had engendered some degree of desperation, and a young man as clever as Will must have prospects. He immediately dismissed the notion. Anne had wit enough of her own, and pleasantness of spirit. This had to be put down to love. 'But what—'

'But what will I do now? How will I come to London and make my way in the world with a wife and child? It is a question I have heard a dozen times or more from Father. I swear I will strike him if he provokes me more.'

'Will, do not be angry with *me*. This is all new. My mouth gallops ahead of my thoughts and I find myself wondering things aloud. That is all. I have always known how much you want to win the world. Ambition burns you up as it always burnt me. It is so hot, sometimes I think it a fever. I know you will never be content confined to this town, pleasant though it be. You bound to domestic duties? You, a schoolmaster or clerk? I cannot see it.'

'No, I will never be a clerk. Come, walk to Hewlands Farm with me. Anne will be overjoyed to see you. And a little anxious, too . . .'

Chapter 16

Boltfoot did not know where to look, or what to say. He was standing in Goodman Whetstone's parlour, while the innkeeper's daughter sat at the table, her head in her hands, crying as though the world would end.

'She had believed he would marry her, you see, Mr Cooper,' Whetstone said. 'But now he is gone away and she fears he will not come back.'

'Buchan Ord was her intended?'

Kat's weeping grew louder.

Whetstone nodded. 'Indeed, he seemed a fine Scotch gentleman from a great family. We had no reason to doubt him, for he had chivalry and good manners aplenty.'

'Had there been a trothing?'

'He pledged that they would wed at Easter. I confess I had a father's doubts at first, but he seemed constant, and so I put aside my worries and welcomed him with good grace. Though he was a Catholic gentleman, he did not appear overly zealous and I thought we could make a satisfactory contract. I was misled, Mr Cooper. We *both* were.'

'Where has he gone? Has he not written?'

Geoffrey Whetstone shrugged his great shoulders. He looked like a man who had strayed too far into the water and now found himself out of his depth. For a minute, the only sound in the room was the sobbing. Boltfoot had no more idea than Whetstone how to deal with tears. He himself had never known mother, sister or wife. For half his life, ship's crews had been his family. He looked away from her and gazed out of the window. Suddenly, there was a snuffle, loud and determined. Kat sat up and wiped the tears from her eyes. She blinked them dry, took a deep breath, then placed her hands firmly, palms down, on the table.

Her mood had changed as suddenly as a squall in the narrow seas and Boltfoot saw that sorrow and despair had turned to anger.

'You ask where has he gone,' she stated, as though it were an accusation. 'He has cast me off and gone south, Mr Cooper, that is where he has gone. And it is my plain intention to find him and stab him through the heart, as he has stabbed me.'

'You mean you *know* where he has gone?'

'I have just said so, have I not?'

'Where then is he?'

'If I were to tell you, would you take me to him?'

Boltfoot looked from the young woman to her father, who shrugged once more.

'Miss Whetstone, if he has abandoned you, how can it be that you know where he has gone? I never knew a mariner to leave a sweetheart in port and tell her truly where his ship was bound.'

'I know where he has gone because I overheard him say it to that French doctor of medicine. It is common knowledge that they were confederates.'

'Were you spying on them? What did you overhear?'

'No, indeed, I was not spying. I overheard them inadvertently. It was an hour or so before Seguin departed. They were in the taproom, in a private booth, talking quietly over goblets of brandy. I approached them with no intention to eavesdrop.

I merely desired to bring more spirit and to plant a kiss on my Buchan's head. And so I crept up on him, like a lover. Which was when I heard them.'

'Yes?'

'Buchan said, "And so we meet at . . ." and he mentioned the place. He said no more for he sensed my presence behind him. He turned and smiled and kissed my hand, but I could tell he was hoping that I had heard nothing.'

'What did *you* say?'

'Nothing. I kept up the pretence, as he desired. At the time, it did not mean anything to me.'

'You have not told me where he planned to meet the Frenchie.'

'Nor will I – unless you take me there.'

'Miss Whetstone, Kat, you know I cannot do such a thing. This is no matter for women.' He turned to her father. 'Tell her this is so, Mr Whetstone.'

'She won't listen to me! Stubborn as a terrier gone to earth.'

'But you wouldn't let her ride away from here with a stranger? Why, she hasn't even told us how far away this place is. Is it ten miles, is it a hundred?'

'Mr Cooper, if you will take her, then I must place my trust in you. So far I have had no cause to mistrust either you or your master. If you do not take her, I fear she might ride alone.'

'I know things about Buchan Ord,' Kat said, 'things that could lead him to the scaffold.'

'And you will tell me these things?'

'When you have taken me to him. I want to see his face when you capture him.'

The hamlet of Shottery amounted to nothing more than a cluster of farms, a small alehouse and a farrier, a little more than a mile from Henley Street. The walk there took twenty minutes. They strode through the orchards, heavy with apples and pears, over ditches and across meadows where cattle grazed. They were in open country again and the air was already sweeter. All around them was the stubble of wheat and barley, and stacks of hay in the fields.

At last they came to the brook at Shottery. Sheep grazed in the broad meadow and scattered at their approach. Shakespeare and his brother leapt nimbly across the ancient stepping stones. Hewlands Farm, the fine house of the Hathaways, stood before them on the edge of a gentle incline. Tom Whittington, the Hathaways' shepherd, hailed them with a wave of his crook. They waved back, then began to climb the stone steps to the farmhouse. Shakespeare felt a stab of envy. Here he was, almost twenty-four and no sign of a woman in his life. Meanwhile his brother, just eighteen, was about to become a married man, with all the joys that entailed. Clearly, Will had already savoured those pleasures.

The shepherd was walking across the meadow to them, at a brisk pace. He increased his speed and broke into a run.

Will stopped. 'What is it, Tom?'

'There is a hue and cry, Mr Shakespeare. They're out in the woods and fields. I would join them, but I have a sick ewe.'

'A hue and cry? What for?'

'They're looking for Florence Angel. She has not been seen in twenty-four hours or more. Didn't come home last night, they say. The widow Angel is sick with worry.'

Shakespeare felt the hairs on his neck prickle. Florence Angel was elder sister to Benedict Angel. *Father* Benedict Angel, foremost of the fugitive priests mentioned by Walsingham and Leicester during their meeting at Oatlands. The Angels, one of the most persistent of the recusant families in the area, were neighbours to the Hathaways, as were that other tainted family, the Dibdales.

Florence Angel had been a close friend to Anne ever since the Angels moved to Shottery as weavers. This was what he had most feared when the mission was initiated: the distasteful business of investigating friends and neighbours with whom he had grown up. This was all much too close to home.

They found Anne and her brother Thomas, who was half her age, in the hall. They were both pulling on boots. Anne's brow beneath her coif was creased with concern, but she managed a smile when she saw Will and his brother.

'John, is it really you?'

He clasped her hands. 'I have heard your good news.'

'Thank you.' She attempted a smile, but it would not come. 'What a time. I cannot bear the thought that any harm has come to her. We were just setting off into the woods, with sticks to beat the undergrowth. You know she has developed the falling sickness?'

'No, I did not know that. Tom tells us that she has been missing twenty-four hours or more.'

'Not so. She was home last night, but went out to market this morning. She was supposed to return by noon, but hasn't been seen since. We must find her.'

'Then it is only a matter of a few hours.'

'But you know Florence. She would not tell her mother she would be home by midday and then be not home by six o'clock. It will be dark soon. Come with us, John. We must find her while it is still light. She could be lying injured somewhere, fallen in a ditch or trampled by kine. These are bad days for the Angel family, as you will discover.'

He shook his head. 'You go with Will and your brother. I will go to the Angel house.' He could see the puzzled look on his brother's face, but he could not explain his interest in the whereabouts of Florence's brother Benedict. 'I want to ensure we have the tale straight. It is my business to inquire, Will. I know how often messages become garbled and altered in the telling.'

'If that is what you think best, John.'

Shakespeare could tell his brother was not convinced.

Shakespeare was shocked by the state of Audrey Angel's home. The path to the doorway was overgrown and the door itself was broken from its hinges, lying askew against the wall. Its centre was stove-in, as though it had been battered by a siege ram.

He called into the gloom. 'Good day, Aunt.' As his eyes became accustomed to the dim light, he saw that the central hall of the farmhouse was a mass of firewood that had once been furniture. He could make out the wreckage of a court-cupboard, the remains of a table and three or four stools. All were in pieces deliberately broken apart. Shards of earthenware crockery lay strewn about, and in the walls, holes were gouged. A spinning wheel lay in pieces.

A woman appeared at the inner doorway which he knew led from the kitchen. She looked a mere shade of the spirited woman he had once known.

'Aunt Audrey, it is John Shakespeare.'

She approached him slowly. 'John?'

'What has happened here?'

'I thought you had gone away, John, into the service of Walsingham and Burghley.' She took him in her arms, as she had always done. But though she retained her warmth and the kindness still shone from her eyes, her frame was wasted and her anxiety was obvious.

'I am home for a visit. But I see plainly that all is not well with you. What is this?' He cast his gaze around the room. 'What evil has happened here?'

'Have they found Florence yet?'

He shook his head. 'I am sure we will hear soon enough when she is discovered. She will be safe and well.'

Audrey was in her mid-forties. Her clothes were as fine as they had always been, but today they hung from her bony frame unflatteringly. She wore her hair loose; now, instead of glowing with lustre and health, it was lank and thin.

'I know she is a grown woman, but so much has happened here of late that I panicked when she did not come home. It is good of the men to look for her.'

'But what has been done here?'

She smiled wanly. 'They say they are pursuivants. They say they are acting in the Queen's name. They come by night; thrice they have been at midnight, once in the hour before dawn. Look around you; they have run out of things to destroy. And so they break it all into ever smaller shards. Last time they carried my loom away and burnt it in the yard. How am I to live now?'

How could such a thing have been done in the Queen's name? Shakespeare thought back to Sheffield and the burning down of Sir Bassingbourne Bole's manor house by Richard Topcliffe's pursuivants. The notion that such practices were now come to his own home county appalled him.

The only person locally with the authority to order such raids was Sir Thomas Lucy, justice of the peace, member of parliament and sometime high sheriff of the county. More than that, he was a ferocious advocate for the reformed Church and despiser of Catholics. It was likely that his men had been hunting for Audrey's son, Father Benedict. But there was more to this wanton destruction than that. You did not need to break apart a cupboard or stool to seek a hidden priest. Nor did you need to destroy a widow's livelihood. No, this was done because Thomas Lucy and those associated with him wished to send out a message to all who clung to the Catholic religion. *We will bring you down.*

'Rafe Rench's boy is one of them. The one they call Badger. You know the boy who was so strong? Well, he's not a boy now, of course. They say they want Benedict, but my son would not be so foolish as to come here.'

'I understand.' He put a comforting arm around her for a brief moment; she did not shy away at his touch. 'We will put this right. Our family, your neighbours . . . I pledge we will find the means to repair the damage and restore your house and fortunes.'

She laughed. 'Do not trouble yourself, John. They will just come and break it again. And again, until they have driven us out. You should take care of your own father. I think it has been noted that he fails to go to church.'

The thought had occurred to Shakespeare, too. While he had happily put aside all allegiance to the corrupt old faith with its superstitions and relics, his father could not so easily cast it off. If he was not careful, it would do for him.

'Why are you so worried about Florence?'

'John, you know what she is like. She was always . . . *fragile.* She communes with God. Talks with Him and receives wisdom. In the past, men would have said she was imbued with the holy spirit and they would have sat at her feet in prayer and devotion. Now, no one understands or cares. Sometimes I wish there was a convent she could go to; she might be happy there.'

'Anne told me Florence has the falling sickness.'

Audrey Angel nodded. 'This summer she has been afflicted by fits. Three times that I know of. And each time more frightening than the last. She drops to the ground, her body rigid, shaking like the throes of death. I have given her bishop's wort, but it is of no help and I know of no other remedy. So far

Florence has escaped injury. But what would happen if she were alone by the water or the well when she fell – or if she hit her head on stony ground?'

Shakespeare set his mouth firm, not certain that he was hearing the full tale. He spoke sympathetically, trying to take her at her word. 'You are beset by many tribulations, Aunt. I would urge you not to be too proud to seek help. Anne would do anything for Florence, and for you. My brother Will likewise, and of course my mother. But Aunt, there is something I am duty-bound to ask you: do you believe Florence's disappearance has anything to do with Benedict? Has he been in these parts?'

She looked at him fearfully, but shook her head vigorously.

Shakespeare was about to delve deeper, but in the distance they heard a shout. Then the shrill blast of a whistle pierced the air. Audrey Angel's eyes widened.

'They have found her!'

'Stay here. I will discover what has happened. You will hear soon enough.' He did not want her to go, in case the news was bad. Sometimes a mother should not see what has become of her child.

Chapter 17

THE BODY WAS at the edge of the wood, half a mile west of the Angel house. It lay straight, like the stone carving on a knight's tomb. Feet together, hands crossed on the chest, blank eyes open as though staring at the darkening sky. A long branch lay close by, broken from an oak.

Shakespeare stood over the wretched corpse. His eyes went to the neck, where a black wooden rosary was drawn taut. The crucifix, also made of black wood, hung to one side of the lifeless throat.

The face was cold and discoloured, but Shakespeare recognised it well enough. He had known it for much of his life: his cousin Benedict Angel. Their kinship was tenuous – Audrey's mother had been an Arden – but it was enough to consider them family of sorts. A group of villagers had already gathered, thirty or so. Some made the sign of the cross in the old way. Two women got down on their knees and began to pray. Another woman wailed and tried to move forward to touch the corpse. Shakespeare stayed her with gentle pressure on her arm, then turned to his brother and Anne. 'Keep everyone back. No one must trample here. There may be footprints or other evidence.'

'They will not listen to *me*, John.'

'Then bring the constable to me. This is important. Do it now.'

Will nodded, took Anne by the hand and hurried away with her towards the town, trailed by Anne's young brother, Thomas.

Shakespeare put up his hand and addressed the assembled villagers in a loud, clear voice. 'Will has gone for the constable. While I wait for him, I must ask you all to stand back away from the body. You all know me as John Shakespeare, but I am now an officer of the crown, and I will be obeyed. This is the body of Benedict Angel, whom you all know. He had become a seminary priest and fugitive, but his death will be investigated in accordance with the law, and if there has been foul play, then the murderer will be hunted down to be arraigned before a court, where he will face trial and retribution. Do you understand?'

One or two grumbled; others nodded to signal their under-standing. Most hung their heads, disgruntled, angry and afraid. A killer on the loose in Shottery? In living memory, none had heard of such a thing. Doors would be locked this night.

'And remember, we still have a missing person – Benedict Angel's sister Florence. You can do nothing here, so it would be better if you resumed your search for her, before darkness makes further progress impossible. We must hope for the best, and pray that she is safe.'

Was Florence further on into the woods? Shakespeare did not hold out great hope of finding her alive. He could not but think that her disappearance was somehow connected to the death of her brother. Getting on to his knees, he looked more closely at the face and neck. He touched the face, then the hands. The flesh was utterly cold, everywhere. Benedict Angel had been dead for many hours. Gently, he pushed two fingers beneath the beads of the rosary. A four-foot length of cord ran from it, but was not tied around the neck. The rosary itself was tight against the flesh, but that did not mean it was the cause of death. He needed one versed in the examination of corpses to look at this body, and the sooner the better.

Standing up, he looked at the footprints in the dust and fallen leaves that littered the forest soil. There were too many of them; no way of knowing which were from the villagers searching for Florence and which might be the prints of the murderer or murderers. He looked at the broken branch and considered whether Angel might have hanged himself from it, dying before it snapped. It seemed unlikely.

At the back of the group of villagers who lingered, reluctant to leave this grisly spectacle, he spotted the bull-like figure of Rafe Rench, the biggest farmholder in Shottery and father to Badger Rench. He was broad, his arms as muscled as the quarters of a plough-ox. Catching Shakespeare's eye, Rench snorted and turned to go.

With wary eyes, a group of farmhands watched him walk away. One of them nudged his friend and jutted his chin towards Rench's back. 'He won't be unhappy.'

'Another poke of the stick.'

Were they suggesting Rench had something to do with this? Shakespeare wondered. It was a question that he would have to put, but first things first. He had to get this body moved before dark, and call for the Searcher of the Dead.

His brother and Anne reappeared with the constable.

'He had heard of the search and was on his way,' Will said, by way of explanation for their quick return.

Shakespeare turned his attention to the constable. 'Mr Nason.'

'This is bad, Mr Shakespeare.'

'Who is Searcher of the Dead these days?'

'Mother Peace in Warwick still, but she lies close to death. Her boy, Joshua, has been doing her work most of this year past, though there are many who call him necromancer, for he deals with bodies in most unholy fashion. It is said he learnt devilish tricks in the Italies.'

'Well, send to him nonetheless. I want him to return straightway, with your messenger. Is that understood?'

Nason took off his filthy, stained cap and scratched his long straggly hair. 'If I may be so bold as to mention it, Mr Shakespeare, it seems that you are directing matters here, whereas the way I see things, it is my place as constable to take control of the inquiry until the sheriff is informed.'

'Don't argue with me, Mr Nason. I have the Queen's authority. Now send for Mr Peace before you do anything else. There is no time to be lost. And then – and only then – will you remove this body to the home of Mr Angel's mother, and inform the justice of the peace and sheriff what has befallen here.' Shakespeare had no doubt that Nason had already sent word to the justice, for Sir Thomas Lucy employed Ananias Nason as a servant in the kitchens when not taking his turn as constable.

'I don't like it. We don't need no Searcher of the Dead here.'

'You don't have to like it, just do it. Or you will spend this night in your own cage.'

Nason grumbled something and wandered off. Shakespeare did not trust him. He would have to find a messenger of his own to ensure that word got through. Across the field, the villagers were still hunting for some sign of Florence, but their efforts seemed lacklustre as if they were searching for a second corpse. He caught sight of Will, with Anne and her brother. Ah, Thomas. He could be despatched to ride the nine miles to Warwick and bring back Mother Peace's son.

Boltfoot Cooper and his new riding companion, Kat Whetsone, arrived at a wayside inn ten miles south of Nottingham. She was wearing doublet and hose and had her hair tied back beneath her cap. But though she rode astride the horse, none could have mistaken her for a man.

'This inn looks fair enough, Mr Cooper. Not as fine as the Cutler's Rest, I would say, but that is no surprise.'

Boltfoot grunted. He averted his eyes from her and shook his head wearily. How had he ever been persuaded to bring this woman with him on such a journey? They had ridden hard all day and, to be fair to Kat, her progress had been as good as Boltfoot's. But her mere presence discomfited him. She was no less comely in man's attire than in woman's.

'It will do, will it not?' she demanded when she received no response.

'We eat, have the horses watered and fed, then carry on. We ride all night,' Boltfoot said. *Sooner this journey is over, the better.*

'No, Mr Cooper, we shall dine well this evening and sleep in feather beds, for your master will be paying. Come, let us give our mounts into the care of an ostler, then warm ourselves in front of a brave fire of oak logs. I shall dine on fried sausage links and roasted fowl.'

Within the hour, they were sitting at a long table in the main hall. Kat had changed into womanly clothing and untied her hair. Boltfoot wondered what deadly sin he had committed that God or Satan should send this creature to beguile him. Sitting beside her, he could smell the promise of her flesh. Twenty travellers were packed along the benches, all talking loudly, laughing, eating and quaffing. A trio of minstrels with tabor, lute and pipe played and sang a rousing melody. Boltfoot noted that Kat kept glancing their way. He felt a pang of jealousy, but then persuaded himself that her interest was natural enough, for they were providing fine entertainment. However, he could not help noting – grudgingly – that the lutist, who was also the foremost singer, was well-proportioned, carried himself with assurance and had a handsome face.

The minstrels came closer so that Kat became the centre of their attention and surrounded her. Suddenly it seemed to Boltfoot that they were serenading her alone. He waved his hand at them like a bullock swatting flies with its tail, but they ignored him. Angry now, he fished a farthing coin from his much diminished purse and dropped it with meaning into their collecting cap. 'Now go,' he said. 'You have what you came for. There is no more.' It made no difference, for they played all the closer.

Kat was enjoying their attention. She began to move her arms in time with the music, smiling at the handsome man, making eyes at him. *Wanton* eyes, as it seemed to Boltfoot. He grasped her right arm and tried to hold her still.

She shook herself free. 'Do not touch me!'

'Remember yourself, Miss Whetstone. Your father has given me dominion over you.'

The song ended and the minstrels took a bow to a thunder of applause from the assembled travellers. Then the singer leant forward and kissed Kat's cheek and put a hand on her breast, inside her linen smock dress. Boltfoot was dismayed to see that she did not resist. In fact, she turned her face towards the singer's so that their lips met. And his hand remained on her flesh.

Boltfoot had had enough. He jumped to his feet and his hand went to the hilt of his cutlass. 'Take your hands away from her.'

The diners were all watching with great interest. They began to jeer Boltfoot. 'Leave her be, cuckold!' one man called out.

Kat removed the man's hand from her breast and turned her attention to Boltfoot. 'Put your strange sword away, Mr

Cooper. If I need your assistance I will request it. In the mean-time, I am well able to look after myself.'

'No. You are betrothed to another.'

'I was – until he spurned me and cast me away. Now I am a free woman again, and if a man pleases me, that is my concern – and none of yours.' She smiled at her new swain. 'Come, sir, will you not ask me to dance?'

Boltfoot slammed his cutlass blade down on the table. 'No. You are here with me for one reason. To lead me to Mr Buchan Ord. You will obey me, or I shall go now and leave you to go where you will – alone.'

'Your master will have you flogged if you leave me. But do as you wish. Do you think I will not find another traveller to take me onwards from here?' She tilted her chin and gave Boltfoot a sweet, defiant smile, then turned her attention back to the singer. She took his hand, clasped it once more to her breast and kissed him full on the mouth.

Sitting on the edge of the bed, the Earl of Shrewsbury smoothed down his nightgown, allowed his breathing to sub-side, then turned and gave a graceful little bow to Elinor Britten. 'Madam,' he said. 'I am indebted to you, as ever.'

'It was my pleasure, George . . . as ever.' She dabbed at her moist lips with a corner of the bedsheet.

'Best remedy for melancholy that ever God devised. If only it worked for the gout. And so, I will leave you, my dear, until morning.' He stood up and seemed about to bow again when there was a discreet knocking at the bedchamber door.

He hesitated a few moments, frowned towards his mis-tress, and then the knocking came again. 'Who is it?' he called.

'It is Gilbert Curle, my lord.'

Gilbert Curle? Why was one of Mary's secretaries here at this time of night? Shrewsbury adjusted his dress once more. 'Enter, man.'

The door opened and Curle stepped into the room tentatively. He gave the impression of timidity, but Shrewsbury knew that his heart was steely enough. It would have to be to put up with the incessant demands of the Scots Queen these long years.

'Forgive me for disturbing you, my lord.' He averted his eyes from the large tester bed on which Elinor Britten lay, her hair spread across the pillows, her pink breasts exposed like a pair of delicious pastries.

'Well? What is it, damn you?'

'You desired to know what had become of Buchan Ord, my lord. Well, I fear we have had word from his home in Scotland. He has been found dead close to his father's estates. Murdered. His father's ghillie found him. It seems his horse had been shot from under him and he had been choked with a cord.'

Shrewsbury stared at Curle incredulously. 'And you thought fit to come to me here, at this time of night, just to tell me this?'

'I had thought you desired to know, my lord. And, in truth, I very much desired to tell you.'

'Well, it is shocking news, of course, but at least we now know the truth. Has the Queen of Scots been informed?'

'Indeed, but there is more, which is the reason I am here. It has now become clear that our Mr Ord was not at all what he seemed.'

Chapter 18

Shakespeare stood in the rubble-strewn chamber of the Angel house. The room was lit by a dozen tallow candles. Audrey was at his side. She had not wept yet; it had always been her way to show strength and stoicism, but her tears would come soon enough, when she was alone. Their eyes were both fixed on the serene face of her son, Benedict, whose body had been laid out on the only surviving piece of furniture, a bed, broken but pieced together as well as could be managed.

'Do you think he is in heaven, John? With his father?'

'We must pray it is so.'

A picture entered his head of a boy of thirteen, back in the year fifteen seventy-one, soon after the widow and her children came to Shottery. Benedict's hair had been lighter then. All the boys were outside the schoolhouse, enjoying a warm summer's day, eating the bread and cheese their parents had given them to get through the long dawn-to-dusk school day. The sun had came out from behind a cloud and framed Benedict's head like a halo.

Because of his name – but also because of his fervour – the other boys called him Archangel or, sometimes, Gabriel. The names were used in jest, but there was an edge of unpleasant mockery in them, too. In truth, they did not like him, partly because he was an incomer, but also because of his stern religion. While they played, he prayed.

He had always been too devout, too close to Mr Hunt, the new schoolmaster. Hunt was indiscreet in his defiant Catholicism and did not disguise his preference for the boys whom he knew to share his faith. Benedict Angel and Robert Dibdale, a year his senior, were chief among them. At times, they stayed in school at the end of the day for extra tuition with Hunt. It was said, too, that the pair of them had gone to a secret mass with Mr Hunt on more than one occasion.

Benedict Angel had the reckless abandon of youth. As he became ever more zealous, he told some of the other boys that their families would burn in hellfire for conforming to the new Church. His classmates were appalled and, in the end, they shunned him. Dibdale had been much more discreet, and he never lost the other boys' friendship. It was a curious thing that Benedict and Robert had never seemed close to each other.

No one was surprised, least of all Shakespeare, when a few weeks before Angel's seventeenth birthday, word reached Stratford that he had gone away to join the Catholic seminary for young Englishmen in Douai. It was rumoured that he had been lured there by Simon Hunt, who had left Stratford and had fled into exile some months earlier. Dibdale followed them a few months later.

The question that Shakespeare could not answer adequately was this: had Benedict Angel been a saint-in-the-making – or a treacherous dupe? Shakespeare was happy to admit he had found him difficult to like; he had the unbending self-assurance of many men of the cloth and could not accept the smallest possibility that his version of the Gospels could be open to doubt or misinterpretation. Benedict Angel was the sort of zealot who would die for his beliefs or kill for them.

But that gave no man the right to murder him.

So *who* had killed him, and *why*? One possibility had to be Lucy's band of pursuivants, perhaps with the connivance of higher authorities.

But Shakespeare could not put out of mind the thought that there could be some connection to the events at Sheffield and the mission he had been ordered to undertake by Walsingham and Leicester. In the brief time he had worked for the Principal Secretary he had learnt enough to know that there was no such thing as a coincidence in his war of secrets.

Or did the motive lie closer to home? What, indeed, was the meaning of the brief conversation he had overheard suggesting that farmer Rench might not be distressed by the killing? *Another poke of the stick . . .*

'There is no word of Florence,' Audrey said at last, as though she had forgotten until this moment that her daughter was still missing.

'Perhaps that is a good sign. It means there is hope.'

'I will not think it good until she is home safe.'

François Leloup stopped at the edge of the town and pulled his threadbare copy of *La Guide des Chemins d'Angleterre* from his packsaddle. His eye traced the course that had been set for him and then looked up at the spire and chimneys of the town. Yes, he was certain: this was Warwick. He stowed the map, kicked his spurs into the horse's flanks and managed to persuade the obstinate animal to limp on into the town.

Around his shoulders, he wore a capacious cloak, so that none should notice his missing arm. At the inn, he dismounted, handed the reins to a groom, and then ordered an ostler to bring in his heavy saddlebags.

Making his way into the well-appointed hostelry, he spent a few minutes talking amiably to the landlord about his life as a travelling merchant in French wines, haggled perfunctorily over the price of a decent – though not the most opulent – chamber, and ordered a splendid meal of English roasts to be brought to his room. He was about to go there when he held back.

'It is possible there is a letter for me, innkeeper.'

'Ah yes, Monsieur Seguin. I recall a courier brought it two days since. Let me fetch it for you, sir.'

'Instructions from my masters in Paris. Have I found buyers for next year's vintage? Can I acquire English woollen stuffs rather than silver? Have I bargained a good price? How they drive an old man in their quest for profit! I tell you, innkeeper, they are harder taskmasters than any wife could be. Should they not give me a pension and allow me to live out my days in peace among my vines and books?'

The landlord produced the letter. The Frenchman glanced at it casually to see the seal was unbroken, then bestowed a little bow upon his host and placed it within his doublet. 'I shall take it to my chamber to read in mine own good time. My body is not what it was and I must take my rest.'

His hand curled around the silver pomander of musk and ambergris that he wore on a chain about his neck, and he breathed deeply of its exquisite scents.

'And, innkeper, have my meats served properly rare. It pleases me to see and taste the blood.'

Joshua Peace arrived at the farm shortly before midnight. Audrey Angel had fallen asleep on her knees, her tears still unwept. Shakespeare had had no supper and no rest, and yet he could not leave this place, not yet. At last Thomas Hathaway appeared in the doorway with a young man, bright-eyed, with short, thinning hair.

'This is Mr Joshua Peace,' Thomas said.

'Thank you, Tom. Go home now. You have done more than

enough this evening.' Shakespeare turned towards the new-comer and shook his hand. 'Mr Peace, thank you for coming this far. It is a pleasure to meet you.'

'And you, Mr Shakespeare. I am told you are an officer of the crown.'

'Indeed.' He indicated the inner room. 'The corpse is through there, in the chamber.'

'Then let us get to work.'

'I can tell you this: at first sight it appeared to me that he had been choked.'

'I will look at him myself, if it please you, sir. I prefer not to have preconceptions when I view a cadaver.'

Shakespeare looked at Peace with surprise. He was taken aback by his brisk manner. Such an attitude was rare in the countryside, where time tended to drift by with the indolence of the stars in the heavens.

'And shall I have beer brought to you, Mr Peace?'

'I would prefer wine, but beer will do if it is all you have.'

'I shall see what Mistress Angel can provide.'

'There is no haste. I will wait until after I have made my initial examination.'

Peace stood back from his work, stretched his narrow shoulders and breathed deeply, as though stifling a yawn. He had been studying the body for more than an hour, sniffing and prodding it. 'I will have that wine now.'

Shakespeare handed him the goblet with the dregs of the wine that the pursuivants had not succeeded in drinking or pouring away. Joshua Peace took a sip, grimaced, shrugged, then sipped again.

'You will see, Mr Shakespeare, that the rigor of death is at its most intense. Try to move an arm. It is stiff as though it had been frozen solid in ice.'

'Which means he has been dead how long?'

'Some time between twenty hours and twelve hours past. It is one o'clock in the morning now, so I would suggest he died last night, an hour or two before dawn. I make that calculation on the assumption that he was murdered somewhere else then left in the place you found him. I doubt many murderers would go about their business in the open air on a bright morning. Especially a murderer such as this one, who had time to place the body just so, fold the arms across the chest and tie a rosary around the neck.'

'Are you suggesting the rosary was placed there after death? Was it not the murder weapon?'

Joshua Peace picked up the black-beaded rosary, gripped it between both his hands and tugged sharply. The cord split and beads flew across the floor. Peace laughed. 'That answers that one, I think. You would not be able to strangle a kitten with it. Anyway, look at the neck.'

Shakespeare held a candle close to the dead man and gazed at the neck. 'What am I looking for?'

'Do you see any indentations that might have been caused by rosary beads?'

'I see marks, certainly.'

'But not bead marks. What you see is the unmistakable spiralling of good English hemp. Any hangman in the land will tell you that this man was choked to death with a narrow rope.'

'So he was hanged? Was that the other cord? The one attached to the rosary.'

'No, no. Look under the jaw, beneath the right ear. You see the bruising and discoloration there? The rope was wound tight around a stick – a garrotte as the Spaniards call it. They use it much in their executions and assassinations.'

'Are you suggesting a Spaniard did this?'

Peace laughed, but not unkindly. 'You range far ahead of the facts, Mr Shakespeare. Though this method of killing is common in Spain, that certainly does not mean they have a monopoly on its use.'

'Forgive me. You must think me a fool.'

'Not at all, sir. It is late at night and we are both tired. What I think is that you were very wise to have called me out so promptly. The more a body is allowed to decay, the more the evidence disappears. You might be astounded to know how often I – and my mother before me – have been called to view a body two or three days after the discovery of a carcass. Sometimes longer.'

'Well, I am pleased you came.'

Peace put his hand into his apron pocket and produced a portion of some sort of paste. He held it up to show Shakespeare.

'What is it?'

'I found it in the mouth. I rather suspect it is unleavened bread, the host, as used in the Roman mass, for I also smelt wine. And as every attentive schoolboy knows, the word "host" is derived from the Latin *hostia* – which can be translated as *sacrificial victim*. I found that rather interesting. What about you, Mr Shakespeare?'

'I think I probably agree, Mr Peace. But that does not get me any closer to finding a motive for his death, nor the murderer.'

'What most interests me, though, Mr Shakespeare, is that I believe the murderer must have put the bread and wine in Mr Angel's mouth, *post mortem*. For if it had been taken voluntarily during the Eucharist, it would surely have been swallowed almost instantly.'

Chapter 19

SHAKESPEARE BEAT ON the front door of the large farm-house that was home to Rafe Rench. Within a minute, the heavy door creaked open. Rench's wife stood there and looked at Shakespeare.

'You know me, Goody Rench. I want to speak with your husband.'

Shakespeare had had no more than three hours' sleep but he had freshened himself with a splash of cold water and a good breakfast at the White Lion.

'He's in the yard with the swine. Go around the back.' She was a short, pinched woman with no trace of a smile or kindness in her eyes. In fact, no expression in her eyes at all. She shut the door.

Goodwife Rench. None of them had ever thought much to her. She was not the sort of woman to hand hot tarts or pies to the neighbourhood boys and girls at baking time.

The Searcher of the Dead had found nothing more of interest on the body. The cause of death was garrotting; there could be no doubt. Shakespeare asked Peace to stay in Stratford so that he might be a witness at the inquest. He also offered to take Audrey Angel to his parents' house so that she could be cared for at this time of great loss. She would have none of it. 'Many folk do not understand grief,' she said. 'They think you need company. But we must all face our grief alone, as we must face our own death alone. The presence of another person does not alter that.'

Shakespeare understood and bade her farewell. 'I will return soon enough,' he said, 'and I hope to hear good news of Florence.' Then he and Joshua Peace had walked the short distance into Stratford, where they managed to raise the inn-keeper from his slumbers. He knew Shakespeare of old and could offer them one spare room with a feather bed. If Mr Peace wanted to share the room, he would have to use the truckle bed. Another room would come free for him later in the day if he required it. Shakespeare had slept as best he could and now, two hours after dawn, he was fed and watered and back at Shottery, at the Rench farm.

With the help of his pigman, Rench was holding down a young male porker, which had been bound and tied to a post for castration. Rench sliced at the ball bag with a sharp blade, then thrust his hand into the sack, ripped out a testicle and held it up in his bloody hand. The panic-stricken pig squealed and writhed. Rench threw the ball into a pail a couple of feet away, then attended to the other one. Finally he spotted Shakespeare.

'Never seen a hog being gelded before, Shakespeare?'

'Now and then. There are more pleasant ways to pass the day.'

Rench lifted himself off the maddened pig. 'Put him in the pen, Joseph,' he told his pigman. 'So, why are you here, Shakespeare? Everyone thought you were long gone from these parts.'

'I saw you yesterday when the body of Benedict Angel was found.'

'You saw me and every man in the village.'

'Someone said something that made me wonder about you.'

'Is that so?'

'They implied that you would be glad Benedict Angel was dead.'

'Well, I'm not *un*happy. Why should I be? He was a papist, outlaw and traitor. Good riddance to him. Cousin of yours, wasn't he?'

'But then another man said something else, something most strange. He said, "Another poke of the stick". Now what could he have meant by that?'

'Did you ask him?'

'No, I'm asking you.'

'Well, my reply to you is, go and geld yourself with a rusty blade before I do it for you.'

Shakespeare stepped forward as though he would grab Rafe Rench by the lapels of his grubby wool jerkin, but immediately restrained himself.

Rench laughed. He was twice as broad as Shakespeare with the strength of a working farmer to go with his size. 'Take me on, will you?' He was like a rock. 'You need to do some honest work, Shakespeare, build up some muscle before you come here trying to throw your weight around. You always were above yourself. Now, get off my land before I have you in court for trespass and common assault.'

Shakespeare didn't move. 'Bad blood between you, is there? Between you and the widow Angel? What's this about Badger? Your boy's one of the pursuivants making her life hell. What are you after?'

Rench spat into the dust and summoned his pigman. 'See Mr Shakespeare off my land, Joseph. And if he gives you trouble, toss him in the midden with the other turds.'

*

It was late morning and Kat Whetstone still had not emerged from her chamber at the inn. Boltfoot had already broken his fast and was pacing up and down in the yard beneath the galleried rooms where travellers stayed.

He could not take his eyes from the closed door of the chamber on the first floor. He would not go up there, though. He could not bring himself to hammer on the door of a maiden.

Boltfoot had left her dancing with the minstrel and had gone to his own chamber. It had been an hour or more before sleep came to him. If this woman truly knew where to find Buchan Ord, then his master would want to talk with her. But what lengths should he go to get the young woman to do his bidding? And then the door opened. She was there, in the open doorway, but she was not alone. The handsome minstrel stepped past her, then leant back and kissed her. Boltfoot felt a shiver of fury – and something else. A stirring of envy and desire.

The minstrel made his way down the steps. She watched him go. She spotted Boltfoot and smiled at him knowingly, as though she well understood the effect she had on him. With her delicate fingers, she gestured to him and called out. 'Mr Cooper, will you not join me up here?'

As the minstrel ambled past him, he made an obscene gesture with his curled fist and smirked. Boltfoot ignored him and mounted the wooden steps to the first gallery.

'Ah, Mr Cooper,' Kat said, 'be pleased to ask the kitchens to provide me with food for my breakfast.'

'Breakfast! It is almost midday. We must be riding on. We have tarried here too long.' Boltfoot gazed at her in horror. She wore a long shirt, to her knees and, seemingly, nothing else.

'But, Mr Cooper, I have a mind to stay here a day or two longer. My business is not quite finished yet.'

'No. We ride within the hour.'

'And if I refuse?'

'You cannot refuse.'

She reached out to him. Her hand went to the front of his hose. He looked down in astonishment. Her hand stayed there.

'Would that make it better, Mr Cooper? Is that what you want?'

As he walked into the village, it occurred to Shakespeare that he kept losing people. So far the only one who had turned up was Benedict Angel, and he was dead. This was not going well. He found his brother in the small village alehouse, which amounted to no more than the front room of a modest thatched cottage – a cramped taproom with dirt and sawdust floor.

'Any word, Will?'

'Florence is home. Safe and sound.'

'Thank God. Where was she?'

'Won't say a word. Not to Anne, nor me. Perhaps she has told her mother. Then again, John, it is possible she does not know where she has been. There have been times these past weeks where I doubted her sanity. The pursuivants destroying her home, the terrible falling sickness. If truth be told, Anne did not sleep last night for fear Florence had cut her own throat or was lying in the woods somewhere, lost to the world.'

'What state was she in when she arrived home?'

'Much as she left, I think. Her clothes were not torn or muddied, if that is what you mean.'

'I shall go to her.'

'Be gentle. She arrived only an hour since. Anne and her mother are with her. It would not take much to tip her over the precipice. She needs to be helped, not rebuked.'

'I understand.' He signalled to the potboy and ordered a

pint of small ale, then told his brother about his encounter with Rafe Rench. 'Do you have any thoughts, Will?'

'Another poke of the stick? That's clear enough. Rench wants the Angels' house and the small strip of land where they grow their food and keep their pig. It abuts his own land. He has been offering to buy it from her this past year, ever since Benedict was first arrested. But she won't sell. And why should she, for we must all eat? Rench believes it is only a matter of time before she is forced to move away, and he wants to ensure that he is the beneficiary. Anything that helps drive out the Angels would suit him. Each fine for recusancy, each pursuivants' raid is a poke. Folk around here believe the raids have nothing to do with religion and all to do with driving an innocent woman from her home. That is why they think the death of Benedict Angel is another prod to force her out.'

'Are you saying Rench killed Benedict? Is that what people believe?'

Will drew in a short breath through his teeth, then shook his head. 'I would not have said so, but who knows?' He tilted his chin towards one of the other drinkers. 'There's Humfrey Ironsmith. He found the body.'

'Bring him over here.'

'As imperious as ever, John? This is just like when you were ten and I was four or five. You were Robin Hood and I was Will Scarlet or some other minion to be ordered here and there, to fetch and carry.'

'You can either assist me, or not, Will.'

Will smiled. 'I suppose being the eldest brother must be allowed its rewards.' He rose from the bench, and went across to the table where Ironsmith sat with two other drinkers. After a brief conversation, Ironsmith stood up and dragged his hanging belly over to the Shakespeares' table.

'Good day, Humfrey.'

'And you, John Shakespeare.'

'Still shoeing horses?'

'Aye. Staying alive in hard times.'

'Will tells me it was you who discovered the body.'

'Aye.'

'Did you touch the corpse?'

'No, didn't need to. I could tell he was dead and gone. Seen enough death in my time.'

'Did you touch the cord or the rosary?'

'No.'

'Did anyone else interfere with it in any way?'

'No. Not as I know, leastwise. As far as I know he was just as you saw him.'

'There were many footprints in the mud and dust when I saw the body.'

'I called out, blew my whistle and the searchers all came running, that's why.'

'But were any footprints there when you found him?'

Ironsmith rubbed his belly, then scraped his fingers through the straggles of his hair. He narrowed his eyes as though trying to recollect something. 'You know, John,' he said at last, 'I really couldn't say. I was looking at poor Benedict Angel, not the earth around him.'

'*Poor* Benedict Angel? Was he a friend?'

'I had nothing against him. Oh, I heard what you lads all thought of him when you were at the school together. I thought he was not treated well, to tell true. I go to the parish church, but I will hold no man's religion against him. And Benedict never did me no harm. I would say, too, that Widow Angel was always a good woman and a respectable neighbour. The pursuivants will take it out on the Dibdales next. Then who? Which one of us is safe if we miss a Sunday or two at church?'

'And you have no fear expressing this opinion to me, knowing that I am an officer of the crown?'

'No, I have no fear. I tell you the old folks are bewildered. Take Widow Boyce. She'll be eighty this December, God willing. She recalls the year Great Henry came to the throne and there was much rejoicing with a fair here in Shottery. She will tell you of the friars and the monks and nuns that walked these lanes, and she recalls being told by the priest at Holy Trinity Church that if she was a good Catholic and attended mass and said confession and lived her life in the ways of Rome, then she would go to heaven. Now she is told that if she were to help that priest, she would be a traitor. How do you reconcile that, Mr Shakespeare? It is a topsy-turvy world where virtue becomes crime.'

'Things change, Humfrey. The Roman Church had become corrupted by avarice and venery. The relics, the sale of indulgences. And so we must deal with things as they stand now.'

'Aye, things change – and so do you. I would say you have become a Queen's man before a Stratford man and I had always held you and your family in good regard, John Shakespeare.'

'What do you think of Rafe Rench?'

'He is a grasping, bullying toad. His son is lower than the belly of an adder.'

'Is that the common feeling hereabouts?'

'You'll be hard put to find any man or woman in Shottery with a better opinion of either of them.'

'Thank you, Humfrey. You will make yourself available to the coroner in due course.'

'Aye. I know my duty well enough. But I would say this to you, John: whatever your fine office, you'd best be wary how you cross Rafe Rench and his boy. They got Sir Thomas Lucy on their side, and he's backed by Lord high-and-mighty

Leicester. Just be wary, lad, that's all I am saying. There's a darkness come over this once pleasant land. You will even find families cleaved clean in two, which is something no one should endure.'

As Humfrey Ironsmith returned to his drinking companions, Shakespeare exchanged glances with his brother and thought of their own family. Whatever their religious differences, such matters had never divided them.

'So now you know, John.'

'Do *you* think there are traitors here? What of Somerville and cousin Edward Arden? What of the Catesbys and Throckmortons and Dibdales?'

'They are fervent in their Catholicism. God's blood, they are more than fervent – they are defiant. They will say a mass, whatever the cost. But *traitors*? No, I will not have that.'

'Are you certain? You do not sound certain. What about the gibberings of John Somerville? That must be treason.'

Suddenly Will made a curious face. 'John, you are worrying me. Do you have some intelligence or evidence against any of these people?'

'No.' Shakespeare was speaking quietly. 'But I can tell you this: they have raised the hackles of the Privy Council. My master, Sir Francis Walsingham, would have it that this place is infested with papists intent on insurrection. The Earl of Leicester speaks as though the county is diseased and needs disinfecting.'

'So that is why you are here.'

'I fear so. My task is not pleasant.'

'Then whose side are you on? Lucy and the Rench family – or the Ardens and the Angels?'

'You cannot put such a question to me. I am on the side of Queen and country.'

As he spoke, he heard a roaring sound, then a clatter of

heavy wood and iron. The low door was flung open, almost ripped off its hinges. The opening was immediately darkened by the shapes of men at arms, pushing their way in as a mass. They were shouting, raging. They seemed like a small army.

At their head was Badger Rench, sword in one hand, pistol in the other. He kicked a stool out of the way, knocked jars of ale and pewter platters flying from a table as he drove forward towards Shakespeare and his brother. Behind him, Shakespeare saw four men. Not an army, but a heavily armed squadron.

He was rising from his stool, his hand going to his sword. But Badger had the advantage of surprise and was already on him, thrusting the muzzle of a pistol full into Shakespeare's face. At his side was another man with a cord curled around his torso. He snatched at Shakespeare's sword arm and prevented him drawing the weapon.

One of Badger's confederates grabbed Will and pushed him down to the dirty sawdust floor, holding him there with a foot on his back and a sword to the nape of his neck. Two other raiders kept the unarmed landlord and drinkers at bay with pistols and swords. One of them picked up a half-full jug of ale and quaffed with seeming indifference.

'No one move or you will die!' Badger ordered. 'And you, John Shakespeare, hands behind your back.'

The one with the cord was behind Shakespeare now. He grasped his left wrist and pulled both arms back. Shakespeare fought and struggled, ignoring the pistol in his face, but he was not fast enough, for he was overpowered as two more hands went to his wrists and dragged them back and upwards, like the strappado torture of the Inquisition, until the joints at his shoulders felt as if they would snap.

Badger drew back his pistol and slammed the stock into Shakespeare's head, knocking him sideways. His legs gave way, he stumbled and flailed, half senseless. His arms were in an iron grip. The cord was looped about his wrists now, drawn taut so that the hemp bit into his flesh, to the bone.

'You are wanted, Shakespeare.'

'No.' Somewhere deep within, he knew there was something he should say, some command he should give, but the words would not come.

Rench turned his attentions to the younger Shakespeare brother. He kicked him in the ribs. 'That's for taking what is not yours.' Will groaned and squirmed. Rench kicked him again, harder. 'And that is for your lewd dealings.' He turned back to the elder brother. 'Your presence is required. Now walk.'

'No.'

'Then you will be carried. Take him, lads. Throw him on the muckwain.'

He was assailed by the hands of three men and lifted bodily, his arms firmly bound behind his back. With the last of his strength, he kicked out violently, but one of the men lashed another cord around his ankles, tying them tight together. And then the butt of the pistol crunched into his head again and merciful darkness came.

Chapter 20

SHAKESPEARE REGAINED CONSCIOUSNESS somewhere in the countryside outside Stratford. All he knew was that he was bound, hand and foot, and that he was in the back of a horse-drawn dung cart. He knew this, because he could smell it. He was being pummelled and battered as the vehicle's wheels lurched this way and that along the potholed highway.

More than that, he knew his head was in a bad way. Blood was clotting around his right eye and it felt as though a smithy had his skull on the anvil and was hammering it into some diabolical shape. The pain was all the worse for the rocking of the cart. Each jolt pounded his bones.

Above him, the sun glared into his bloody eyes. And then they were in woods, with a canopy of green, which was some relief, but not enough.

How long would this go on? Where were they taking him? Surely it must still be morning – in which case, the position of the sun told him they must be travelling eastward. The cart suddenly tipped into a deep rut, hurling Shakespeare against the wooden side panel on the right, then back to the left. With his hands bound tight behind him, unable to protect himself from the fall, he let out an involuntary gasp of shock and pain. The cart ground to a halt, listing like a beached ship and his ill-used body came to rest for a brief moment of respite.

He heard cursing, then the tailgate was pulled down and he was dragged out by two men and dumped at the side of the path, beneath a hedgerow.

'Too much ballast,' Badger Rench said. He had climbed down from his horse and was directing the operation. His carter had climbed down from his perch and was busy trying to lift the small wagon from the rut, assisted by two of Rench's men. 'Get on with it or you'll have no pay. You two' – he pointed his dagger at two men who were still mounted – 'come off your nags and help them.'

As the men battled to heave the cart's wheel out of the furrow into which it had fallen and stuck hard, Shakespeare managed to raise himself on to his elbows. He was breathing like a runner, but the words were beginning to form. 'You have committed grievous assault, Rench.' He gasped out the accusation. 'In the Queen's name, I demand to know what this is about. Where are you taking me?'

'You'll find out soon enough, Shakespeare. Now stow you or I'll stop your mouth with my fist and a wad of mud.'

'Do you know who I work for?'

'Aye. But does *he* know the truth about *you*? Does Walsingham know you give succour to papists? Maybe you're one of them.'

'Succour to papists? What nonsense is this?'

'You know well enough.'

'I know what you and your father are about, if that is what you mean. And you will pay the price. Riding with Sir Thomas's men will not save you. You should have stayed at the farm, shovelling out the slurry, doing something useful.'

Rench picked up a handful of dirt and stones from the verge, and was about to thrust it into Shakespeare's mouth and nose when he thought better of it. He threw the mud away, then raised his fist. 'You'll find out how strong I am if I hear another word out of you.' He kicked Shakespeare in the ribs, then turned his attention to the cart, which was finally up and out of the pothole. 'Is that damned wheel done? Is it sound?'

'Sound enough, Badger.' The carter, who was panting from his exertions, grinned. He took off his wool cap and wiped his sweating brow. 'It'll get us to Charlecote.'

'Well, get this bag of dog turd back aboard and we'll be on our way.'

Through the haze of his aching head and body, Shakespeare acknowledged ruefully that, yes, Badger was almost as strong as his father, and well deserved his nickname. His brutal power had won him many wrestling matches around the county. So feared had he become that other men now refused to join him in combat. He was a shade taller than Rafe and a little leaner, but that would change. With age he would fill out and then he would be an even more daunting prospect. It was a thought that gave Shakespeare no pleasure.

The hands were on him again, lifting him without ceremony, dumping him into the back of the wagon. And then the carter cracked his whip and and they lurched forward once more.

As they rolled beneath the arch of a magnificent gatehouse, Shakespeare recognised the twin octagonal turrets of Charlecote Park, the home of the Lucy family for more than four hundred years. The latest incarnation of their seat was a great country house which had been built in the year Elizabeth ascended the throne and had, to its lasting fame, played host to Her Majesty for two days when she visited the county.

The wagon was hauled around the property to the stableyard where it lurched to a halt and Shakespeare was dragged out, landing heavily on the flagstones. The fall jarred his backbone and the back of his already aching head. He nipped his tongue with his teeth and tasted blood.

Rench snorted, amused. 'Trussed up neat for the spit, ain't he?' He stooped down, dagger in hand, and cut the cord that bound his captive's legs, but left his hands still tied. 'Get to your feet. You're coming with me.'

Shakespeare did not bother to argue.

Sir Thomas Lucy was in the hall, rapier in hand, poised to strike. Opposite him was Ruby Hungate in his harlequin doublet, also with rapier. Suddenly, Sir Thomas lunged forward, thrusting his sword towards Hungate's chest. With barely a flick of the wrist, Hungate parried the thrust, then whipped the point of his own weapon to Sir Thomas's throat, where it rested, within a whisper of his flesh. 'You are dead.'

'I will have you next time, Mr Hungate.'

'Once you are dead, you are meat. There is no next time.'

A flicker of irritation and injured pride crossed Sir Thomas Lucy's brow. At the age of fifty, he considered himself at the height of his powers. He knew Hungate's reputation as England's finest shot and swordsman well enough, but still he did not like being bested by the man. As if suddenly aware that there were two figures in the doorway, he turned to the newcomers.

'What have you brought me, Badger?'

Badger was standing in the doorway, behind Shakespeare, whose hands were still bound behind his back. He stepped forward, and with an ingratiating sweep of his arm, said, 'You asked me to bring you John Shakespeare, Sir Thomas.'

'Well, what has happened to him? Did you find him in a ditch? He smells of horse-dung.'

'He was in the alehouse. He resisted arrest.'

'And what were you arresting him for? I trust he has committed no crime.'

'He has consorted with a papist, to wit the widow Angel.'

Rench's eyes alternated between the face of Sir Thomas Lucy and the sword of Ruby Hungate. Was it possible, Shakespeare wondered, that there could finally be a man in the world whom Badger feared?

'God's death, Badger, I wanted you to ask Mr Shakespeare to join us so that we might converse, not drag him through mud and manure.' Sir Thomas Lucy glanced at Hungate and they both began to laugh. 'I think you had best cut him free.'

Rench blanched and his great bulk seemed to develop a tic. He hesitated, his eyes now firmly on Hungate and his sword, as though computing his next move. Suddenly decisive, he drew his dagger once more, stepped back behind Shakespeare and sawed through the cords that bit into his wrists.

'You will leave us now,' Sir Thomas said, nodding curtly at Badger. 'And on your way out, you may order brandy brought to us, with three goblets. We shall be in the dining parlour. Oh, and have a basin of water and towels brought for Mr Shakespeare.'

Blinking furiously and clearly bewildered, Badger bowed again and backed out of the hall. Shakespeare was astonished to see the change in him. From being cock of the walk, strutting his muscular bulk around Stratford, he was suddenly like a fawning puppy in his eagerness to please and his hurt at being shunned.

'Come, Mr Shakespeare, let us withdraw to the parlour where you can wash away the worst of the grime and where we may all sit down. You seem to have endured rough treatment.'

Shakespeare stepped forward slowly and painfully. He did indeed want to sit down. Even better would be a feather bed and a night's sleep. Every part of him felt damaged and bruised. He brushed the dust from his hair and felt the blood on his face and the sharp tenderness where the pistol stock had first hit him. Licking his lips, he tasted the blood from his tongue. He had a longing to tell Sir Thomas Lucy what he thought of him, but then a pain stabbed him at the shoulder blade and all he could do was suppress a groan.

'Forgive my man. It seems Mr Rench not only has the strength of a badger, but the wit of one, too. When I commanded him to bring you to me, I meant him to escort you here, no more. We have much to talk about.' He motioned his rapier point towards Ruby Hungate. 'I believe you have already met my fencing partner. I would have preferred it had you not seen him besting me in such humbling fashion, however.'

'I know him,' Shakespeare said, gritting his teeth to suppress the pain and weariness. 'What is he doing here?' As he said the words, he knew his tone was sharp, but he was in no humour for niceties.

Hungate answered the question in kind. 'Keeping an eye on dog's arses such as you, Shakespeare.'

Sir Thomas slapped his rapier into the palm of his hand. 'Gentlemen, gentlemen, let us be easy with each other, for I am sure we share the same aims: the hunting down of traitors and the weeding out of conspiracy. As to the first, it seems we have no longer any need to seek the egregious Mr Angel, for he has generously placed his body at our disposal.'

'You mean he has been murdered, Sir Thomas.'

'We will discuss the fate of Mr Angel in due course.' An edge of irritation entered Sir Thomas's voice. 'Come.' Shakespeare knew Sir Thomas's reputation well and had seen him often enough at important events in Stratford. He was a well-made man with a taste for country sports – hunting and hawking – and a keen sense of his own exalted place in the world. His birthright put him above the local populace, but below the Earl of Leicester and other senior courtiers. He had no ambition but to maintain things the way they were. If God had placed the earl above him, then he would give him his total loyalty. And if others had been placed below, then he would treat them with the scorn their rank merited.

They sat at the table in the parlour. A basin of cold water and towel were brought by a servant and Shakespeare cleaned away the worst of the blood and dirt. More than anything, he was grateful to take the weight off his feet. The fog of his brain was clearing and he directed his mind to the question of Ruby Hungate. Clearly he had been sent here by the Earl of Leicester to delve in the same dark waters as Shakespeare. And who was to say there weren't traitors here? There were certainly papist sympathisers aplenty.

But nonetheless Leicester's employment of Hungate nagged. What was it Walsingham's steward Walter Whey had said? *I fear there is little to amuse about Mr Hungate.* And he had intimated that it were better not to ask about him. Well, Shakespeare had no time for such discretion. 'Tell me about yourself, Mr Hungate. What, precisely, is your position in my lord of Leicester's household?'

Hungate's mouth smiled, but his eyes did not. He stared at Shakespeare as a cat might watch a bird in a cage. 'Why, Mr Shakespeare,' he said at last. 'I kill people for him.'

Sir Thomas Lucy laughed, but the sound was forced. 'Come now, Mr Hungate, our guest has no appetite for your jests. He has suffered quite enough this day.'

'Then I shall avoid killing him until another day, Sir Thomas. In deference to your hospitality and the unsightliness of blood on your fine floor. Also, because I have a few questions to ask the malodorous cur while he yet lives. Tell me, Shakespeare, what do you know of Benedict Angel and his family?'

'I know that Benedict was a popish priest and fugitive. I

know, too, that his sister and mother are sore troubled by the wanton destruction of their home by pursuivants.'

'How else are you to seek fugitives but by seeking out their hidey-holes? If they crawl like lice into the cracks of houses, then the houses must be pulled down to get at them. But tell me more: when did you first meet them?'

With Benedict dead there seemed no harm in answering. 'I think it must have been eleven or twelve years ago, when they arrived in Shottery and Benedict joined me at the King's New School in Stratford.'

'Where had they come from?'

'I do not believe I was ever told. From their voices I might deduce they were southern. But I believe they came to Warwickshire because Mistress Angel has kin in this region.' He did not mention that those relatives included his own family.

'And their name was always Angel, not Angelus?'

'You will have to ask them that yourself. What is your interest, Mr Hungate, now that the supposed traitor is dead?'

'And the father, what of him? Is he still alive? What is his business?'

'Mistress Angel was already a widow when they arrived. It is said the father had been murdered. But this is all a long time ago, and that is all I know.' Shakespeare turned away from Hungate and directed his attention once more to Sir Thomas. 'Was there some reason for asking Badger Rench to bring me here?'

'It is the matter of this priest, the ill-named Angel. It has come to my attention that you have thought fit to assume some sort of authority in the investigation of the death.'

'As you must know, I am in the service of Her Majesty. I will not explain myself to anyone save Sir Francis Walsingham, my master, and certainly not the likes of Ananias Nason.'

'I heard that the Angels are kin to you.'

Shakespeare shrugged. He had been expecting the question. 'What of it? Most folk around here are kin if you go back far enough.'

'But Audrey Angel has Arden blood, does she not?'

Shakespeare ignored the question.

'And I heard, too, that you had called upon the son of the diabolical Mother Peace to try his necromancy and devilish tricks on the corpse.'

'Mr Peace has a fine, inquiring mind. It was he who discovered that Benedict Angel was murdered by garrotting with hempen rope.'

'That is not the story I heard and nor will I believe it. But this is certain, Mr Shakespeare: *I* am the authority in these parts and I will not have you dealing with local matters that are no concern of yours. The death will be dealt with by the coroner and myself, in my role as justice. No other inquiries will be made by you. From what Mr Nason tells me, there is no cause for inquiry anyway. It seems the papist traitor choked himself to death or hanged himself with his superstitious beads. Whether he caught himself inadvertently on some low branch or whether it was deliberate is for the coroner to decide. His accidental death – or suicide – saved the hangman a task. My lord of Leicester will not be displeased by the news. Is that understood?'

'No, Sir Thomas, it is not understood. I have been sent here by Mr Secretary, who is your superior in all things. I will not be diverted from my inquiries by you or any man.' He met the gaze of Hungate and repeated the last two words. '*Any man.* Is that understood?'

'God damn you, Shakespeare, I am trying to be civil!' Sir Thomas Lucy rose from his seat and hammered his fist on the table. 'I *know* why you are here. My lord of Leicester has sent

✝ 189 ✝

me letters requiring me to assist you in sniffing out popish treason. But you will be working for me and you will do *my* bidding. You will not go your own way.'

'Sniffing out popish treason . . . is that what you were doing when you sent Rench and a band of pursuivants to destroy the house of Audrey Angel and her daughter? Or were you tormenting an innocent family for the benefit of your ally Rafe Rench?'

Sir Thomas was speechless. Blood rushed to his face and a vein began to throb in his forehead.

Shakespeare rose from his seat. He had had enough of this place. He would find a way back to Stratford, even if he had to walk the five miles unaided.

'Sit down, Shakespeare. I have not finished with you yet. Hold him, Mr Hungate.'

'I am going and you can do nothing. You have no power over me. Everyone knows I was brought here. Harm me further and there will be a heavy price to pay – even for one as notable as you. Do not underestimate the reach of Mr Secretary.'

Hungate did not move from his seat. His feet were on the table, ankles crossed, hands behind his head. He appeared to be enjoying the spectacle.

Sir Thomas grasped hold of Shakespeare's shoulder, but Shakespeare spun round and his hand went to the other man's throat. 'Do not trifle with me, Sir Thomas. I have had enough of your foul hospitality this day.'

Breaking free from Shakespeare's grip, Sir Thomas Lucy's hand went to the hilt of his dagger. But Hungate's hand shot out and grasped his wrist. He shook his head.

Sir Thomas held back from Shakespeare, though he still seethed with anger. 'You are Arden through and through. Like a plague of flies. I should have let Badger have his way with you.'

'Then you both would have been arraigned for murder and hanged from the same gibbet. As it is, I shall see that Rench is brought before court for what he has done.'

'No man here will arrest Badger Rench. That I can promise you. And if you try, then you and yours will feel the lash of my fury. Your brother might have escaped justice once, but it will not happen again.'

Shakespeare turned once more, and swung his aching body towards the door.

'Your brother is a mongrel, do you hear me?' Lucy roared behind him. 'Take the filthy dog in hand or I will do it for you soon enough.'

Shakespeare turned violently. 'My family has nothing to do with any of this!'

'He has too great an interest in country matters, I say. First he poaches my stags, now he plucks the doe Hathaway. He will make her honest in short order, or I will have them both in the stocks. We are not brute beasts in this county; there will be no bastards born here without consequences.'

A bluecoat arrived with brandy. Shakespeare took a goblet from the tray and downed it in one. 'My brother was found *innocent* of poaching, as I recall.'

'The jury were dogs, too. They will also suffer.'

'I thought you believed in the rule of law, Sir Thomas, being a justice of the peace.'

Sir Thomas Lucy ran a hand through his hair, his back arched and stiff with wounded dignity. 'Then the matter of the stag is forgotten, for the law is always right. But he is not forgiven. Nor will he escape a charge of fornication so easily. You come from tainted stock, Shakespeare. Your father is a recusant, your brother is a debauched mongrel and your cousins Edward Arden and William Catesby are traitors, which I will prove. They harbour priests and those who would do our sovereign lady harm. They are a disease upon the body of Warwickshire and England. Get you gone, sir.'

Shakespeare did not look back. Had he done so, he might have noted a movement behind the inner door of the parlour. He might have seen a pair of eyes and a shock of white hair. And had his nostrils not been clogged with dust and clotting blood, he might have noted the unholy stench of a man he had hoped never to see again. A man who had watched and listened to all that had gone on in this room between Shakespeare and Ruby Hungate and their host, Sir Thomas Lucy.

But Shakespeare did not see him, nor smell him. He would do so soon enough, however.

Chapter 21

A HORSE WAS saddled in the Charlecote stables, ready for Shakespeare as though he were an honoured guest departing. He was surprised but, not relishing a five-mile walk, he took the reins from the groom with good grace and accepted the offer of a leg-up. Without a word or a backward glance, he kicked on and rode for Stratford and the White Lion at a steady pace.

Joshua Peace was at the long table, eating his midday meal a little away from the other diners. He looked alarmed when he caught sight of Shakespeare's dishevelled appearance.

'Don't ask, Mr Peace.'

'I heard you had been taken. I confess I was at a loss who to turn to.'

'I will tell you about it in due course. For the moment I want nothing more than a bed.'

'Would you like me to examine you? I have medical knowledge from my mother, and have garnered a great deal more during my travels in Italy.'

'I thought you dealt with the dead, Mr Peace.'

'How can I determine a cause of death if I do not understand the effects of injury and disease in the living?'

'True enough.' He smiled. 'Yes, indeed, Mr Peace, I would be most grateful if you could put me back together.'

*

Shakespeare stood naked in the centre of his chamber, while Joshua Peace washed him down with remarkable gentleness, taking extra care to use a light touch at the sites of bruises and lesions, particularly on the face and head.

'I do not think I have been washed by another since I was a babe, Mr Peace. Thank you.'

'Washing bodies is part of my job.'

Shakespeare laughed. 'Do I look like a corpse?'

'No, but I will tell you that you are fortunate to be alive and in possession of your senses. The blows to your temples could have done severe damage, if not killed you. I have seen men suffer lifelong palsy from such injuries.'

'That is most reassuring.'

'I can tell you more, too, when you are rested.'

'Tell me now.'

'Very well. I have heard men talk, here at this inn. There is great fear in town.'

'Who do they fear? The pursuivants? The priests?'

'Perhaps both. They speak of change and distrust. Uncertainty has become a malaise. They have seen murder and violence and they fear for their own safety. They speak of Sir Thomas Lucy's ruffians in hushed tones. I heard them talk of your abduction, but none thought to help you. They know something bad is happening, but they do not know what. In particular, they do not know who is on their side.'

'Well, perhaps they are right to be afraid. But that is why you and I must keep clear heads and bring these matters to a speedy and just conclusion. Have you heard from the coroner? Is there any word of an inquest?'

Peace shook his head and wrung out the linen cloth with which he had been cleaning Shakespeare. A trickle of pink-brown water dripped into the pewter bowl on the coffer at his side. He studied Shakespeare's lean, muscular body for a moment, then smiled. 'You will survive. Now take to your bed, Mr Shakespeare, and sleep.'

'No, I cannot yet. There is something I must do.'

Shakespeare ate in his room, then took leave of Peace and headed for Arden Lodge, one of his cousin Edward's homes, three or four miles to the west of Stratford. As he rode along the pathway to the front of the large manor house, a pistol shot split the air. His horse jinked and whinnied but he tugged at the reins to bring the animal to a halt and under control.

He looked right, for that was where the sound seemed to have come from. Was it his imagining, or was that the shadow of a man disappearing around the far wall of the house? He looked left. A hole had been gouged into the yew tree not three feet from his shoulder. Someone had shot at him, and had not missed by far.

Kicking on into a canter, he rode hard for the corner of the stone-built house where he thought he had seen the figure. A small gate barred his way. In one smooth movement, his injuries forgotten, he jumped from the saddle, knotted the reins together and slung them over the gatepost to tether the horse. He then drew his sword and eased the gate open.

An exquisite garden lay before him in intricate patterns and colours. In a square, perhaps ninety feet at each side, was a dizzying arrangement of borders and small hedges, all made of herbs, exuding a heady late-summer fragrance. Lavender and thyme, rosemary and marjoram and bay.

Kneeling with his back to him, clippers in hand, was a man in a wide-brimmed hat, whom he took to be the gardener. Shakespeare approached him silently. 'Turn around very slowly. Do not make a move.'

The man froze, but obeyed. His eyes were wide. He looked timid and uncertain, but that did not mean he was unarmed. A man could easily conceal a loaded wheel-lock pistol in a capacious sleeve, or behind a bank of box hedging.

'Who are you?'

'My name is Hall, sir. Hugh Hall. I am the gardener.'

'Stand up, with your hands open to me.'

The man did as he was bidden. He was not tall. Perhaps four inches over five feet. There was little in his appearance to suggest he was a gardener. His skin was pale, as though deliberately protected from the ravages of the summer sun. True gardeners cared nothing for such vanity.

'Where is Mr Arden?'

'In the house, sir, I do believe.'

'You heard a pistol report?'

He seemed about to deny it, but the shake of the head turned into a nod of reluctant confirmation. 'I heard something, sir, like the crack of a whip. I did not know what it was.'

'Was it you?'

'No, sir. No, indeed, I promise you.'

'Who then? I saw someone run into this garden.'

The gardener hesitated a moment too long. 'I saw no one. There was no one.'

Shakespeare touched his swordpoint to the man's chest. 'You are lying. Come, Mr Hall – if that is your name – take me to your master. Be careful how you go, lest you slip on to my blade.'

They found Edward Arden in his library on the far side of the house. A pistol lay on the table, still smoking. The stink of burnt gunpowder was sharp to the nostrils.

'Cousin John, you must accept my apologies.'

Shakespeare lowered his sword and replaced it in the scabbard. Arden took his hand in greeting. 'My fool of a son-in-law thought you were a squirrel, so he says.'

'You mean John Somerville?'

'He has the wit and eyesight of a worm. Believes he saw movement in the yew and fired. Then he heard your horse and realised his error before scuttling away like a frightened rabbit.'

'I do not call that poor eyesight, cousin, I call it blindness.'

Arden tapped his head twice with his forefinger. 'I think he is not sound . . . if you take my meaning.'

Shakespeare nodded towards the spent weapon. 'In which case, do you think it wise to allow him access to that?'

'Forgive me. I must take responsibility for this unfortunate incident. Happily he would be hard pressed to hit an oak tree from two feet, so I suspect you were never in danger.'

No, Shakespeare thought. No, you cannot write off this incident so easily. *John Somerville shot a pistol at me and I could have been killed.* And if Somerville was deranged, then the man who allowed him the liberty of his house with a gun was either equally mad, or culpable. This was nothing to do with squirrels.

'I have offered to have some spectacles made for him, but he will not have it,' Arden continued. 'He says his eyes are as good as a hawk's. Hah!' He laughed lightly.

'Where is he now?' Shakespeare was unamused.

'I will deal with the pig's pizzle in my own way.'

No, thought Shakespeare, I will deal with him in *my* own way. But there was time enough for that. 'I suggest you relieve him of his pistol permanently,' he said. It might be wise, too, he thought ruefully, to remove his tongue if everything Will had told him about Somerville's threats to the Queen were true.

'You have met Mr Hall, the gardener? He has constructed a fine example of the art, do you not think?'

'A most agreeable garden, but that is not the reason I am here.'

'No, I rather thought it was not.' Arden glanced towards the gardener. 'You may go, Hugh. Ask for some wine to be brought, if you would.' He turned back to Shakespeare. 'Now, tell me, why *are* you here?'

Arden's voice was still cordial, but Shakespeare detected a hostile edge to it. Shakespeare pressed on. 'You have heard of the death of Benedict Angel, no doubt, and the attacks on his home. I assume, too, that you know of the invective hurled at you by Sir Thomas Lucy and those who ride out for him?'

'What of it, John? Do you think I give a rotted turnip for the opinion of Lucy or his puppet-master?'

'I take it you mean the Earl of Leicester?'

'You know I do. The whole world knows what I think of them. Leicester pulls the strings and Lucy jumps like a monkey on hot coals. His plan is clear: with Walsingham's aid, he will keep the Queen unwed, put Mary's head on the block and raise up his own kin to be king of this realm.'

'This is absurd. Leicester has no claim to the throne.'

'But his sister's family does. Katherine Dudley is married to the Earl of Huntingdon, who must be first in line if the Stuarts are discounted.'

Shakespeare laughed dismissively. 'This is old and hoary. The mad delusions of Cardinal Allen and his acolytes who accuse Leicester of every sin known and many more invented in the dark sweaty nights of a single man's seminary cot.'

Edward Arden gave Shakespeare a hard look. 'You have turned from the true path, John. I had thought you better than that. When you were a boy, I had great hopes for you.'

Arden looked exactly what he was: a gentleman of middle years with standing among the gentry. A former high sheriff of the county, he was still undisputed head of his family. As a child, Shakespeare had been here at Arden Lodge each year for the summer fair, an annual event for Arden's workers, parishioners and extended family. The Ardens were a family who had long dominated this county. He recalled being picked up and displayed by Arden when he was five or six. The great man had laughed and shown him off as though he were a prize pup. 'So this is your fine fellow, is it, Mary? I say he is an Arden through and through,' he boomed. 'Arden blood, not Shakespeare.'

Here and now, in this room, he noticed that while his elder cousin still looked the county gentleman, there was an unfamiliar weariness, as though the defiance had turned to recklessness. Perhaps the long-standing and relentless feud with the Earl of Leicester and Sir Thomas Lucy was taking its toll on Arden's reasoning.

The feud between Edward Arden and Robert Dudley, Earl of Leicester, was the stuff of legend in these parts. Arden, very publicly and very clearly, had called the earl 'whoremaster'.

Whoremaster!

It had come about seven years ago when Arden had heard that the Earl of Leicester was idling away the night hours between the legs of Lettice Knollys, who was another man's wife. And nor did he stop there. When summoned to appear at a grand pageant in Kenilworth attired in the earl's livery – the blue coat and silver badge of the bear and ragged staff – Arden refused.

No one refused such an honour. No one insulted Leicester and slept well.

And now, it seemed, that blood feud was being waged on Leicester's behalf by his lackey Sir Thomas Lucy. Was Arden beginning to understand what he had done? His defiant Catholicism must be costing him a great deal in recusancy fines – the penalty for refusing to attend the parish church. The truth was, Edward Arden was badly tainted by his past. Words that might have seemed like knightly boldness and audacity now sounded like treason. A great deal had changed in England in recent years and it was becoming increasingly difficult to cleave to the old faith. The days when the Queen refused to make windows into men's souls were gone. *Regnans in Excelsis* – Pope Pius V's Bull of Excommunication – had seen to that even before Arden's ill-judged insult to the Queen's favourite. The excommunication meant Catholics were now told it would be no sin to murder her. And so they became her enemy.

'It is not my place to give you advice, cousin,' Shakespeare continued, 'but I would be failing in my duty to you as a kinsman if I did not come to warn you that I fear for your safety. As your friend and cousin I must tell you that the Earl of Leicester is a dangerous man, and he has not forgiven you. He bears a grudge, and if you are not exceeding careful, he will have his revenge.'

'And you came here to tell me that, did you, John? That is no news to me.'

'Then I will now address you as a government officer. And I will ask you this: who has been harbouring Benedict Angel?'

A curious expression crossed Arden's brow, but he quickly recovered his composure. 'What makes you think I know anything of Benedict Angel?'

'He must have been staying with the Catholic gentry in these parts. If not you, then with the Catesbys or Throckmortons. And I know *your* wife to be a Throckmorton.'

'Bull's bollocks, John, I will not listen to this. Are you a pursuivant now? Do you ride with Lucy's men?'

'At the moment, I am your cousin, for I am not persuaded that you are a traitor. But if I had proof otherwise, my attitude towards you would change very quickly. And I must tell you this: there are those on the Privy Council who are not persuaded of your innocence.'

'Hah. Let me guess their names – Leicester, Walsingham, Burghley. The unholy trinity.'

'Mr Secretary Walsingham is my master. I will not hear ill spoken of him.'

'He is the devil.'

'I will not tolerate such talk. Once I have left this house, our kinship will be no more. We will not be cousins. I will investigate you as hard as any pursuivant, for I fear you have secrets. This son-in-law of yours – Somerville – he goes into the world with threats against Her Majesty's person. He fires shots at riders walking their horses up to your front gate. And your gardener, Mr Hall, what precisely is he? What is going on here at this house?'

'Go, Shakespeare. Get out. I said once that you were an Arden, but you are not.'

'Will you answer me? I have other questions, too.' *Has a one-armed Frenchman been here? Who is hiding at your other grand properties such as Park Hall in the north of the county? What secrets are concealed here at Arden Lodge?*

'Go. I will not trim my religion to suit you or Leicester or any other damned heretic. Go, I say.'

It seemed for a moment that Arden's hand was moving towards the spent pistol on the coffer. Shakespeare's own hand went once more to his sword. Arden's hand hovered and stopped; so did Shakespeare's.

Though the very thought made the bile rise in his gullet, a bitter conclusion was forming in Shakespeare's brain: that Leicester and Sir Thomas Lucy were correct in their estimation of the bubbling treason in the county. There *was* a problem here – and it *did* involve Edward Arden.

Without another word, he turned away and strode out. He felt sick. Until this day, he had always liked cousin Edward. Now he realised the cold truth: they were enemies.

Chapter 22

'A MAN HAS been looking for you. He says his name is Harry Slide and that you know him.'

Shakespeare gave his brother a puzzled look. Out of context, he did not immediately recognise the name. Harry Slide? Then he remembered. Slide had been the one stalking him in the woods in Sheffield. The man who claimed that he spied for Walsingham and had a mission to discover the bedroom secrets of the Earl of Shrewsbury. The man who had slithered away like a serpent into a hole.

'Slide was here at Shottery?'

'Not here. It was at Henley Street, no more than two hours since,' Will said. 'Margery answered the door and called me. He seemed a charming enough fellow.'

'Where is he?'

'He wouldn't tell me. He said he would find you later.'

'Did he say what he wanted?'

'No. It may be my imagination has caught an ague, but I rather thought he might be a spy. This is what your presence is doing to me, John! And though he was pleasant, I did not invite him in.' Will paused and assessed his elder brother. 'But let me look at you. What damage has the villainous Rench wrought upon you? Mother would worry herself to an early grave if she knew what was happening.'

'It is nothing, a sore head. And what of you? You were kicked senseless yourself. What was he talking about when he accused you of lewd dealing and taking what was his? Was he talking of Anne?'

'I fear so. He has believed himself her swain these eighteen months past, yet she never gave him cause nor encouragement. He asked her to marry him, an invitation that she found all too easy to forgo. And now he resents her – and even more does he resent me.'

'Well, he may be witless, but he is dangerous nonetheless, so take care.'

'It is the reason he dislikes us so much. As far as Rench is concerned, this is nothing to do with the Ardens, this is merely jealousy.'

Shakespeare was barely listening. It was Harry Slide who held his attention. If Slide was here, then his story about spying on Shrewsbury for Walsingham was horse-manure. This was something to do with the Frenchman François Leloup. Slide must be hunting him, too. Perhaps Walsingham or Phelippes had sent messages to Slide to that effect. The hundred-mile gap between Stratford and Sheffield was closing all the time. The connection was as visible as a heavy cable between two vessels in dock. It tied treachery and murder in Warwickshire to conspiracy in Yorkshire. And yet the nature of the connection was as cloudy as an Avon fog. He focused once more on what Will was saying.

'John?'

'Forgive me, Will, I was elsewhere.'

'Where did Rench and his men take you?'

'Charlecote Park, trussed up like a lamb to the shambles. I was guest of Sir Thomas Lucy and I must tell you, Will, that you have made a bad foe there. He wants vengeance against every Arden in Warwickshire, but especially you and cousin Edward and the Angels.'

Will was indignant. 'I cannot speak for Edward Arden, but John, let me be straight with you: I did not poach deer on Lucy's estates. I have never poached deer in my life. My most heinous crime thus far has been to scrump apples in the orchards and to get Anne Hathaway with child outside wedlock. In the case of the deer, the jury believed me because I told the truth. And yet I had already been punished, for the gamekeeper gave me a beating.'

'Fear not, I believe you, too.' Shakespeare smiled at his brother. They were in the parlour at Hewlands Farm. Anne walked into the room, having cleared the empty platters of food, and then sat on the bench beside her betrothed.

Shakespeare was sitting opposite them. They made a fair couple. With his tufts of beard, Will looked a little older than his eighteen years, whereas Anne could still pass for a girl. He smiled at them both again, for they seemed a little apprehensive. 'Anne, Will, has Florence told you yet where she went and where she stayed overnight?'

Anne Hathaway's hand went to her belly and she averted her gaze. *She has something to hide.* Shakespeare suddenly felt the prickles rise on his neck. He looked at the flush rising up his brother's neck. What was going on here?

'Anne? Will? Do you have aught to tell me? If you have something to say, then for your own sake say it now. It is better to be questioned by me than others who might take an unwholesome interest. I beg you, Will . . . Anne?'

Anne took a deep breath and sighed. 'I have feared that Florence is losing her sanity. She hears voices and sees ghosts. I am afraid for her.'

'It is becoming worse,' Will said.

'But none of this explains where she went yesterday – or why you both seem so reluctant to confide in me. There is something you are not telling me. I ask again: where was she?'

'She will not tell us, brother, but we have our fears. This all began in the summer when Benedict Angel returned.'

'You saw him?'

'Once. He was dressed in broadcloth, like a Calvinist, but it was no sort of disguise. I recognised him instantly.'

'So the pursuivants were right to search his mother's house! They knew he was here.'

'But Florence told us that he never stayed there. He feared bringing the law down upon his mother and sister, which is just what happened anyway. And he knew that he would be instantly recognised in Shottery. I believe he moved around from village to village – Lapworth, Edstone, Wilmcote – among the recusant Ardens and Catesbys and Throckmortons. I believe they all have hidey-holes now, for the concealing of priests, their vestments and silverware.'

'Where was he when you saw him?'

'North of here. He could have been heading for Lapworth, but that is mere surmise.'

'Sir William Catesby?'

'I had considered the possibility, but—'

'I understand. Could Florence have been there, too? Or could she have been at Arden Lodge, perhaps?'

Anne had been silent. Now she intervened. 'I think you have said too much, Will. It is not only idle surmise, but dangerous tittle-tattle. We know nothing of Benedict Angel or his murder. All I care about is Florence. The way she talks . . . what will become of her?' She stood from the table. 'Will, John, you will forgive me if I ask you to make your way home now. This talk . . . It is late and I am tired, and since my father's death, I must be both parents in this house.'

Shakespeare rose from the bench. 'And I must take my leave

of you. I also need sleep.' More than that, he had a slippery fellow named Slide to seek out.

Anne woke in the hour before dawn, gasping for breath. At first she thought it was the nightmare that had disturbed her. In her dream, a stream of chanting men and women, all dressed in white robes, walked piously through the night, their hands held together in prayer. And all the while, a blood-red rosary was being tightened about her neck. She was kicking and writhing, but her hands were bound and she could neither breathe nor scream.

The relief of discovering that the nightmare was nothing but a dream soon evaporated, for she realised that something else had woken her: the close sound of splintering wood. Someone was breaking into the house.

She shook her sister. 'Catherine, wake up.'

Anne jumped up and began pulling her two younger sisters from the bed they all shared. She shouted out for Thomas and the boys. Not for the first time it dawned on her how vulnerable they were in this house since the death of their father a year ago, and the departure of her brother Bartholomew to farm land to the east of Stratford. Anne was the eldest now and must not only run Hewlands Farm but care for her two young sisters and three small brothers. Only Catherine, now nineteen, was of an age to be of real help. Bartholomew would surely have to return soon, for he was needed here.

She shouted again and then there was a crash as though a heavy cabinet had toppled over. Clutching little Joan and Margaret to her, she shepherded them into hiding behind the bed. 'Stay with them, Catherine. I will go and see what is happening.' She feared she knew already, for she had seen the horror visited upon the home of Florence and Audrey. She moved towards the doorway. Before she could lift the latch, the door flew open.

*

There was no time to saddle horses. Shakespeare and his brother ran through the dark streets of Stratford, their way lit by guttering torches of pitch. Ahead of them ran Thomas Hathaway, desperate with panic. He had managed to slip out of a window and fled to seek their help: Anne and the children were being held at Hewlands Farm by pursuivants. On the path between the orchards on the outskirts of town, Will stumbled in a ditch and yelped. Shakespeare caught his arm and prevented him from falling further.

Five minutes earlier, Will had beaten his fist on the door to Shakespeare's chamber, waking him from a deep sleep. Bleary-eyed and a little dazed, Shakespeare had woken quickly and opened the door.

'John, get dressed. You must come instantly.'

'What is it, Will?'

'Thomas Hathaway is outside. The pursuivants have come to Hewlands Farm and are running rampage through the house. He managed to get away, but Anne and the others are all held by the men.'

By the time they reached the farm, the pursuivants had gone, leaving behind a scene of weeping children and distraught women. Anne and Catherine tried to comfort the little ones, but they were shaking and could barely contain their tears. The house itself had not suffered much damage, and certainly nothing like the destruction wreaked on the home of the Angel family. The front door had been battered open, but was still on its hinges. A dresser had been cast down to the floor. Earthenware pots, pewter platters and jugs had been scattered, many of them shattered or cracked.

The entrance hall was lit by candles and rushlights. The children were collecting up broken pieces from the floor.

Young Richard Hathaway, a sturdy seven-year-old, was weeping with frustration as he attempted vainly to lift the dresser back into position.

Anne came forward, holding Joan and Margaret by the hand, and Will folded them all in his arms.

'Was this Rench?' he said, spitting the name.

'Will, it was terrifying. They came into our chamber like ravening wolves.'

'I will kill him.'

She disengaged herself from his arms. 'Don't say that, Will.' She indicated the small children in earshot. 'There has been more than enough violence in this place.'

'No, I won't kill him. But I *should* do.'

'I beg you, Anne, tell us exactly what happened.' Shakespeare walked around the room, examining the chaos and disarray. 'What was their strength?'

'There were a dozen of them, all dressed in black leather doublets, emblazoned with the Lucy crest. Rench was among them, but he was not their leader. I thought it would never end. They were turning out coffers, rifling through linen and clothing, scattering food in the pantry. It seemed like hours but it was no more than ten or twenty minutes. Everything was emptied, all cupboards searched, but little damage was done. No one was harmed, thank the Lord.'

Shakespeare stopped. 'If not Rench, then who *was* their leader, Anne?'

'I know not. He was a man I have never seen before. Rench obeyed him like a pet dog.'

'Did he wear a coloured doublet, like a harlequin? A slender fellow with a foul tongue.'

'No, he was attired like the others and I would call him squat, not slender. He scared me, John. He scared me much more than Badger Rench ever did. He was older – perhaps fifty

– and he had white hair. He knew I was with child and he mocked me and called me—'

'What? What did he call you?'

She lowered her voice so that the children could not hear. 'He called me *Shakespeare's whore*. I could not bear the smell of him. He stank so and smacked his blackthorn stick into his hand.'

Shakespeare felt his hands curl into fists and a horrible sensation churned in his stomach. How could Richard Topcliffe be here in Shottery in the heart of the Midlands? And yet, the white hair, the fear he engendered, the foul insults, the stench, the blackthorn – was there any other man in England who fitted such a description? Why was Topcliffe in Warwickshire? And what was he looking for at Hewlands Farm?

'What else did he say?'

'He said this was but the beginning. He told me I would never sleep sound again.' Anne hesitated, then lowered her voice. 'He tried to touch me, most lewdly.'

Will's hand went straight to his dagger. Shakespeare restrained him. 'Did you hear his name, Anne? Did anyone call him Topcliffe?'

'No. Why, John, do you know him?'

'I fear I do. If I am right, then you have had the misfortune of encountering Richard Topcliffe. He is a rabid priest-hunter. I met him in Sheffield and travelled with him as far as Tutbury Castle in Staffordshire on orders of Mr Secretary. We parted there and I thought he had gone on to the royal court. I had hoped never to cross his path again, for there is darkness and cruelty in his soul. If he is here, it is bad news. And if he is working with Badger Rench, it is even worse . . .'

Will looked away, avoiding his brother's gaze yet again. Shakespeare watched him a few moments, and then suddenly gripped his younger brother by the shoulders and made him meet his eyes. 'Will, if there is anything you are holding back from me, anything at all, now is the time to speak your mind. We must have no secrets between us. Anne is right to be afraid. There is grave danger here.'

Chapter 23

A N HOUR LATER, as the sun was rising, and the children were back in their beds, the truth finally came out.

'Florence gave me a letter for safekeeping,' Anne said. 'I was consumed with fear when I saw it, but I did not know what to do. Florence herself was scared. She could not hide it in her own home, for the pursuivants would have found it.'

'What letter? Show me.'

'I no longer have it.'

'Well, where is it? Have you destroyed it?'

Anne was silent. She gripped Will's hand.

Shakespeare stared at his brother and waited.

At last Will let out a long sigh. 'Very well, John. I insisted Anne give it to *me*. I understood the peril.'

'Will, get to the heart of the matter! You still haven't told me what this letter is. Who wrote the thing? To whom is it addressed? What is its content?'

'It is in cipher, but the mark at the end is clear enough. It is signed by Mary Stuart. I have no idea of the intended recipient.'

Shakespeare thought his blood would run cold in his veins. A secret letter from the Scots Queen? God in heaven, the import and peril of this would be obvious to anyone. Mere possession of such a document was tantamount to treason.

No one but a conspirator would conceal such an object. How had such an item surfaced here in the sleepy Warwickshire countryside? And why was it now in the possession of his brother?

'Give it to me.' He held out his hand. 'You could hang for this.'

'It's not here. I hid it.'

'Then let us go and fetch it now and burn it. Where did you put it?'

'Is this necessary, John? You are acting like a law officer, treating me like a criminal. Am I not your brother?'

'You are my brother, but you are also a subject of the Queen of England and are liable to be held accountable before the law. So believe me, this is necessary. Where is it?'

'I have it at home, concealed within a book.'

'God's blood, Will, I had thought you a young man of wit!' Shakespeare exploded. 'I now think you are totally insane. You hid it within a book! Did you think they would not look there? Did you not see how they tore the widow Angel's house to pieces? How could you think that the Shakespeare house was safer than Hewlands Farm? Perhaps the pursuivants are there even now. And Will, if what you say is true – and I still cannot believe it – then you have brought your own mother and father into peril. How could you do such a thing? You must realise you could both be hanged for this, and worse.'

'Worse?'

'Tortured by rack for the names of your accomplices, bowelled and quartered. Tell me you understand the danger, for pity's sake.'

'I am sorry. Anne was scared. Would you have not helped *your* betrothed in any way necessary?'

'But Anne, what possessed you to accept this thing from Florence? You must have had doubts.'

'I was worried for her. I wished to help a friend. What else was I supposed to do?'

'Who else knows about this letter? Who knows that Florence gave it to you, Anne?'

'No one. Not that I know of.'

'And yet Topcliffe and his pursuivants come *here*. That is a mighty coincidence, is it not? They have no notion that there is a letter, nor that it was given to you – and yet they come beating at your door at dead of night. Anne . . . Anne . . . of course they know something.' A hideous thought was taking shape. What if Benedict Angel had been captured by Richard Topcliffe before his death? Topcliffe had already told Shakespeare that he was not averse to the use of torture. Was it not possible that Topcliffe and his men had used pain or threats to obtain information incriminating Anne and Will? 'Where do you suppose they will go next, Will?'

Will's face was pale. He was shivering. 'Are you thinking of our home?'

'Yes, I am. They will go as certain as night follows day and death follows life. They will go to Henley Street and rip our home apart. Come, Will, we have no time to lose.'

Shakespeare stood by the window in the chamber that he had once shared with Will and Gilbert. He could not believe Will had been so reckless and foolhardy. He clenched his fists and hissed through his teeth with rage and fought the instinct to club his brother to the ground.

'Do you know what you have done?' he repeated. 'You have endangered this whole family. Your mother, your father, your brothers and sisters.'

Will was chastened. 'You have made the point forcibly. And yet still all I can say is that I am sorry.' He removed a large book from the bottom of a pile near the bed. He held it up and tried to lighten the mood. 'It is called *A Brief Discourse of the Late Murder of Master G. Saunders*. It is a poor thing concerning the death of a London merchant. Even a pursuivant would find no entertainment there.'

'God damn you, Will. There is no mirth to be had this day and I have no interest in your book. Give me the letter.'

Will placed the tome on the bed and flicked through the pages. Somewhere in the middle, he found what he was looking for: a letter with the seal broken. 'Here, John, take it. I never wish to see the thing again. It will give me many sleepless nights as it is.'

Shakespeare studied it closely. It was scraped in a small, neat hand, filled from top left to bottom right, with no margin space. The only thing fathomable was the name, *Marie R.* He held it up to the window light. It certainly looked like her hand. He had seen her letters before, in plain script and in cipher, but none encrypted in this manner, with a strange mixture of letters, numerals and Greek symbols.

'Will you burn it now?'

He did not reply. Every instinct told him to tear it up and throw the pieces on to the fire until each shred was utterly consumed and then take out the ashes and throw them to the wind. But he could not do it without knowing what the letter said. Not while the Duke of Guise prepared his invasion fleet in the ports of Normandy and while François Leloup was on the loose in England.

Angrily, he folded the letter, thrust it into his doublet, and stalked from the room. He could not bear to speak to Will, nor even look at him.

The coroner observed the state of Widow Angel's house and refused to go inside. 'We will hold the inquest at the alehouse.' He beckoned two witnesses, the farrier Humfrey Ironsmith and Constable Nason. 'You two, bring the dead man to the alehouse. Quickly.' He spotted Joshua Peace. 'Who are you?'

'I am the Searcher of the Dead, sir. Joshua Peace.'

'Help them, and then be on your way. I have no need for a searcher. From what I am told, this case is cut, dried and in the jar.'

'I have been commanded to stay by John Shakespeare, who is an officer of the crown.'

'Well, he has no authority here. This is my court. Carry the body and be gone with you.'

Joshua Peace walked into the ruins of the house with Ironsmith and Nason.

Ananias Nason put a hand to his face. 'Too sweet for me. Smells like last month's pork in here.'

Peace looked at him with disdain. 'Have some respect in the company of the departed, Constable.'

'You tell me to have respect? I've heard how you prod and cut bodies. You've learnt your mother's witchcraft, so folks say. And one day you'll have your neck stretched for it. Now get carrying, you and Ironsmith.'

'The coroner told us *all* to carry the corpse.'

'That was outside. Now we're inside and I'm in charge, so what I say goes. And what I say is that you two worms can shift the cadaver.'

'We'll need a cart.'

'No, you'll need your hands and the strength God gave you.'

A light rain was falling. Boltfoot reined in his horse on the edge of town and slumped his shoulders.

'I do believe we are here, Mr Cooper.'

She was smiling at him. A smile that said, *Here we are and I have got you to do just what I wanted.*

Boltfoot patted his horse's neck. He had an uncomfortable

feeling that he and Kat were not going to be at all welcome here in Stratford-upon-Avon. Most likely, he would be dismissed from Mr Shakespeare's employment by day's end and be reduced to scouring London docks for a berth by Saturday.

'Why, Mr Cooper, you do not look at all happy. Now that we are here, you can be rid of me. I had thought you would be glad to see the back of me.'

'Where is he, then? Buchan Ord? You said he was here.'

'Patience, Mr Cooper. First let us find an inn where we can feed ourselves and the horses and wash this dust from our mouths and eyes. Then we can seek out your master, and all will be revealed.'

The inquest was under way by the time Shakespeare arrived at the alehouse. He was surprised to see Joshua Peace standing outside in the drizzle.

'What is going on here, Mr Peace? Why was I not informed of the inquest – and why are you not participating?'

'The coroner does not want me. He has made up his mind already, or someone else has made it up for him. He will not allow me in there.'

'I know whose work this is. Sir Thomas Lucy.' Shakespeare spat the name. 'Follow me, Mr Peace.' He pushed open the alehouse door and felt the eyes of twenty or so men looking at him. A group of them – perhaps fifteen – were jurors; only two were witnesses – Humfrey Ironsmith and Ananias Nason. At a table, dominating the small room, was the coroner, with a clerk at his side.

The coroner was a slight man with red hair, cheerless eyes and grim lips. In any other setting, no man would note him. Yet here, as master of his court, he had a stern presence that cowed the men ranged before him. He was accustomed to being obeyed when he held an inquest.

In front of the table, laid out on a sheet on the floor, was the corpse of Benedict Angel. The smell of beer and woodsmoke could not quite conceal the early waft of a decomposing body. Two of the jurors were standing looking down at it, having been ordered to examine the dead man.

The coroner pointed a long, slender finger at Joshua Peace. 'Mr Searcher, what are you doing here? I ordered you to go away. If you do not do so now, you will be arrested and held in contempt until such time as the justice orders you clamped into the pillory.'

'No, he stays.' Shakespeare strode forward to the coroner's table. 'I am John Shakespeare and I am in charge of the investigation into Mr Angel's death – murder, as it seems to me. What is your name, Mr Coroner?'

'No, damn you, I am in charge of this investigation. And you have no need of my name, for you, too, are leaving this hearing.'

Shakespeare turned to the clerk. 'What is your master's name? I need it, for it will be reported to Sir Francis Walsingham, as will yours. The Privy Council will hear how you have interfered in the inquiries of an officer engaged on Queen's business.'

The clerk looked to his master for guidance. Suddenly, the coroner hammered his fist on the table, making his Bible and several papers jump. 'Rot in hell, Shakespeare. My name is Bagot. Henry Bagot. Stay if you must with your necromancer. Stand by the wall and be silent, for this is a solemn proceeding and I will brook no interruption.'

Shakespeare stayed at the hearing for one reason alone: so that the coroner should know that his corrupt justice was noted, and that it would be reported.

'You mentioned a broken branch not three feet from the body, Mr Nason,' the coroner said.

'That is so, sir. It was a main lower branch of an oak.'

'Would it have been high enough to suspend him? Is it possible that the dead man hanged himself from that branch and that it broke away from his weight after he had died?'

'I cannot deny that is a possibility.'

'And this thing.' He held up the rosary, which had been restrung. 'This thing of papist superstition could have borne his weight and choked him to death?'

Nason seemed to accept the suggestion, but he was clearly uneasy. No one in the taproom dared gainsay him or the coroner, however. Except Shakespeare, who snorted with scorn. The coroner gazed at him with undisguised contempt. 'Be careful, Mr Shakespeare, lest you wish a week in the cells.'

The verdict was always a foregone conclusion. Directed by Bagot, the jury decided unanimously that the dead man must have taken his own life. Somehow, Benedict Angel must have tangled his rosary on a low branch and choked himself to death. It was so implausible as to be laughable. Even a playwright would not have devised such a plot.

'God has seen fit to strike down the popish traitor,' the coroner concluded. 'So die all the Queen's enemies. Bury him in unhallowed ground.' He swept up his papers and Bible and, with his clerk in his wake, tottered from the alehouse on his dainty legs.

Shakespeare watched him go. The coroner and his clerk kept their eyes firmly ahead, refusing to meet his judgemental gaze.

The jury also averted their eyes. They knew they had colluded in a scandalous episode and were ashamed.

'Come, Mr Peace,' Shakespeare said at last. 'Brave the rain and walk with me to the Angel farmhouse. I would speak with Florence and I would like you there, for I would be grateful to have your opinion on the matter of the young woman's health. Her mother says she is afflicted by the falling sickness.'

*

The countryside was rich and lush in this part of England, and the rain only served to make it seem greener. Since leaving this place, it had become in Shakespeare's imaginings a heaven on earth, full of wildflowers and the scents of summer. Now it seemed tainted and full of foreboding, as though a cloud shaded the land.

'I would value your thoughts, Mr Peace, on what is happening here in Stratford. Am I alone in thinking we are caught up in lunar madness? Everywhere is rage and hostility. No one is safe.'

Peace shook his head. 'No, you are not alone. But are you surprised, Mr Shakespeare? In the space of half a century, this realm has supplanted one religion with another. How can that be achieved without conflict? There are too many interests at stake, and it seems this county has more resistance to change than most.'

'And your own religion, Mr Peace? Where do you stand?'

Peace threw Shakespeare a puzzled smile. 'Do you really wish to ask me that?'

No, thought Shakespeare, that would be unfair. He rather suspected that Mr Peace was without religion. Such a man would be seen as heretic by Catholic and Protestant alike and condemned by both. 'Forgive me, Mr Peace. Your religion is none of my concern.' Suddenly it came to him, like a ray of sun through a break in the clouds. This letter within his doublet, burning his body: there might be a way of dealing with it after all.

For the past two hours he had been wrestling with his conscience. His duty to his sovereign and his country told him that he must despatch the letter to Walsingham so that Mr Phelippes could attempt to decipher it. People did not bother to encrypt letters unless they had something to hide. It would be treason to withhold such a letter.

And yet . . .

And yet he knew Walsingham well enough by now. He would insist on knowing the precise manner in which the letter was discovered. How could Will and Anne be protected from the storm that would then break? The weak link would always be Florence Angel. There was every chance that she would be apprehended in the near future. A seasoned questioner would easily break the resolve of someone so fragile and vulnerable. Shakespeare gripped Joshua Peace's arm and pulled him beneath the canopy of a huge oak tree, out of the rain.

'What is it, Mr Shakespeare?'

Shakespeare looked at the young man with keen, inquiring eyes. One question pounded in his brain like rolling thunder: could he place his faith in this man? His intuition told him that he had never met a more trustworthy person in his life. But that ran counter to all that Walsingham had taught him.

'Mr Peace, I want to trust you.'

'Is that wise?'

'No. No, it is not wise.' Shakespeare glanced up into the leaves as though guidance would come dripping with the rain. As he did so, he had a bleak vision of himself accoutred like a pursuivant, hammering down doors in the name of the Queen. Was he *really* suited to this world of secrets and suspicion?

'And yet I *am* a man of honour.'

'Yes, Mr Peace, I truly believe you are.' His hand went to his chest as though feeling for his pulse. The letter was secreted just below his heart.

There was silence between them for a few moments.

Sometimes in life, a man must strike out into the dark and trust his judgement, otherwise nothing would ever get done. Just as the great explorers of the oceans set to sea with no certain idea of where they are going and even less hope of returning home safely, so he must broach this subject now, or never. Shakespeare put his hand into his doublet and pulled the letter halfway out so that Peace caught a glimpse of it, then thrust it back into the warm pocket between his shirt and flesh.

'Mr Peace, that paper is a letter. It could take innocent people – *good* people – to their grave.'

'Then place it on a fire.'

'I cannot. It is encrypted and I need to discover its contents. The only way to do that is to give it to my master, Sir Francis Walsingham, who has men skilled in the breaking of codes. But if I do so, he will rightly demand to know where I came by it.'

Peace understood it all, in an instant. 'Then tell him that I found it within the clothing of Benedict Angel. I will confirm it.'

'You would do that for me?'

The Searcher of the Dead shrugged. 'Father Angel is beyond pain. Better taint *him* than the living.'

'Thank you, Mr Peace. You have promised more than I could have asked.'

'It is my pleasure, Mr Shakespeare.'

From a distance of a hundred yards, Harry Slide strained to see what Shakespeare and Peace were doing. He could hear nothing and see little enough through the grey drizzle, and yet he gained an impression that something of importance had passed between the two men. And then he saw them shaking hands, like two market traders doing a deal for the sale of cattle.

Slide rubbed his own soft hands together with a smile. This was like fishing with human bait.

Chapter 24

Florence Angel and her mother were doing their best to clear up the chaos of their home. They looked up from their work without a word when the two visitors entered.

Shakespeare smiled at the widow in greeting. 'Good morrow, Aunt Audrey.'

'John,' she said, her voice flat.

'And you, Florence.'

'Why are you here, John?'

'I am investigating your brother's death, for which I offer condolences.' He hesitated. 'How are you, Florence? I know that all has not been well with you.'

'I mean what brings you to Stratford? I had believed you were gone from here into the service of the heretics. Should you not be there, writhing in the pit of snakes?'

Shakespeare was astonished. Was this really the Florence Angel considered best friend by Anne Hathaway? He looked at her expressionless face, then to her mother, who seemed pained.

Suddenly, Florence seemed to soften. 'Forgive me, John. I have not yet welcomed you to our home.' She swept her arm around the debris of the hall. 'Perhaps you can understand why I do not feel hospitable.'

'Yes, I understand your anguish. But I am not your enemy.'

'No?'

'No.'

'But nor are you my friend. Tell me, do you bring word from the inquest?'

'A verdict of death by his own hand was returned. The jury only did what they were directed to do. I fear they had no say in the matter.'

'So justice is dead, along with my brother.'

Shakespeare could not disagree with her, so he merely shrugged. He was studying her demeanour, wondering what Joshua Peace might see there. She was not as plump as he recalled. And she no longer wore her golden hair loose, but tied up beneath a close-fitting pynner, which made her look a little severe. Her eyes were bright, but distant. She was faded. No, more than that . . . she was *spectral.* As though she were already gone beyond this world. Only her sharp words and her rich crimson lips retained her link with the temporal. Around her neck she wore a rosary that looked exactly like the one tied around her brother's neck.

'I will investigate this, Florence, and I pledge that I will do all in my power to bring the murderer to court. It will help me if you would talk with me. When did you last see Benedict?'

'Save your breath, John. I am not interested in your questions.'

'You must have suspicions. Tell me this at least: who do you believe killed him?'

'This heretical regime. Oh, I had quite forgot – that is *you.*' She had reverted to the accusatory tone and it came as a jolt.

'I understand your anger and grief. I would prefer to come to you when you have had time to bury your brother and mourn, but I do not have the leisure of waiting.'

'Perhaps you should talk to him, Florence,' her mother cajoled. 'I do believe he is trying to assist us.'

'No. He *says* he is our friend, but I know he is not. Benedict came to me last night in my sleep and told me you are my enemy and were never his friend. You come in a good man's guise, but you are not with us, John Shakespeare, and so you are against us.'

Shakespeare was at a loss for words.

Joshua Peace stepped forward from the shadows. 'Miss Angel, you do not know me. I am the Searcher of the Dead for these parts and I was called in to examine your brother's body. Like Mr Shakespeare here, I know that he was the victim of a violent attack and that the verdict of the inquest jury was a travesty. I know, too, that Mr Shakespeare is your only hope of finding justice. I would beg you to listen to your mother and answer his questions.'

For a few moments, she appeared to be wavering. There was something wholly innocent about Joshua Peace that was difficult to resist. 'Mother told me of you.'

'Help us, I entreat you.'

'No. I cannot go against my brother. He sits now, all pale and shining, with Holy Mary. I thank you for your help, Mr Peace, but I must ask you and John Shakespeare to go now, and not disturb us again.'

Shakespeare could barely contain his frustration. He turned once more to her mother. 'Aunt Audrey, for one final time, I entreat you: make your daughter see sense and cooperate with me, to your advantage and mine.'

'She is almost twenty-six years of age, Mr Shakespeare. She will not be influenced by me.'

Joshua Peace put his hand on Shakespeare's shoulder. 'Come, sir, there is nothing more for us here.'

'Well met, Mr Shakespeare!'

Shakespeare swivelled in surprise, his sword halfway out of its scabbard.

'No need for your sword, sir. We work for the same man and have the same ends.'

Shakespeare relaxed. 'Mr Slide. I heard you had been looking for me. What are you doing here in Stratford?'

'Why, the same as you. Hunting traitors, earning a dishonest crust from the silver platter of Mr Secretary.'

Shakespeare had just taken his leave of Joshua Peace on the outskirts of Shottery and was on his way back to Hewlands Farm. His last hope of learning anything from Florence Angel was to enlist the aid of Anne Hathaway. 'You have no notion why I am here, Mr Slide, and you know it.'

'Oh, I know well enough. You wish to find a one-armed Frenchman and a Scotsman named Buchan Ord, and now you have complicated matters by stumbling into murder and conspiracy.'

'Conspiracy?'

'This town is febrile with plotting. I believe you need my assistance, sir.'

'Why would you expect me to trust you, Slide? You followed me covertly in Sheffield, and then you dodged away like a common criminal.'

'Mr Shakespeare, I assure you, I am a most *un*common criminal. And I can prove my worth to you this very instant, by bringing you intelligence that will both delight and astonish you.'

Shakespeare studied Harry Slide. As in Sheffield, he was attired in a yellow satin doublet that would not have looked out of place at Elizabeth's court. 'I should take you by the neck and drag you to the town gaol, Slide. I am certain a dozen lashes at the whipping post would do you good.'

'Do you not wish to know my intelligence?'

'Very well. Tell me. If it disappoints me, you will have the whipping.'

'Then prepare to be astounded, sir, for I bring you most remarkable news: your little friend has arrived in Stratford this very day.'

'What little friend? Do not speak in riddles.'

'The lame one. He rode in not two hours since.'

'Boltfoot Cooper?'

'Yes, indeed, I am certain that is the name. He arms himself like one of Drake's pirates and grunts where better favoured men might utter a word or two.'

Shakespeare drew his dagger. Slide put up his hands defensively. 'I beg of you, is this not good intelligence? Worth a groat of anyone's money, I would say.'

'You will not insult any man of mine. Where is he?'

'He is at the White Lion, and nor is he alone, which I am sure is even more remarkable and welcome news for you.'

'Slide, you risk wearing out my patience utterly.'

'He is with Kat Whetstone. Surely you remember her? Few men do forget her once they have seen her.'

'She is here with Boltfoot? What manner of nonsense is this?'

'The very finest sort of nonsense: true nonsense.'

Shakespeare grasped Slide by the nape of his neck and pulled him. 'Come with me, we will go to them.'

'Mr Shakespeare, unhand me. I have come to you of my own free will to offer intelligence, with no expectation of reward, though one always hopes. You do not need to treat me with brute force.'

It was true, of course. Shakespeare released his grip.

Slide rubbed his neck. 'Thank you, Mr Shakespeare. But before I go, a word of warning for you, sir. There is one Hungate hereabouts. Ruby Hungate.'

'I have met him. I need no word of warning.'

'And therefore you must know his strange tale.'

'What tale?'

'The stuff of legend, Mr Shakespeare. It is said he came from Surrey and was orphaned, that he lived in the woods alone, honing his skills as huntsman and archer. When Elizabeth was staying at nearby Loseley Park, there was a great fair with tumblers and minstrels, fighting and horse races. All the great courtiers were there, including Robert Dudley, the Earl of Leicester. As was often his habit, he offered a purse of five pounds for the finest archer in the region.

'Ruby Hungate heard about it one day when he came from the forest to take rabbits to market. He was thirteen years of age, but had not yet grown to manly size and could well have passed for a boy two or three years younger. When he asked to try for the archery prize, the arbiter refused. "You're not even as tall as a longbow and you certainly couldn't pull one. Go watch the clowns and jesters." "No," Hungate said. "I will shoot my arrows. I'm as good as any man." Something in Hungate's eyes must have unnerved the arbiter, for he relented. I have seen Hungate's cold eyes myself and I know why this might have been. Have you seen his eyes, Mr Shakespeare?'

Yes, he had seen them. 'This tale – this *faerie* tale – how long does it take, Slide?'

'A minute or two of your time. "Go on, boy," the arbiter said. "Get in line and see if you can shoot an arrow. Good fortune be with you, because you'll need it. And serve you right if you make yourself a laughing stock." Hungate's arrows flew true. Everyone said he had the strength of a young bear, the eye of a falcon and the steadiness of a great cat. He beat the finest archers in Surrey and more from even further afield and won the five-pound prize. But more than that, he won the interest of the Earl of Leicester, who soon learnt of his prowess.'

Shakespeare laughed. 'I have heard this tale before. It is the story of Robin Hood.'

'Not so. This is the history of Ruby Hungate. He was summoned to the earl's presence. The boy did not bow nor show fear. "Are you not scared of me, boy?" the earl demanded. "No. And I am not a boy, for I say fuck, cunny and dog turd, and will use those words to any man who speaks to me so." "You have a coarse tongue ... boy. What *are* you scared of?" "Nothing," Hungate replied.'

Despite himself, Shakespeare was enthralled by the story.

'And this is the way they spoke: "You will address me as *my lord* – or *sir*," quoth my lord of Leicester. "Have you killed?" Young Hungate hesitated but a second. "Foxes, birds ..." "Deer?" "That would be poaching, and against the law." "A man?" "I have killed animals." "There are those who say man is an animal." To which Hungate gave no reply. "Well?" "I had not realised it was a question, *sir*." And he laced the word "sir" with heavy disdain. The earl then laughed. "What is your name ... *boy*?" "Hungate. Ruby Hungate." "Then you shall have a ruby as an extra prize. And you shall join my household and learn all the soldierly arts. And you will learn to call me sir. You have a cold, killing eye." For the first and last time, Hungate bowed. "Thank you, *sir*."'

'And how do you know this fine story, Mr Slide?'

'It is a tale the earl himself likes to tell – to like-minded people. It is perhaps embellished, but I have heard it more than once and it is the same in essence. Anyway, Hungate was accorded a special place in the earl's retinue, under the tutelage of his personal bodyguard. For the next three years he was educated in the skills of shooting, bowmanship, fencing and hand-to-hand fighting. He was told that the earl wished him to be trained to such a degree that one day he, too, could aspire to be his personal bodyguard. Later, when his loyalty was beyond doubt, he was sent to Rome and Venice to finish his education. He became versed in the subtle ways of belladonna, hemlock, arsenic, nux vomica and the Destroying Angel mushroom from an old alchemist who, it is said, boasted that his father and grandfather had prepared venoms for both the Borgias and other great families, so they might kill each other. He learnt the different techniques of strangulation and throat-slitting. He was taught how to kill without a sound and without leaving a trace of evidence. But still Hungate had not been asked to kill. On his return from Venice, he was summoned once more to the earl. "If I had an enemy who wished me harm, Mr Hungate, what would you do?" "Whatever you asked of me." "Would you harm this man?" "If you wished." "Even to the point of death?" "Yes, I would kill him." "What if my enemy was a woman?" "When I shoot dead a goose, I do not ask its sex." "And what would you expect in return for this service?" "A harlequin doublet, my lord, to show that I am your jester. And a ruby for my ear."' Slide smiled as he waited for a reaction to his story.

Shakespeare said nothing. Was there any truth in this? It had the symmetry of an old wives' tale or a myth of the ancients. And yet . . .

'And so I bid you good day.' Slide bowed low, with a sweep of his arm, then sprinted like a hare for the cover of the woods. Shakespeare found himself laughing at the man's temerity, but let him go. He had other, more important matters to deal with than to chase after the slippery Mr Slide.

At the White Lion, he found Boltfoot about to depart in search of him. Shakespeare shook his assistant by the hand. 'I am mighty pleased to see you. Does this mean you have news of the missing Buchan Ord?'

'I believe so, master. I trust so.'

'Have you found him? Is he apprehended?'

'No. I am told he is here, in the shire of Warwick. There is a meeting place . . .'

Shakespeare's eyes narrowed. 'A meeting place. Where? When? With whom?'

'With the Frenchie. They are to meet here. Somewhere. That is what I was told by Kat.'

'Continue, Boltfoot. Tell me everything. I have heard some fanciful talk that Miss Whetstone has accompanied you here. Put my mind at ease if you please.'

Boltfoot shifted uneasily. 'Aye, it is true enough. I brought her here with me. She made me bring her. I had discovered that Mr Ord was betrothed to her, but that he had cast her off. Before he disappeared, she had overheard him telling the Frenchman to meet him at a secret place. As I was later to learn, the appointed place for their meeting is in this county.'

Shakespeare wondered if the whole world was not going mad. What manner of fool would ride a hundred miles through England in the company of a strange – if beautiful – young woman? 'Boltfoot, you will have to explain this to me more clearly. How did she *make* you ride with her? Did she hold a pistol to your head?'

'I did not want to bring her and did all I could to dissuade her, for I feared you would be greatly displeased. But she would not tell me where Mr Ord had gone unless I pledged to accompany her. What was I to do, master? I was charged by you with discovering the whereabouts of the Scotsman, and Kat offered me a way.'

'And has she told you about this proposed meeting place?'

'Not precisely, only that it is in this town or close by. She refused to tell me more. When we arrived, I demanded the information of her, but she said she would reveal all to you.'

'Where is she?'

'She has taken a chamber here in this inn. She must be there now.'

Shakespeare tried to soften the hardness evident in his tone and face. Boltfoot had done what he believed to be correct. And who could tell, perhaps it would turn out that way. 'Thank you, Boltfoot, you have done well.'

'It was not easy, master. I have used up all the coin you left me, and I have discovered that Kat Whetstone has a wayward spirit.'

Shakespeare raised an eyebrow. 'Boltfoot?' He shook his head. 'Never mind, you can tell me in due course. I must go to her now. If she can reveal to me where Buchan Ord is, then all our problems may be solved. And, Boltfoot, stay here and get some rest. I will have a task for you this night.'

'Yes, master.'

Kat Whetstone was not in her chamber, but the innkeeper told Shakespeare where she had gone. 'You'll find her in the meadows by the river at Tiddington Lane. She asked me for somewhere that she might wash away the mud and grime of her travels. I gave her towels and soap.'

Shakespeare thanked him and walked out. The rain had ceased, but the day was still grey and cool. He crossed the bridge and strode as briskly as he could along the churned-up riverside path, past the osier beds, catching his hose and netherstocks on brambles and thistles. It was a path he knew well from his childhood, where his father brought him to learn angling and where he, later, brought Will for the same purpose. He recalled the day they landed a ten-pound pike and Will almost lost a finger in its vicious jaws.

A quarter of a mile on, there was still no sign of her. He wondered whether she had misunderstood the innkeeper's directions. The path entered thick woodland, with trees that overhung the water's edge. A little way on, he heard splashing and smiled to himself. The thought of her kneeling at the water's edge, washing her face, perhaps scrubbing at her riding habit, was enough to entice any man.

But she wasn't kneeling at the water's edge. She was in the water, and she was clearly wearing little or nothing, for Shakespeare spotted a pile of women's garments on a dry patch of grass beneath the trees. And he could see that her shoulders were bare. She was swimming slowly against the gentle flow, so that she seemed almost motionless.

She was facing upriver, away from him. He turned away and prepared to walk back to the inn. He would talk with her on her return.

'Mr Shakespeare, is that you?'

He stopped, but he did not look around.

'Forgive me, Miss Whetstone. I did not expect to find you unrobed. You realise there is more than a little river traffic at this time of year . . .'

'I am sure there is nothing about me that they have not seen before. And, Mr Shakespeare, I would consider it mannerly if you were to turn around, for I do not like talking to your back. Fear not, I am not about to die of shame if you should see my shoulders.'

Slowly, he turned. She was in the centre of the stream, with only her head above water. Beneath the surface, he could not fail to see the motion of her breasts, light and swaying in the clear, green waters, and he could imagine her arms and legs moving in the way swimmers do when they wish to stay in the same place.

'Mr Cooper tells me that you have important information for me.'

'Does he? Oh, he is a strange man your Boltfoot Cooper, but a sound travelling companion. I always felt delightfully safe with him.'

She sounded a little out of breath from the effort of paddling her arms and legs. 'And the information, Miss Whetstone?'

'You are to call me Kat. Do you not remember?' Her hair was dripping wet about her face. Her right arm rose from the river, slender and pale gold, and she ran her fingers through the tresses.

'Indeed I do, Kat.' He coughed awkwardly. 'I think it best if I leave you to your ablution now and return to the White Lion, where we can discuss these matters a little more easily.'

'And I shall call you John, for we are practically wed now that you have promised to show me the lion-cats in the Tower.'

Shakespeare closed his eyes and took a deep breath. He had almost managed to forget about the lions in the Tower.

'How long did you say their teeth were? Four inches? Five inches? No, I do believe it was six. It makes me tremble with terror just to think of them.'

He bowed awkwardly. 'I shall see you in two hours' time, in the hall at the inn.'

'You cannot leave me here, John. I had thought this place would offer me some privacy. But if you have found me, so may others. And what of the wherries bringing the harvest to market? You must look after me and bring my towels and underthings to the water's edge, that I may not be espied in my naked shame.'

As she spoke, she struck out for the river bank and within a few seconds was stepping from the water, uncovered and showing very little in the way of shame.

Chapter 25

SHAKESPEARE STOOD AND looked at her because he could not take his eyes away. He knew there was nothing perfect under the heavens, for only God was immaculate, but Kat Whetstone's body came very close.

'My towels, John, if you please.' She smiled with too much knowing and made no attempt to cover herself with her hands, nor move towards her garments. She was no more than five feet from him.

Suddenly, he scurried for the clothes and picked up two large linen towels, which he handed to her at arm's length, looking away.

She wrapped one of the towels around her waist, and then used the other to dry herself. 'For a moment, John, it seemed you had quite forgot yourself.'

'My apologies. I should not have stared so.'

'Did you not like what you saw?'

'I shall go now.'

'Will you not accompany me back to the inn? I would feel much safer with you. What if someone were to chance upon me in these woods?'

'Two hours' time. In the main hall.' With an immense effort of will, he began walking back along the path through the meadows to the town. He had a curious feeling that she was laughing at him, behind his back.

Leloup's purse was heavy with gold sovereigns. He tied it closely inside his doublet, then walked down to the hall of the coaching inn. He raised his proud wolf's nose in greeting to the innkeeper, and then to his visitor. He clasped him by the shoulder and ushered him away from the innkeeper and his staff.

'Mr Ord, I received your letter. This is the day, is it not?'

'Indeed, Monsieur Leloup.'

'Then I am ready.'

'And the gold?'

'The gold, too. Safely stowed. But more importantly, are our *friends* ready?'

'I believe so.'

'But that is for me to decide, yes?'

'Indeed, Monsieur Leloup.'

'Then take me to them without delay. The sooner all is organised and we have freed Mary, the safer she will be.'

At the White Lion, Shakespeare took quill and paper and wrote a careful letter to Sir Francis Walsingham giving news of the death of Benedict Angel and explaining the enclosed document.

Mr Angel was found murdered, as I thought, a judgement that was readily agreed by the Searcher of the Dead, Mr Peace. The coroner and jury disputed this finding and a verdict was returned that the deceased took his own life by hanging or self-strangulation. I shall, however, continue to investigate the death for I fear he was part of some disturbing activity in this county, which is connected in some way to recent events at Sheffield. This is reinforced by the letter herewith enclosed, which was found by Mr Peace among the dead man's apparel. By its hand, seal and mark, this missive appears to be from the Scots Queen. The cipher, however, is beyond my wit, so therefore I commend it to you for the attention of Mr Phelippes.

Shakespeare sealed his letter with the cipher letter enclosed and handed it to the innkeeper, whom he trusted of old, to be sent to Oatlands by special courier.

'My boy will take it, Mr Shakespeare. He is the best there is.'

'He will have a mark on departure and another on his return. He is to give it to no one but Walsingham or his steward, Mr Whey.'

'I understand, sir.'

'Then have him ride at speed.'

In the early evening, Shakespeare woke Boltfoot. Like any sailor roused for his watch, he was instantly alert.

'I know you are still fatigued, as am I, but I would have you follow after me. We must walk through the town, a little way north to a village. Walk a good distance behind me so that no one can tell that we are known to each other. Be inconspicuous. Do you understand?'

Boltfoot grunted.

Shakespeare clapped him on the shoulder. 'This is important. You are to keep watch on a house. In that house is a young woman named Florence Angel and her mother, Audrey Angel. You will hide yourself in the spinney to the north of the house. After I have gone, you will stay there and observe everything that happens. If the younger of the two women goes out, you will follow her, unseen. I want to know exactly where she goes and I want a description of whoever she sees. You will then report back to me. Is that clear?'

'Yes, master. How long shall I watch her?'

'Until dawn. And you will leave your cutlass and caliver here, otherwise I think you will attract too much attention as you walk through town.'

Walking at an easy pace, Shakespeare once again traversed the streets of Stratford towards the village of Shottery, ensuring that Boltfoot could keep within distance.

When he arrived, Audrey Angel came to the door.

'I would speak with Florence, Aunt. I must give her one more chance to help me. You must persuade her of the danger she faces if she will not cooperate.'

'She is not here, John.'

'Where is she?'

The widow wiped her eye. 'If I knew, I swear I would tell you – for I am afraid for her also.' She had clearly been weeping. 'This is all my fault. After their father died, I brought them up in the old faith. It would have been so much easier to conform. But how could I betray him, having sworn to him that I would raise them in the Roman Church?'

'You have no need to explain your religion to me, Aunt.' Shakespeare reached out and touched her shoulder. 'I seek out traitors, not Catholics. But I beg you, be wary, for there are many who would spill the blood of you all. Now tell me, how long has Florence been gone?'

'An hour, no more.'

'Did she walk out on her own, or did someone come for her?'

'No, she went alone. She is going to die, John, I am certain of it. She is bent on her own destruction, and there is nothing I can do to save her.'

*

Shakespeare found Boltfoot in the woods. 'All has changed,' he said shortly. 'There is another house I want you to watch. In it, there is a woman named Anne Hathaway. As before, you will observe her carefully. And likewise, if she goes out, you will follow her. If she meets another young woman – a woman of slightly broader girth with golden hair – you will tell me precisely where they are. Do not disturb them or reveal your presence to them in any way. Can you do that? Will you remember the route?'

'Yes, master.' Boltfoot nodded without enthusiasm.

'I will go into this house and bring Anne Hathaway to the door so that you will know what she looks like, for there are others within.'

Shakespeare left his assistant once again in an area of woodland, near enough to see the door, and walked up to Hewlands Farm. There were more ways than one to accomplish his ends. If Florence was not there to be followed, there was someone else who might lead him to her.

As he approached the door, he felt deceitful and dishonest. This was what he had feared at Oatlands when Mr Secretary had given him this task: here he was, spying on his own. And yet what was he to do? Anne was already up to her delicate neck in the mire. So was his brother. They needed protection and he was the only one to give it. By whatever means available – even by spying on them.

Anne was serving food to the younger children in the hall. She invited him to sit down with them and eat.

'A beaker of ale will serve me well enough, Anne. Where is Will? Is he not with you?'

'He has been tutoring Alderman Whateley's young children. We will need the money soon enough.' Her hand went to her belly.

'Well, it was *you* I wished to talk with. Florence has gone again. Her mother is distraught and fears she will come to harm.'

'I wish I were surprised.'

'Do you know where she is?'

'No, John.' She looked at him askance.

'I ask, of course, because no one is closer to her. Because she entrusted that letter to you.' He watched Anne's face closely, noted the strain in her wide eyes and taut forehead. He still could not fathom why she had agreed to hold the Mary of Scots letter for Florence. 'I want to enlist your aid. Come outside, away from the earshot of the little ones.' He picked up his cup of ale and they went out into the damp air and stood by the bread oven. Chickens and geese scattered across the muddy yard. A cock crowed incessantly. Ahead of them were the barns and byres and sties. To their right the fields and the woods. Shakespeare stared hard into the fern and brambles but could not spot Boltfoot. He made sure Anne was in a position just beyond the door where she would be clearly visible to him.

'What can I do to help, John?'

'You must have heard what happened at the inquest. It was a grotesque injustice, but Florence refused to help me. I am certain she knows more than she will reveal, but she will not talk to me. She said Benedict had come to her in her sleep and that he had said I was not to be trusted.'

'And is that not true? I had thought you boys felt nothing but scorn for him in your younger days.'

'There is a world of difference between disliking someone and wishing them harm. He was fervent in his faith and stood apart from us. But that is all long gone. I am telling you no secrets when I say that the Privy Council considered him a traitor. That, too, need no longer concern us. Whatever he did in his life is now between him and God.'

'Then, John, what do you want from Florence?'

'A solution to a murder.' *But also, I desire to know the source of the Mary Stuart letter, and I want to discover those with whom Benedict was involved.* But that was not what he said. 'I desire justice for her brother in this world. Florence does not – or will not – understand that. I also want to protect her. Her innocence does not come untainted. I cannot help wondering whether she has any idea what is involved here. Does she know that I could have her arrested for hard questioning on the suspicion that she is withholding evidence?'

'But you will not do that.'

'No, I will not. But there are others who might. My lord of Leicester has it in mind to clear the county of papists, as does his creature Sir Thomas Lucy. I fear the work of the pursuivants has barely begun. And so I would ask *you* to make inquiries on my behalf. She trusts you, Anne. You are perhaps the only person she trusts apart from her mother. Find out where she went when she disappeared. And where is she now? With whom is she involved? This letter – this missive from the Queen of Scots – tells us that she is delving into dangerous and murky waters. Find out who she believes killed her brother – and the motive. I know she is your friend, but Anne, I must tell you . . . I have suspicions. I am not sure I trust her. Help me on this.'

Anne hesitated. She had her own ideas but was not at all certain she dared to share them with John Shakespeare. She had always been wary of him, even when they were young. It was as though he had authority over them. Perhaps that was why she had never seen him as a possible swain. She sighed and said what she could in safety. 'Florence has changed. She is not the person she once was. She hears voices and sees ghosts. I worry about her constantly. That is why I agreed to help her with the letter. We must protect her from herself, or I fear she will do something rash.'

'For the sake of common justice, we cannot allow a murder to pass unremarked.'

'Very well, I will do what I can. But it may be that I end up losing her friendship.'

'Thank you. Better to save a life than a friendship.'

'Is this the place, Mr Ord?'

It was early evening. They had come through the gatehouse, which was unmanned, and were riding up the long driveway to Arden Lodge.

'This is the place, Monsieur Leloup.'

Leloup reined in his horse and gazed towards the house. 'It is fair. *Très belle*. Go through it with me. Who is in there now?'

'This is Mr Arden's home. He is the prime mover, a man driven to do this holy work by the sacrilege he has witnessed this past quarter of a century. Also here you will find his wife Mary and daughter Margaret. They are devout and loyal Catholics, who will travel with Queen Mary as her companion ladies as she passes through England to the southern coast. Arden and the gardener, Hugh Hall, who is in reality a seminary priest, will both be party to the escape at Sheffield, along with myself and Miss Florence Angel, whose brother was most recently murdered. She may be but a woman, but I would say there is no man more steadfast among all the seminaries of France and Italy. Also here is Mr Somerville, Arden's son-in-law. They are a most remarkable and committed band. You will find none finer in all of England.'

'And you are certain none of them is a spy? They are all devoted to our cause?'

'I am certain.' The soft Scottish voice was reassuring for he could see the doubt in the Frenchman's eyes. 'Arden, Somerville, Hall and Florence Angel are all willing to die in the cause of the Holy Father and the Catholic League, as am I.'

'So five of you will effect her freedom in the manner we have already discussed? And Arden's wife and mother will play their part when Mary is safe?'

'No, there will be four of us at Sheffield. Somerville has a separate mission. He is charged with travelling to court to kill the usurper.'

Leloup looked at his companion in disbelief. 'And he can do that alone?'

'He has a confederate within the royal court and is certain there is a way. I have no reason to doubt Mr Somerville. But you must hold your nose, monsieur, for he is a difficult man, a man on fire. Such a man as we require.'

'You make him sound a little mad.'

'Some might think him so. But he is God's instrument, and he will not waver. If he fails in his mission, it will not detract from our other plans. Anyway, others will come after Mr Somerville. All we need is for one assassin to get through. If not this week or month, then the next . . .'

'Indeed. And so,' Leloup said slowly, 'in the absence of Mr Somerville, we are left with four of you to break Mary from her cold prison. Is that sufficient?'

'If all goes well with the northern lords, then that will be more than enough. All we need now is your authority – and the return of the ring to Mary. For if she hesitates, all will be lost.'

'Tell me a little more of their characters, Mr Ord. I must be wholly convinced.'

'I understand. Mr Arden is an English country gentleman. Like so many of his ilk, he feels betrayed by the changes he sees. Where once he took pride of place in the Church of this county, worshipping in the true faith, now he feels himself cast away by the new order. These ideas from the Germanies, from Switzerland, from the Low Countries all seem alien to him. He is full of rage.'

'And the priest, Hall?'

'A timid man, ordained in France and obedient to God. He would rather tend his garden, but when called on, he will not fail. And then there is the woman . . .'

'Florence Angel. I met her brother in Paris. A most zealous priest, ripe for martyrdom. Do we know who killed him?'

'The pursuivants. I am sure they committed this cruel and bestial crime. Sir Thomas Lucy's men have been ranging wide in their hunt for priests. They are Godless men. Cold murder is a day's merriment to them. Father Benedict's death has only stiffened his sister's resolve. You will find her a most inspiring woman, for she has visions and communes with the Maid of Orleans.'

Leloup raised an eyebrow. 'You paint a curious picture, Mr Ord. They seem a most singular band. Tell me true, for much is at stake: do you trust them?'

His companion bowed low in the saddle. 'I do, *monsieur le docteur*. Truly, I do.'

At Hewlands Farm, Anne Hathaway watched her future brother-in-law depart with fear in her heart. His reaction to the letter signed by Mary, Queen of Scots had scared her more than he could know, more even than the visit of the pursuivants. It was not the letter that terrified her so; it was the other document, the one she had not dared confess to him, the one she would now have to reveal to Will. She would need his help in retrieving it. Please God, they could retrieve it.

The problem would always be Florence. John had identified that accurately enough. She was the broken link in the chain.

In the heat of summer, when love disturbed the mind and turned sane men and women mad, Florence's quirks had seemed charming. She was more faerie than angel, a soaring spirit not quite of this world. And then her brother had appeared, and there was excitement and secrecy in this quiet backwater. Why should a young man be a fugitive for his religion? Why should every man and woman not be allowed to worship as he or she pleased? Anne and Will were agreed on that. And though they were not convinced by Father Benedict's homilies, they enjoyed all the furtiveness their clandestine meetings entailed. Nor were they the only ones in these parts who had succumbed to his holy aura. When attending his masses, they felt they were part of some dangerous underground. But that was then, and this was now. Everything had changed. The long hot summer of sacred passion and carnal desire had become an autumn of brutal reality and murder.

And if only that was the sum of it. But there was more. There was the secret document, the so-called Spiritual Testament.

Anne recalled with horror and shame the mad night she had signed the Testament. She knew now it was a death warrant, a pathway to martyrdom for a cause in which she did not believe. Why, in the name of all that was holy, had she put her name to such a thing?

For a year now it had become a treasonable offence to assist a Catholic priest in his mission and yet she had signed a document stating that she had entrusted her soul to the Catholic faith. Why had she done it? The truth was she did not know whether she was Catholic or Protestant. What was the difference between them? Both worshipped one God, both believed He sent His only son Jesus Christ into the world to save mankind, and both adhered to the teachings of the same scriptures. Protestant or Catholic? Two names for the same religion with but minor differences.

There had been midsummer madness that night. In other places, maidens gave away their virginity, sober men became drunk and wise men spoke like fools. But at Arden Lodge, there had been ecstasy of the spirit. All who were there – and there were many – signed the documents that promised their eternal soul to the Church of Rome and to God. If only Will had been there to stop her. If only she had never agreed to go with Florence.

Where was the fateful six-page document now? Why had they not allowed her to keep possession of it? The very thought of it made her sick inside, for it had been used against her already – and would be used against her again. And again.

Her carefree days were done. A child was on its way, and so no more could she dabble in such matters. Somehow, she had to extricate herself, and quickly; for the child's sake as much as hers. Somehow she had to find the document – this accursed Spiritual Testament – and destroy it.

Against his wishes, Shakespeare sat down to supper in the White Lion. He had wanted Kat Whetstone to tell him everything she knew there and then, but she had other plans.

'I have travelled a hundred miles to bring you this information, Mr Shakespeare. I desire nothing more than to savour it and make merry with you for just this one evening. For I know you will cast me off as soon as I have told you what you wish to know, just as Buchan cast me off. It is the way of you men.'

The door of the inn clattered open, letting in a blast of chill air. Shakespeare and Kat both turned to see who was coming in. Badger Rench was there, broad and tall. He slammed the door shut and came over to them.

'Well, well, what have we here?' He stood above them, swaying slightly.

'Get you gone, Rench, you are not welcome.'

He ignored Shakespeare. Instead, he pulled up a stool and sat at the side of their small table. He held out his hand to Kat

Whetstone. 'Thomas Rench,' he said. 'You must call me Badger, for the whole world does so.'

Kat did not take his hand. 'Mr Shakespeare said you were not welcome here, Mr Rench.'

Darkness clouded his eyes, and he grabbed her small hand and put it roughly to his lips. He held it away from him, his grip still tight, then sniffed the air. 'Smells like a bitch hound's arse.' He dropped the hand.

Shakespeare stood up and drew his dagger. 'We both asked you to leave, Rench.'

Rench looked at the dagger as though it were a child's toy, and then clapped his hands to summon the potboy.

'Yes, master?' The potboy glanced nervously from Shakespeare's dagger to Rench's enormous hands and arms.

'A gage of beer and make it quick. I have work to do this night. Godly work.' He turned back to Shakespeare. 'I ask again, who's your scraggy whore?'

Kat Whetstone lashed out at him with the hand he had just kissed. Her fingernails were as sharp as claws and she dug them into Rench's face, drawing three bloody lines down his cheek beneath his left eye. He was taken by surprise, but he recovered instantly and shot out his hand and gripped hers by the wrist. Hard.

'You have cut me, bitch. Lick it clean.'

Shakespeare knew this could only end badly, especially for Kat. He sheathed his dagger and pulled out a kerchief, which he proffered to Rench. 'Use this. It's a small scratch. You insulted her; she retaliated as any honest woman would.'

'An honest whore? That's a pretty paradox if ever I heard one.' Badger Rench laughed loud, but released Kat's wrist and snatched the kerchief. As he dabbed at his cheek, his ale arrived and he gulped it down, banging the empty blackjack down on the table. He dabbed once more at the blood on his cheek, then flicked the bloody cloth at Shakespeare's face. 'For the moment I must bid you farewell, but you'll pay for that soon enough. No one cuts Badger Rench. There's something for you to look forward to in the long night with your knees about your ears.'

Rench stood from the table, upturning it so that food and ale and all the platters were strewn across the sawdust floor. Laughing again, he stalked out.

Boltfoot lay in the damp undergrowth. The rain had ceased, but he was soaked through and stung by nettles. He kept watch on the house with the woman named Anne Hathaway indoors. He knew nothing more about her than her name and that he must observe her and follow her whatever happened between now and dawn. Boltfoot was accustomed to receiving orders without demur, and obeying them. At sea, there was no other way if one wished to survive, and such habits lingered.

It was probable that nothing would happen. That the shutters of the windows of the pleasant farmhouse would be closed and curtained, that the lights would go out and all the occupants would go to bed, and sleep until daylight.

Something crawled on to his neck and he shook his head like a dog emerging from the water. He had not been this wet and miserable since the storms of the Pacific, west of the strait that led their little ship into that vasty sea. He plucked his rough fingers at his neck and picked off a foul black centipede, which he threw into the depths of the wood.

And then he saw movement at the house. Somebody was coming. At first he thought it was Mr Shakespeare, but this man was a little younger and not so tall. And yet there were similarities – a brother, a cousin? But why would his master wish him to spy on a woman associated with a member of his family? Boltfoot put the thought to the back of his mind; it was none of his business.

The door opened and the man was welcomed with a kiss by the woman named Anne Hathaway, then ushered inside.

Boltfoot was beginning to wish he had brought a flagon of ale. While the damp was seeping into his body and soul, his mouth was dry and parched. It was late, and there was little light save the horn lantern that hung at the side of the farmhouse door.

A few minutes after the man was admitted to the house, he emerged again, with the woman, who was now coated and booted. She lifted the lantern from its hook and they began walking down a path in Boltfoot's direction.

As the couple walked past within two yards of him, he nestled deeper into the undergrowth and stilled his breathing. He let them go on ahead, their lamplight fading into the woods, then rose to his feet and followed. All he had to go on was the well-worn path and the speck of light swaying ahead of him like a ship's stern lantern.

For a minute he lost the light and was seized with panic as he tried to limp on faster, but then he saw it again. They were coming out from the woods into a meadow. Boltfoot had to hold back now, for the moon had emerged from the clouds and there was more light. And then he realised that they were making their way to a bridle path. The going would be a great deal easier there, but he would have to remain even further back, for there would be less cover.

On they walked, at a steady pace, for almost an hour, before turning left across a series of ploughed fields. With his clubfoot, Boltfoot began to toil in the thick, rain-sodden soil. The going was slow and hard. Eventually, they came to an orchard, laden with apples, red even in this silver light. Then a low stone wall, which the man and woman climbed over. Once more, Boltfoot hung back until he was sure they were not waiting to ambush him on the other side.

Keeping himself bent double, he approached the wall and peered over. Ahead of him was parkland and a large house with leaded windows that blazed candlelight. Anne Hathaway and her companion approached the front door and hammered at it. After a long time, perhaps a minute, they knocked again and a few moments later the door was opened by a man who appeared to be brandishing a pistol. The two visitors stepped back in apparent alarm.

What did Mr Shakespeare expect him to do now? He was to watch Anne Hathaway, follow her wherever she went and then report back at dawn. But he could not follow her inside this grand manor house. He could, however, creep up to a window and try to spy who was inside and what was happening.

Just as he began to crawl forward, he saw something move beside the stables to the east. Another figure was approaching. A large man. From this distance, he seemed to be trying to conceal himself. Was he a guard watching over this house? Boltfoot stayed where he was. His eyes strayed from the house to the guard and back.

Not for the first time, he felt uneasy at being without his caliver and cutlass. A knife was a poor weapon against a sword or pistol, especially when your potential opponent was built like an ox.

Chapter 26

ANNE WAS MORE scared than she had ever been. In the summer, when she had come to this house, she had experienced an electric thrill like dry lightning. The saying of the mass in the warmth of a June night, the candlelight, the serene procession of the communicants, like some holy dance, moving as one as though they all floated on air. The crystal singing in the cathedral of the trees. As she sipped the wine and imbibed the host, she had felt the blood and flesh of Christ enter her. There had been a mystical quality and she had felt at one with her God. Later, in the light of day, she had been less certain. Now she knew she had been deluded. This place was cold and all her memories seemed like dust.

'Enter,' Somerville said, waving his pistol in their faces. 'Mr Arden is in the library with the Scotchman. I'll see if he will receive you.'

Anne looked at Will. His face was drawn. She knew he liked this even less than she did. He had come here this chilly autumn night because he was loyal to her, and because he was concerned for her.

Earlier, when she confessed to him the existence of the Spiritual Testament, he had been consoling, but could not conceal his horror. Though he did not say the words, she knew what he was thinking: Anne, how could you do something so foolish?

'I was beguiled by them. No one refused to sign. They said it was a Spiritual Testament – the Last Will of the Soul, to keep me safe from the temptations of the devil in the hour of my death. They said it would save me from any unconfessed sins, should I die suddenly, and that I would for ever be communed with the Church of Rome and that Holy Mary would be my guardian. It was designed for those forced to conform to the new Church, but loyal to the old faith in their heart.'

'And you signed this with your own name or mark?'

'Yes, my own name. They said they would look after it for safekeeping until the evening's end, but when it was time to go home, I could find no one who knew where it was. That was when I felt the first shiver of fear. I did not know what to say.'

'They? Who were they? Father Benedict and who else?'

'Your cousin, Edward Arden.'

'Not Florence?'

'She was there.'

Will had put his arms around her then. 'My brother will know what to do.'

'No! We cannot tell him. He thinks me a fool already.'

'Well then, we shall find it and destroy it. I know of these things. It is a formulary. The Jesuit Campion was given these or similar ones in Italy by Cardinal Borromeo. Campion brought them to England. Many were distributed here in Warwickshire when he travelled through the county in the weeks before his arrest and execution. I would think that the ones Benedict Angel brought were the same or similar.'

'How do you know this, Will? I had never heard of such a thing before midsummer.'

He waved away her question. 'We must destroy it. In the wrong hands, well . . .' He let the possibility dangle.

She knew well enough who he meant by the wrong hands. 'Whatever you do, Will, I beg you not to tell John of this. He was torn enough by the Mary of Scots letter. I know he would do nothing to endanger us, but . . .' It was a statement, but there was doubt, too. John Shakespeare had a new master. Where, now, did his loyalties lie?

'Tell me, Anne, is this the reason you agreed to look after the coded letter for Florence?'

She had turned away from him, unable to meet his eyes. Yes, that had indeed been the reason. Florence had not threatened her, but there was something implied in the way she asked, *demanded*.

And now they were here in Edward Arden's hall to throw themselves on his mercy and plead kinship.

'Follow me,' Somerville said. He looked down and pointed his pistol at their mud-encrusted boots. 'After you've taken those off.'

As Anne tugged at her boots, she could not take her eyes away from the weapon. Was it her imagination or did it smell of recently spent gunpowder? Why did he wave it around so threateningly? And what was that dark patch nearby on the stone-flagged floor, a few feet in from the door? She looked at Will to see if he saw it too, and he clearly had, for he tilted his chin and moved his eyes slightly to the right. The patch looked as though something had been spilt and hastily cleared up with a rag. Something dark and sticky. This place was malign.

Somerville took them through to the library where they found Edward Arden standing beside the hearth, a smouldering log throwing out welcome warmth. In his hand, he had a goblet of yellow metal, probably latten. Anne noticed another, similar, goblet on the table and wondered where the Scotchman Somerville had mentioned had disappeared to.

'Good evening, cousin,' Arden said with an unconvincing

smile, then acknowledged Anne's presence. 'This is a most pleasant surprise.'

Will shook hands. 'Cousin Edward, we wish to speak to you in private.'

Arden flicked his fingers irritably. Somerville did not take the cue and so he spelled it out. 'John, would you leave us alone for a short while?'

Somerville looked a little bewildered, but edged towards the door.

'Shut the door after you, if you please.'

When he had gone, Arden gave Will another forced smile. 'Well, cousin?'

'We have come here to recover something.'

'Indeed? I had no notion that anything was lost.'

'Anne here is now my betrothed. This summer she came to your house with her friend Florence Angel. There were many others here and she – like the others – was asked to sign a certain document . . .'

'That is so. I recall the night well. You are referring to the Spiritual Testaments brought here by Father Benedict.'

Anne was astonished by the openness with which Edward Arden spoke of such secret matters. Had he no idea of the peril such talk could bring if overheard by agents of the state? But he had never been one to hold his peace, much to the fury of Lord Leicester and others. Perhaps he still imagined himself high sheriff of the county, and beyond the law as it applied to ordinary mortals.

'Yes. Anne signed one of the documents and believed it was to be kept by her, but at the end of the evening's celebrations she did not receive it. She would like it now.'

Arden knitted his brow into lines of puzzlement. 'Forgive me. I have not offered you refreshment. It is a difficult ride by night.'

'We came by foot.'

'Well, you must needs have wine or brandy. Or perhaps a cup of mead to warm you . . .'

'We cannot stay. It is getting late and we must make our way home. If you could just give us the document – the testament – we will leave you in peace.'

'My dear Will, of course Anne should be in possession of her own Spiritual Testament. But I am afraid I cannot help you, for I do not have it. Have you asked Florence?'

On the table she noticed a rosary – the same rosary that Florence and her brother always carried. Was she here, now? Anne nodded her head. 'Yes, I have asked her repeatedly. She says you must have it. My recollection is that I did give it to you.'

Arden seemed genuinely mystified. 'I am sorry, but I fear you must be mistaken. If I did have it, I would happily hand it to you this very minute, just as I am sure you would do little favours for me.' He smiled at Anne. 'Think carefully. What exactly happened when you had filled in the formulary and signed it?'

Little favours. He meant the Mary, Queen of Scots letter. How did he know about that? Had Benedict or Florence told him? Had he suggested her in the first place? Had he used her because he knew she felt trapped by the Spiritual Testament? She wondered what he would do if he learnt she had given it to John Shakespeare, government agent, and shuddered.

'Father Benedict was there. He said I should have it looked at to ensure it was completed correctly.'

'That is understandable. One cannot be too careful with one's immortal soul.'

'And so I showed it to you.' Anne had a sudden horrible thought that he was jesting at her expense. But if he was, it was not evident in his face, which showed nothing but honest concern.

Arden looked pained, as though trying to recall the event. He sighed deeply. 'I do not remember this,' he said at last. 'If indeed you did hand it to me, I am certain I would have given it back, for it was not mine to hold.'

'You must see, cousin,' Will put in, 'that if such a document were ever to get into the wrong hands it could put Anne in grave danger.'

'Yes, yes, I see that well enough. I cannot imagine what has happened to it. Would you like me to ask about among those who were there that fine night?'

'No. We wish no attention drawn to it.'

He nodded. 'I understand.' His voice was sympathetic and consoling, but his eyes were not. 'If only Father Benedict were still with us, for he might have a notion. What a monstrous business it all is. Who would murder such a gentle soul? Such brutality. It has shaken all of us at Arden Lodge. You know he stayed here these past months? I am sure it is safe to entrust you with that knowledge. My wife and daughter are inconsolable. We are waiting for word from the inquest.'

'They returned a verdict of suicide.'

Arden tutted. 'I wish I were surprised. It is a travesty. What has become of our once fair country? These are dangerous days. Beware nothing untoward happens to you . . .'

Boltfoot was wondering how he would describe this place to his master. It was a large, stone-built house with a fine garden to one side, and isolated. But beyond that he had no notion of its name, or whose it was. His only hope would be to bring Mr Shakespeare here, for he was almost certain he would be able to retrace his steps.

The front door opened in a stream of candlelight. The woman named Anne and her companion emerged. Boltfoot glanced left and saw that the guard was shrinking back into the shadows and he, too, moved away from the wall, into the depths of the orchard.

The man and woman clambered back over the wall. Boltfoot waited until they had passed. He was about to follow them when he spotted the immense figure of the guard scaling the wall after them. Boltfoot ducked back into cover and waited again. The guard was following the couple. Boltfoot tagged on behind the three of them, a chain of runagates passing into the night.

After Will Shakespeare and Anne Hathaway had departed, the inner door to the library opened. Edward Arden lifted his chin to the man who emerged. 'They've gone, Buchan. Did you hear it all?'

'Aye. You did well. She will be like clay in our hands now. They both will. But the other Shakespeare is the hurdle we must cross. Perhaps it is a shame Mr Somerville missed.'

'Somerville is a fool. He will do for us all.'

'Oh, his heart's in the right place. He will be of value when the time comes.'

From the orchard, they crossed the first of the fields, mud clogging their boots so that every step was as though they were shackled by ball and chain. They were tired now and their energy drained into the unforgiving earth, making their progress slower and slower. Boltfoot adjusted his pace to match. But then things changed. Ahead of him, the guard was lengthening his stride, moving closer to the couple. And now his sword was drawn, and another weapon dangled in his left hand. It was hard to make out in this poor light, but Boltfoot had seen enough battles and skirmishes in his time to know that bloody horror was about to be unleashed.

The signs were all too clear now; had the large man wished

to take these people prisoner, he could have done so easily. But he was on a mission to mete out death; that was why he had ventured this far into the countryside, to a place where none would hear but the birds in their nests and the foxes on the prowl. He needed the lonely silence of this remote killing field.

Do not let yourself be known. Do not interfere, merely watch. That was what Mr Shakespeare had told Boltfoot. But how could a man observe a savage murder – two murders – and do nothing?

He drew his dagger and tried to break into a run, but his club-foot dragged in the thick, cloying soil. He was wading, not running. He tripped and almost fell, emitting an involuntary grunt. It was not loud, but in the quiet of the night it was enough to alert the three people ahead of him. He regained his footing and ploughed on through the mud, stumbling forward with the strength and resolve of a plough-horse.

Boltfoot was fifteen yards away now, and the large guard was almost upon the young couple, his short sword ready to strike. Looking over his shoulder, the young man grabbed the woman's hand and pulled her into a loping run.

Behind them, the attacker lifted his left hand. Boltfoot saw the pistol, its muzzle dark and foreboding. He let out a guttural roar and charged. It served to distract the assassin just enough, and alerted the intended victims who threw themselves sideways. The attacker turned round to confront Boltfoot, his sword poised to strike home into his belly and rip the life from him.

Boltfoot was slow and ill-armed and nowhere near as powerfully built as this man. But he had courage and the cunning of a warrior who has survived many fights. He had no intention of allowing his blood to fertilise this black soil.

The sword jabbed at him viciously. He sidestepped it. He would never be a runner, but he was lithe enough and fit. The sword thrust again and this time Boltfoot let it come. The blade skimmed his ribs and Boltfoot drove his dagger down into the forearm. The attacker made a noise, half growl, half groan of pain.

Boltfoot pulled out his dagger and the man's blood rushed up, spraying across his hand and arm. The attacker kicked out at Boltfoot's chest, sending him sprawling backwards into the mud. He knew he was done for. He looked up into the cruel, shining eyes and saw the sword raised for a downward strike into his throat. But suddenly the attacker lurched to the left, as if he had been hit violently on the side of the head, and the sword spun away.

Boltfoot did not need a second chance. He rolled to the right. Taking his weight on his left arm, he gained enough purchase to thrust upwards with his right hand, plunging his dagger into the attacker's belly, just beneath the ribcage. This time there was no groan, but a howl of rage.

The man was not done. Using his undamaged arm, he brought the muzzle of his pistol up and aimed it square into Boltfoot's face. So this was how he would die, his face blown into blood and torn flesh. Unarmed, with his dagger buried deep in the other man's body, Boltfoot squirmed backwards.

Another blow struck the attacker's head. He tried to turn again, realising too late that he was under assault from the young man he had been following. He dropped the pistol into the dirt and his hand went down to the dagger protruding from his upper abdomen. He pulled it from his body and moaned. Blood poured from the wound like a slit pig in the moments before death. He looked at it in disbelief, then looked down again at Boltfoot, sprawled on the ground before him, and seemed about to say something. His lips flapped soundlessly and then he collapsed forward.

The body fell, dead-weight, on to Boltfoot's left leg, trapping him. Struggling on to his elbows, he leant forward and grabbed hold of the corpse's hair and shoved him off, then sat in the wet mud, panting with exhaustion.

The young man stood ten yards away. Behind him, shielded by his body, crouched the young woman.

For a few moments none of them said a word. Finally, the young man spoke. 'You've killed Badger Rench. We've killed him.'

'You know this man?'

The young man was still gasping for breath. In his hand, he clutched a length of rusted old harness chain. 'It's Thomas Rench, known as Badger. I – I don't know what has happened here. Or why.'

'He was trying to kill you.'

'Who are you?'

'No. Who are *you*?'

'My name . . .' He hesitated. 'My name is Will Shakespeare.'

Boltfoot said nothing. So this must indeed be his master's brother, or cousin.

'Why were you following us? Mr . . .'

'You don't need my name. I have protected you, that is enough. We must leave here quickly. There will be a hue and cry as soon as this body is found at daylight.'

Will shook his head helplessly. 'They will come straight to us. We will be suspected. He must have been sent to spy on us. Or worse . . . they will know we were involved. We will stand no chance.'

'Then you had best get horses and leave this region immediately.'

'Could we not bury the body?'

'Here? In this field? It is neatly ploughed. Any farmer would see the disturbance in these furrows.'

'What are we to do?'

Boltfoot looked beyond Will Shakespeare. In the glow of the moon, he saw they were twenty yards from the edge of the field and, beyond that, the woods. Wiping his bloody dagger on his hose, he thrust it back into his belt then limped across and looked about within the margin of the trees. He scuffed the leaves and undergrowth, hoping to find a decline or burrow, but there was nothing. They would just have to do this the hard way. He walked back to the corpse and grabbed hold of the legs. He signalled to Will. 'Help me lift him. Don't drag him or he'll leave a trail. We'll carry him to the verge and bury him there as best we can. You, Mistress Hathaway, cover the tracks where the body fell.'

'You know my name.'

'Aye, I know your name.'

'How?'

'Never mind that. Let us deal with the corpse.'

Badger Rench weighed close to three hundredweight, but Boltfoot was strong and Will was young. After a couple of stops, they got him to the edge of the field where the ground was covered in a layer of leaves.

'Now,' Boltfoot said. 'Fashion yourself digging tools from fallen wood, and we shall begin. Best thing would be to bury him eight foot down, but we'll never manage it. Three feet is the most we'll do, so let us work. We disperse the excess when we've covered him. Then we recover the ground with leaves. Is that understood, Mr Shakespeare?'

'Why are you helping us? Why did you follow us? Is this something to do with my brother?'

'Your brother? You'd better ask him that. I am a common man and I do what I am told and keep my thoughts to myself. There's many another might do well to follow such advice.' Boltfoot collected Rench's sword and pistol, then returned to the corpse. He kicked away the leaves with the side of his foot, then, with the tip of the sword, he drew a line in the mud, about six and a half feet by four. 'That'll do. Now, let's dig.'

Chapter 27

T HE CANDLE WAS almost burnt away. Its flame guttered and the wax dripped. By the fading light, Shakespeare looked down at the woman who lay in his arms, her hair falling across his chest. How had he ended up in her narrow bed? The answer was obvious: strong ale and brandy, the wit of a sheep and the uncontainable urges of a ram. He should feel shame, but he didn't.

Kat snored softly. Her face was turned to him and her lips were parted to reveal the gap of her teeth. It would be daylight soon. He slid his arm from beneath her head, trying not to wake her. The candle died, but the first rays of dawn came into her chamber. She turned away from him with a low moan, and pulled the sheet and blanket about her. He turned and sat at the edge of the bed. His garments and hers were everywhere, scattered like straw across the wooden floorboards.

'John?'

'I must return to my chamber. It is almost light.'

She laughed. 'Come back to bed. There is no hurry.'

'No. I must go.'

He pulled on his clothes and fumbled with the ties, then hesitated.

'You have something to say, John?'

'I was hoping you might have something to say to me. The questions you avoided last night . . .'

'You are a most insistent man. I have come all this way to see you. We have time enough for serious matters.'

'No, you came to help me find Buchan Ord, your betrothed, the man who abandoned you. Is he here, or was that all but jest?'

'He's here and when I find him, so shall you. Have a little patience. All will be well.'

'I do not have time.'

She laughed again. 'You had time enough last night.' She reached out from the bed and tried to pull him to her. 'One kiss before you go . . .'

Six giant coaching horses stood patiently in the early morning air. Each of them was tethered to a peg, which was driven into the ground. Vapour shot from the animals' nostrils. Occasionally, they stretched their long, muscular necks forward and grazed on the tufted grass of the heath at the edge of the highway.

They were twenty-five miles to the north and east of Stratford-upon-Avon. Close by the horses a magnificent carriage shimmered in the dawn light.

Newly crafted and decorated in lustrous gold and royal blue, it was clearly made for someone of extreme privilege. Atop the coach, on the driver's seat, a man on watch huddled into his cloak. The muzzle of a loaded petronel gun poked forth from the folds of cloth.

He had stayed awake and alert for every second of his six-hour watch. There were too many vagabonds, too many robbers along this highway north. And the cargo they had been commissioned to transport was too precious to be lost: it was the carriage itself. A conveyance fit for a queen.

Inside the great coach, the other driver woke from a short sleep on a bench upholstered with soft cream hide and farted like a trumpet blast. He emerged into the wan light, yawned and stretched his arms. 'Nothing?' he asked idly.

'Nothing but foxes, squirrels and hedgepigs. The only other thing I heard was your snoring and farting.'

'Got to keep the carriage fragrant for Her Scottish Stinking Majesty.' He slapped his comfortable stomach. 'Hey-ho. A piss in the woods, a cup of ale and some bread and we'll be on our way then.'

'Aye, and make it quick.'

Back in his own chamber, Shakespeare found Boltfoot sitting naked on the floor beside a basin of cold water. His face and hair were muddy. The pile of clothes that lay on the floor at his side was dripping wet.

'Boltfoot, when I asked you to hide and keep watch over Hewlands Farm, I did not mean you to dig yourself into the mud like a mole.'

But Boltfoot did not smile at his jest. 'Master, something bad has occurred.'

Shakespeare found his brother and Anne at Hewlands Farm. Neither of them had slept, but at least they had changed from their muddied clothes, rinsed their hair and washed as much soil as they could from their nails and eyes and ears. Will sat with his head in his hands. Anne had fetched food for the younger children and spilt a jug of milk across the floor. Shakespeare looked on the scene with a mixture of irritation and horror. How had they come to this pass?

'Will, Anne, we must talk. Now. Send the children out to play.'

Anne shuffled her young siblings out into the fresh air, and shut the door behind them.

'He's your man, isn't he?' Will said. 'You set him to follow us. Was he supposed to protect us – or discover our destination?'

'His name is Boltfoot Cooper. I set him to find Florence Angel. He has told me everything about the unfortunate incident with Badger Rench. I don't have time to have Boltfoot retrace your trail for me. Tell me everything.'

'We went to Arden Lodge,' Will said.

'And was Florence there, too?'

'I believe so,' Anne said. 'Though we did not see her, I saw her rosary – or one very like it. Something is happening at that house.'

'Who else was there? John Somerville with his pistol? Cousin Edward?'

'Yes. And perhaps one more.'

'One more? Who?' Shakespeare's questions came urgent and fast.

'A Scotsman.'

'Buchan Ord?'

'I don't know his name. We did not see him, but Somerville mentioned him.'

Shakespeare clenched his hand into a fist and looked for something – someone – to beat. 'You realise that I have come a hundred miles to find this man? Was there a Frenchman there, too? Will, Anne, what are you involved in? This man Buchan Ord is a courtier to Mary, Queen of Scots. I believe he and the Frenchman I seek are plotting to free her. From what you say, Edward Arden, John Somerville and Florence Angel are part of the same conspiracy. And then –' he could barely speak for the spit and fury that flecked his mouth – 'and then you kill a man and bury him in a field.'

'Badger was about to kill us,' protested Will. 'Your man saved us and stabbed him to death.'

'I truly hope you buried him deep.'

'Not deep enough. We had naught but sticks for spades.'

Shakespeare sighed. 'We will deal with that presently. Now, let us go back. My man Mr Cooper says Badger Rench was outside Arden Lodge.'

'That is what he told us, too.'

The question that had to be answered was why Rench was there. Was this Sir Thomas Lucy's doing? Or had he been looking for Will and Anne, consumed by jealousy? Lucy seemed the most likely option, which meant he had at least a powerful suspicion of what was going on at Arden Lodge – if not the whole story. By now he was probably aware that his man was missing, and would soon believe him murdered. Where did that leave Will and Anne? On the scaffold . . .

'If they don't find the body, no one will know we were there or even that he is dead,' Will said hopefully.

'Will, at times your mouth belies the wit you keep closeted in your head. When Arden and Somerville and Florence Angel are arrested and racked, do you not think they might mention who else was there at the house last night? God in heaven!' Shakespeare slammed his fist down on the table in front of Will.

'What can we do?'

'First, you must start being honest with me. Everything. Not little scraps of information like grain fed to chickens. Hold nothing back, nothing at all. Why were you there? How deeply are you involved? Who else knows? What did the Mary of Scots letter really say – and why did you have it? I need honest answers and perhaps then we can begin to devise some route out of this blood-drenched maze.'

At last Shakespeare sat down. The bliss of the night with Kat Whetstone had evaporated faster than water thrown on fire. 'Anne, bring me a cup of something strong. Beer, brandy . . .

anything.' As she went to the kitchen, he jabbed his finger at his brother. 'Will, I know you understand my anger and my fear. I know that you have been led into this unwittingly. But you must now become a man. You have no time to ease into this new role. And you must play your part to perfection, not just for your own sake, but for Anne's, too, and for your unborn child. Look after them. Anne is as taut as linen on a tenter. If we are not careful, she will lose the babe.'

Will exhaled loudly. 'Brother, there is another matter I must confide in you . . . the reason we went to Arden Lodge. Our cousins have a hold over Anne.' He paused. 'Do you know of the Spiritual Testaments?'

'You mean the ones brought over by the Jesuits Campion and Persons? How could I not know, Will? They brought them over by the thousand.' Shakespeare threw back his head. 'She didn't sign one, did she?'

Will nodded slowly, his face etched with pain.

'I had no idea she was even a Catholic.'

'She isn't. She went to mass with Florence. Many people from hereabouts were there. They all became inflamed with the fervour of the moment and signed the damnable testament.'

Shakespeare did not try to conceal his bewilderment. 'Why do people do this? At best, it is like walking about with a sign around their neck saying "Look at me, I am a recusant and care nothing for your laws". At worst, it is like walking about with a noose around your neck. And most certain of all, your name will be added to the list of potential enemies, to remain there for evermore. The list is everything . . .'

Will smiled ruefully. 'The old man signed one last year.'

'Our own father?'

'He showed it to me and asked me what I thought. I told him to destroy it.'

'Did he do so?'

'I do not know. As to the one Anne signed, she regretted it immediately, for it is now in the possession of Edward Arden and whoever else inhabits that seminary of conspiracy he runs at Arden Lodge. That was why she agreed to look after the Mary of Scots letter. That is why we went there again last night. I even pleaded kinship, though the Lord knows I never liked the man.'

Shakespeare sighed and clasped a hand on his brother's right shoulder, his anger gone. If any of them were to survive, they must bring cold logic to bear. 'Will, we must deal with this piece by piece. My first duty is to my master and my sovereign, but we will find a way out of this for you and Anne. For all of us.' He knew he must concentrate on Arden Lodge, for that was at the heart of this unholy mess. He would have to pay it another visit, this time armed and with Boltfoot at his side. He gripped Will's shoulder tighter. 'You called it a seminary of conspiracy?'

Will snorted. 'That's what it is. Everyone knows it. The supposed gardener, Hugh Hall, is a popish priest sent from Rome or Rheims. Benedict Angel was there for months. Dibdale has been there; and it is said Campion spent time there before moving on to Lapworth. I tell you, John, I do believe that Catholics in this county outnumber Protestants by two to one. No one knows which way to turn.'

'If everyone knows of the events at Arden Lodge, Sir Thomas Lucy must know it, too.'

'I am sure he does.'

'Then why have the pursuivants not been in to tear it apart? Why have they not all been arrested and slung in the Tower?'

'That is a good question – and one for which I have no answer.'

Just then Shakespeare and his brother heard a cry. They looked towards the doorway to see Anne standing there, cup in hand. But she was not alone. At one side stood Richard Topcliffe, white-haired and grinning with yellow teeth, his blackthorn stick idly tapping the floor. At the other, with his pale hand on her shoulder, stood Ruby Hungate, his harlequin doublet bringing unwelcome colour to a drab day.

Hungate pushed Anne forward. She stumbled. As she tried to regain her footing, Hungate's sword flashed and swirled in a steel spiral of light. A thick lock of Anne's hair flew from the back of her head and Hungate caught it. He kissed it elegantly, put it in the palm of his hand and blew so that the strands dispersed into the still air like a dandelion clock. 'You see how simple that was? Next time I'll prick the bastard from her belly.'

Will roared and tried to lunge at Hungate, but Shakespeare shot out a restraining arm. 'No, Will.'

Anne turned and faced Hungate with contempt.

'Well, well,' Topcliffe said, 'what do we have here? Huggermugger like conspirators. And who is this?' He jutted his white grizzled head towards Will. 'From the vague similarity, I would take him for your brother. Is this the dog that did the dirty deed with comely Miss Hathaway and got her with child?' He slapped Anne's arse, making her jolt.

Will tried to throw himself forward again, this time at Topcliffe, but again Shakespeare held him back.

'Who is this man? I'll kill him, John.'

'He is a dog's turd, Will, pay him no heed.'

Will lunged again. This time he came face to face with Topcliffe before Shakespeare managed to pull him back.

Topcliffe sneered. 'Your brother is more man than you, Shakespeare.'

'The trainband prizes him. He has a way with blades. Don't test him, Topcliffe.'

'He thinks himself a swordsman in more ways than one

then. But he has met twice his match this day. I do think his whore would like a piece of Uncle Dick now she's got a taste for it. Is that not so, my pretty little trug?'

'Leave her be,' said Shakespeare, indicating to Anne to get behind him. 'Why are you here, Topcliffe?'

'Why, paying a neighbourly visit, that is all. My very good copesmate Mr Hungate and I were wondering how your inquiries into papist conspiring were progressing. Sir Thomas Lucy is most anxious to have every last traitor in his county apprehended. And you know what I mean by the word "traitor", Shakespeare. Perhaps we could be of some assistance.'

'I need no assistance from the likes of you.'

'Likes of me? There is no one like me, Mr Shakespeare. None at all, as you shall discover if you continue to try to cross me.'

Shakespeare looked from Topcliffe to Hungate and back again. They were two of a kind. 'Do you have a purpose for being here, or are you merely come to irk us and insult a good woman?' Shakespeare was standing now, his hand on the hilt of his sword, which remained stowed in its scabbard. He had no fear of Hungate, but knew that a wrong move could end in the spilling of the blood of his brother and Anne.

'I have a purpose,' Hungate growled. 'Where is the bitch sister of the dead priest? I heard she had returned home, but now she is gone.'

'If you mean Florence Angel, then I have no knowledge of her whereabouts.'

'I mean the treacherous bitch sister of the dead priest. One dead Angel is not enough. My lord of Leicester will not be pleased to hear she is loose in his county, for she is up to her scrawny bird's neck in all the evil goings-on of her brother. I will deliver her to the scaffold, where she will be despatched. Tell her that when you see her, Shakespeare. She will be despatched.'

Topcliffe clapped Hungate about the shoulder. 'Well spoken, friend. Like a true Englishman.' He sniffed the air. 'Will you not offer us ale or beer, Miss Hathaway? Do I smell partridge pie?'

'The only smell is your stink, Topcliffe,' Shakespeare said. 'One day you will discover the joys of bathing and the world will be a better place. And you, Hungate – why do you have such hatred in your heart for Florence Angel? How has she ever harmed you?'

'She harms me by being alive. As do you, Shakespeare.'

'Come, Mr Hungate,' Topcliffe said. 'Let us leave these maggots to their squalor.'

Hungate shrugged. 'And what of the other matter we came for, Mr Topcliffe?'

Topcliffe thrust his stick in the air. 'Ah yes, the body. Truly, I had almost forgotten. Indeed, yes, a body has been found this morning, Mr Shakespeare. And as justice of the peace, Sir Thomas Lucy instructs you to inquire into the matter. He says that the investigation of unexplained deaths is your line of work.'

Chapter 28

As Topcliffe and Hungate departed, Shakespeare looked at his brother and Anne. Their mouths had dropped open, their eyes wide in shared horror.

Will shook himself, as though to shed the soldier that resides in every man when his blood is up. He looked at Anne. 'What are we to do? Should we depart this place?'

'No, for that will paint you as guilty as your mark scratched on a confession. They have told us nothing. Where is this body now? Is it still at the field or has it been taken to the Rench farm for laying out? No one but cousin Edward and his household can know you were at Arden Lodge last night, so we have time to think and plan our move.'

'But, John, they are playing with us. If we stay, we will be climbing the scaffold ladder by week's end.'

'Did anyone see you return home with your garments all muddy?'

'No. It was before daylight.'

'Then Will, Anne, you will both listen to me. You will go about your daily business until you hear otherwise from me. Do you have tutoring this day?'

'Yes, Whateley's daughters again.'

'And you, Anne?'

'I have children to care for and farm work to be done. There is hay to be stored—' Shakespeare silenced her with a brisk wave of the hand. 'Will, go to Alderman Whateley's, do your work as best you can. Anne, stay here and keep the farm going and the children fed. We will confer again later. Say nothing to anyone. Smile, frown, pass the time of day, talk of the apple harvest, of the weather and your wedding plans. If someone mentions the death of Badger Rench shake your head, and ask what has become of the world. Do you understand all this?'

They hesitated, then both nodded, unconvinced.

'Good. Then I must go.'

Walking briskly along Meer Street, Shakespeare spotted his father and hailed him.

'Where are you off to at such a pace, John?'

'I'm looking for a body.'

'Yes, I had heard. What is happening to this town? And what has any of it to do with you? Your mother is sick with worry and fear and your fool of a brother seems out of sorts, too. I have never known him so taciturn. And why did he not come home until dawn? There are certain standards of behaviour to be upheld. I still have a position in this town.'

Shakespeare gripped his father's arm a little too hard. He lowered his voice. 'Do not say that Will came home at dawn to anyone. Say nothing.'

'John, what is this? You are frightening me.' The fear in his father's eyes was all too obvious. A body found . . . Will out all night. How could he not draw conclusions and be afraid?

'I will explain all in due course. Now is not the time or place. Just make sure that neither you, nor Mother, nor the younger ones discuss Will or his whereabouts with anyone.' He offered his father a reassuring smile. 'Now – this body. Where was it found?'

His father shook his head. He was clearly disturbed. 'I don't know, but I do know it was being taken to the White Lion. Please, John, tell me—'

Shakespeare embraced his father. 'All is well. I promise you. But say nothing. Nothing at all. There are those who wish us ill – and we must not give them arrows to shoot at us.' He only wished he possessed the confidence his words were intended to convey.

It seemed to Shakespeare that the whole town was going down Henley Street towards the White Lion. Enveloped by a throng of townsfolk, he had to push his way through the swelling ranks.

A man tugged his arm. 'What's going on, John Shakespeare? What are you doing to our fair town?'

Shakespeare shrugged him off.

'You bring naught but bad luck and trouble,' another said, pointing an accusing finger.

Shakespeare pressed on. The crowd murmured. Someone pushed him.

'The necromancer's in there. He should be hanged as a witch. And his crone of a mother.'

'The moon turned red last night, I saw it. Blood red. Been like that since John Shakespeare came home.'

'One of my ewes collapsed and died this morning. Not a mark on her.'

Finally, Shakespeare managed to force his way into the stableyard at the back of the inn. The Searcher of the Dead was walking towards the storehouses.

'Thank God you are still here, Mr Peace.'

Joshua Peace smiled grimly. 'Perhaps I should take up permanent residence. There are enough cadavers to keep me busy. But listen to that . . .' The hubbub, occasional whistles and shouts of the mass of people outside in the street provided an unwelcome background noise. 'I confess I feel under siege in here.'

'Where is this new body?'

Peace tilted his head. 'Back there in an empty storeroom.'

'Who summoned you to look at it? Was it Sir Thomas Lucy?'

'No, Mr Shakespeare, Alderman Whateley asked me to look at it. He seems to think kindly of you and your judgement, unlike that crew out there.'

'They are scared, that is all. Two unexplained deaths within days will unnerve any man or woman. They begin to look at their neighbours askance. They lock their doors at night when such a thing was never done before. Come, show me what we have.'

The body was laid out on a pile of empty crates. Shakespeare looked upon it with relief and the blood flowed back into his veins. It was not Badger Rench.

His first reaction lasted all of two seconds. His next reaction was one of astonishment. The corpse had only one arm and a hole where its nose should be.

'Shot in the face at close range,' Peace said. 'No doubt at all what the cause of death is here. The arm was long gone. Even that dirty-dealing coroner could not dispute a finding that this man was shot dead with a bullet to the brain. As no weapon was in evidence, and as the muzzle must have been no more than six inches from his face, I suggest that murder is more likely than suicide.'

Shakespeare wasn't really listening. He was trying to make sense of this. Surely this was the body of the Frenchman, Leloup or Seguin or whatever he called himself these days? He gazed down at the figure. Naked and pale, the body was that of a man in late middle years, perhaps fifty or so. The legs and arm were still muscled, but the belly, hairy and speckled with blemishes, was expanding. The prick hung sad and forlorn in a forest of grey.

'Cover him, Mr Peace. Allow him some decency.'

Peace draped a linen sheet across the body's nether regions.

'Was he like this, naked?'

'No.' Peace pointed towards a stone shelf at the back of the store. 'His garments and other accoutrements are over there. It occurred to me this man was not of common stock, for his clothes are good and he wore a silver pomander around his neck – something I have not seen since I was in Italy. People in these parts cope well enough without such things.'

'I believe I know who he is. If I am correct – and I have a way of checking – then he is a Frenchman named François Leloup, an associate of the Duke of Guise.'

Peace raised his eyebrows, and then emitted a laugh of astonishment. 'You are full of surprises, Mr Shakespeare. These are deep waters.'

'It was said he had a nose like a wolf's snout.'

'No more.'

They both gazed at the bloody wound. Shreds of flesh and gristle hung loose where once there had been a proud nose.

'Where was the body found?'

'In the river, by the bridge. The constable, Nason, had it brought here. When I came out this morning, it was lying in a handcart in the yard out there. No one seemed to know who it was or what to do with it. I think it fair to say that no one wanted to make any decisions. Nason scurried off. I rather think he wished to carry the news to his master at Charlecote.'

As Peace spoke, Shakespeare rifled through the dead man's possessions. A capacious riding cape, doublet of black and gold, shirt of fine white cambric with lace cuffs, fine knee-length hose, netherstocks and riding boots. Nothing too lavish or gaudy, nothing to draw the attention of strangers. He might have been a government officer, a lawyer or merchant. Such men usually travelled with servants to guard them and do their bidding, but at the Cutler's Rest in Sheffield they had insisted Leloup had no lackey. He felt all the seams for hidden coins or papers, but there was nothing.

Beside the clothes, on a platter, there was a dagger with a jewelled hilt and the silver pomander that Peace had mentioned. Shakespeare picked up both items and studied them. They were fine artefacts, expensive. He returned to the body and examined the hand. No rings or other jewels.

'Was there no purse?'

'No. Nor any sort of baggage.'

'Curious that the murderer took his other possessions, but not this dagger and pomander. They are items of considerable value.'

'There was one other thing that interested me, Mr Shakespeare.' Peace pointed his index finger at the chest of the man, and traced a line around the front and side of the body. 'You see this line like a thin surcingle? And here, halfway up the ribcage, a small indentation in the flesh. No bigger than a farthing coin. It is clear he has kept something tied close to his body. Whatever it was, it has gone.'

'It must have been something of extreme value. Will you wait here, Mr Peace? I want someone else to see the body.'

Kat Whetstone was dipping her spoon into a bowl at the long refectory table in the hall. She greeted Shakespeare with a smile. 'This is the latest I have ever broken my fast in my life. Taste this.' She held out the spoon. 'Frumenty with little pieces of apple and raisins and cinnamon.'

'Thank you, Kat, but no. I will eat later.' He looked down at her seriously. 'For the moment, please come with me. I must show you something.'

'This is very mysterious, John. Do you intend taking me to your chamber to show me this wondrous object?'

Shakespeare was not in a mood for mirth. 'A body has been found in the river near here. I want you to see it.'

She placed her spoon in the bowl, stood from the table and smoothed down her skirt.

Her dismay was clear enough to see. She put a hand to her mouth as though she would gag at the horror that lay before her.

'Is it the Frenchman?'

She nodded hurriedly, and then turned away. 'Yes, it is Monsieur Seguin. Even without . . . even so horribly muti-lated, I recognise him.'

Shakespeare was surprised. He had thought that Kat Whetstone did not have a squeamish bone in her body. She was tough, resolute and had the stomach of a hardened soldier. What was it about the death of François Leloup that so unsettled her? Was she afraid?

'Who did this?' She had retreated to the doorway and held her head averted from the corpse.

'That is what I mean to discover. And to do so I need to find Buchan Ord. If you truly have the information that you prom-ised Mr Cooper, then end your games now and give it to me without further delay. Ord must know something about this man's fate.'

'John, I have not been playing games. All I know is that they planned to meet here in Stratford.'

He looked at her coldly. 'I believe you know more.'

She met his eye. 'Very well. Perhaps I led Mr Cooper to think I had more detailed knowledge, for which I beg forgive-ness. But one thing you cannot deny: Mr Seguin's presence here – even in death – must indicate that Buchan is somewhere nearby. And it is my desire to find him as much as it is yours.'

Chapter 29

THE BURIAL OF Benedict Angel was a grim, dirty affair. The gravedigger excavated a ragged hole at the crossroads near the place where his body was found. His mother stood at the edge of the pit, her head hung low, her despair complete.

Few townsfolk had dared come, for they knew the dangers of being associated with papism or treason. Shakespeare and Boltfoot stood beneath an old gibbet, charred where someone had tried to burn it down many years ago. They were a few yards from the grave. Will, Anne and her siblings were there with Shakespeare's father and mother. So were the Dibdales, who farmed the land near Hewlands and whose son was also a fugitive priest. A score of the braver souls from Shottery and Stratford stood their ground with courage, all too aware of the problems that could be heaped on their families by being recognised as papists.

On the other side of the grave, twenty yards from the proceedings, Richard Topcliffe watched with Ananias Nason. Topcliffe had a black book in his hand, a quill and a horn of ink. Ananias pointed to each of the mourners in turn and muttered. As he did so, Topcliffe followed the pointing finger with his eyes, then scratched away in his book.

'That man could give the reformed religion a bad name,' Shakespeare said to Boltfoot.

Boltfoot said nothing. He was wondering about the hole he had dug just a few hours earlier. He had gone to great lengths to ensure it was deep enough, but given their poor tools and the lack of time, he was unsure it was adequate. How deep was it? Three feet, perhaps. Four at the most. He did not feel easy.

Shakespeare sensed his anxiety. 'I know what you are thinking, Boltfoot,' he said quietly. 'We will talk of it later.'

Just as the coffin was about to be lowered into the grave, Topcliffe handed his book and writing implements to Nason and walked forward. He shook his head. 'Put it down. You're not wasting good English oak on a traitor.' The pall-bearers nervously set the coffin on the ground. Topcliffe pulled out his dagger and prised open the lid. Without ceremony, he upended the casket and the body rolled into the grave with only the winding sheet to cover it. Topcliffe pulled the coffin to one side, and then spat into the grave. 'Now fill it in.'

One or two mourners crossed themselves and Topcliffe took back his black book and made more marks in it.

Shakespeare was surprised Florence Angel wasn't here. He had been certain she would have heard about the funeral and would have come. No one from Arden Lodge had appeared.

Rafe Rench arrived just as the earth was being piled into the hole on top of the corpse. He walked up to the widow Angel, who was now on her knees, her hands clutching at the mud. She was being comforted by Shakespeare's mother, who held an arm around her bony shoulder. Rench bent down and rasped words into Audrey's ear. His words were clearly audible.

'Ready to sell now? Name your price and I'll halve it.'

Audrey Angel buried her face in the dug soil, clutched handfuls of mud and wiped it all across her face, in her mouth and eyes, as though she would join her son in the earth.

Shakespeare felt sick. How had this quiet town and village,

this corner of Eden, been rent asunder like this? Neighbour against neighbour, and all in the name of religion and greed. He watched the hole being filled. As the mourners drifted away, so did Topcliffe and Nason and Rafe Rench.

Shakespeare's mother came over. 'You must do something about this, John,' she said as she clutched his hands.

'I will do all I can, Mother.'

'I know you will.' She smiled at him, and then turned away to join her husband on the walk back towards Stratford. At last, only the widow Angel was left. She made a final sign of the cross over the grave and whispered some words. Her face was covered in mud and she was shivering and seemed short of breath.

Shakespeare approached her. 'I want to help you, Aunt, but you must help me.'

'Help? There is no more help. My life is done.'

'No. There must be some small speck of light. For you and Florence. Anne will come to you. Please, listen to her and do what she says.'

Audrey Angel wiped her wrist across her cheeks, but the tears would not stop. 'For the sake of Florence, I will listen. But if anything happens to Florence, then I will block my ears and eyes and mouth for ever.'

She hung her head again and they watched her walk off across the meadow. She looked ill and thin. These events were taking a heavy toll on the woman. When the soul despairs and rots, the body will never be far behind.

'Come, Boltfoot, I have seen enough.'

He turned away, and was startled to come face to face with Harry Slide. Shakespeare stared at him for two seconds, then grasped him by the arm. 'Load your caliver, Boltfoot, and shoot this man in the leg if he tries to get away.'

Boltfoot unslung his gun and began to load it.

'Mr Shakespeare,' Slide protested, 'there is no need for this. I have come to you of my own volition.'

'If you have something to say, say it.'

'What I have to say, Mr Shakespeare, is that events are proceeding. Fast.'

'What do you mean, Slide?'

'I mean the conspirators are almost on the move. They mean to free the Scots devil and carry her away to France.'

'How do you know this?'

'It is my business to know such things. It is what Mr Secretary pays me for. And I shall hope for a recommendation from you that he gives me twenty marks at least for this intelligence. Now, please, will you ask your man to stop pointing his gun at me? Such things have a tendency to go off when least expected.'

'Who is on the move? Who are these conspirators?'

'You know as well as I do who they are. You are no fool, for Mr Secretary would never have employed you if you were. Now, I beg you . . . before Mr Cooper does me some damage.'

'No, you will run again – and I have questions to ask.'

'I promise I will not run. I came to you because my inclination is to ride for Sheffield Castle, which is a sieve. We must stop it up. We could ride together.'

Shakespeare sighed. 'Put up your gun, Boltfoot, but if he moves without my say-so, cut him down. Now then, Mr Slide, tell me more.'

Slide bowed low, like a courtier. 'Our meetings thus far have been too short, but now I am yours and you must consider me your servant. Mr Shakespeare, you can do with me as you please in the service of Mr Secretary and Her Royal Majesty, and all for a small price in silver.'

'I'm promising you nothing. Get to it, Slide. Tell me what you know.'

'I know what is happening at Arden Lodge. Horses are being readied, weapons polished and oiled. It cannot be long. Yes, they could be stopped here. You could arrest them all here this very day. But you would have no evidence against them. And nor would you know the names of their co-conspirators in the north. From what I know of Mr Secretary, I would suggest he might prefer us to surprise them in Sheffield, where the whole conspiracy will unfurl and their fellow plotters will reveal themselves.'

'Why do I have such difficulty believing a word you say?'

'Because you have been well taught by Sir Francis Walsingham. You are right not to trust me, or any other man. But that does not signify that I am untrustworthy.'

For a moment, Shakespeare felt himself sinking into Slide's lure, but then he shook his head. 'No, Mr Slide, go alone to Sheffield if you wish. If you are who you say you are, then report to the Earl of Shrewsbury. He will know what to do with your information – if you have any.'

Shakespeare's first duty lay here, finding some way to protect his family against lethal forces that assailed them on all sides.

They tethered their horses in the woods and made their way to the outskirts of Arden Lodge on foot. Approaching from the northern side through the trees, they avoided the woodland paths and nearby farmland where they were more likely to be spotted.

The edge of the forest was thick with ferns. Together they crawled through the dense foliage until they had a good view of the back of the house. Over by the stableyard Edward Arden was talking with a man, perhaps a groom. Arden was dressed in a heavy riding coat. He had a petronel in one hand and several swords in the other. Close by, horses were being saddled and loaded with packs.

Shakespeare peered closer. No, Arden wasn't talking to a groom. He was talking to Harry Slide, who was also dressed in a heavy riding coat and boots. What was Slide doing here? Was he playing some sort of double game? Was it possible that he did dirty work for both sides, with loyalty to neither? Perhaps that was how he paid for his expensive silk doublets and his sapphire buttons. Shakespeare touched Boltfoot's arm and gestured towards the trees to the west of the property. They inched their way round until they had a view of the gardens and there they saw what they were looking for: Florence Angel.

She had just emerged from the house and was walking purposefully through the ornate gardens towards the woods. At her side was the mouse-like priest Hugh Hall. Both were dressed for riding.

'Have your caliver ready,' Shakespeare whispered.

Boltfoot unslung his weapon and checked that it was still fully loaded. It was a fine, ornate weapon, won from a Spaniard on the far side of the world. It had a wheel-lock mechanism, was light enough to carry slung across his back and was his most prized possession. He pushed it out in front of him and gazed down its short muzzle.

'What are your thoughts, Boltfoot?'

'Too far for a certain kill.'

'I don't want anyone killed. I want to rescue the woman.' Shakespeare had no doubt that Edward Arden and John Somerville and their fellow conspirators were digging their own graves, but it was Florence who was the greatest threat to Will and Anne. The problem was, he very much doubted whether she wished to be rescued.

'Are there others inside the house?' Boltfoot asked.

'Probably two men and two women. There could be more.'

'And you do not wish any of them killed?'

'No. If they are engaged in treason, the law must take its

course. What I want is to seize the woman and spirit her away without the others knowing what has happened. It would be best if they thought that her disappearance was of her own doing.' He touched Boltfoot on the arm and pointed. Boltfoot took his finger from the trigger. John Somerville had emerged from the back door waving his pistol. Florence and Hall turned and began to increase their pace.

'Come away, Hall,' Somerville shouted. 'Mr Arden wants you.'

'We must make our peace with God,' the priest called back.

Florence took the priest's arm and continued towards the woods.

'Not now, you lazy arse! Pray later.' Somerville aimed the pistol at Hall, but then appeared to change his mind and pointed the weapon at a wagtail as it pecked its way across the lawn. He pulled the trigger. The weapon recoiled and Somerville fell backwards. The shot blew away a lavender bush and the bird flew off at speed.

'That man is more a danger to himself than anyone else, Mr Shakespeare,' whispered Boltfoot.

'He can cause harm enough. He almost did for me.'

Somerville had regained his footing. He looked around as though he had lost what he was looking for, spotted Hall, who had stopped, and beckoned him with the spent pistol.

Hugh Hall stepped forward timidly and began to follow Somerville back towards the house. Even from this distance he did not look like the stuff from which conspirators and assassins were made. Shakespeare touched Boltfoot's arm again. Florence had resumed her walk and was heading off on a woodland path. There would be only one chance, and this was it.

'Cover my back, Boltfoot. Come behind me at a distance.'

Shakespeare moved soundlessly through the trees, keeping

twenty or thirty yards to Florence's right, almost parallel. Occasionally he looked around to ensure Boltfoot was behind him. After five minutes, the woods gave way to a small green clearing. At its centre, like a child's toy, stood a small chapel. Without hesitation, Florence went in.

Shakespeare stopped. He had never seen this building, nor heard of its existence. Yet from its worn stones, it was clearly ancient. It was well hidden; no one but a poacher would be likely to find it by chance. He watched and listened. Boltfoot was with him now. They could see that the door was open. 'I'm going in,' said Shakespeare. 'If I shout, follow me, caliver first.'

She was on her knees, praying at a small side altar, which had the appearance of a personal shrine, with two candles, a shred of red cloth and a lock of hair. A shrine to her brother? It was possible.

Shakespeare looked around the chapel and was astonished. It was a relic of another era, before the reforming iconoclasts tore the Roman glitter and trimmings from the churches. The main altar was high and decorated with gold and silver. A full-sized Mother of Christ statue, carved from marble, stood close to the sacristy door. Shakespeare had never seen an artefact of such magnificence. The faces of saints gazed at him from every corner. The whole space was filled with dazzling coloured light from a multitude of stained-glass windows. This chapel might be small, but it was exquisite, dripping with religious images and artworks.

He hurried down the aisle, his boots clicking on the flag-stone floor. She turned, alarmed, and began to rise to her feet, lips parted as though she would scream, but he was already there, clamping his hand over her mouth, and clasping his other arm around her waist.

'Do not say a word, cousin. Do not make a sound.'

She was struggling, fighting him with more strength than he imagined possible in one who seemed so fragile and ethereal.

'Hush, hush,' he tried to soothe her. 'Don't fight me.'

She tried to bite his palm, her fingernails clawing at the back of his hand, like a mole scratching at hard earth.

'Ssshh. You must trust me. I am here to save you.'

She was growling, her breath coming shorter and more desperate.

'I am taking you to a place of safety. Your mother will be there. Anne will be there. You will be cared for. Help me take you from this place. I will do you no harm. Arden Lodge, this house, is doomed. All in it are doomed.'

Suddenly everything changed. Her fingers went rigid and flew away from his hand. Her mouth closed like a vice. Her shoulders quivered. As her arms began thrashing wildly, and her back arched, her head was thrown back so violently he feared her neck would snap. Shakespeare went cold. She was having a seizure.

Chapter 30

As gently as he could, he laid her to the ground, feeling utterly helpless. He had heard of paroxysms but he had never seen one. He ran to the door and signalled to Boltfoot, then ran back to her and tried to calm her violent jerking. He turned to Boltfoot. 'We have to get her out of here. Anyone could come.'

'Can't move her, master, not while she's having a fit. Blueboy the coxswain on my first ship had them. Never knew when they'd come.'

'How long did they last?'

'Usually two or three minutes, but you can't be sure. Sometimes a few seconds, other times it was half an hour. The danger's in the falling. You need to put cushions or something beneath her head. Don't want her banging herself on this stone floor.' He picked up some of the hassocks from under the pews. 'Put these around her head. They'll protect her.'

Shakespeare built up an elaborate cushion beneath her head and neck and to the sides. 'How will she be when she comes around?'

'Quiet. Drained of all energy. Easy as a kitten.'

As Boltfoot said this, Florence suddenly slumped. Her eyes were closed. The tip of her tongue was caught between her teeth, dripping blood.

Shakespeare was calculating the distance to the horses. Probably the best part of half a mile from here. Could they carry her that far through the woods? What if she screamed?

'I'll go for the horses,' Boltfoot said, reading his mind. 'I can move quicker alone and it will give her a little time to recover.'

'Yes, do that. I'll carry her to the woods to the west of the church door. No one should see us there.'

Florence Angel put up no resistance as Boltfoot lifted her up into the saddle so that she was sitting in front of Shakespeare, and supported by him. She was as lifeless as a doll, so docile that the only real danger was that she could simply fall sideways. Shakespeare put his arms around her and took the reins. She said nothing and he was grateful that the seizure had taken away all her defiance and resistance. He did not wish to gag her or bind her, but he was worried how long her compliant state would last.

Once away from the Arden Lodge estate, they rode at a sedate pace. Instead of taking the road to Shottery or Stratford, they headed north and east, keeping to less travelled paths and tracks through woods, away from fields where men and women would be working. They saw a few people at a distance, but took circuitous routes to avoid them. It had been years since Shakespeare had seen these ancient ways, but he knew his route as though he still rode them day by day.

Audrey Angel was at the Black House with Anne and Will. She quickly took her daughter in her arms and helped her into a corner to comfort her. Shakespeare watched them with an uneasy churning in his belly. His aunt did not look well and the daughter was in a bad way. He turned to Will and Anne. 'What have you brought?'

'Food, bedding and candles,' Will said. 'The plan is that

Anne stays here while I return to Stratford and come back later, by horse, bringing more supplies.'

'Yes. It is better that Anne stays with them, at least to begin with.' It would make it seem more like a friend helping friends than an illegal abduction. 'This is a good place, Will. What made you think of it?'

Will gave him a wry look as if to say: *You know what made me think of it.*

Shakespeare took a swift look around the dilapidated, over-grown building. There was a partially covered area at the back where a rough mattress of straw and canvas held the eye. It was almost a habitable room. If the roof could be restored, it would also be watertight. In one corner, Will had already laid a fire, and had set out the foodstuffs and candles. They could stay here – but for how long? It depended on what influence Audrey and Anne could bring to bear on Florence. She was in desperate need of care and the danger of returning home was too great. They must stay here until a better option presented itself.

He went over to Florence, who was still in her mother's arms and knelt down. 'Florence, answer me one thing: what was in the Mary of Scots letter?'

He didn't think she had heard him, but then her face emerged, heavy-lidded, from her mother's breast. 'It was a letter to the faithful, not to you.' She turned her wretched face back into Audrey's body, like a snail drawing back into its shell.

Shakespeare's face stiffened. He walked over to his brother.

'This isn't going as you hoped, John.'

'No. I open one door and another closes. I may have to leave Stratford at a moment's notice. If I do, I will send messages via Henley Street. Boltfoot will stay here with you for at least today and tonight. He was a cooper by trade, so if the roof leaks, he may be able to fix it. Whatever you need, I trust he will do all he can. You already know his fighting skills . . .'

'Thank you, John.' Will paused and then added awkwardly, 'I know what agonies you are going through, trying to protect us. You are split down the middle.'

'No, Will, you don't understand. For me, this is very simple. It is about my family and my country. Anyone who threatens either is my enemy. Whatever Florence believes, this is not about religion. I cannot pretend to like the Roman Church.' He lowered his voice to a whisper. 'Nor can I pretend to like Florence Angel or to have liked her fool of a brother. And yet that does not give the murderous Hungate the right or liberty to hunt down her or any other Catholic like a dog. It is treason I abhor, not religion. Which is why I must now hold my nose and go to Charlecote Park.'

Sir Thomas Lucy lounged back in his throne-like chair of carved oak and allowed himself a smug moment of triumph. 'So you come as a supplicant, do you, Mr Shakespeare? It is always gratifying to see a self-satisfied young man brought so low that he begs me for assistance.'

'Have it as you wish, Sir Thomas.'

'And you say you want me to raise a squadron of pursuivants for you to search Arden Lodge.'

'Yes. Treason is being plotted. There is little time.'

'Treason? That is a strong word. A mighty unpleasant word. I had thought Edward Arden to be kin of yours.'

'My loyalty is to England and the Queen.'

'So what is your evidence for this supposed plotting? I am a justice of the peace, charged with upholding the law of the land. I cannot order searches of men's houses on *your* whim.'

'I have reasons, good reasons.'

'Then name them.'

Shakespeare frowned at Lucy. He had the leisurely, disinterested air of some eastern potentate, who cared nothing for such small matters. And yet Shakespeare knew that Sir Thomas very much wished to destroy all the Ardens, and Edward Arden in particular. And his master, the Earl of Leicester, had said the Ardens were all vipers. So why would Sir Thomas balk at the opportunity to authorise a raid on Arden Lodge? Had he not himself called Edward Arden a traitor – and was it not Sir Thomas who sent Badger Rench to watch Arden Lodge? He *must* know about the conspiracy.

'The fugitive priest Benedict Angel was hidden there,' Shakespeare said. 'And there is a powerful connection to events at Sheffield Castle. The dead man found in the river this day is a Frenchman named François Leloup, who recently came from the Queen of Scots. I believe, too, that one of her courtiers, a young man named Buchan Ord, is at the house. These are dangerous men who wish ill to England.'

'Oh, what a tale you weave, Mr Shakespeare! Frenchmen, Scotsmen, fugitive priests and dead bodies. Next you will be writing plays for the stage.'

'This is no play, Sir Thomas.'

'Then *prove* it to me. Show me the evidence of mischief. How do you know these French and Scots demons have taken possession of Arden Lodge? Where is the evidence of conspiracy?'

Shakespeare glared. What evidence did he have, other than the testimony of Anne Hathaway, an encrypted letter bearing the name *Marie R* and the dubious word of an intelligencer named Harry Slide, who now seemed to have thrown in his lot with Arden? He had no evidence that he could reveal. Only suspicion, and the evidence of his own eyes.

'I saw them saddling up, loading armaments.' He tried to keep his tone even. 'If I take a band of pursuivants, we will find evidence aplenty. If I am right, then they are about to ride north to secure the release of the Scots Queen. We could stop them now.'

'No. That is not enough. Edward Arden is an important personage in this county, not some vagabond to be hauled in at will.'

'Are you willing to risk this? Do you want this brought back to you when I report to Mr Secretary that you refused me assistance? If we go now, this plot can be nipped in the bud. And you will have Edward Arden where you and my lord of Leicester have always wanted him: beneath your heel.'

Lucy was tapping his fingers on the arm of his chair. 'Bring me proof, then I will act.'

Shakespeare was stunned into silence. A short while ago, Sir Thomas Lucy would have happily stretched any law to bring about the demise of Edward Arden. Why, now, was he refusing to move against him? Shakespeare snapped his head into a curt bow, then turned away.

'Wait, Mr Shakespeare. I am glad you have come, for there is one other matter . . .'

He stopped. 'Sir Thomas?'

'It is about one of my men, Mr Thomas Rench, known as Badger. If you recall, he was the man who escorted you to me. It appears he is missing.'

'Tell me more.'

'I was hoping *you* might know what became of him.'

'No. I have no notion. Why would I know anything?'

'He had some history with your family. I believe he was unhappy when your disreputable brother took up with Mistress Hathaway. What do you think might have happened to him?'

'Are you accusing me of something, Sir Thomas?'

'Should I be?'

'I did not come here to be insulted. I know nothing of

Badger's whereabouts. If I discover anything, I will let you know.'

'Do that, Mr Shakespeare. Despite Badger Rench's faults, he has served me well. Perhaps you would find out what is said. Dig about a little . . .'

Chapter 31

Night had fallen. The moon was almost full and the sky clear. In the Black House, Anne was heating a pot of broth over the fire. Florence sat at her side, huddled into a blanket, watched over from a distance by Boltfoot. The widow Angel had ventured into the woods to relieve herself.

Anne smiled apprehensively. 'We are really doing this in your best interests, Florence. I hope you understand that.'

'I have nowhere to go. It is too late.'

'What do you mean?'

'Nothing.' Florence shook her head dismissively. Close by, an owl hooted and she shivered. 'This place is full of ghosts.'

'No, that's a tale for old wives. It is just ancient and ruined.'

'I see them all around me. Spectral beings. I see them as clearly as I see you or that strange cripple over there.'

'Do you hear voices?'

'Not since Benedict died. I believe I will never hear them again. I sensed the Maid of Orleans leaving me. I felt the heat of the flames and heard her last breath. She drowned in fire.'

'What of Benedict?'

'I see him in my dreams. He is throned in gold and sits with the Lamb.'

'Who killed him?' Anne asked softly.

At first Florence ignored the question and leant forward to

stir the broth. But then she turned and smiled. 'I don't know. I thought at first it must be Badger Rench or one of his men, but I have had other thoughts. This is not how it was supposed to be. None of it is. Did you see the blood on the floor when you came to Arden Lodge?'

Anne thought back, remembering the stain on the floor and the one on the wall when she and Will removed their muddy boots. There had been something else, too, the acrid scent of black powder. 'What blood?'

'The blood of a Frenchman. He was the man we had been waiting for, the one who brought all our hopes. He was introduced to us all, but he was not impressed. He said that we would not suffice. He called Mr Ord an imbecile – *un imbécile* – for bringing him to Arden Lodge. He spat at him, and then turned to leave, taking the gold and the ring with him. But Somerville went after him and shot him in the face. It was his blood in the hall that we wiped a few minutes before you arrived. If Somerville could kill like that, what else could he do?'

'You think he could have killed Benedict?'

'I don't know. But he scares me.' Florence peered again into the broth, but she seemed far away.

'You must give all this information to John Shakespeare,' urged Anne. 'He is our only hope. If you turn Somerville in, John will ensure you are safe.'

'And will he save us from the ghosts? Will *you* sleep sound here this night?'

Arden Lodge was quiet. No windows were lit. Shakespeare rode up to the front of the house and dismounted. He banged his fist on the door. There was no answer. He drew his sword and walked around to the left, where he knew the stables to be. No one was there. All the horses were gone.

Behind the stables, there was a servant's cottage. It, too, was in darkness. That did not mean there was no one there. Servants could not afford candles and when they were not needed in the big house, they tended to take to their beds with nightfall and rise with the sun. But the very silence everywhere told Shakespeare that everyone had gone; family, servants, stable-hands.

At the back of the house, he tried the latch on a postern door. It was locked from the inside. He tried it with his hands; it seemed weak. He stepped back, and then ran at it with his shoulder. The door burst open.

Holding his lantern in front of him, Shakespeare began walking through the house towards Arden's library. The lantern light gave out an even glow in the stillness and Shakespeare imagined Arden and his fellow conspirators all gathered here, plotting treachery. He shook off the image and began looking closely at the piles of documents and ledgers that every large estate must keep for efficient working. There was a great deal to go through, but most of it could be dismissed with ease. All he wanted was one thing: the Spiritual Testament that Anne had signed. Surely it must be here. Working at speed, he looked through the documents as well as he could. All he found were household accounts, letters of no consequence and books, many of them in Latin. No sign of any Spiritual Testaments. He went to other rooms, threw open coffers and cupboards, and then climbed a flight of stone steps to the first floor. In the bedchambers, his search proved no more fruitful. Perhaps there were secret nooks and hiding places behind panelling, but he did not have the means or the time to search them.

He cursed. This search was going to reveal nothing. To all intents and purposes Arden Lodge was the house of a wealthy country gentleman, a stalwart of the county. There was nothing incriminating here; nothing that could offer relief from the fears of Anne and Will. Perhaps a band of pursuivants would find something, but one man alone at night was unlikely to discover anything.

So where were Arden and his band of traitors now? It had been perhaps five hours since last he was here. He imagined they would have spent some time looking for Florence before giving up on her, but a group of four or five men could have travelled twenty or thirty miles north by now. He would have to follow them as best he could. But first, he had one more matter to attend to.

He found Kat Whetstone at the White Lion. 'I need answers about Buchan Ord. The story you told does not fit well with that of a woman of substance who cares not a jot for marriage. You were not betrothed to him, were you?'

She could see that he was serious. She sighed. 'I have never been betrothed to any man, nor ever intend to be. Anyway, Buchan Ord would make a poor sort of a husband. I do believe such a man would sell my inn from under me, steal my birthright and leave me destitute. Deceit is in his nature. But the story enticed Mr Cooper to bring me here, did it not?'

'Then what is your connection to the man?'

'He paid me. He wanted you both away from Sheffield. If you wish to know why, you must ask him yourself.'

'Was it true that you overheard him saying he intended to meet the Frenchman?'

'Yes. And you must know now that I did not dissemble – for you have found poor Mr Seguin. Or what is left of him.'

'Why did *you* wish to come here?'

'To see you again. What else?'

Shakespeare ignored the challenge in her voice. 'You flatter me, but I do not believe you.'

'Then you have a puzzle that you must solve.'

'Kat, this is no game. You are dealing with desperate men; you may even be an accessory to treason. I believe Ord and others are even now riding north with intent to free the Scots Queen. If anything you have done is seen to assist them – even by omission – then you would be liable to prosecution and everything that entails. It is essential that you be straight with me.'

'I know nothing of any plot regarding Mary Stuart. Do you have no faith in me?'

Shakespeare did not answer her, but pressed on with his own questions. 'Describe Buchan Ord. What is his appearance, his manner and his attire?'

'Well, he is a high-born Scottish gentleman with a pleasing Scottish accent to his voice.'

He snorted. 'Any mummer from the Theatre or a travelling troupe of players could mimic a Scottish voice. I could probably do it myself. It means nothing.'

'He is well dressed, as you would expect of one of Mary's fine young courtiers. He favours silks and bright colours. He is a very handsome, ostentatious young man. Some would call him immodest and might suspect him of profligacy. I liked him.'

'He is Harry Slide by another name, is he not?'

A frown crossed her brow, and then a curious little smile curled the edges of her pretty lips.

Shakespeare glanced at her. 'I want the truth from you. Now. Damn you, Kat. I want to know everything. What is your part in this? What is going on? Your deception puts you in grave danger, Kat Whetstone.'

'I thought it a marvellous jest.'

'Jest? You saw what happened to the Frenchman. Now tell me, whose side is Slide on? Is he Walsingham's man?'

'Why, he is on *your* side, John. Has he not said as much?'

'How did you discover that Harry Slide was Buchan Ord?'

'He told me. He had to – for I would never have helped a Scotchman or friend to the Queen of Scots. That would have been treason.'

'What do you know of Slide?'

'I know that he gave me silver for my part. I know no more than that.'

'You should not have concealed this from me. It is a most hazardous game. I would like to think that you had no notion how dangerous he is. With two men dead – murdered – you must now see that.'

She hesitated. Watching her closely, he thought he detected something different in her manner. She still feigned a brazen exterior, but beneath the surface there was something else. Not contrition, nor fear, but doubt. 'Kat, if you have done wrong, this may be your last chance to set it right.'

Now it was Kat's turn to sigh. 'Very well. It was all a foolish stratagem. Harry wanted you and your man Boltfoot to come here to Stratford. He told me what to say. And I told the ostler at the Cutler's Rest to reveal the Frenchman's destination to you.'

'Why did Slide want me here? He must have given you a reason.'

'I didn't ask. I didn't want to know. He paid me silver. And promised . . .'

'Promised what?'

'Promised to show me the world outside Sheffield.'

'So it was his idea for you to come, too?'

She nodded. 'It all seemed a fine game, and believe it or not, I have been pleased to renew your acquaintance. That is all. I had not expected murder, or treason. Now I am worried. I liked Monsieur Seguin or whatever his name might be, and seeing his lifeless body has scared me. Whoever killed the

Frenchman might also kill me, fearing that I know too much. I think Harry Slide has overstepped himself and he could bring me down with him.'

It could only mean one thing: a trap was being laid. But a trap for whom? And was he bait or prey? The more Shakespeare tried to unravel the threads of this strange web, the more tangled it became.

As he saddled up, Kat remained at his heels, begging him to take her with him to Sheffield. He ignored her tears and protests, although he could not prevent her saddling up another horse and riding out of the White Lion stableyard with him. He drove his own mount on at a reckless pace and by the time he reached Snitterfield, four miles from Stratford, he had lost her. He felt a surge of relief. She would turn tail and go back to the White Lion, where the innkeeper would provide her with safe escort when next he learnt of a trustworthy traveller going in the same direction.

As he headed north, the weather began to change. Clouds scudded across the dark sky and blanked out the moon. The lack of light made progress slower and increasingly perilous. But he pushed on, his biggest concern that his horse could stumble in an unseen pothole.

Hour followed hour and the highway seemed to stretch into everlasting blackness.

In the event it was not a pothole that proved his undoing, but his own exhaustion and a heavy, low-hanging branch, unseen by horse or rider. It smacked into Shakespeare's forehead with bone-crunching force.

He toppled from the saddle, still clutching the reins, dazed but conscious. The horse dragged him, bumping along the stony way until he managed to get a footing and pull it to a halt. His head throbbed in a line along the eyebrows and the highest point of his nose. He put his hand to his face and felt a sticky smear of blood above his eyes. He knew he couldn't carry on. Still unsteady on his feet, he led the horse to the side of the highway and fastened its reins to a sapling. Then he slumped down against a tree and, through the haze, tried to plan his next move. But he did not have the strength. Within seconds, he slithered sideways into the warm earth where sleep or unconsciousness came.

Boltfoot Cooper swung his caliver at the noise. A horse was approaching. He relaxed. It was only Will Shakespeare.

'Fresh bread,' Will said as he dismounted. 'One of Mother's beef pies – and some news.'

Boltfoot grunted and waited.

'My brother left a message at Henley Street. He says that Edward Arden and the others have gone from the Lodge and he has ridden north after them. However, he believes there is still great danger to Florence from Sir Thomas Lucy's men and he wants her to stay here until his return. You are charged with her safekeeping, Mr Cooper.'

Boltfoot grunted again. He had endured worse.

Anne did not look happy. 'People will begin to miss us.'

'You and I are to resume our normal lives. We can take turns to come here with supplies and news. Aunt Audrey and Mr Cooper will remain here constantly with Florence. When John returns, he will find a way to safety for them.' He turned to Boltfoot. 'Is all well?'

'An ounce or two of tobacco would not go amiss, young master.'

Will looked at him blankly.

'For smoking in a pipe.'

Will laughed. 'There is kindling aplenty in the woods. I do not think the fire will fail for want of wood.'

Boltfoot did not bother to explain. He glanced across at Florence Angel, her pale face glowing in the light of the fire. Her eyes flickered left and right, high and low, seeking out ghosts. Every sight of her made him uncomfortable.

It was not the ghosts that haunted Boltfoot, but the woman herself. She disturbed him and he did not trust her. How, he wondered, was he to keep her safe when she had no concern for herself? He recalled his crewmates' opinion of the Bible tale of Jonah and the whale. The mariners all said the seafarers of old had been justified in casting Jonah into the waves to quell the storm. How would they feel about this woman Florence, whose presence endangered them all? Would they have thrown *her* overboard?

Chapter 32

SHAKESPEARE WOKE WITH a start. He had heard a sound. Breathing in sharply, he tried to calm himself, not really sure if he was yet awake or still in deep slumber. He gazed into the darkness but could see nothing. The horse whinnied softly and Shakespeare exhaled. How long had he been asleep? He had no idea whether it was midnight or the hour before dawn. He opened his eyes again and saw a flicker of light. Was that the first glow of the new day?

He shivered, cold and damp, then went rigid. He tried to scramble to his feet, but he was unsteady, and his head felt as though it had been hammered by a siege ram. What *was* the light? It danced in the darkness like a firefly, moving ever closer. And then a face appeared, a human face. This was no dream. He reached into his belt for his dagger.

'John?'

'Who is there?'

'It's Kat, you fool.'

His knees gave way and he clutched at the tree for support. How much punishment could a head take? Battered at the temples by Badger Rench, and now this. 'Kat, you're in Stratford.'

'And you are babbling. Let me see that.' She held the dim lantern close to his face and sucked in air between her teeth.

'That isn't good.' She moved away with the lantern and he saw that her horse was tethered next to his own. She unhooked her water flask and brought it back to him and made him drink, then she touched his wound. 'I'll clean it. It may hurt a little.' She poured some water in her hand, then hitched up her petticoats, dampened a corner of the hem and dabbed at Shakespeare's face with it.

Her ministrations were tender and he felt himself drifting. He heard her say something, which sounded like 'You're cold,' and then he felt her take his head in her arms and nestle her warm, slender body close to his, and the pain gave way again to sleep.

They awoke with the light and she helped him on to his horse. No words passed between them. They began to ride, very slowly. He knew he must go faster, that they were losing valuable time, but every pace of the horse's hoofs on the dusty highway jolted his head and increased the pain.

A little over five miles along the track, they came to a small wayside inn. The smell of woodsmoke belching from the chimney was a welcome promise of warmth and cooked food. They handed the horses over to an ostler and then Kat helped Shakespeare into the warmth of the inn where she ordered a chamber and asked for food and ale.

'You are treating me like an invalid,' he said as she insisted he lie down on the bed.

'You *are* an invalid.'

'It's a scratch and I have a headache. It is nothing. We must ride on.'

'We?'

'You have followed me this far, Kat. We may as well ride on together.'

'If I am to ride with you, then you will do as I say, for I am now your physician and you are my patient. And what I say is this: you will lie here for at least three hours, perhaps more, for you have not yet slept enough. You will eat heartily, the horses will be fed and shod – and then we will ride until nightfall. If the going is good, we will be at the Cutler's Rest by then. If not, then we will sleep where we may. Is that clear enough for you, John? You are no use to anyone in your present state.'

He eased back into the pillows. Yes, indeed, she made perfect sense. Even if he could go now to the stables and ride non-stop to Sheffield, the horses most certainly could not. He yawned and closed his eyes.

The youth with the long red hair and red velvet suit shook Harry Slide by the hand. 'They now know you are not Buchan Ord,' he said quietly. 'Word came from Scotland of a body, found by his horse, garrotted.'

'And so I am no longer to be trusted?'

'She assumes you to be a spy, sent by Lennox or the Protestant grouping in Edinburgh, a notion that has been reinforced by her secretaries. So well did you play your part, it has not occurred to them that you were English. Why, you might even have fooled me, Mr Slide.'

'What of Leloup?'

'Oh, she has complete faith in him. And why should she not, for he is what we believe him to be, the Duke of Guise's man.'

Slide nodded. 'Indeed, Mr McKyle, indeed.' He did not bother to mention that François Leloup now lay dead in a tavern outhouse a hundred miles from Sheffield. For that would take some explaining. He moved the conversation on. 'Has the carriage arrived from the French embassy?'

'Aye, it has, and a wondrous thing it is to behold. Her Royal Majesty enjoyed her first excursion in it yesterday.'

'And all went well, Mr McKyle?'

'She was surrounded by guards. As secure as a prisoner in the Tower of London.'

'Good. Then Shrewsbury will be happy with the arrangements and the guard will be less alert. And so will she. The question now is – will she go along with the plan? After the betrayal, as she must see it, by Buchan Ord, will she allow herself to be rescued?'

'You have her ring?' asked McKyle.

'Yes, I have it.'

'Then she will do everything required of her. She is desperate. This is her only hope of redemption.'

Slide dug the ring from his purse and handed it over to McKyle. 'Give it to her tonight. Tell her that tomorrow is the day. Be sure to say that. She must beg leave of the earl to use the new carriage again. Tell her that her redemption – her salvation – is now certain if she does this.'

Shakespeare and Kat arrived in Sheffield at noon the following day. They had endured a gruelling journey and had been forced to make an overnight stop within twenty miles of Sheffield.

He had wanted to go on, but realised that she was right; any further progress in the pitch darkness of a cloud-covered night was simply unfeasible. And so they ate well, drank a little too much, took leisurely pleasure in each other's bodies and then talked in the soft quietness of their feather bed.

'You are different, Kat,' he said. 'I was brought up to believe that a woman wanted a good home, an able husband and sons. It seems you have other ideas. Will the Cutler's Rest be enough to hold you?'

'I have a heroine, John, a woman I would emulate.'

'The Queen of England?'

'The Countess of Shrewsbury. She has come from nothing

to a woman of riches and independence. That is what I will be one day. The Cutler's Rest is my beginning.'

Shakespeare had to laugh. 'But you say you don't want a husband! The countess garnered her wealth through four advantageous marriages.'

'And her own wit. Anyway, I might make an exception if a man was rich enough. Do you have a coffer full of gold?'

'Whole galleons weighed down by diamonds and pearls, and a castle in every county. Is that what you want to hear?'

'Kiss me again. Let me have no dreams.'

Some time in the middle of the night, there was nothing left for them but deep, untroubled sleep. When, at first light, he awoke, he felt his body was halfway healed. And then he remembered where he was going and why.

The Earl of Shrewsbury was in effusive mood. 'Mr Shakespeare, sir, you are returned to us.'

'With alarming news, my lord.'

'I do not want to hear it. My enemy the papist is happier than she has been in years, and so I am happy too. What is more, my own dear sovereign has given me leave to attend court for a season. I cannot tell you, sir, how I long to meet old friends and be at the centre of the world once more. The Queen of Scots complains that this place is no better than a prison. Well, if it is a prison for her, I contend it is the same for me.'

Shakespeare stabbed the bubble of his good humour. 'There is a plot to free her. I am certain the conspirators are here, now, in Sheffield and will act imminently.'

The earl produced one of his tired, resigned smiles. 'Mr Shakespeare, you do not discomfit me so easily. There is a plot to free her every week of every year. She is closer guarded than the Queen of England.'

'No, this is different. This time it is real, not imagined. This involves the Frenchman Leloup – Seguin as you knew him. He is now dead, shot through the face. It also involves the man you knew as Buchan Ord. Except that isn't his name.'

Shrewsbury raised his hand to stop Shakespeare's flow. 'Please, sir, you do me a disservice. Have I not ensured this woman's security for a dozen or more years? Give me some credit, sir. I know that Ord is not the man he claimed. News has reached us from his family in the Highlands of Scotland. The real Mr Ord is dead, choked to death with rope and flayed. His body had been lying undiscovered for two months or more. His family had been sick with worry, failing to understand why he did not write to them. It is assumed that he was killed by one of the Duke of Lennox's spies, who took his place here.'

'No. His place was taken by a man named Harry Slide, who claims to work for Mr Secretary, though I doubt that is true.'

Even this did not appear to disconcert Shrewsbury. He peered at his guest more closely. 'Mr Shakespeare, you look wretched, sir. What has happened to your head? Shall I call for help to have a bandage applied? Perhaps a poultice?'

'I fell foul of an unpleasant man named Badger Rench, and then I fell foul of a tree. But, my lord –' Shakespeare struggled to remain calm – 'we must take action to counter this plot! I swear it is real enough.'

'Then tell me. How is it to be effected?'

'We will find out soon enough. For the moment, keep her under lock and key. Double and re-double the guard.'

Shrewsbury laughed. 'She is as heavily guarded as ever. Perhaps you would have me muster the county militia and surround her with culverins. I say you underestimate me, Mr Shakespeare. We have known from the day she arrived that she would not want to be held captive, and so we have lived with the threat of escape ever since. Unless you bring me details of something new and definite, there is nothing more I can do. You must see this, sir.'

'Yes, I see it.'

'Then take some cider with me and tell me everything you know. I confess I am sorry that the French doctor of medicine is dead. I found him most charming and entertaining.'

Something still wasn't making sense. Whose side was Harry Slide really on? If he was on the side of Edward Arden, why would he have colluded in the murder of a young Catholic gentleman in Scotland? If he was on the side of Leicester and Sir Thomas Lucy, why was he assisting Edward Arden in his treacherous actions? Did the answer lie in the encrypted letter? No word had come from Walsingham. Perhaps the code-breaker Thomas Phelippes had failed to decipher it. Little made sense in this mission. And yet . . . he sensed that the solution was only a thought away. It was there, at the corner of his brain, like a butterfly in its chrysalis. He just needed to break the husk, let it fly – and then catch it. And then he would understand everything.

He shivered. Perhaps he did understand. Perhaps . . .

He had thought they were laying a trap, but they weren't. They were laying a *trail* – and he had followed it, just as they wanted, like a hound with the scent of a royal hart in its nostrils. The question was *why*. He was no longer listening to Shrewsbury but thinking. His eyes stared at the earl's moving lips. He was talking but it was difficult to take in what he actually said.

'My lord, you said something when I arrived. You said you were happier than you had been in years – and you said it was because the Queen of Scots was happy.'

'That is so. I have great hopes that her ailments will vanish like the wind now that she has the fine caroche and six, courtesy of our own dear sovereign and the French embassy, that she has wanted for so long.'

'A carriage and six horses? Why? Where will she go?'

'She can take the air, see the countryside.'

'And do you consider that safe?'

'The paths they are taking have been scouted. And with her bad legs, there is no fear that she could run. Nothing can happen.' The earl picked up a paper from the table. 'Here is the ordinance from the Privy Council. It says that Mary is to be allowed to go up to three miles outside my parkland, provided there is no concourse of people to look on her. And she is, of course, heavily guarded, as always.'

'How can you be certain? Your chief of guards Mr Wren inspired no confidence in me. And are these the same guards who failed to stop my man Mr Cooper entering this castle?'

'I can be certain, Mr Shakespeare, because we have received two men from court whose credentials as sentries and fighting men could not be bettered anywhere in England. One of them, Mr Topcliffe, you already know. The other is Hungate, my lord of Leicester's own best man. I do believe no papist renegades will get past them.'

'And when do you plan to allow the Queen of Scots to venture out?'

'Why, she is already taking the air, Mr Shakespeare. I believe they have been gone ten minutes or more.'

Mary Stuart sat back on the sumptuous cream leather bench in her carriage and felt like a queen. She always made sure she looked like a queen and acted like one, but it was many years since she had *felt* like one. The years of captivity, silk-lined though it was, had taken their toll on her belief that she would ever reign again, either in Scotland or here in England, her birthright.

She had the leather blinds rolled up on all four windows and could not take her eyes off the earl's rolling acres of parkland. As the horses drove on, the grey walls of the castle – her prison – receded behind her.

'It is a holy day, Your Majesty.'

Mary removed her gaze momentarily and smiled at Mary Seton, her old friend and attendant, who sat on the bench opposite. 'Indeed it is.' She held up her hand to show the two rings she wore: her own phoenix, now restored to her by Mr McKyle, and the cross of Lorraine from the Duke of Guise. 'All my ailments are gone. The pain has vanished. I truly believe I could dance.'

'Your skin is glowing, ma'am. You look no older than you did the day you wed the Dauphin. I would swear you are not yet twenty.'

The Queen held a fan of peacock feathers. She tapped it on her companion's knee. 'You are foolish, Mary Seton. It is my birthday soon and I shall be forty.' But the truth was, she liked the compliment. She held up the looking glass that hung from her waist on a slender silver chain and gazed at her face and hair. Mary Seton had busked her a beautiful new periwig using nun's tresses sent from France. It was set with a dozen little pearls, all framed by a hooded cape of royal blue velvet for the coming journey. In her arms, she held her favourite little dog.

'I slept last night, the first time in many weeks.'

'I am certain it has done your health nothing but good.'

'But I fear I am still a little fat and stooped.'

'Ma'am, I promise you, there is none more comely in this land. No looking glass nor portrait can ever do justice to your beauty.'

'I have often wondered if that is the reason my cousin will not receive me at court. She fears she will be outshone by me.'

'Your Majesty, you are the sun to her moon. Your brightness would always eclipse her dull glow.'

'But my legs and gut: they are sore swollen. Tell me true, Mary Seton, how will my beauty play in Paris?'

'You will be loved and feted wherever you go.'

'I have been so lonely and forgotten that I no longer know my standing in the world.'

'That will be put to rights today with the ending of your confinement.'

'Is this really the day, Mary?'

'I am certain of it, ma'am. Mr McKyle said that all was ready, did he not? I am sure that Monsieur Seguin would not have sent the ring to you unless he was satisfied that all was well. All you need do is open the carriage door when the time is nigh.'

'Then let us play our part. We have a long journey ahead. To think that in a few days we will be in France at the Hôtel de Guise . . .'

Mary Seton shook her head. 'Not *we*, ma'am. You must go alone. I cannot accompany you, for I would slow you down.'

'But we have been companions since childhood! Do you think I could do without you now? Who would dress my hair and set my periwig? I could not survive in Paris without you.'

'You will survive very well, Your Majesty.'

Mary was thoughtful, then smiled. It was a smile of such warmth and joy that it had won her many admirers over the years. These days it was rarely in evidence. 'Yes. Yes, I shall. But I will miss you, nonetheless.'

'I will come to France in good time. I will not be wanted here, or in Edinburgh. They will not keep me against my will.'

'Mary Seton, you are more kin to me than ever was this cousin, Elizabeth. I think her closer kin to the Indies tigers.'

The Queen stroked her pet dog and breathed in the fresh air.

Her eyes were on the horizon now, searching. Searching for salvation. High in the sky, a buzzard circled. She followed its lazy, lonely trail, its enormous wings catching the late warmth. She was that bird. High-born, destined to fly above the world, alone and majestic. Always alone. It was the curse of sovereignty.

The carriage clattered along the stone path that led from the castle away from the parkland. Its canopy was tan leather with gold-leaf edging. The lower panels of wood were painted blue, with yet more gold trim. At each corner was a sturdy wheel, shod in hammered iron. Everyone who had seen it on the long journey north had known that this was a vehicle for royalty, so how could Mary Stuart not now feel that her day was come?

And yet every glance from the window told her that she was indeed still a prisoner. Ahead of the coach rode four guards, with four more outriding. Close by the doors rode four more, and six bringing up the rear. All of them were heavily armed with loaded petronels, swords and axes. It would take an army to get past them and seize their charge.

The day was so quiet, the parkland so empty. The only sound was the thud of horses' hoofs and the rattle of iron-shod wheels. How, in the name of the Holy Father, was this escape to be effected? No one had told her what was to happen. All she knew was that she must be in this carriage, in this park, on this day, at this time, and that she must step down from her cabin at the sound of a whistle.

And then she heard another sound: the shrill cry of a hunting horn.

Chapter 33

THE HUNT CAME over the rise in full flood. Scores of horses and dogs, men in the saddle, men on foot, advancing like great ocean waves. The hounds and spaniels bayed and whined and sniffed, the horns blew. Ahead of them, the stag darted and stumbled in blind panic.

Within moments, the carriage holding Mary, Queen of Scots and her lady-in-waiting Mary Seton was surrounded and buffeted by hounds and horses and huntsmen. The stag was away, no more than sixty yards ahead of the main body of the chase, but its cause was doomed; it would never make cover.

The guards surrounding the carriage were lost in confusion. Sergeant Wren was supposed to be in control, but he had never expected something like this. His orders were clear: if anyone comes close – especially a band of men – then aim your petronel and fire. Fire and fire again. Kill them all without question or mercy. Those were his orders, but no one had mentioned a hunting party chasing a stag across their path. Was he supposed to shoot down a large body of men comprising at least half the aristocracy and gentry of this part of Yorkshire? And all for chasing a stag across land that was not even part of the earl's estates? Huntsmen never took note of boundaries or property rights when hot on the scent of a fine stag. Wren couldn't start shooting at these gentlemen; it would be sheer bloody murder.

Anyway, he and his men were vastly outnumbered and lost in the mêlée. He looked for Mr Hungate, hoping for some guidance, but could not see him.

By the time he had hesitated, it was too late. His control over his men was lost and they were chaotically mingled into the body of the hunt. And then he caught sight of Hungate, adorned in the Earl of Shrewsbury's livery, riding away from the hunt. Wren rode towards him but was waved away and signalled to stay back. Wren bowed with more than a little fear, for it was said Hungate was the Privy Council's own man. Best not to ask questions. Some things were better left unasked and unknown.

Suddenly, the carriage broke from the confusion of horses and men. The coachman lashed the six coursers with his long whip and they broke into a powerful gallop, in the opposite direction to the stag. The carriage was heavy, but the stallions were broad and strong and he drove them mercilessly.

Inside the coach, the Scots Queen clutched her dog as they were rocked and tossed from side to side. Her companion tried to help her, but she herself was thrown to the floor. The carriage rattled and lurched. It was a stately construction, never designed for such violent movement.

Onwards it flew. Mary's heart was pounding. She managed to grip the sill of the window. She looked out and ahead, the wind in her hair, her vision blurred by the bone-rattling motion of the charging vehicle. Where was this carriage going? Where were her rescuers? Surely the coach would not be able to go far before the guards regrouped and cut it down; horsemen will always be faster than a wagon drawn by horses – even horses as superb as these.

On the brow of the hill she saw three horsemen and she caught her breath. There they were: the rescue party, not more than a hundred yards away. She could see their weapons of war. They had another horse with them, riderless. That would be her mount. But still she was bewildered. How could three men fight off a squadron of heavily armed guards with orders to kill? And then she recognised the face of one of them: Buchan Ord. Her heart lifted at the sight of her charming courtier, then fell. How could that be Ord? That man, whoever he was, was someone else, for Ord, she now knew, had been murdered in Scotland . . .

John Shakespeare had thrown himself on his horse and ridden harder than he had ever ridden before. His thoughts were as clear as daylight. He knew now. He understood. A trail had been laid for him and he had followed it, halfway across England and back again. What had not been clear was where the trail led and what its purpose was. All along, he had believed he should be seeking to foil a papist plot to free Mary, Queen of Scots. But that wasn't it.

Yes, a band of deluded and hapless conspirators at Arden House had sought Mary's freedom, but their efforts were laughable. That was the reason Sir Thomas Lucy had refused to send pursuivants against Edward Arden; he had to be at liberty if he was to be taken seriously as a papist conspirator.

The true purpose of all that had happened was a great deal more sinister.

The real plan was Mary's murder.

She was to be shot dead in the act of escaping. The bosom serpent was to be cut down as she tried to slither away. That was where Hungate and Topcliffe came in.

The problem with that proposition was the matter of his part in it. *Why go to such great lengths to involve me? How could my investigations help anyone? And who was the paymaster? Whose gold paid for Harry Slide's exploits?* These were questions that would have to wait. Time was running out, and Shakespeare had to save a Queen – the 'Scots devil' as Shakespeare's own master, Walsingham, called her.

There might well be powerful forces who wished her dead, but that was not John Shakespeare's way; he was not about to condone the cold-blooded murder of any man. Or woman.

Ahead of him he saw a mass of riders, footmen and hounds. He estimated two hundred men and twice that number of beasts. They were bearing down on a stag. The kill was certain. A pair of hounds snapped at the deer's heels and it stumbled. A crossbow bolt thudded into its rump; another caught its flank. The animal's hind legs dragged, then its forelegs gave way and it was down.

The hounds and huntsmen descended on it to quench their deathlust. Their blood up, the hounds would eat well this day and the huntsmen would copulate hard with wives and mistresses and get falling drunk. All would sleep like children. The joy of the kill.

Shakespeare was looking way beyond them. The carriage and six had sprinted away from the hunters and the guards and was heading towards a rise where three horsemen waited. Even from this distance, Shakespeare fancied he could recognise them: Harry Slide, Edward Arden and one other. Narrowing his eyes, he believed he knew the third one, too, the hapless gardener and priest, Hugh Hall. So the trap was about to be sprung. Just like the stag, Mary of Scots would be torn apart. She was as good as dead.

He kicked his horse and urged it on. It was fresh and fast, and Shakespeare had always had a taste for race-riding against the other youths in the fields and lanes around Stratford.

Cutting through the press of men and animals, he crouched low into the saddle, goading his mount ever onwards, ever faster. He was clear of the huntsmen now. But twenty or thirty yards ahead of him one of the guards was closing on the carriage. Was that him, the killer? He had to beat him there.

Suddenly, his horse found another turn of foot. It was at the quarters of the guard in a matter of strides, then past him and alongside the carriage. Through the window he saw a blur: Mary and her lady-in-waiting, being thrown about like peas in a pan of boiling water. He had to stop this coach.

Shakespeare didn't even think about his next move, for if he had, he would never have attempted such a thing. He removed his right foot from the stirrup, edged the horse left, brought the animal within a yard of the coachman's seat and committed himself.

His left hand caught the iron support rail at the end of the driver's bench, his foot pushed off from the stirrup and suddenly he was free of the galloping horse and swinging in space. His other hand grasped the rail, but his lower body and legs were dangling loose, close to a front wheel. If he touched it, he would lose his grip on the rail and he would be dragged down and crushed beneath the wheel. He swung his left foot up on to the protruding board of the undercarriage, then had the leverage to pull his right leg up towards the coach driver's seat.

The coachman had other ideas. Holding the reins with his left hand, he grabbed up his petronel and tried to slam the butt of the weapon down on Shakespeare's fingers. As he did so, Shakespeare saw the face beneath the coachman's cap: Richard Topcliffe. He also saw the blow coming.

His hand broke free of the rail and snatched at the gun as it came down. The movement jerked Topcliffe sideways and, simultaneously, Shakespeare raised his right leg further on to the footboard. In the same movement, he pulled himself up and held the middle of the petronel like a spear, thrusting it forward, smacking the muzzle of Topcliffe's weapon back into his own face.

Crying out and falling sideways, Topcliffe instinctively let go of the reins and clutched at his face. Blood seeped through his fingers from his torn cheek. Shakespeare needed no more prompting. Throwing the petronel down from the careering coach, he got hold of the lapels of Topcliffe's coat, wrenched him from his seat and flung him down to the ground after his weapon.

He snatched up the reins and jerked the lead horse violently right. Kicking up a cloud of dust, the horses veered sharply away and the carriage went up on two wheels. He had driven carts and wagons before, but never a majestic coach such as this with six strong and speedy coursers. For what seemed like half a minute, but was probably no more than two or three seconds, the carriage teetered over and Shakespeare feared it would upend. But then the horses found their new line and the carriage came down with a jolt on all four wheels. From behind the panel he heard a scream.

Shakespeare lashed the horses with the long whip. He looked around him, horribly aware that the guard must be close. Though he had not yet seen the man's face, he feared, too, that he knew who it was.

Other guards were making headway now, but it was the closest one that held his attention, for he was almost parallel. Surely he would not have the courage to leap aboard the carriage. Surely he would not be steady enough in the saddle to loose his weapon.

He continued to turn the carriage; he had to drive it back towards the castle. One thing was certain: if he stopped, they were all dead. The guards would consider him their enemy, trying to abduct Mary, and would not wait to ask questions before blowing him to dust.

Then he saw the face of the guard in his wake: he wore the Shrewsbury livery, but he was no guard. It was as he had suspected: this was Ruby Hungate.

All was lost. He knew what Hungate could do with sword and pistol. Had Walsingham's steward not told him with awe that Hungate could shoot a bird from the saddle of a galloping horse? And even if that were an exaggeration, six horses in harness and a man in the driving seat were an easy enough target for a pistolier of such skill.

He cracked the whip again, trying to drain every last ounce of energy from the superb stallions. If only he could make it to the castle gatehouse, there might still be a chance. Hungate would not want to kill Mary there, for how could anyone think she had died in the act of escaping if she was clearly being driven back to her prison?

Now Hungate was level with Shakespeare. This was it. Would the bullet strike him in the head or in the heart – or would Hungate shoot the horses to bring the whole carriage crashing to a bloody halt?

And then they came, streaming out from the castle gatehouse. A body of guardsmen, some on foot, some on horseback. Above them, on the battlements, Shakespeare saw the Earl of Shrewsbury looking down in grim silence on the unfolding drama. Glancing sideways, he saw that Hungate too had spotted the earl and the advancing guardsmen.

Hungate reined in. For a few moments, he gazed on the approaching horde of castle guards, then he looked up at the commanding figure of Shrewsbury again. Finally, he bared his teeth at Shakespeare and shook his head as if to say, *This isn't over*. He thrust his pistol into his belt, wheeled his horse a half-turn, and spurred it into a ferocious gallop. His game was done; he had lost this round.

As the guards swarmed around like wasps on the scent of

sweet syllabub, Shakespeare slowed the horses and at last brought them to a halt. Steam rose from their flanks and their great barrel chests heaved.

Shakespeare took a deep breath and climbed down from his perch, handing the long reins to one of the guards. He went to the carriage door. The blinds had been rolled down, blanking out the interior. One of the locked doors had been flung open by the violence of the chase. He stepped up and peered inside. A dog yapped. In the gloom, he saw two women, huddled into their cloaks. One was hooded in blue velvet. He could not see her face. She was shying away from him, shrinking into the corner of the seat, clutching at the dog. '*Ne me regardez pas! Ne me regardez pas!* You will not look at me, you will not!'

Her companion moved from her seat to block the intruder's view of her mistress.

'You are safe now, ma'am,' Shakespeare said. 'My lord of Shrewsbury's men are here to escort you back to your apartments.'

From the depths of the huddle, an arm appeared. The ungloved hand hung limp, sickly and pale and a little too fat. A hand with rings, one showing a phoenix, the other a cross of Lorraine. Shakespeare understood that he was supposed to genuflect and kiss this blotched, unhealthy piece of royal flesh. Instead, he closed the coach door and stepped away.

Chapter 34

THE EARL OF Shrewsbury cut a miserable figure. It
seemed to Shakespeare that he would do well to command a seamstress to take in his fine old doublet and have his
steward order new ruffs from London. For a man known to be
among the wealthiest in the land, there was no reason to worry
about the cost. Perhaps he had merely lost interest in his
appearance through being away from court so long.

They were sipping fine French wines in his library.

'I wish I was surprised,' the earl said after Shakespeare had
explained all he knew of the conspiracy. 'The question is: what
will you tell your master about these events?'

'The truth, my lord. Mr Secretary can sniff a lie at a hundred
paces.'

'Yes, I believe he can. Well, I am sure you cannot lay all the
blame at my door. It was the Privy Council and the Queen
herself who authorised the carriage for the papist. And in the
event, very little harm has been done. Would you not agree?'

Shakespeare smiled without comment. No, he would not
agree at all. He believed a great deal of harm had been done –
and the danger was far from over. It had been a shocking
episode that left many questions unanswered, and one in particular unasked. Perhaps Shrewsbury was afraid to ask it
because he already knew the answer: who was the paymaster?

Who had planned this conspiracy to murder the Queen of Scots? Certainly not Hungate, Topcliffe or Harry Slide. They were but spokes in a bigger wheel.

That was a question to be asked in due course. For the moment, the overriding thought in Shakespeare's head was the problem of Edward Arden, John Somerville and Hugh Hall. What had become of them? They may have been gullible fools, but their conspiracy to free Mary and kill Elizabeth had been real enough in their own minds. They had intended harm to the realm. So where were they now – and did they still have plans? If they were at liberty, then they must be considered dangerous.

And where, too, were Hungate, Topcliffe and Slide? This all felt far from complete.

As the question formed in his mind, the door opened and Richard Topcliffe strode into the library. His visage was grim, his cheek bloody where Shakespeare had gouged him with his own weapon.

The earl glared at him. 'Dick, what has been going on? Do you know anything about this?'

'I believe it has been a poor day's hunting, George. A fine stag was taken, but there was a yet greater prize that slipped us.'

'Dick, if you are part of this, then you are not my friend.'

'You mean do I dispose of vermin? All true Englishmen must do their part to cleanse this land.'

'No, that is not good enough. You treat me with discourtesy and abuse my hospitality and friendship.'

'George, I am your very blood brother. No one does more at court to promote your reputation and kindle love for you in Her Majesty's heart.'

'Words, words, words! Mr Shakespeare has laid accusations that there was a plot to murder the Queen of Scots – and you do not deny you knew of it. Perhaps you were a party to it.'

Topcliffe glared at Shakespeare. 'He speaks gibberish. I was hunting with my friends. There was some commotion, that is all. No one tried to kill the heifer.'

Shakespeare beat his fist on the table. 'You are a liar, Topcliffe. It was you who drove the carriage.'

'And you are a dung-beetle of very small wit and too great an attachment to Rome. I would have *you* investigated, Shakespeare. You keep unsound company.'

'How many others were involved? What of the huntsmen? Did they believe they were assisting a murder – or an escape? Mr Secretary will hear the truth about you. You believe yourself favoured by Her Royal Majesty but I will ensure your days of preferment are numbered.'

'You talk out of your arse, Shakespeare. It is one long fart that needs be stoppered with goodly cork.'

Shakespeare had a mind to strike Topcliffe down and do yet more damage to his face. Instead, he clicked his heels and gave the Earl of Shrewsbury a curt bow. 'My report will be in Sir Francis Walsingham's hands within the week. I must go now for the stink in here has become too great. Good day to you, my lord.' He did not look at Topcliffe, merely stalked from the room. More than anything, he needed a good night's rest.

In the morning, Shakespeare rose from a long sleep at the Cutler's Rest and broke his fast in company with the innkeeper, Geoffrey Whetstone.

'I must thank you for bringing my daughter safe home,' the landlord said.

'The truth is, she brought *me* safely here.'

Whetstone took in the damage wrought on Shakespeare's head. 'Yes, she mentioned that she had found you in a bad way. Well, I thank you all the same.'

'She is a remarkable young woman.'

'The word you seek is *spirited*.'

'You make her sound like a headstrong horse, Mr Whetstone!'

The innkeeper laughed and his large frame shook. 'She was ever wont to go her own way.'

'Yes, I had noted it.'

'I often think she will go from me, for her ambition knows no bounds. Her desire for life is too big for Sheffield town. But what would I be without her? The light and warmth would go from here if she went away.'

'She will stay, I am certain.' Shakespeare smiled, uncertain that he truly believed this.

'My problem, Mr Shakespeare, is that I can deny her nothing. When she demands something of me, I cannot say no. The truth, as you now know, is that there was no Scottish man. I pray our dissimulation did no harm.'

Shakespeare sighed. It had only been at the last moment in Stratford that it dawned on him that Slide and Ord were one and the same; the fact that Slide was at Arden Lodge where he would have expected Ord, the way Slide kept disappearing and had been desperate not to be taken to Sheffield Castle where he would have been recognised – and finally Kat's own description of the man. At last it had all added up.

What now? Leloup and Angel were dead and their killers still not apprehended. Badger Rench, too, lay in his grave. But none of the three deaths could be laid at the door of Mr Whetstone or his daughter. Kat came into the taproom with a jug of weak cider which she set down on the table between her father and Shakespeare. 'What are you men talking of? Not me, I trust.'

'I need answers from you, Kat. I need to find the whereabouts of Harry Slide.'

'Harry? Nothing could be easier. He is here at the Cutler's

Rest. Came at midnight and the night porter put him in a chamber.'

Shakespeare was aghast. 'And you did not think to alert me to this? Take me to him.'

'He's going nowhere in a hurry. Sup some cider with your breakfast first and let me examine your head. I think you have been more than a little concussed.'

Shakespeare downed a cup of cider. 'The devil take my head. Let us go to him now.'

Harry Slide was fully dressed, lying on a bank of pillows atop a large feather bed. He was snoring softly. Kat shook him. 'Wake up, Harry. Mr Shakespeare is here to see you.'

He yawned but didn't open his eyes. 'I'll need a kiss, Kat.'

She pecked his cheek. 'Come on, Harry, rouse yourself.'

'*You* rouse me.'

Kat rolled her eyes. 'I will leave you two gentlemen together to fight out your differences.' She began to open the door. 'And if you come to blows and damage anything, you will pay for it.'

Shakespeare approached the bed and touched the point of his dagger to Slide's throat. 'Perhaps this will wake you.'

Slide recoiled from the cold metal, but brushed the blade aside with the back of his hand as though it were a bluefly. He looked at Shakespeare, then to Kat. 'What is this?'

'Just talk to him, Harry.' She walked out and shut the door behind her.

Slide raised his eyes to the ceiling. 'She was happy enough to take my silver, wasn't she? Just like a woman; looks like an innocent lamb and has the teeth of a wolf. Just like my wife and sweethearts.'

'That's enough.' Shakespeare put the dagger back in his belt and began searching the room. 'I want answers from you. What treason have you been involved in here? You planned to kill the Scots Queen, but what were your plans for me? Was I to be killed next?'

'*Kill you*, sir? Indeed not. I bear no enmity for you, nor wish you harm. As far as I am concerned, this was only ever about doing for the Scots devil and serving my country like a good subject of Her Majesty.'

Shakespeare rifled through Slide's clothing, and then spotted a leather bag leaning against the table leg. He picked it up, aware of Slide's eyes following him. 'Why did you think it necessary to lure me to Warwickshire and back here again?'

'Ah, yes . . .'

'Well? Speak, man, for I *do* bear you enmity and *do* wish you harm.' He unbuckled the bag. 'What have we here?'

'Mr Shakespeare, these are delicate matters. Great men are involved, as I am certain you must be aware.'

Shakespeare tipped up the contents of the bag and a set of large documents fell to the floor. He picked them up: official maps of Sheffield and south Yorkshire carrying the Shrewsbury crest. He glanced at Slide and raised his eyebrows. 'My lord of Shrewsbury will be pleased to see these.'

Slide shrugged. 'They were borrowed, not stolen. I had always intended returning them to the castle.'

'You walk a dangerous line, Mr Slide. Give me the whole truth. Now. Or I will have you hauled to the town gaol in irons. Topcliffe and Hungate may have protection elsewhere, but I rather think you will find yourself alone and exposed, for I know my lord of Shrewsbury is mighty discomfited by these events and requires a scapegoat. I think you will fit his purposes nicely. Your fine yellow silk doublet will be pleasingly eye-catching as you swing on the gibbet.'

Harry Slide spread his arms, palms up. 'What can I say? I am at your mercy.'

'Indeed you are.'

'Very well. You were to have been an honest witness. You were supposed to tell the world that there had indeed been a conspiracy to free the Scots Queen and so prove that her death was not assassination, but justifiable homicide. The notion was that you would place your hand on a Bible and would swear that you had uncovered a plot to snatch her to freedom. And not only that: that she was also to be placed on her cousin's throne. And you would have spoken all this with the gloss of truth, for you had indeed uncovered such a plot.'

Shakespeare laughed. 'Why should anyone believe me?'

'Because you are honest and worthy of respect. You have done nothing to sully your reputation. Anyone who questioned you would believe you.'

'This is preposterous.'

'Trust me, you are plausible. I am certain your testimony would have played well across the capitals of Europe. The masters of the Vatican, the Escorial, the Hôtel de Guise – all would shake their heads and shrug their shoulders and say, "Well, the English had no alternative but to kill the mad witch." And even if they had their doubts and made protest, they would be able to prove nothing. I do believe a great deal of thought and discussion went into choosing you for this role. Why else was I required to bring you and your man to Stratford if not to involve you in the events at Arden Lodge?'

Slide's story had a strange ring of truth to it. If the Catholic plotters were clearly identified, then the Privy Council would be able to point the finger at Cardinal Allen and the Duke of Guise. *Those are the men to blame; they sent the traitor Benedict Angel and the wolf's snout François Leloup into our midst to seduce Edward Arden and others to their foul design on England. We did our best to protect Mary, but Arden and Angel and their masters in Europe gave us no choice . . .*

No one in the wider world would have heard tell of Harry

Slide or his intrigues. He would simply slip back into the stinking sewer whence he came. Edward Arden, John Somerville, Hugh Hall, the Angels and all the other recusant families of Warwickshire and Yorkshire – they were the ones to blame. Men like Sir Bassingbourne Bole, with whom Buchan Ord was said to have conspired. The evidence was there for all to see.

And he, John Shakespeare, would have proved it. Young and biddable, he would have provided the link from Arden Lodge to Sheffield. That was the plan, but they had underestimated him. He may have been untested in the world of secrets, but he was no fool.

As for those in Warwickshire, Arden and his band were merely hapless tools, each one of them damned by his or her own hand, duped and played for gulls.

'Tell me: what has happened to Edward Arden and Father Hall?'

'They are limping home to Warwickshire.'

'You were with them. Why did you not arrest them once the plot to kill Mary was foiled?'

Slide shrugged. 'What can I say? They will hang soon enough. Once our little plan failed, it was best their link with Sheffield was severed, so I sent them on their way. Don't want folk going around saying we had it in mind to kill the Queen of Scots.'

'Why should I not arrest you, here and now?'

'Because you and I are on the same side, Mr Shakespeare. We work for the same man. It is Arden and Hall and Somerville – and Mary of Scots herself – who are the enemy.'

'Are you saying Mr Secretary ordered you to do this?'

'I am saying nothing of the sort.'

'But your implication is clear.'

'No, it is *your* imagination. You seek a head to a snake, but perhaps you are dealing with a hydra.'

Shakespeare glared at Slide. Short of the rack, was there any way to extract the truth from this man? He battled to contain his fury. 'Let me put the question this way: who commissioned you to trick your way into Mary's court here in Sheffield? Who fills your purse?'

Slide spread his hands. 'Mr Shakespeare, you cannot ask me questions like that. When I do the bidding of a great man – or woman – I pledge complete discretion. As I shall prove to you one day when, as I pray, you ask me to do some stealthy work for you. Trust me, Mr Shakespeare, I beg you. I will answer all your questions but not that one.'

'Was it Walsingham?'

'That is all I will say on the subject.'

Was there a hesitation? 'You told me you were his man.'

'I have many bills to pay – gaming debts, tailors. I am but a hireling, and so must find work where I can. I work for other men – and women – when the right price is offered. And when they are on the side of loyalty to England and Elizabeth.'

'And yet Walsingham would happily see Mary dead.'

'You have my answer.'

'Burghley? Leicester?'

Slide did not even shake his head.

'Then at least answer me this honestly: if your plan had been successful – if Hungate had killed the Queen of Scots – what would have happened to Arden and Hall?'

'What do you think, Mr Shakespeare? Would the Council have wished them to appear in a court of law and admit their felonies, or would it have preferred them dead at the scene of the crime?'

'You tell me.'

'I think one of each.'

Shakespeare's anger subsided and he looked at Slide with something approaching respect. He was sly and calculating and lived up to his name. In fact, he had all the attributes of a Walsingham intelligencer. This had all been worked out very carefully in advance. The timid Father Hall would have been arrested and then transported to the Tower, where he would have endured the rack, hot irons and the scavenger's daughter. Then he would have been hauled into court, so that he might confess to the world that there had, indeed, been a papist plot to snatch away Mary. Shakespeare would have backed up his testimony in court. What a sweet conclusion that would have been for those who wished the Queen of Scots dead. What a sweet killing.

Arden, though, would have been of far less use, for he would *not* have gone tamely to the scaffold. He would have raged at the Earl of Leicester and Sir Thomas Lucy and Elizabeth. His evidence would have served to open windows into secret practices that the Privy Council would rather wish to remain obscured. A quick bullet in the head or a sword thrust to the belly would have been his fate – and indeed might well already have been carried out. Slide, he was sure, would have been more than capable of dispensing such swift retribution.

'What of John Somerville? I am surprised he was not with you.'

'Oh, you know Somerville. He is like a crazed weasel, uncontrollable. He left us just outside Stratford. Said he had to go and kill the Queen. Can you picture that gibbering ape of a man getting within a mile of Elizabeth with his pistol?'

'God's blood – you mean he is on his way to murder Her Majesty?'

'He said he had a friend at court, one with influence who could grant him access to the presence chamber. He had convinced himself that from there he could burst into her privy apartments and shoot her dead. I did not bother to disabuse him.'

'But this is—'

Slide put up a hand. 'Fear not, I sent word to Mr Secretary. Somerville will get nowhere near court.'

Shakespeare did not feel reassured. 'Madder things have happened, have they not? Why, I have even heard tell of an Englishman who rode to Scotland to kill a young man named Buchan Ord so that he could adopt his name and voice and be taken into the bosom of the Queen of Scots. Why did no one bother to disabuse *that* man?'

'I take your point, Mr Shakespeare. But for your information, I did not kill Buchan Ord. And you might like to know that Ord was himself a greased priest, ordained in Douai with so many other traitors.'

'And if you did not kill him, then who did?'

'I know not. I was merely commanded to learn to say the mass, adopt a Scottish mode of speech, dress and character – and was told all I needed to know about his past. These were simple matters for one who has trod the boards, for I knew that none of the courtiers at the castle had ever met him.'

'And the Frenchman, Leloup – who killed him?'

'That was Somerville. That's when I knew for certain he was insane and incapable of rational thought or action. Leloup had brought us a large quantity of gold for arms and equipment. Also Mary's ring, to prove that she bestowed her blessing on the enterprise. These things were necessary to keep the faithful inspired.'

'Then why kill him?'

'Poor François – whom I liked a great deal – took one look at my little band of conspirators and decided they were without merit. I had searched the country high and low for these people, and yet he dismissed them out of hand! I tried to persuade him that the plot could work with Arden and Hall and Florence, but he would not have it. He told me he could not believe that in the whole of England I was not able to find a more competent and soldierly body of men. I think more than anything it was Somerville and Florence who disturbed him. Florence was seeing ghosts and Somerville was leaping up and down like a monkey, moon-mad. He thrust the muzzle of his damned pistol in François's face and pulled the trigger. I was appalled.'

'I suppose Somerville killed Benedict Angel, too.'

'It is possible, of course. I know nothing of it, except that the death is a mystery and one that caused great consternation at Arden Lodge.'

Shakespeare thought he detected some flicker of discomfort in the man's expression, but perhaps not, for he was smiling and seemed as light-hearted as ever. But that seemed to be Slide all over. On the surface, he was an amicable man, the kind anyone would be happy to work with; he had certainly charmed his way successfully into Mary Stuart's heart. And yet Shakespeare was certain he was capable of almost anything, if the price was right. 'What do you think?' he asked.

'If I knew, I would tell you.'

'Very well, answer me this: what is your connection to the murderous Ruby Hungate and the foul Topcliffe?'

'At times a man must consort with verminous bedfellows in this war of secrets. Mr Secretary will have told you that, I am certain. Did he not ask *you* to work with Topcliffe? I would prefer to work with someone like you, Mr Shakespeare, for Topcliffe is not to my taste. But there is one thing I will tell you, unasked. You mentioned Mr Hungate, a man I would never cross and I believe you should know this of him: he has a most unwholesome disliking for the papists of Warwickshire. In particular, he has sworn to kill Florence Angel.'

'Just because she is a papist?'

'Something more. Something buried in his past.'

'Her kinship to the Ardens?' He recalled that Walsingham's secretary had mentioned Hungate bore a grudge against the family. He remembered, too, the intense questioning Hungate had subjected him to. He had been desperate to know how long the family had lived in Stratford. *Had their name once been Angelus?* Perhaps they were people he had known before, in another place. It might explain his resentment.

'And,' Slide went on, his expression now serious, 'Mr Hungate has also developed a deep loathing for *you*. I think it fair to say that his rage was as explosive as powder yesterday when you foiled his plans for the Queen of Scots.'

'Well, I can look after myself,' said Shakespeare. 'And he will not find Florence.'

Slide sucked in air through his teeth. 'Forgive me for being the bearer of bad tidings, but I fear you are mistaken. He had your brother followed before we rode to Sheffield. The unpleasant Constable Nason was his tracker. Despite his sluggardly demeanour, he has some little talent as a stalker, for he found what Mr Hungate was seeking. Apparently, Miss Angel is hiding in the woods in some ruins.'

Shakespeare went cold. 'Hungate knows this?'

'Yes, he does. And he has a start on you of several hours. He is most cheery at the prospect of what lies ahead. Sees it as some consolation for yesterday's failure to do for Mary of Scots. Perhaps he will win another red stone for his ear.'

John Shakespeare had a problem with Harry Slide. He could not raise the question of the Mary of Scots letter or the Spiritual Testament for fear of incriminating Anne and Will. But even more worrying was the matter of Badger Rench. Slide must know that Badger Rench had been watching Arden House. And he would know, too, that Will and Anne had visited the manor the night that Badger disappeared. A man like Slide would quickly come to a conclusion.

Such matters were better left unspoken. In return, Shakespeare would not delve too deeply into some of Slide's methods. It was a devil's pact, for he had no idea how far Harry Slide could be trusted.

It was time to test him. 'Mr Slide, you say you would work for me.'

'Indeed, Mr Shakespeare, it would be a great honour. It is said Mr Secretary has extraordinary plans for your future.'

'I do not need your flattery,' Shakespeare snapped. 'Five minutes ago you were telling me I am considered so pliant that I could be played like a puppet. What I need is for you to ride post to court and warn Mr Secretary in person about Somerville. We cannot be certain that your message arrived – and such matters must not be left to chance. I will ride with you part way. I must be in Stratford by nightfall.'

'And how much will you pay me for this menial task?'

'Nothing,' Shakespeare said curtly. 'You owe me for trying to gull me with no concern for my welfare. But carry out this task in good faith and I may forgive you. I may even bear you in mind for future missions.'

'You deal hard, sir.'

'You have no notion. But you will find out.'

Chapter 35

WILL SHAKESPEARE UNSLUNG his saddlebag. The contents clattered out, all objects of the blacksmith's art: axe, saw, bolts, nails, hammer, hinges. Boltfoot grinned at the sight of the tools and set to work. For hours, he hewed, shaped and hammered. Slowly, he fashioned a makeshift roof and the portion of the ancient ruined Black House that they had made their refuge became more habitable. Nothing that would last, but enough to keep most of the rain out for a day or week, as necessary.

He also addressed the defences of the place. The Black House was remote and the likelihood was that no one knew they were there, but he had to think of all eventualities. What if a gamekeeper spotted them and alerted the pursuivants?

When Will Shakespeare departed, his place was taken by Anne who had come to try to raise Florence's spirits. She could spare little time from her young siblings, but while she was there Boltfoot decided to make use of her.

'Help me,' he said gruffly. 'Can you tie a knot?'

Anne laughed. 'Mr Cooper, of course I can tie a knot!'

'Sailor's knots?'

'Farm knots.'

'That'll do. Bring old pans and string when next you come.'

When she returned, they worked through the woods, twenty

yards out from the house in all directions, tying string from tree to tree with pans containing stones hanging in the spaces between.

'If someone comes by night, they'll trip it and I'll hear a rattling.'

'You'll be up all night shooting fox and boar.'

'Boar will suit me. We'll eat well enough.' Boltfoot cut at the string with the penknife Kat Whetstone had given him and which he had left, almost forgotten, in his jerkin pocket. It was sharper than his dagger.

'I am worried about Florence and Audrey Angel,' Anne said, her voice low. They both looked over to the open doorway. Florence's lips were moving, as if in prayer. A little to her right, her mother was lying on a mattress, huddled into a blanket.

Boltfoot was worried, too. The widow Angel had been sick in the night and was not faring well. The daughter was not making things any easier. For one who was supposed to be best of friends with Anne and of a holy disposition, she was being mighty quarrelsome: the two were scarcely on speaking terms. 'Do you think she'll walk away?'

'Yes, it seems likely.'

'And if she does walk out?'

'John said we couldn't hold her.'

Boltfoot did not push his questioning.

Anne tugged at Boltfoot's sleeve. 'Walk with me a little, Mr Cooper.' They moved further into the wood, perhaps fifty yards from the old house. 'As your life is in peril,' she said when they were out of earshot, 'I think I should tell you my concerns. For as long as I can recall, I have imagined that Florence and I were best friends, but this is not the Florence Angel I once loved like a sister. She is rigid, like iron. Unbending, unforgiving. We share nothing. She is zealous, I am wayward. She says I am in error and calls me heretic.' *She also demands to be given the Mary of Scots letter, but that is not something to be mentioned to John's assistant.* 'I say this because I will speak up for you to your master if you feel you have no cause here.'

Boltfoot shook his grizzled head. He felt much the same about Florence Angel, but this dark wood was his place until told otherwise by his master. Yes, he was discomfited by her gasps and sudden movements at night, but he could live with that. What he found more galling was that she treated him as though he were a servant to be used and ignored. Even Drake, who dealt harshly with his men, had never shunned him or anyone else, however menial.

Anne smiled weakly. 'But there is nothing we can do, is there, Mr Cooper? You are here because your master has commanded you to stay.' *And I am here because I have no alternative. The prospect of Florence being arrested and questioned is too terrifying. And still there is no sign of the accursed Spiritual Testament.* As they walked back towards the house, Anne stopped and looked around at their system of alarms. 'The pans may let you know that the pursuivants have arrived, Mr Cooper, but what will you do then? You have but one caliver and two women to protect. How will the clanging of pans help if a squadron of a dozen men arrives? What will your one gun do for you?'

It was a question Boltfoot had already asked himself. So far, he had come up with no satisfactory answer. 'Better to be prepared than not,' was all he said. 'I've also started making a door of sorts. Should afford a little protection, I hope.'

Anne kissed his cheek. 'You are a marvel, Mr Cooper. But now I must leave you until tomorrow. There are children and chickens to be fed and cows to be milked. Will intends coming with food soon after dusk. Please do not mistake him for a pursuivant or wild boar . . .'

*

For the third time in an hour, Boltfoot heard one of the pans clinking outside the house. Instinctively, he swivelled the muzzle of his loaded caliver towards the doorway, where he had built his makeshift door, cut from the bough of a mature oak.

This time there was a low curse. Foxes and deer don't utter profanities.

Boltfoot looked over in the direction of Florence and raised his hand to indicate silence. She did not acknowledge him, merely went back to mopping her mother's hot brow.

There were two knocks at the door, silence, then a third knock. Boltfoot rose and walked over, his caliver still in front of him, his finger still on the trigger. He opened the door, and then lowered the muzzle slowly as he came face to face with Mr Shakespeare's brother.

'Master William.'

'Is all well, Mr Cooper?'

Boltfoot indicated the two women. 'No, sir, can't say that all *is* well. The mother ails. Naught but a common cold, I hope, but she's been sickly and seems weak. The daughter won't let me near her, but I suppose it's giving her something to do. At least she isn't seeing ghosts at the moment. Only one thing to scare us now: the rattling of the pans.'

Will was abashed. 'I'm sorry about that. Anne told me about them, but they were too well concealed. I couldn't make them out, even with my lantern.' He ran his hand down the edge of the door and swung it on its hinges, then examined the wooden bar that secured it from the inside. 'I like this. You're a fine carpenter, Mr Cooper.'

Boltfoot eyed his handiwork. He had made a raft-like structure from strips of oak, binding them together with battens. 'Bit rough, but it's heavy, so it'll do. My line's casks, not doors, but the skill's similar. Any man that can fashion staves can make a door. Not much in it.'

'I've brought another of my mother's pies. Pigeon this time.'

'Thank you, sir. And be pleased to tell her that I've never tasted better than the beef one. But what we need is some medicine for *her*.' He tilted his head towards Audrey. 'Truth be told, it would be best to get her in her own bed and take advice from an apothecary.'

Will opened his bag and produced two stoppered jugs. 'Anne has prepared infusions: camomile and feverfew.'

'Better hand them to her.' Boltfoot indicated Florence. 'Make her do something useful. Keep her away from ghosts and prayers a while longer.'

They were talking in low voices, but sound carries at night. Florence stood up. Her face shone in the light of her candle and the lanterns. For a few moments she said nothing, but they knew she had heard them.

'Florence, Mr Cooper didn't mean anything—' Will began.

'Give me the feverfew. Camomile will do nothing.'

Will handed over the jug. 'These are difficult hours, Florence. People say things they don't mean.'

'I don't say things unless I mean them. I don't commend my spirit to God and then turn away from Him.'

'Be careful, Florence. We have put ourselves in grave danger to protect you.'

She snorted with scorn. 'Do you think I do not know why I am here? Do you think I do not know why you abducted me like thieves? You cloak what you have done in talk of my welfare – of saving me from the pursuivants – but I know that this is about your necks. Your trip to Arden Hall the night Rench disappeared, the Spiritual Testament, the letter from blessed Mary Stuart. You fear I will use these things against you both.'

'Florence . . .' Will's voice was soft, but nothing could disguise his urgency.

'And why should I not use them against Anne Hathaway?' she shot back. 'She is a traitor to God – an apostate.'

'Florence, do you know where this testament is?'

'How would I not know? I have always had it. It should be sacred, but she has defiled it. Why do you think she fears me so?'

'Does Anne's friendship mean nothing to you? When you came to Shottery she treated you like a sister. She only signed the document to please you, that is all.'

'Do you not know her at all, Will Shakespeare? The error is there plain to see, in her eyes, as it is in yours. You are all damned for your pseudo-religion, but there is a special place of eternal pain for apostates; like Lucifer, they have fallen from grace. I saw Anne walk with Jesus at midsummer, and then the next time I saw her, she had fallen.'

Will stepped forward, hands held out in appeal. 'Florence. I am appalled that you talk thus! Think of God's love. Think of forgiveness and sisterhood. Think of the virtue and nobility of the Samaritan.'

'She was trifling with God! Only repentance and fire – in *this* world – will save her. This is doctrine, which is truth.'

There were no more alarms. Will Shakespeare, his heart heavy following the harangue from Florence, took his leave of Boltfoot and disappeared into the night.

Half an hour later, Boltfoot was jolted into alertness by a sound above his head. A sound like an arrow thudded into the patchwork of wood roof he had constructed. Then another and another.

And then silence.

But someone was out there and wanted those inside to know they were no longer alone.

Boltfoot motioned with his hand to Florence to stay down.

There was no point in trying to pretend they were not there; Florence's voice, normally so soft, had become loud and angry as she prayed into the night, imploring the heavenly father to care for her mother. Her voice would easily have been heard out in the woods.

'We're heavily armed. Six of us,' Boltfoot shouted out. It was a poor strategy, but he had no other. For the moment, all he could think to do was to keep his caliver trained on the door and then, when it was battered in, to pull the trigger and take at least one of the enemies with him. If he could rush forward with his cutlass amid the smoke of gunpowder, he might at least make a fight of it with a second man. But that was all; the end was certain.

'They don't want you, they want me,' Florence said and began walking towards the door. Boltfoot dragged her back. She screamed and struggled and tried to bite him.

'I'm going to bind you else you'll kill us all.' Boltfoot picked up the unused twine that remained from the setting of the alarm system. 'I can't fight you and them.' He indicated the door.

He could smell something. There was burning. They had shot fire arrows into the roof, but the wood was green and wet, so he was sure it wouldn't catch. The smell was the pitch in which the arrows had been dipped.

What do we do? he asked himself, then gave answer. We stay here and wait. If one of them wants to give up his life, he can come first through that door.

Chapter 36

SHAKESPEARE RODE A hundred miles before dusk and it was dark when he arrived at Stratford. He intended to go to Henley Street first, for he needed news of the encampment at the Black House – and also word of Hungate. But before he got there, he spotted Ananias Nason, passing a few words with the lamplighter. Shakespeare watched him a few moments as he concluded his conversation, then turned left into the High Street. Shakespeare kicked on after him and stopped him outside the shuttered butcher's shop.

'Mr Nason.'

Nason turned with the jerky movement of a startled pheasant. He held up his lantern. 'Mr Shakespeare. Thought you was gone.'

'Well, I'm back. And I've been hearing things about you.'

'Yes, and I've heard things about you, too. None of it good.'

He made to move off, but Shakespeare leant over and grasped the straggle of long hair that fell out of the back of Nason's cap. 'Wait.'

Nason was stopped in his tracks. He tried to shake himself free. At last, Shakespeare released his grip.

'That'll be assaulting an officer of the law in the execution of his duty.'

'Stop your mouth, Nason, or I'll do it for you. I have been

told you've been doing dirty work for a hired killer named Hungate.'

Shock registered in the constable's eyes, glowing in the light of his own lantern. 'Where'd you hear that?'

'That's my business.'

Nason stiffened and pushed out his chin defensively. 'Well, what if I have done a favour or two for Mr Hungate? Hired killer? That's dog turd talk, that is. He's my lord of Leicester's gentleman and a guest of my master, Sir Thomas Lucy. Mr Hungate is a respectable Christian gentleman.'

'You followed my brother.'

'He's going to end up with a noose about his neck, and not a moment too soon. Poaching Sir Thomas's deer, getting the Hathaway trug with child. And there's another matter, too. The matter of Badger Rench. He's disappeared and I have my suspicions.' Nason touched the side of his nose. 'There are rumours about town. Way I hear it, Badger was betrothed to Miss Hathaway when your brother stepped in and did his grubby fumbling. If anything's happened to Badger Rench, we'll know where to look for a suspect sure enough.'

'You are gibbering.' Shakespeare looked down at the man with contempt. 'Badger is strong enough to look after himself against any man, as you well know. If he's disappeared, then fine riddance to him and pity the poor folk where he's gone.'

'Aye, well, Sir Thomas believes he's likely dead and buried.'

'Ananias Nason, enough of this. I want to talk about Hungate. I have known you all my life and though I have always thought you a poor excuse for a man, and cowardly, too, I had never thought you to be an accessory to a possible murder. And that is what you are about if you have been helping Hungate. He is a devil, Mr Nason, and he will take you down with him. Now tell me this, is Hungate here in Stratford?'

Nason grinned, confident now. 'Why, yes, I do believe he might be hereabouts.'

'Damn you, what have you done?'

'Me? I've done nothing. Look to your own family before you accuse others, Shakespeare.'

'Where is he?'

'If you're talking about the fine Mr Hungate, then I do believe he said something about taking the country air. I recommended some woodland paths he might wish to sample. Perhaps he will do a little hunting, too, for I have heard he is a remarkable fowler, shot and trapper. That's the way to fill the pot at supper. A fine hare or a brace of partridges . . .'

Shakespeare had stopped listening. He wheeled his exhausted horse and rode for Henley Street. He found his father returning from a business meeting and looking ill at ease. The old man's mood changed to concern for his son when he noticed the state of his injured head. 'John, what has happened to you?'

'I met the branch of a tree. It is nothing.'

'Gloving is a great deal safer . . .'

Shakespeare smiled briefly. 'I had heard things were not going as well as once they did, Father. Maybe you need some more cold winters. Now, where's Will?'

Boltfoot heard a rustling and snapping sound outside the door and realised the attackers were building a bonfire in front of the door. They would be hoping to engender panic among the besieged but the sound was competing with the chanting of Latin prayers from the lips of Florence Angel. He wondered whether he should bind her mouth, too. She was a menace.

Florence was kneeling by her mother. Her hands were tied in front of her and she had them raised, across her chest. Her eyes were turned upwards, like a penitent seeking guidance from the heavens.

Maybe He will answer her prayers, Boltfoot thought. He was surprised by his own scepticism, for he had never been one to doubt the existence of God. But then another thought struck him. She was not praying for salvation, but martyrdom.

By the faint light of the moon Ruby Hungate sharpened his long butcher's blade. On the ground in front of him lay the body of a stag. He had felled it with a single crossbow bolt.

He had brought it here to this dark place in the Forest of Arden not as food but as display. Many people, he knew, felt uncomfortable – even fearful – in the woods by night. But this was his place, his kingdom, and he felt at ease. This was his place of remembering: the strong grip of his father's hand, the soft light in his mother's eyes and the dancing smile of his beloved sister.

Hungate had never needed the company of other boys. His father was his only friend. Their time together in the woods was his apprenticeship. They would set off at dawn and spend all the hours until nightfall among the trees and ferns and wild animals. And the boy learnt all their ways and all his father's skills.

By the age of ten, he could track down an adult fox and kill it with his own hands, wrenching apart the forelegs to tear its vital organs, then removing its skin and fur whole. Only at sunset did they return home, hands red with blood, to his mother and sister, with meat for the pot.

That was his joy. Killing in the wild. Proving to all the beasts of the forest that he was the most cunning of all God's creatures.

At the age of twelve, everything changed. He was alone.

And he killed his first man.

Now, here in this wood, in the dark, he was in his element. This was the world where he was king. No man or beast could match him here. He worked methodically and alone, without haste. The chase and kill were to be savoured, not hurried.

He took his right ear between thumb and forefinger and counted the ruby earrings set there. Nine in all, and each one payment for a killing. He knew each of them intimately.

From the top: death by poison of an enraged husband whose wife had been seduced by his lordship; a plunge from a cliff for a creditor, made to look like suicide; a drowning in a lake, the body weighted to disappear for ever; a sword thrust to the belly outside a Southwark tavern for one of Walsingham's dangerous spies looking in places where he should not have been; a dagger through the heart, in the man's own bed, for another jealous husband; a sword thrust to the belly and neck while stalking deer; the garrotting and skinning of a priest in Scotland; pistol shots to the heart of a man who had insulted Leicester, in the bed of his concubine; likewise the concubine.

Each one had won him a red ruby from the hand of Robert Dudley, the Earl of Leicester.

But for these ones, these deaths in the forest, there would be no ruby, no payment. These were not for his lordship. These deaths were personal and special. The blood debt of his boyhood was about to be paid in full.

With exquisite agility, Hungate scaled the walls of the house to the roof. He stood for a few moments on the rough timbers newly erected by those inside, listening for voices or other sounds. Hearing nothing but the mumbling of a prayer and the crackling of the greenwood fire, he stamped about deliberately to create an echo in the rooms below. Thick plumes of white, acrid smoke billowed up from the blaze he had set in front of the door. He found a small gap in the makeshift roof and looked down. In the dim light, he could make out the two Angel women, the older one lying down, perhaps sick. Standing further off was the lame mariner he had heard about, the crippled assistant to John Shakespeare. He was the only one armed. It would have made no difference to Hungate if they had all been armed with heavy petronels, crossbows and cannons. The pleasure would merely have been that much greater.

For the moment his only desire was to extend their fear for as long as possible.

Above him, Boltfoot heard footsteps. He listened closely to the sound, tracing the progress of the man above as he trod noisily across the roof. Boltfoot aimed the caliver as best he could and pulled the trigger, shooting blind. He had nothing to lose. The weapon belched forth flame and the smoke of burnt gunpowder. Stinking and malevolent. The bullet smacked into the roof and sent a shower of splinters raining down. That and the coarse sound of a man's laughter.

Boltfoot set about reloading his weapon with the speed born of many skirmishes at sea and on land. Skilfully, he poured in the powder and shot and tamped them home. And waited.

Still laughing, Hungate climbed down from the roof and walked purposefully through the woods to his two horses. He patted the neck of the one he rode, then turned his attention to the sumpter, a large dray horse with heavy baskets draped across its back.

Reaching into one of the baskets, he withdrew two iron spheres, the size of naval cannonballs. Each had been packed full of gunpowder and weighed about six pounds.

He carried no lantern or rushlight. It was not that he could *see* in the dark, but that he could sense his way. The meanest of moon slivers was enough, even in woods that he did not know, such as these. It was an accomplishment he did not understand, but he knew that it gave him a lethal advantage over beasts and over other men.

Returning to the front of the ruined house, he picked a taper from the fire at the door, then went to the far side of the building. He walked silently. He wanted this to be a surprise. Without a sound, he placed the two bombs together against the wall, in the weakest spot, where the old stones and lime mortar had crumbled away. He tied the two fuses together, and then applied the taper before walking back into the woods to shelter behind a tree. Within ten seconds, a huge flash of flame lit the forest, as though daylight had returned for the briefest of moments.

Boltfoot and the women did not hear the devastating thunderclap. It was too loud and too close. But they felt its force as they were flung across the ancient floor, knocked back by a welter of stones and fire. Smoke bellowed like a furnace unleashed. Boltfoot had experienced the cannon's roar and the blast of black powder more than once, but nothing like this. This was a peaceful English woodland by night, not hot battle between opposing armies. His ears rang. He was still clutching his caliver, but he had unintentionally pulled the trigger and it had discharged its bullet unaimed. Through the haze, he was vaguely aware that his shoulder and forearm had been hit by something, probably by rocks. He had no idea if any bones were broken. All he could think of was the ringing in his ears.

The woods were full of maddened birds, woken from sleep. A woodpecker flew past his head and crashed into the fire. For a moment it seemed to rise from the flames, its wings ablaze, but then it flopped soundlessly to its death.

As Boltfoot's vision cleared, he saw a man standing over him, arms and legs akimbo, staring down with insolent curiosity. Smoke wafted about him as though he were Satan, come to collect his own.

He had a coil of rope in his left hand and a dagger in his right. Without a word, he knelt down at Boltfoot's side and looped the rope around his wrists. Boltfoot was still not thinking and did not resist, but then the pain came in as the hemp bit into his injured arm. He tried to pull away, but the knot was already tied, tight.

Hungate surveyed the scene with pleasure. The bombs had blown a most impressive hole in the wall, and the three occupants of the room were exactly where he wanted them – dazed, battered, sprawled across the floor and unarmed.

After binding the grizzled mariner's wrists, he looped another section of rope twice around his ankles and secured it with two half-hitches.

He gazed down at his captive, neatly parcelled up. 'Don't wander off. I have plans for you.'

Florence Angel was regaining her senses. Hungate watched her as she tried to crawl towards the hole he had blown in the wall. Her clothes were in shreds, her bindings torn away, her face dark with soot and blood. He thought of his mother and sister and for a moment felt some pity. The feeling evaporated as soon as it came. Why should these women have life and hope when his mother and sister had been afforded none?

He grabbed Florence by the hair and dragged her back into the midst of the rubble and ruins. She fought and scratched, but he re-tied her hands with ease then held his smooth hand beneath her jaw and made her look into his eyes. 'Know this. Your father did for my family, and so will I do for you and yours.'

The old woman, Audrey, was unconscious, her breathing shallow and laboured. Hungate thought of killing her there and then, but decided there had to be more. He tied her as he had tied the other two, then dragged all three of them from the wreckage of the building, through the hole created by the bomb, to the tree he had already selected.

It was a tall ash with a strong lower branch that stretched horizontally ten or twelve feet above the ground. One by one, he attached long ropes to the bound ankles of his three captives, then tossed the loose ends over the branch and lifted each of them up, suspended by their feet, until their heads and bound hands hung down, swaying, a foot or two from the earth. The women's skirts were bound to their ankles so they did not fall, and so they could still see.

He left them there and walked away to his horses, where he removed a flask of brandy and a loaf of black bread from his saddlebags, then returned to his three prisoners. He sat down against the wall, amid the rubble of stones, and began to eat the bread, occasionally sipping at his brandy flask.

'You will burn in hell,' Florence gasped as she twisted.

'Save your dirty breath. You will need it for screaming.'

'What is this?' Boltfoot demanded, attempting to jerk himself upright. 'If you are a pursuivant, you cannot do this.'

'What is your name?'

'Cooper.'

'You are John Shakespeare's man.'

Boltfoot did not reply.

'I would rather he were here than you. It is unfortunate, for you have strayed into something that is none of your doing. This is about these worthless popish baggages. It took me all these years to discover their place of abode. This is so my mother and sister may finally rest in peace.'

'What do you want of them? One is a sick old woman, the other a defenceless daughter. They can do you no harm.'

'Not now they can't, strung up like rabbits. But they

prospered while my mother and sister starved. And so now *they* will suffer – and then, bit by bit, they will die. And so will you, Mr Cooper, simply for being here. The only question that remains is which of you will take the longest.'

Hungate stood up and unsheathed his long butcher's knife.

Boltfoot realised that the only thing that could possibly save them was someone's intervention. But that was not likely to arrive this night and by dawn, he was certain, it would be too late. Their only hope was to keep this madman talking.

'What happened to your family, sir?' His voice was nothing more than a strained whisper. The blood was rushing to his head like a tidal current, filling him up, throbbing.

'*Sir?* I am not a sir. I am a common man like you, Cooper. Do not be fooled by my jewels and my fine doublet, for I have spent all my years red with blood and I have waded through shit.'

'If I am to die here, at least let me know what this is about.' Even upside down, Boltfoot could not take his eyes off Hungate as he hoisted the dead deer off the ground by its legs and attached it to the branch of another tree, so that it, too, hung down.

'Watch, Cooper. See my skill.' He made an incision just below the fetlock of one of the animal's hind legs, then at lightning speed made a further series of cuts.

Boltfoot had seen animals being skinned before, but never with such accuracy and so quickly. Within five minutes, Hungate was pulling off the whole skin of the deer, like a tight glove being peeled from a hand. Boltfoot watched without saying a word. At his side he heard the rasping breath of the mother and the moans of the daughter, like some sort of religious ecstasy. He could not see them, but wondered if they, too, were watching this.

'And so you see, Cooper, that was a *dead* animal. It did not squirm or bleed. Simple. I have skinned a thousand animals or more. Blindfold me and I could do it by my sense of touch. But it is not so easy when the animal is still alive. How long would that take, would you say?'

'Is that what you are planning for us?'

'The women. You can have a bullet in your head, for I wish you no ill will.'

'What have they done to you?'

'They prospered. Let us ask them. Mistress Angelus, tell me of your husband. How did he live? How did he die?'

Boltfoot sensed the older woman's breathing coming faster, and then he heard her faint voice. 'He lived well and was murdered. Brutally.'

Hungate laughed. 'Let us go back a bit. Let me tell you about my family. Like the Angelus family, it consisted of a father and mother, a son and a daughter. I was the son. We lived in the county of Surrey, south-west of London. My father kept and nurtured the game at Loseley Park, a great seat of Sir William More, a house often visited by the Queen. Our life was good, until Robert Angelus—'

'Who was he? What happened?' Boltfoot spoke with great effort.

'He was the destroyer. He killed my father.'

'But why?'

'By bearing false witness against him. Angelus was a treasurer and steward to Sir William, who was a man of great wealth. By the year fifteen sixty-seven, Angelus – a secret Catholic in a good Protestant household – was stealing gold from his master, and sending it to William Allen in the Low Countries to help in founding a seminary for English papists. He came to realise, however, that this theft could not continue undetected for much longer and decided to find a scapegoat.

That was my father, a more innocent soul than you will ever find. Angelus had formed a disliking for him ever since he refused to enter into a scheme whereby venison would be sold to local butchers and the money split between them.'

'This is a sorry tale, Mr Hungate.'

'I was barely twelve years old. We came home from the woods, as always, and the sheriff was there with his men. They searched our property and found fifty pounds in gold hidden away in our barn. My father was taken to court, found guilty of stealing all the gold that had gone missing from Sir William's coffers – though this was twenty times the amount found at our home – and hanged the next day. I was forced to watch it, as were my mother and sister. We were then cast out from our home, with nothing. No money, no livestock, no land. My mother was beyond despair. By nightfall, she had hanged herself. The next day, my sister threw herself to her death in the lake. And I was alone.'

Boltfoot forced his engorged lips to move. 'How did you survive, Mr Hungate?'

'I returned to the woods, Mr Cooper, and lived among the wild beasts and the birds. I was already a skilled hunter, but now I dedicated my life to the art of war, with but one thought: one day I would do to Robert Angelus what he had done to me.'

'Where is Robert Angelus now?'

'Dead. Before I was thirteen, I had killed him. I watched and I waited and I learnt that the saintly Robert Angelus had taken a local wife as his mistress. Each Tuesday, he rode out alone to meet his filthy woman, a weaver's wife. I waited outside her cottage and watched him arrive. I listened at the shuttered window and heard their foul grunts as they copulated the afternoon long. At last, he departed, his business done. I watched him from the woods, my longbow ready. I trailed him as he sat astride his mare, adjusting his dress. My hands did not shake, nor did my eye blink as I drew back the bowstring and let loose the arrow that split the man's throat. He fell from his horse without a sound and died in a sea of his own blood. And then I stripped him of his skin and hung it, stretched between two saplings, like washing hung out to dry. I rejoiced. Yet I soon discovered that I was not satisfied. The blood debt had not been paid.'

'But the injustice was caused by Robert Angelus, not his family.'

'They prospered. Old Sir William ensured they were taken care of. Again I watched and I waited and then, one day, they were no longer there – and I had no notion where they had gone. I had no way of finding them until I heard of the quest for the fugitive Benedict Angel and began to wonder. And now here they are, ready to pay their debt in full.'

Chapter 37

JOHN SHAKESPEARE FOUND his brother at Hewlands Farm. He was supping ale with Anne and the elder of her siblings, Thomas and Catherine, before they retired to their beds for the night.

Will was clearly relieved at his brother's arrival. 'Thank God you are here. Audrey is sick, and Florence Angel quite mad.' He turned to Anne. 'Is that not so?'

'It is true. She despises me and calls me apostate. I had thought her frail, but she is hard. I do believe she would happily bring me to the Inquisition and have me burnt for heresy.'

'Tell him about the Spiritual Testament, Anne.'

'She has it, but she won't tell me where it is hidden. She has been holding it over me for weeks. Now she says she wants the Mary of Scots letter back. I have not told her it is burnt, for I fear what she might do with my testament . . .'

Shakespeare said nothing. He did not wish to tell them he had sent it to Walsingham. 'There are ways and means of finding things. But for the present, we must worry about the presence of a man named Ruby Hungate – one of those who came to your house. It seems he knows about the Black House – and very much wishes to kill Florence. When were you last there, Will?'

'No more than two hours ago. There was no threat. Your

man Cooper has set up a system of alarms and has his caliver loaded at all times. The women could not be in better hands. He is a fine fellow.'

'That may be so, Will, but I must go to them now and get them away to some place safer.'

'Let me come with you.'

'No.' Shakespeare clasped his brother to his chest. 'You will remain here. If I am not back by dawn, raise a search party.' Their eyes met. They both knew what he truly meant: *If I am not back by dawn, search for our bodies* . . .

Shakespeare trod slowly through the damp undergrowth and twigs that carpeted the floor of the forest. It was late. The moon scarcely penetrated the canopy of leaves. All he had to guide him was an oil lantern, which was guttering fitfully. The only weapons he carried were his sword and poniard. He had considered bringing an old fowling piece from Hewlands Farm, but it was so heavy and unreliable that he decided it would be safer without. Here among these trees, there was such silence and such magnification of sound that any but the lightest of footsteps would be audible.

Somewhere in the distance, he heard a cry and stopped. Was it an owl, a dying animal, or his own overheated imagination? He walked on, along the familiar woodland path, across a moonlit glade where coppiced logs had been piled and then back into the woods. An animal scurried away into the darkness. Shakespeare felt his own heart beating as hard as a hunted beast.

And then, through the trees, he saw the faint glow of a fire, no more than three hundred yards in the distance and close to the Black House. He snuffed out his own lantern and discarded it on the floor of the forest, then stood still, listening and looking. Unsheathing his sword, he crouched down and began moving, tree by tree, through the woods, placing each footstep with great care. He was fifty yards away when he saw the horror: three human figures, bound, hanging upside down from the branch of a tree, their still bodies lit by the flames of a fire.

With all the finely tuned senses of a wild animal, Hungate smelt the man and heard him almost simultaneously. He slipped away, into the woods. *If you are being hunted, become the hunter.*

Shakespeare edged closer. He had known these woods since childhood; he must have an advantage over Hungate. He was thirty yards away now and recognised the three hanging figures as Boltfoot and the Angel women. Were they alive or dead? There was no sign of Hungate, or anyone else. Shakespeare tried to calculate his next move. Once he went into the open to cut down the three figures – alive or dead – he would be exposed to attack himself.

Crawling on his belly, he came to within ten yards of the edge of the house. He now had a clear view of Boltfoot whose eye was attracted by the movement in the undergrowth. Shakespeare was certain his man shook his head slightly, but it was so insignificant that, at first, he was not sure whether he had imagined it. Then Boltfoot's eyes moved to the right. He was telling Shakespeare that that was the way Hungate had gone.

Shakespeare held up five fingers. Boltfoot closed his eyes once in response, and then opened them. So Hungate was alone.

Are you a fighting man like Mr Hungate? Good with blade and pistol and fists? Leicester's words haunted him now. Was he a fighting man? He had fought as a boy, but that was not to the death, nor was it with real weapons. And if even half the stories told about Hungate were true, then no man in England would have a chance against him.

Shakespeare slid his right arm forward, the blade pointing ahead. Then his left leg, then torso. As close to the earth as a serpent. He was more alert than he had ever been, but he did not hear Hungate until he spoke.

'So you've come to collect your second arsehole, Shakespeare.'

Shakespeare tried to twist around and stab upwards. But Hungate's foot stamped down on his sword arm, pinning it to the ground. He stood over him, pistol in hand, pointing down towards Shakespeare's belly.

'Just there, that's where I'll put the hole. Takes a man a good while to die, shot in the stomach. Churns your bowels into shit and blood, for you to watch. Another Arden turned to dust. My master will be pleased.'

Hungate kicked away his victim's sword, then knelt down, astride him, and placed the muzzle of his pistol at his navel. He grinned and pushed the cold metal hard into Shakespeare's belly. 'Feel it. You cost me a pretty ruby in Sheffield, saving the papist bitch. And now here you are trying to save yet more Romish rubbish. As you die, you may ponder this: was it worth it?'

There was an explosion and a sudden violent lurch. Shakespeare gasped, certain he must have been shot in the gut. He had heard that the agony did not hit instantly, that the numbing of the pain is God's gift to the dying. But it was Hungate who slumped forward, blood flowing like a cataract from his shattered head. Even so, Hungate's pistol was still wedged into his belly. His finger might still be on the trigger. It would take very little pressure to fire it.

Shakespeare tried to see, but Hungate's blood was in his eyes. He pushed against the weight of the twitching corpse, but it was pulled from him. His arms now free, Shakespeare wiped his sleeve across his brow, blinked away the blood, and looked up into the face of Harry Slide. Slung beneath his arm he held a smoking wheel-lock petronel.

'Come, Mr Shakespeare,' he said, nodding towards Boltfoot and the women. 'Let us cut down those poor wretches.' He leant forward. 'And remember, Mr Shakespeare, to these people I am still Buchan Ord . . .'

'You know, John, sleep no longer comes easy.'

'What did you say, Will?' Shakespeare was distracted, saddling up his horse for the long ride to court, wondering exactly how much he should reveal to Walsingham.

'It haunts me, the knowledge of what lies –' he lowered his voice – 'what lies buried out there.'

Shakespeare stopped tightening the girth strap and looked into his brother's eyes.

'Anne, too.'

He sighed and managed a small smile. 'You have nothing to feel guilty about. Rench was about to murder you. Remember this well: you did nothing but save yourself and the woman you love. He suffered the fate he deserved. Mr Cooper will have no nightmares, and it was *his* blade that did the deed.' Shakespeare hugged his brother. 'Come, be strong and let me take my leave of you. I shall return for the wedding.'

Shakespeare was more worried about another body interred in the vicinity of Stratford: the corpse of Ruby Hungate, buried in woods a mile from the Black House. Few would care a jot about Badger Rench, but the powerful figures of Sir Thomas Lucy and the Earl of Leicester were certain to take a keen interest in the whereabouts of Mr Hungate. And Constable Nason would be sure to assist them with what he knew of the Black House and its occupants. Well, they were not going to find the body and that was an end to it. Hungate was buried eight feet deep. As for Florence and Audrey Angel, they no longer posed any risk.

Will hesitated. 'Anne feels she should apologise to you, John. The letter . . . the Spiritual Testament . . . She was foolish and her foolishness put us all in danger.'

'Tell her to forget it.' Shakespeare climbed into the saddle, put his boots in the irons, then wheeled his horse about.

Chapter 38

S IR FRANCIS WALSINGHAM was almost cheerful. No, Shakespeare corrected himself, not actually *cheerful*. That would be too much to hope for; the Principal Secretary had the permament look of a bloodhound that had been denied its supper and was not given to smiling. But certainly remarkably even-tempered and at ease.

They were in Walsingham's office at his mansion in Seething Lane, London. It was an austere place, much like his country retreat, Barn Elms. The chairs were plain, unadorned oak, as was the table. There were no hangings on the wall and little light, for the windows were often kept shuttered through the day. The table and shelves were a litter of papers, books and maps. Only Mr Secretary knew what they all were; only he could locate a particular document or letter, for there seemed to be no method to the disarray.

The only symbol of Walsingham's power and position was the painting that adorned the wall opposite the window. It was modestly sized, perhaps six feet wide by four feet high, and it showed the eighth King Henry in splendour on his throne, with Queen Mary and her husband Philip of Spain to his right, and his son King Edward VI and daughter Queen Elizabeth to his left. The divide between the Catholics and Protestants was sharply evident. Shakespeare's eyes strayed to the picture. He knew well that it had been a gift to Sir Francis from the Queen. It always surprised him to see Philip of Spain among the Tudors.

'Keep your enemies close,' Walsingham said when he saw the direction of Shakespeare's gaze. 'It is a lesson for us all.' He poured two silver goblets of sack. 'You have done well, John. Very well. I thank God you were there to save the Scots devil.'

Shakespeare could not disguise his incredulity. He was expecting to be berated; this was not at all the reception he had expected. 'Sir Francis . . .'

'I know. You imagined I would have wished Mary Stuart dead.'

'Indeed, I assumed so.'

'Well, you would not be far from the truth, John. But do you not think I could have ordered her throat slit before now, had I so wished it? No, that is not the way for a civilised country to go. I want the woman to be condemned for her crimes in open court and to suffer the full force of the law of England. She came here as a guest and she has repaid our generosity by conspiring against us. When eventually she faces the executioner, the capitals of Europe will know that her death was lawful, just and deserved.'

Shakespeare saw no sign of dissimulation, but that meant nothing. He knew enough about Mr Secretary to realise that he could call an apple a pear and have you believe it. 'Mr Slide suggested—'

Walsingham tapped his right index finger twice on his table. It was an impatient gesture. 'Pay no heed to Harry Slide. He has a mind of his own. The problem is he thinks he knows *my* mind. Harry Slide is a useful man in his own way, but he is limited. That is why he is the hireling and you are my apprentice and my great hope. Consider this your blooding.'

'You flatter me, Sir Francis.'

'I flatter no one, not even Her Royal Majesty.'

'But someone paid Slide to organise this assassination attempt.'

'Indeed they did.'

'And if not you, then why send me to both Sheffield and Stratford?'

'Do you think to interrogate me, John? Is this wise?'

'When first you took me on as your assistant secretary, you told me you liked plain speaking. Forgive me if I now talk out of turn, but I was lured along a merry trail and I would like to know who set me on it.'

'You were blooded and you survived. Yes, I knew some mischief was brewing, but I was not certain what form it would take. When it was suggested to me that you might investigate the papist conspiracies in your home county, I was naturally interested. Yet I had no notion as to what you would find.'

'Then this is my lord of Leicester's doing.' *It made sense, of course. Had not Hungate mentioned a ruby he might have won had Mary died?*

'I did not say that.' Walsingham paused and tapped his finger on the table again. 'As you know, he has interests in Warwickshire, but that does not mean he was involved in the attempt on the Scots devil's life. The important thing is that you discovered the plot and stopped it, for which I have already commended you.'

Shakespeare was not wholly convinced, but there was little advantage in pressing the point further. 'Indeed you have, and I thank you.'

Walsingham nodded. 'But you are still fretting. I see it in your eyes. You don't understand exactly why I did not tell you my fears *before* you left Oatlands. And my answer is that I trusted you to solve this puzzle yourself and bring the answer to me. And now you have proved me right. However, I must say this: not everyone is happy with you . . .'

Shakespeare held Walsingham's gaze. 'Sir Francis?'

'There is the matter of the Earl of Leicester's man, who has disappeared. What do you know of him?'

'Ruby Hungate? Very little. I met him at Oatlands, then Stratford, and then at Sheffield where he seemed primed to do murder. Why?'

'Sir Thomas Lucy says he returned to Stratford and went into the Forest of Arden to discover the whereabouts of the sister of the priest Benedict Angel. Sir Thomas suspects the young woman was up to her own pretty neck in conspiracy.'

'I know nothing of that.'

'Well, then I must accept what you say. Just as you must accept that I had no knowledge of this conspiracy against Mary Stuart.'

So this was how it would be, Shakespeare thought. A stand-off.

'And with that settled,' Mr Secretary went on, 'let us now move to other matters. Tell me your thoughts regarding these disgraceful traitors, these Ardens. What are we to do about them?'

'Edward Arden and Hugh Hall are returned to Warwickshire.'

'Should we arrest them?'

'On what charge?'

'Conspiracy.'

'It is possible, but then Harry Slide would have to give evidence against them. There is no one else. Would you like to see Slide in court testifying?'

Walsingham almost seemed to laugh at the thought, but there was no humour in his eyes. 'You are right. Men like Slide must always be kept in the shadows. But there are other ways.

With persuasion, Arden and Hall will confess. I am sure Mr Topcliffe could extract the truth from their lips.'

'Topcliffe is a cruel and savage man. I have seen him beat a man halfway to death without cause. He destroyed the home of a Yorkshire gentleman named Bassingbourne Bole for no reason other than brutal vengeance. Forgive me for speaking plain yet again, but I cannot stomach Topcliffe.'

'I know all about Bole and the priest he harboured. Bole has since denounced the Pope and all his agents and has been pardoned. The priest, Edenshaw, has been hanged in Sheffield, convicted of treason. As for Mr Topcliffe, I told you, he is strong meat. But we need such men. We are fighting a foe that tortures and burns men and women simply for not being Catholic. No one is killed in England for their beliefs, only for treason.' Walsingham fixed Shakespeare with a stare. 'But still –' his voice softened – 'I believe you are probably right about Arden and the priest Hall. Leave them be for the moment. They are best watched, for they may lead us to other conspirators. As for Somerville, he will be arrested as soon as he comes within a furlong of the court.'

'If he does not shoot himself first.'

Walsingham rose from his hard chair and walked across to a bank of shelves at the east of the room. He hunted through a pile of official papers and dragged out a large map, which he brought back and unfolded across the table. 'Now, to the matter of the bosom serpent. I am pleased that you and Mr Topcliffe managed to agree on this at least, that she is no longer safe at Sheffield.' He placed his slender finger upon the point where the rivers Sheaf and Don converged. 'This is a map of England, John. The question is, where are we to put the Scots devil if Sheffield is not suitable?'

'Not Tutbury. It is rotten and would take a great deal of work to be brought to a good enough standard to house a queen.'

'One could almost think you had a soft spot for the witch. Be careful, John, for she has a way of beguiling men, as Norfolk found to the cost of his head.'

'And yet she is a queen, and a cousin of our own dear sovereign. She has her own court and privileges. Is she not to be treated as a monarch?'

Walsingham ignored the question and continued to stab his stiletto finger at various places on the map. 'Wingfield Manor? Fotheringhay? What of one of the great Norfolk houses? Or Suffolk – Framlingham Castle?'

'There is a great deal of coastline around Norfolk and Suffolk.' Shakespeare leant over the map.

The Principal Secretary looked up. 'You are thinking well. I like that. Anyway, this is for the Privy Council to talk over at another time. I have your report and it will most certainly be used in our debate. For the moment, I have one more matter to discuss: the letter from the Scots devil that you say was found in the clothing of the priest Benedict Angel.'

'Has Mr Phelippes deciphered it?'

'No, nor is he likely to. He says it is meaningless, that the cipher is no cipher at all but a muddle of letters and insignificant symbols. He says too that the signature is not the hand of Mary Stuart, but a poor forgery. I rather suspect Mr Slide's hand in this. It is the sort of thing he would use to gain the trust of those whose company he intended to infiltrate. As it is, he was most fortunate that his guise as Buchan Ord was not uncovered by Arden and the others, for what he did not know – and what Mr Phelippes has since discovered – is that the real Mr Buchan Ord and Benedict Angel knew each other well.'

'They knew each other? How can that be? Harry Slide could not have infiltrated the conspiracy if he was known.'

'Buchan Ord and Benedict Angel were ordained together at Douai.'

Shakespeare rapidly ran through the implications. It was the death of Benedict Angel that saved Harry Slide from discovery. Was that mere chance? 'Then . . .'

Walsingham nodded. 'Harry did what he had to do, John.'

Shakespeare's blood ran cold. Benedict Angel must have realised Slide's deception as soon as he saw him – and so Slide killed him there and then, without compunction.

What Walsingham did not know was that thanks to Shakespeare, the deadly Mr Slide had been entrusted with the lives of Florence and Audrey Angel . . .

The grey seas of the Channel were whipped into a frenzy by gales. All ships were confined to harbour and even there they were not safe from the storm. Harry Slide had the shutters open in his small, top-floor room at the Buckland Arms, the squally rain lashing his face. Below him was a scene of devastation, with broken masts and spars. Two packet boats had capsized, their shattered hulls drifting into other shipping.

It had been like this for two days. The inns of Dover were full of would-be voyagers waiting for the storm to cease. Slide was sharing his loft-room with three other men, all travelling alone. They took it in turns to have the truckle bed to themselves while the others shared the tester bed. There were no comforts here.

Behind him he heard the latch being lifted and did not bother to turn around to greet one of his fellow travellers.

'Mr Slide . . .'

The voice jolted him and he turned a little too suddenly. John Shakespeare was in the chamber, the hair on his head scraping the low ceiling. He had closed the door and had his back firmly against it.

'Mr Shakespeare, you gave me a fright! I beg you do not creep up on me so.'

✝ 369 ✝

'And how would you like me to creep up on you?' Shakespeare's voice was soft. These walls were mere partitions.

'Not like an assassin.'

'If I were an assassin, you would be dead. But I think you probably know more about assassination than I do, Slide.'

'Mr Shakespeare.' Slide spread his hands out in appeal. 'I had to do what I did. Hungate was about to kill you, and then he would have done for Mr Cooper and the women in the most horrible manner, flaying them alive.'

'That's not what I'm talking about and you know it. I am referring to the murder of Benedict Angel. Garrotted. By you.'

Slide gasped, as though horrified by the accusation. 'That, too, was Hungate, I swear it. He had to have his revenge against the whole family.'

'Not so,' Shakespeare said grimly. 'You killed him because he knew you were an impostor. When you took on the guise of Buchan Ord, you had not realised that he and Angel had known each other at the seminary in Douai. It was a foolish and careless error by your master, but one you corrected by committing murder.'

'I deny it absolutely.'

'Yes, I rather imagined you might. But your denial does not make it untrue. I am certain, too, that you sought to muddy the waters by adding the rosary to the neck *post mortem* and the host and wine to the mouth – as though this crime was committed with some religious motive, which it was not. But I am not here to fight with you over this, nor have you arrested or taken to court. I know you have courage and that you saved my life. I know, too, that you put yourself in grave danger infiltrating the court of Mary Stuart and fomenting conspiracy at Arden Lodge. But I am here to protect Florence Angel and her mother, and to ensure that you earn your rubies diligently.'

'Why should I wish these women harm?'

'Because they know too much about you. Soon, they will learn the truth about the fate of the real Buchan Ord and they will guess that you killed him and Benedict. It is an assumption I would make myself, certainly in the case of Father Angel. And believe it or not, Mr Slide, there are still people with power in this country who believe that murder can never be justified and will come after you.'

'You are, indeed, making out a good case for me to kill them.'

Shakespeare smiled. 'You do not need *me* to put such notions in your head. I am sure you have thought all this through yourself. And that is why I have come here. An accident at sea, a highway confrontation with supposed robbers while travelling through France to Brabant. It would be all too easy for them to disappear. But I will not let it happen. Within the past hour, I have spoken to Florence and my Aunt Audrey, whom I am pleased to find almost restored to health, and I have told them they must send word to me when they are safe arrived at St Ursula's in Louvain. I have taken a sample of their handwriting and we have agreed a number of words that will be included in their missive, so that I will be certain the letter is truly from them. Do you understand?'

'Yes, Mr Shakespeare, I understand.'

'And Mr Slide, I promise you this. If I do not receive word that you have delivered them safely and in good order – using gold from your own engorged purse, as agreed between us – then I will break you. And that will be easier than you might imagine, for I will find a way to let the Earl of Leicester know what happened to Mr Hungate and, just as importantly, who sliced the ear from his body to take possession of his rubies. Would you really like my lord Leicester as your enemy?'

Chapter 39

A Wedding

'IS SHE READY yet?' Bartholomew Hathaway's voice boomed up the ladderway through the hatch to the first floor.

From above came the sound of girls' laughter. 'He's written her a poem!' Catherine called.

'What does it say? What does it say?' a young voice squealed.

'Shall I compare thee to a horse's arse!'

More female laughter filled the upstairs rooms at Hewlands Farm. Down below, Bartholomew groaned. This was his lot now that he had returned to the farm to take it over and, with it, assume responsibility for all the young children. Anne was well out of it, he decided. He turned to young Thomas. 'Is the gate decorated?'

'Aye, brother.'

'Do I hear the tabor and pipes?'

'You do – I can see the groom's procession across the meadow. They'll be at the brook in two minutes.'

'Well, stay them, for the bride is as tardy as ever she was. If she's not ready soon, we'll have to get up there and drag her down.'

All the young men of Will Shakespeare's age were with him, in their best clothes. His brothers were there, too. Will wore a new doublet and hose, all green and gold, and decorative gold garters above the knee to hold up his new netherstocks. Around the crown of his head he wore a garland of green leaves.

Two drummers banged their tabors, four pipers blew their pipes and six men shook their tambourines. Other young men swirled ribbons of silk and sang songs.

The most soberly dressed of the party was John Shakespeare, who had ridden through the night from Dover to be here. He had not slept. He had dusted himself down, thrown water over his face and rubbed himself with a linen towel, but he was ill-prepared for these celebrations.

'Bring out the bride!' one of the men shouted.

'Bring out the bride!' the others chorused. 'Bring her out, bring her out.'

There was a fluster of activity at the front door of Hewlands Farm as half a dozen village girls emerged giggling in their finest clothes, clutching posies and osier flaskets of flowers.

And then Anne came out and John Shakespeare was stopped in his tracks. This was not the girl he had grown up with, running in the fields and hiding in the byres. This was a beautiful woman on her wedding day. Her hair was loose and had been combed about her shoulders by her maids. They had tricked a pair of thin plaits into her hair, tying chains of small wild-flowers to them. The top of her head was decorated with a crown of laurel, lit up with gold leaf.

In her hands, she carried a large bunch of pink roses with tendrils of blue silk. She looked up and her eyes met Will's. They both smiled. The men all applauded and cheered. Will stepped forward and stood in front of her for a few moments, his head bowed. Then he took her hand and the procession to church began.

Shakespeare's mother and father were already at Holy Trinity, as were Uncle Richard and his brood and various other

Shakespeares, Ardens and Hathaways from the surrounding villages and farms.

Boltfoot Cooper stood apart. He had been invited to join the procession across the meadows, but had declined and Shakespeare had not pressed the invitation.

The three younger Shakespeare boys – Edmund, Richard and Gilbert – were all dressed as pages, decorated with sprigs of rosemary, bound up with bride-laces of golden silk. They stood by the church door nervously, waiting to accompany the wedding couple and the maids inside for the contracting of the marriage and the solemnisation.

Shakespeare broke away from the party and walked across to his father. John senior pretended he had something in his eye, but Shakespeare saw that in truth he was wiping away a tear.

'What do you think of the young fool now, Father?'

'He's still a fool, but all's well. She reminds me of your mother on our own day.'

Mary Shakespeare nudged her husband. 'You're the fool, John Shakespeare. You should have said something to Will, let him know you're happy for him.'

'There'll be time enough for that later, when we're all cup-shotten.'

But Shakespeare's smile had disappeared. Across the road he saw two men on horseback: Richard Topcliffe and Sir Thomas Lucy. Catching Shakespeare's eye, they trotted their horses over to him.

'So the brute beasts will cloak themselves in human hide.'

'You're not welcome here, Topcliffe.'

'I am a servant of the Queen. I go where I like, when I like.'

Shakespeare turned away, disgusted. As he did so, Topcliffe raised his cudgel-like blackthorn stick. Shakespeare feinted sideways, but the stick still caught him a painful blow on the shoulder. Turning back, he swiftly withdrew his sword and held it inches from Topcliffe's chest. At his side now was Boltfoot, his caliver in his arms, also pointing at Topcliffe.

'Put up your arms.' Sir Thomas Lucy's voice was quiet but insistent. 'I'll have no bloodshed on the streets of my town.'

'Then remove your dog, Sir Thomas. He fouls the very air. Do you not note the stink?'

Topcliffe was silent, glaring at the sword and gun that threatened him, but Lucy wanted to have his say. 'I have said it before and I will repeat it now. You Ardens are all the same. You may be protected now by Walsingham, John Shakespeare, but your kin are not. Tell Edward Arden and his satanic gang that I *will* do for them. They will reap the bitter fruit of their treachery very soon.'

'Do as you wish. If Edward Arden is a traitor, then he is my enemy as well as yours.'

'They are all back here in Warwickshire, up at Park Hall. Arden, the priest he calls his gardener. Even the insane Somerville came there yesterday. As bedraggled as a cat crawling from the water, I am told. Never even got as far as Oxford on his miserable quest.'

'As you say,' said Shakespeare evenly, 'he is insane. He has no notion of the season, let alone the lie of the land. I doubt he could find his way from the kitchen to the jakes. If you wish, we can discuss this another day, for the stable needs sweeping. But for today, I have a wedding to celebrate. So I bid you good day.'

'What of Mr Hungate? What of Badger? What do you know of these disappearances?'

'Nothing. What is there to know?'

Topcliffe touched Lucy's sleeve. 'Come, Sir Thomas, there will be time enough for this.'

'Listen to your talking dog, Sir Thomas.'

Topcliffe glared at Shakespeare, then spat on the ground at

his feet. He wheeled his horse's head, kicked its flanks hard and cantered away along the banks of the Avon. Sir Thomas Lucy seemed about to say something else, but then he too turned his horse and spurred it on after Topcliffe.

As the riders receded into the distance, Shakespeare put a hand on Boltfoot's shoulder and smiled at him. 'Thank you. Your caliver saved the day. I do believe we shall rub along well enough, you and I.'

At last they said the words that joined them together in the eyes of God and man. 'I, William, take you, Anne, to be my wedded wife and therefore I plight you my troth.'

They exchanged the rings and he kissed her. Not a peck, but a full-blooded kiss that brought cheers and applause from the witnesses and guests. Cups of spiced wine were distributed to all those in the packed church, and the celebrations truly began.

The maids led the way, dancing through the streets of Stratford towards the White Lion. The whole town turned out to cheer them on their way, for the newlyweds and their families were known to all.

Shakespeare was about to enter the inn when he spotted a familiar figure skulking in a doorway halfway down the street. For a moment, he considered turning away, but then he strode down the street to confront him.

'Good day, Mr Rench.'

'Is it?'

'Have you come to toast my brother and his bride?'

'I have a pig to slaughter for bacon. I should have stayed home.'

'I hear you are about to acquire the land you so desired.'

'It affords me no pleasure.'

Shakespeare looked at the man. There was not even a vestige

of the bold Rafe Rench he had always known. 'No. Well, the ancients tell us that what we desire the most, once achieved, is but dust through the fingers.'

'I know what you think of me. You see me as a tyrant. But it was not me who drove the widow Angel from her property.'

'Your boy Badger played his part, though, did he not?'

'Not at my behest. It never gave me pleasure when he rode with Lucy's band. We argued about it, almost came to blows. I wanted him on the farm.'

'You're right. He should not have ridden with those men.'

'Truth is, Shakespeare, he went bad long before that. I'm a hard man, but I built him up the way my father built me. As for the widow's land, well, I am a man of business like your own father. When her son became a fugitive and when the pursuivants began to call, I thought she might wish to leave Shottery behind. But I never wanted a falling-out with her or any other neighbours. Now it seems I am an outcast, not welcome in my own town.'

'Give them time, Mr Rench. Treat them fair and with courtesy they'll come around.'

'More than that, I want my boy back. I'd give all my land and the widow's for his return. The loss of a son . . . that is a thing I will never become accustomed to. I wish to God I knew where he was. Ananias Nason believes your brother did for him and buried him in the woods, but that don't sound likely to me. Badger could take ten Will Shakespeares.'

Shakespeare kept his expression carefully neutral. 'No, Mr Rench, nor does it sound likely to me. Best thing you can do is to pray for your son.' *And pray, too, that Boltfoot has buried the body so deep that no man will ever discover it.*

In the White Lion, the ale and wine and spirit flowed freely. The tables were laden with beef and mustard, pork and apple, frumenty, quinces, mince pies and a dozen other sumptuous dishes. The older men went bowling in the yard and the young men went to the field for an hour to hurl for goals, returning bruised and battered for another round of drinking.

Shakespeare's father gave a new pair of gloves to all the guests. The women and girls had two lefts, the men and boys two rights. 'Now sort them out between you. But no swapping without a kiss.'

And then the singing and jesting began. Hamnet Sadler, Will's best man, was standing on a table, telling his third story involving farts and nuns when a gust of wind blew in to the hall. Shakespeare, who was sitting close to the door, talking with Joshua Peace about the sciences, turned to see Kat Whetstone standing not a yard from him.

She took her cap from her head, shook out her long fair hair, and smiled at him. He rose unsteadily and ushered her in, closing the door after her.

'Kat Whetstone . . .'

'John Shakespeare.'

'How—'

'What fortune, to come on a day such as this.'

'Then it wasn't planned?'

'This is but a convenient stopping-off point on my way to London.'

'I trust you did not ride alone.'

'My ostler escorted me, and he shall have two marks for his efforts. But come, fill me a cup of strong beer, for I have ridden a hundred miles to be here today and have a thirst greater than any fish. And then you must introduce me to your brother and his bride.'

At their side, Joshua Peace smiled to himself; he would have to find a new drinking companion this day.

*

As darkness began to fall, after many hours dancing and drinking, Hamnet Sadler clapped his hands for silence. 'And now the bedding!' he announced. 'Let the virgin be deflowered.'

The men and women all bellowed with laughter.

'Make a man of him, Anne!'

Kat kissed Shakespeare's cheek, then moved her lips to his ear. 'And who will deflower *me*, handsome prince?'

'You are doomed to eternal spinsterhood, Kat Whetstone.'

The maids dragged Anne by the hand and the young men all pushed and pulled Will towards the best chamber in the inn. It was a large room with a four-poster bed with a decorative canopy. The bedding was strewn with rose petals and the air had been sweetened by a perfumed bowl of dried flowers and herbs. A log fire gave out a fierce heat.

'Perhaps he does not know what is expected of him. Shall we give you instruction, Will?'

'It is like a dovetail joint or a little finger in one of your father's gloves.'

'All you need is the key to the door, and then go through.'

Will grinned inanely and did not bother to respond to the bawdy jests of his friends.

His bride, meanwhile, was ahead of him, being undressed by her maids, until finally she stood naked. 'Now into bed with you, Goodwife Shakespeare,' said Judith Sadler. 'And be sure to take pleasure as well as give it.'

Will was pushed into the room. His bride was sitting up in bed against a bank of pillows, the bedclothes pulled up about her swelling breasts. The men tore Will's clothes from his body, then hoisted him on to the bed beside his bride.

'Now,' Shakespeare said, clapping his hands. 'You are all to leave and close the door. I have something to say to my brother and his bride before they settle down to their first night's slumbers.'

'First we'll see that he's up to it.'

'Come on, Will, rise to it!'

Shakespeare pushed them back, laughing, through the low doorway. Then he closed the door and leant against it.

'I will not keep you from your pleasures more than a moment, but I have a gift for you.' He delved into his doublet and pulled out a packet. 'Here, Anne, is the Spiritual Testament you signed, given to me not two days since by Florence Angel. Her mother persuaded her to hand it over to me and I do believe that at the last she knew that she had done wrong in abusing your trust so.' He held up the stitched sheaf of papers. 'What would you have me do with it?'

Anne and Will looked at each. 'The fire?' Will said. Anne nodded.

Shakespeare threw the deadly document into the hearth and they all watched as the flames rushed up and consumed it.

'And so I bid you both good night and a happy life.' Shakespeare opened the door. 'Treat each other well.'

Chapter 40

Aftermath

S HAKESPEARE'S HEAD WAS full of Spanish grammar and vocabulary as he walked along Seething Lane. For a month past, he had been travelling each day to Clerkenwell, to the home of Julio-Maria Lopez, a Lutheran fugitive from the Inquisition hired as his tutor. Shakespeare enjoyed languages and seemed to have a natural flair for them and these lessons – ten hours a day, every day – were proving fruitful. He could converse in the language and believed he would now be able to translate most of the intercepted messages sent between Madrid and the capitals of Europe.

It had been difficult to fit these lessons in with his work, but Mr Secretary had insisted. 'Your time with me has barely begun, John. You must learn the European tongues and you must understand their laws and politics. More than anything, you need a comprehensive knowledge of the people who wield influence. As well as the Spanish language, Señor Lopez will teach you much about the workings of the Escorial.'

But what of France? Shakespeare wondered. Was that not the greater threat? The machinations of the Guise faction and the Catholic League had not abated since the attempt to free Mary Stuart. It seemed clear that Henri of Guise had not given up on his plans to assassinate Elizabeth and have Mary usurp her throne. The other certainty was that Guise would not allow the death of his man François Leloup to go unavenged.

As Shakespeare entered his office, Sir Francis Walsingham raised his head from a bundle of papers and signalled with a flick of his fingers for him to sit at the table opposite him. He seemed, if not exactly ebullient, slightly less dour than usual. As always, he did not waste words on greetings.

'Edward Arden has been arrested, along with the rest of his household. He is even now at the Guildhall being tried for treason. When he is convicted, he will be taken to Newgate to await execution on the morrow.'

Shakespeare had no reason to be surprised by the news, but it had been so long since the events at Stratford – a long, busy year – that he had put it out of mind. 'I suppose it was inevitable. How did this come about, Sir Francis?'

'His son-in-law, Somerville, was at an inn near Oxford, brandishing his dag and declaring to anyone who would listen that he intended to shoot the Queen with it. His very words were that he wished to stick her head on a pole because she was a serpent and a viper. When he was arrested, he finally confessed and implicated the others. They were all taken to the Tower. Sir Thomas Lucy picked up the priest Hall and the two Arden women. Mr Topcliffe plucked Edward Arden from the house of the Earl of Southampton, here in London. They will not escape justice.'

Shakespeare sighed. 'May I ask, Sir Francis, who drew the confession from Somerville?'

'Are you trying to make some point, John? Beware men do not think you sympathetic to your treacherous kinsmen . . .'

'A man will confess to anything and implicate anyone when he is racked.'

'That does not mean it is not true.'

'And I think it is fair to say that John Somerville is mad. What manner of assassin would brag to strangers about his intention to kill the Queen? Such a man may as well be in Bedlam as the Tower.'

'John, I will not listen to a sermon from you. I told you this matter because I wish you to go to Newgate to interrogate these traitors yourself. You have local knowledge and you know these people. More than that, you are always telling me that a quiet voice can often draw out the truth where torment brings forth only lies. Well, let us put it to the test: see what you can find. This will be their last night on earth. Help them make their peace with God and Queen – and discover who else is involved. Do this well and we can make a bonfire of the rack.'

'Forgive me for speaking out of turn.'

'No, you misunderstand me. I respect your methods. But I know, too, that Mr Topcliffe has had much success in weeding out treason. He is more than a tormentor of bodies. Whatever you think of him, no one learns more from the streets of London. He has men in every prison and every stall and work-shop. Apprentices come to him with little dishes of intelligence. You can learn from him. I need you both, but I believe you must grow harder. I would bring out the iron in your soul.'

'As you say, Sir Francis.'

'I do. Now go to Newgate and do my bidding.'

He found Edward Arden in a small, stinking cell, in irons. He was clearly very weak and could not move from the fetid straw in which he lay.

Shakespeare stood inside the door holding a rushlight, look-ing down at the pathetic remnants of his cousin, the once proud sheriff of Warwickshire. He knelt at the condemned man's side and put a cup of ale to his lips. Arden sipped at it and nodded his thanks.

'What word of Mary and Margaret?' His voice was very faint.

'I have been to them. Your wife and daughter are well.'

'You are on the wrong side, John Shakespeare.'

'We have been through this. I warned you of the danger you faced, but you would not listen. Now I want names from you. Show yourself a true Englishman before you die. Do not go to your death with deceit in your heart.'

'Names? You want names? How do these names sound: Thomas Lucy, Robert Dudley, Francis Walsingham, William Cecil. Traitors all. Will they serve you?'

'Listen. Help me on this and I will assist Mary and Margaret's cause. It is the foreign connections I seek.'

'There is no foreign connection, only the priests. Benedict Angel is dead and Hugh Hall will soon join me at Paddington Green with John Somerville.'

'Have you been racked?'

'Thrice. I believe I am a foot longer. At dawn, I will be a head shorter.'

'How did it all come about?'

'Ask the man who calls himself Buchan Ord. He is *your* creature is he not?'

'Did you truly believe any of this would work?'

Arden tried to laugh, but the effort made him gasp with pain. He shook his head slowly. 'Never.'

'Then why, cousin?'

'Because you took it all. I had nothing left.'

'I took nothing from you.'

'Your pseudo-religion. It changed my England beyond recall. Everything is laid waste.'

Shakespeare was silent for a few moments. There was nothing more to be learnt, with or without torture. 'Shall I take messages to Mary and Margaret? I believe they are to be spared. A pardon will be issued. Mr Hall, too.'

'My love in Christ, that is all. Tell them to walk with God always.'

'I will do that. And God be with *you*, cousin.'

Outside the cell door, Shakespeare breathed deeply. He closed his eyes and said the Lord's Prayer in his head. God was all-powerful and could see into the human heart. Why should He need to hear the words spoken aloud? *Amen.* He mouthed the word, then opened his eyes and summoned the gaoler with his hand.

'Now take me to Somerville.'

'He's dead, master.'

'How can he be dead?'

'Hanged himself in his cell. But they'll still have his head on a spike above the Bridge. He don't escape that easy.'

Shakespeare did not sleep that night. He listened all the while to the soft, warm breathing of Kat Whetstone at his side. What sort of fool was he to allow this woman into his home and into his life? He did not love her and she did not love him and nor would they ever marry.

At dawn he heard the sound of rain on the shutters. He made no move to rise from the bed. All his thoughts now were with his cousin, Edward Arden. Very soon he would be taken from his cell to the yard below, where he would be strapped to a hurdle, his head hanging down at the back, close to the rocky road, and then he would be drawn by a horse along the long, pitted road to Tyburn, where the Godly butchery would begin.

What part had he played in the destruction of this man? What sort of a fool was he to work for a man like Sir Francis Walsingham?

He gazed across at the beautiful woman at his side, her hair splayed across his pillows. She warmed his bed and there was food in the house. At least this was normal life, not the savagery of men who would protect princes and those who would depose them. She stirred, as though sensing his eyes on her. 'Hold me, John,' she said, and so he did.

Acknowledgements

As always my thanks go to my wife Naomi for putting up with me, my agent Teresa Chris for doing the difficult stuff and my editor Kate Parkin for showing me the way when I go wrong. I must also mention Jennie Dobson (www.jenniedobsonwriter. com) for her wonderful efforts seeking out maps. Thanks, too, to the NNGTL for keeping me sane and everyone at John Murray – Roland, Caro and Lyndsey – for their unfailing professionalism and good humour.

Books that have been especially helpful include: *Martyrs and Murderers* by Stuart Carroll; *My Heart is My Own* by John Guy; *Will in the World* by Stephen Greenblatt; *Shakespeare: The Biography* by Peter Ackroyd; *Shakespeare's Wife* by Germaine Greer; *The Time Traveller's Guide to Elizabethan England* by Ian Mortimer; *Shakespeare's Warwickshire Contemporaries* by Charlotte Carmichael Stopes; *Historical Account of the Rise and Progress of the English Stage* by Edmond Malone; *Danger to Elizabeth* by Alison Plowden; *Mary Queen of Scots* by Antonia Fraser; *Bess of Hardwick* by Mary S. Lovell; *Plots and Plotters in the Reign of Elizabeth I* by Francis Edwards.

Historical Notes

The plotters William Shakespeare would have known
The county of Warwickshire was a seething pit of conspiracy and treason during the lifetime of William Shakespeare – and he would certainly have known or been aware of most of the characters involved, including several who were executed.

As a man whose own father may well have been a secret Catholic, Shakespeare must have been painfully aware of the trials and punishments inflicted on these relatives and neighbours:

Edward Arden: cousin to Mary Arden (mother of William Shakespeare), Edward Arden was principally associated with Park Hall in Castle Bromwich, twenty-five miles from Stratford. Arden, a former sheriff of the county, married Mary Throckmorton, daughter of Sir Robert Throckmorton of Coughton Court, Warwickshire. She was the sister of Anne Catesby, of Lapworth, Warwickshire, mother of the gunpowder conspirator Robert Catesby. Arden, a Catholic and sworn enemy of the Earl of Leicester, was implicated in the plot of his son-in-law John Somerville to kill the Queen and was executed at Smithfield by hanging, drawing and quartering in December 1583. His head was placed on a pike on London Bridge. His wife, also convicted of treason, was pardoned.

John Somerville: brought up at Edstone (six miles from Stratford), the son of a landowner, he married Margaret, the daughter of Edward and Mary Arden and they had two daughters. In 1583 he set out to kill the Queen, hoping that she would be supplanted by Mary, Queen of Scots. But even before he got to court, he could not restrain himself from boasting about his intentions to fellow guests at an inn. They testified that he said he 'meant to shoot her and to see her head on a pole, for that she was a serpent and a viper'. He was quickly arrested and, under interrogation and probably torture, confessed that he had been incited by his father-in-law Edward Arden and his priest, Hugh Hall. At the age of twenty-three, Somerville choked himself to death (or was murdered) in his cell before he could be executed, but his head was still severed and placed on a pole. Some historians have suggested that Somerville was mentally ill and that his ramblings were used by the Earl of Leicester as a means to gain revenge on his old enemy Edward Arden.

Hugh Hall: a priest in the household of Edward Arden. Like many such Catholic priests, he disguised himself as a servant, in this case a gardener. He had various conversations with John Somerville and spoke approvingly of a notorious plot to assassinate the Prince of Orange, pointing out that the would-be killer would be absolved of any sin if he did the deed for God, not gain. After Somerville's plot to kill the Queen was foiled, Hugh Hall was among several servants and family members arrested. He was convicted of conspiring to 'compass the death of the Queen'. After the deaths of Somerville and Arden, Hall was questioned again, but was eventually pardoned.

Simon Hunt: schoolmaster at the King's New School in Stratford from 1571 to 1575, where he would have known and taught William Shakespeare until he was about eleven. Hunt, a devout Catholic, then went into exile to the English College at Douai, where he was closely associated with Thomas Cottam (see below) and where they were both joined by Hunt's former pupil Robert Dibdale of Shottery, which is a mile from the centre of Stratford and was the home village of William's bride Anne Hathaway. Simon Hunt later became a Jesuit and travelled to Rome, where he became English Penitentiary at St Peter's.

Robert Dibdale: close neighbour of Anne Hathaway in the tiny hamlet of Shottery, which is now a suburb of Stratford-upon-Avon. He was the son of John Dibdale, a Catholic farmer, and attended the King's New School, like William Shakespeare, though he was certainly a few years older than the poet, probably born in the mid to late 1550s. He would have been taught by Simon Hunt and in 1576 followed him to the seminaries of Europe, at Douai, Rheims and Rome, also becoming good friends with Thomas Cottam. Dibdale returned to England in 1580 and was promptly arrested, being held at the Gatehouse prison in Westminster from July to September, when he was freed. He was next heard of in the spring of 1583 when he entered the English College at Rheims, being ordained a priest a year later. Returning to England once more, he became close friends with the Jesuit priest William Weston and together they conducted exorcisms at Denham in Buckinghamshire, until both were arrested in 1586. Weston was held prisoner but Dibdale was executed with two other priests at Tyburn.

The Cottam brothers: John Cottam was one of the schoolmasters who succeeded Simon Hunt at Stratford. He was elder brother to Thomas Cottam, also a schoolmaster, who went to Douai in 1577 and later Rome, where he became a Jesuit priest in 1580. Thomas returned to England but was recognised and arrested on arrival at Dover. He was found to be carrying a letter and Catholic artefacts (including a crucifix and rosary beads) from Robert Dibdale to deliver to his father in Shottery. After being tortured by rack and scavenger's daughter, Thomas was hanged, drawn and quartered at Tyburn in May 1582. John Cottam left the King's New School in the same year.

Francis Throckmorton: he was a member of the powerful Midlands family who held property in Warwickshire. Francis was brought up at Feckenham, fourteen miles from Stratford and close to the most important of the family's homes, Coughton Court, which is associated with two great conspiracies: Francis Throckmorton's own plot to kill the Queen and the Gunpowder Plot. By 1580, several members of the Throckmorton family were already in trouble for persistent Catholicism and refusal to conform. Francis went to France where he became involved with various angry English exiles. He returned to England and entered into secret correspondence with Mary, Queen of Scots until Walsingham learnt of his activities through a spy in the French embassy. Under torture, Throckmorton confessed to knowing of a plot by the Duke of Guise to invade England, free Mary and kill or kidnap Elizabeth. He was executed at Tyburn in July 1584. Twenty-one years later, in 1605, Gunpowder plotters took refuge at his family's home, Coughton Court.

Robert Catesby: leader of the Gunpowder plotters, Robert Catesby was brought up in Lapworth, Warwickshire, twelve miles north of Stratford. He was the son of the recusant Sir William Catesby and Anne, daughter of Sir Robert Throckmorton of Coughton Court. Robert was cousin to that other notorious conspirator Francis Throckmorton and related by marriage to Edward Arden, through whom they were all related to William Shakespeare. The Catesby family was said to have harboured the Jesuit priest Edmund Campion before his arrest and martyrdom. Robert Catesby's first taste of rebellion came in 1601 when he was part of the Earl of Essex's ill-fated insurrection against Queen Elizabeth. He was wounded and fined £3,000. Four years later, aged about thirty-three, he conceived the idea of blowing up parliament and King James. He recruited other conspirators, including Guy Fawkes, but the plot was foiled and Catesby died in a shoot-out as he tried to escape.

Religious strife in the late sixteenth century

Queen Elizabeth I declared that she did not wish to open windows into men's souls, but once the Pope had excommunicated her and intimated that it would not be considered a crime for Catholics to kill her and usurp her, Catholics found themselves persecuted throughout England.

In all, it has been estimated that 250 priests and other Catholic dissidents were executed for their faith (though treason was invariably the crime cited) in the last twenty years of Elizabeth's reign.

This is how the iron vice of the law was tightened.

1570: Pope Pius V issues a papal bull, *Regnans in Excelsis*, which calls the Queen of England a heretic and releases her Catholic subjects from their allegiance to her.

1571: in England, the government retaliates against the Vatican by enacting a law making it high treason to describe the Queen as a heretic. Treason is always punishable by death. Importing rosary beads, crucifixes and declarations from the Pope becomes illegal. Anyone leaving the country without permission for six months can have their property confiscated. This is to deter Catholics fleeing persecution in England.

1581: Edmund Campion is executed for adhering to the Pope against the Queen, compassing and imaging the destruction of the Queen and entering England to disturb the quiet state of the realm. Fines are increased for refusing to attend the parish (Protestant) church. The penalty for saying mass is £133; for hearing it £66 and imprisonment; for neglecting to attend church £20 a month in fines (increased from sixpence). Priests or others trying to convert anyone to Roman Catholicism are guilty of high treason. Anyone helping them is guilty of treason. New powers are given to magistrates to order raids on recusants' houses on the slightest suspicion.

1585: it is declared a capital offence merely to be a Catholic priest entering England or to harbour a priest. Any priest ordained by the Pope since the start of Elizabeth's reign must leave England within forty days or face a charge of treason. Anyone sending a child abroad to be educated at a Catholic school can be fined £100. Anyone knowing the whereabouts of a priest and failing to report it to the authorities within twelve days can be jailed indefinitely.

1593: you can be jailed for non-attendance at the parish church. Known Catholics cannot go more than five miles from their home without a licence.

Were the Shakespeares secret Catholics?
To be a Roman Catholic in England during the late sixteenth century was always uncomfortable and often terrifying.

As tensions grew, so did the penalties for not complying with the religious settlement dictated by Queen Elizabeth's government. Everyone was required by law to attend the parish church with its Protestant prayer book and services – and you were liable to face heavy fines for refusing to go.

You could be jailed simply for hearing mass and, worst of all, you could be executed for treason for harbouring Catholic priests or assisting them to convert people.

And so papists – as the Catholics were called – tended to keep themselves to themselves, avoiding making any display of their faith and hearing mass in utmost secrecy. Yet despite the danger, it is certain that many people living in Stratford-upon-Avon and the surrounding countryside at the time did still adhere to the old religion.

The question that has intrigued historians for centuries is whether their number included William Shakespeare and his father, John.

The evidence is compelling. In 1757 a builder named Joseph Mosely was working on the roof of the Stratford-upon-Avon house in which William Shakespeare had been born almost two hundred years earlier, and he found an ancient religious document hidden between the tiles and the rafters.

It consisted of six small pages, stitched together, each page signed *John Shakespeare* – or a variant of the spelling. What it amounted to was a declaration that the poet's father was a Roman Catholic and that he would remain so until death. It was, in effect, his spiritual will and testament entreating God to consider him among the faithful even though he might die unconfessed and without extreme unction because of the difficulty in finding a priest to administer the sacraments.

In the fourteen articles of faith contained in the document, John Shakespeare asked that the testament be buried with him. But of course that did not happen. Perhaps it was too well hidden for his widow and children to find when the hour of his death arrived.

What we know is that the house in Henley Street, Stratford-upon-Avon, where the testament was found had stayed in the Shakespeare family, passing to William Shakespeare's sister Joan, who married William Hart, a hatter, and then on through five generations to the Thomas Hart who lived there when master-bricklayer Joseph Mosely was repairing the roof.

Mosely, who was described as an 'honest, sober and industrious man', gave the paper to an alderman named Peyton who passed it on to the Reverend James Davenport, vicar of Stratford, who in turn sent it to his good friend Edmond Malone, the renowned Shakespearean scholar and man of letters who had spent much time researching Shakespeare's life and works.

The document is now lost, but fortunately we know all about it from Malone, who copied it and put it into print. Malone wrote: 'I have taken some pains to ascertain the authenticity of this manuscript and after a very careful inquiry am perfectly satisfied that it is genuine.'

Others were not so sure and for the next century and a half the testament was treated with scepticism by scholars and historians. And then, in the 1920s, a Spanish version of the document turned up in the archives of the British Museum. Known as a 'Last Will of the Soul', it was devised by Carlo Borromeo (1538–84), the Cardinal of Milan, as a 'formulary' – a religious statement drawn up in a set form with blank spaces for the recipient's signature.

What is also known is that the English Jesuit and martyr Edmund Campion stayed with Borromeo in Milan on his way from Rome to England in 1580. It is known, too, that before he was captured and executed, Campion stayed in various houses in Warwickshire, including the home of Sir William Catesby in Lapworth, a mere twelve miles from Stratford. Catesby was related to the Shakespeares by marriage.

It seems highly likely that Father Campion could have brought dozens – perhaps hundreds – of these formulaic testaments, translated into English, to distribute to the beleaguered faithful of his homeland.

I can see no reason to doubt the authenticity of the John Shakespeare Spiritual Testament. Why would Joseph Mosely have conceived and forged such a document – especially as he received no money for it? And isn't the loft space between the tiles and rafters just the sort of place that a worried man would have hidden something he considered hazardous to his health? After all, the pursuivants charged with rooting out Catholic priests, books, vestments and crucifixes were horribly thorough in their searches, often smashing through walls and panelling in their quest for evidence.

The historian Peter Ackroyd writes in his scholarly book *Shakespeare: The Biography* that the document's provenance 'seems genuine enough'.

He adds, intriguingly, that one passage in the testament bears a striking resemblance to a quote from *Hamlet*.

In the testament, John Shakespeare puts his name to a declaration including the words 'that I may be possibly cut off in the blossom of my sins'. In *Hamlet*, Ackroyd points out, the ghost laments that he was 'cut off even in the blossoms of my sin'.

It would not take a conspiracy theorist to wonder whether William Shakespeare might have read through his father's Spiritual Testament – or even signed one of his own.

Here is the full text of John Shakespeare's Spiritual Testament, as recorded by Edmond Malone. *NB: I have modernised and regularised various spellings.*

I

In the name of God, the father, son, and holy ghost, the most holy and blessed Virgin Mary, mother of God, the holy host of archangels, angels, patriarchs, prophets, evangelists, apostles, saints, martyrs, and all the celestial court and company of heaven, I John Shakespeare, an unworthy member of the holy Catholic religion, being at this my present writing in perfect health of body, and sound mind, memory and understanding, but calling to mind the uncertainty of life and certainty of death, and that I may be possibly cut off in the blossom of my sins, and called to render an account of all my transgressions externally and internally, and that I may be unprepared for the dreadful trial either by sacrament, penance, fasting or prayer, or any other purgation whatever, do in the holy presence above specified, of my own free and voluntary accord, make and ordain this my last spiritual will, testament, confession, protest-ation, and confession of faith, hoping hereby to receive pardon for all my sins and offences, and thereby to be made partaker of life everlasting, through the only merits of Jesus Christ, my saviour and redeemer, who took upon himself the likeness of man, suffered death, and was crucified upon the cross, for the redemption of sinners.

II

Item, I John Shakespeare do, by this present protest, acknow-ledge and confess, that in my past life I have been a most abominable and grievous sinner, and therefore unworthy to be forgiven without a true and sincere repentance for the same. But trusting in the manifold mercies of my blessed Saviour and Redeemer, I am encouraged by relying on his sacred word, to hope for salvation and be made partaker of his heavenly king-dom, as a member of the celestial company of angels, saints and martyrs, there to reside for ever and ever in the court of my God.

III

Item, I John Shakespeare do by this present protest and declare that as I am certain I must pass out of this transitory life into another that will last to eternity, I do hereby most humbly implore and entreat my good and guardian angel to instruct me in this my solemn preparation, protestation and confession of faith, at least spiritually, in will adoring and most humbly beseeching my saviour, that he will be pleased to assist me in so dangerous a voyage, to defend me from the snares and deceits of my infernal enemies, and to conduct me to the secure haven of his eternal bliss.

IV

Item, I John Shakespeare do protest that I will also pass out of this life, armed with the last sacrament of extreme unction: the which if through any let or hindrance I should not then be able to have, I do now also for that time demand and crave the same: beseeching his divine majesty that he will be pleased to anoint my senses both internal and external with the sacred oil of his infinite mercy, and to pardon me all my sins committed by seeing, speaking, feeling, smelling, hearing, touching, or by any other way whatsoever.

V

Item, I John Shakespeare do by this present protest that I will never through any temptation whatsoever despair of the divine goodness, for the multitude and greatness of my sins; for which although I confess that I have deserved hell, yet will I steadfastly hope in God's infinite mercy, knowing that he hath heretofore pardoned many as great sinners as myself, whereof I have good warrant sealed with his sacred mouth, in holy writ, whereby he pronounceth that he is not come to call the just, but sinners.

VI

Item, I John Shakespeare do protest that I do not know that I have ever done any good work meritorious of life everlasting: and if I have done any, I do acknowledge that I have done it with a great deal of negligence and imperfection; neither should I have been able to have done the least without the assistance of his divine grace. Wherefore let the devil remain confounded; for I do in no wise presume to merit heaven by such good works alone, but through the merits and blood of my lord and saviour, Jesus, shed upon the cross for me most miserable sinner.

VII

Item, I John Shakespeare do protest by this present writing that I will patiently endure and suffer all kind of infirmity, sickness, yea and the pain of death itself: wherein if it should happen, which God forbid, that through violence of pain and agony, or by subtlety of the devil, I should fall into any impatience or temptation of blasphemy, or murmuration against God or the Catholic faith, or give any sign of bad example, I do henceforth and for that present repent me, and am most heartily sorry for the same: and I do renounce all the evil whatsoever, which I might have then done or said; beseeching his divine clemency that he will not forsake me in that grievous and painful agony.

VIII

Item, I John Shakespeare, by virtue of this present testament, I do pardon all the injuries and offences that any one hath ever done unto me, either in my reputation, life, goods, or any other way whatsoever; beseeching sweet Jesus to pardon them for the same: and I do desire that they will do the like by me, whom I have offended or injured in any sort howsoever.

IX

Item, I John Shakespeare do here protest that I do render infinite thanks to his divine majesty for all the benefits that I have received as well secret as manifest, & in particular for the benefit of my Creation, Redemption, Sanctification, Conservation, and Vocation to the holy knowledge of him & his true Catholic faith: but above all, for his so great expectation of me to penance, when he might most justly have taken me out of this life when I least thought of it, yea, even then, when I was plunged in the dirty puddle of my sins. Blessed be therefore and praised, for ever and ever, his infinite patience and charity.

X

Item, I John Shakespeare do protest that I am willing, yea, I do infinitely desire and humbly crave, that of this my last will and testament the glorious and ever Virgin Mary, mother of God, refuge and advocate of sinners (whom I honour specially above all other saints) may be the chief executress, together with these other saints, my patrons, (Saint Winefride) all whom I invoke and beseech to be present at the hour of my death, that she and they comfort me with their desired presence, and crave of sweet Jesus that he will receive my soul into peace.

XI

Item, In virtue of this present writing, I John Shakespeare do likewise most willingly and with all humility constitute and ordain my good Angel, for Defender and Protector of my soul in the dreadful day of Judgement, when the final sentence of eternal life or death shall be discussed and given: beseeching him, that, as my soul was appointed to his custody and protection when I lived, even so he will vouchsafe to defend the same at that hour, and conduct it to eternal bliss.

XII

Item, I John Shakespeare do in like manner pray and beseech all my dear friends, parents, and kinfolks, by the bowels of our saviour Jesus Christ, that since it is uncertain what lot will befall me, for fear notwithstanding least by reason of my sins I be to pass and stay a long while in purgatory, they will vouchsafe to assist and succour me with their holy prayers and satisfactory works, especially with the holy sacrifice of the mass, as being the most effectual means to deliver souls from their torments and pains; from the which, if I shall by God's gracious goodness and by their virtuous works be delivered, I do promise that I will not be ungrateful unto them, for so great a benefit.

XIII

Item, I John Shakespeare do by this my last will and testament bequeath my soul, as soon as it shall be delivered and loosened from the prison of this my body, to be entombed in the sweet and amorous coffin of the side of Jesus Christ; and that in this life-giving sepulchre it may rest and live, perpetually enclosed in that eternal habitation of repose, there to bless for ever and ever that direful iron of the lance, which, like a charge in a censer, forms so sweet and pleasant a monument within the sacred breast of my lord and saviour.

XIV

Item, lastly I John Shakespeare do protest that I will willingly accept of death in what manner soever it may befall me, conforming my will unto the will of God; accepting of the same in satisfaction for my sins, and giving thanks unto his divine majesty for the life he hath bestowed upon me. And if it please him to prolong or shorten the same, blessed be he also a thousand thousand times; into whose most holy hands I commend my soul and body, my life and death: and I beseech him above all things, that he never permit any change to be made to me John Shakespeare of this my aforesaid will and testament. Amen.

I John Shakespeare have made this present writing of protestation, confession and charter, in the presence of the blessed Virgin Mary, my angel guardian, and all the celestial court, as witnesses hereunto: the which my meaning is, that it be of full value now presently and for ever, with the force and virtue of testament, codicil and donation in case of death; confirming it anew, being in perfect health of soul and body, and signed with mine own hand, carrying also the same about me; and for the better declaration hereof, my will and intention is that it be finally buried with me after my death.

Pater noster. Ave Maria. Credo.

Jesu, son of David, have mercy on me.

Amen.